The Used and Abused

Available from Moreclacke Publishing

Books by Robert Armin

The Flash of Midnight

Sheva, the Benevolent (A Play)

The Used and Abused

Books by Sherman Yellen

Cousin Bella — The Whore of Minsk

December Fools and Other Plays

Spotless: Memories of a New York Childhood

Rediscovery Series

Mabel Wynne and Other Tales of the Romantic Age
by Nathaniel Parker Willis (Robert Armin, Editor)

Why They Married
by James Montgomery Flagg

The Used and Abused

Fyodor Dostoyevsky's
The Insulted and Injured
Retold

Robert Armin

MORECLACKE PUBLISHING
New York City

For information, contact Moreclacke Publishing at
info@moreclacke.com
or
325 West 45th Street, Suite 609
New York, NY 10036-0075

Printed in the United States of America

First Paperback Edition:

Library of Congress Control Number: 2020923513
Moreclacke Publishing, New York, NY

ISBN-13: 978-0-9960169-7-1

For Alexander Zhurbin

Principal Characters

Ivan Petrovich, the 25-year-old narrator (called "Vanya")

Nikolai Sergeich Ichmenyev, landowner of Ichmenyevka, facing financial ruin in a lawsuit with Prince Valkovsky

Anna Andreyevna Ichmenyeva, his wife

Natalia Nikolayevna Ichmenyeva, his daughter (called "Natasha")

Prince Peter Alexandrovich Valkovsky, landowner of Vassilyevskoe

Alexey Petrovich Valkovsky (called "Alyosha"), Prince Valkovsky's impressionable and easily influenced son

Katerina Fedorovna Filimonova, Alexey's wealthy young fiancée (called "Katya")

Jeremiah Smith, a once prosperous businessman, now old and dying

Elena, Mr. Smith's 13-year-old granddaughter (called "Nellie")

Elena's mother, whose life story is shrouded in mystery

Philip Philippich Masloboyev, a private investigator and friend to Vanya

Alexandra Semyonovna, Masloboyev's common-law wife

Anna Trifonovna Bubnova, a whorehouse Madame and lowlife

Princess K., Alexey's godmother, a wealthy dowager

Count Nainsky, a wealthy aristocrat and patron to young Alexey

Countess Zinaida Filimonova, Katya's stepmother

Sizobryukhov, a wealthy but debauched young drunkard

Arkhipov, a fat, licentious degenerate leading Sizobryukhov astray

Mitroshka, a dashing young con artist and friend to Masloboyev

Matroyna, the Ichmenyev's housekeeper

Mavra, Natasha's housekeeper

CHAPTER ONE

Last year, on the evening of March 22nd, I was involved in a very bizarre incident. I had been searching around the city all day looking for a new apartment. Mine was damp and I'd caught a bad cold there. I had wanted to move since the previous autumn, but had put off making the change until then, in the early spring. I'd been searching about, as I said, all day, but found nothing suitable. Above all else, I wanted my new home to be isolated from other people. If necessary, one room would do, but it had to be spacious and, at the same time, I didn't want to pay a lot of rent.

I've always observed that in a confined space one's ideas do not flow freely. I like to pace up and down a room as I meditate upon my novels. And while I'm on the subject of my novels, I confess that I've always found far more pleasure in dreaming them up than in writing them down. Why is that, I wonder, for I'm by no means lazy by nature?

I had been feeling poorly since early that morning and as evening approached, I felt even worse. I was feverish and, after having been on my feet all day, extraordinarily tired when I arrived on Voznesensky Prospect a few minutes before sunset.

I love the March sun in St. Petersburg, especially as it is setting on a calm, pleasant evening. When the weather is frosty, the whole street, inundated with floods of light, bursts into glory in an instant. The houses—grey, yellow or dirty green—suddenly erupt into a fountain of sunbeams and lose their sinister aspect in the blink of an eye. A man's soul lights up, as well, and a cold chill runs through his veins and he wakes with a jolt, as though someone had nudged his elbow. New ideas come with the new light. It's astonishing what power a ray of sunshine has on the human soul!

Meanwhile, the sun had set, the frost was growing sharper and beginning to prickle my nose, the darkness grew deeper and the gaslight streamed from the shop windows. I was passing Mueller's pastry shop, which stood on the opposite side of the street, when I suddenly came to a dead stop as though struck by some presentiment that an extraordinary event was about to take place. I felt a most disagreeable shudder run through me as I observed an old man and his dog moving toward the pastry shop. I am certainly no "mystic," and I have little patience with those who claim powers of divination, but I have observed in my lifetime certain circumstances that are difficult to explain. This old man, for example. Why did I feel at the very sight of him that something was about to happen to me quite different from my usual daily experiences? It occurred to me that I was feverish and that one's impressions during illness are often deceptive.

As the old man proceeded toward the shop, he advanced with slow and uncertain steps, moving his limbs without bending them as though they were blocks of wood. He stooped and tapped the stones of the pavement with his cane as he went along. I had seen him before in Mueller's shop and each time he had left a sad, disagreeable impression upon me. In all my life, I had never seen so strange and ridiculous-looking a figure: tall, but with a crooked back; a pale octogenarian face that looked like that of a corpse; a worn-out coat, torn at the seams; a round hat, bruised and broken, which might well have seen twenty years of service, covering his nearly bald head which retained only a few strands of yellowing hair at the base of his neck; his automaton-like movements; all these things were quite shocking to people meeting him for the first time.

It was certainly strange to see this old man slogging through a solitary life, seemingly without a soul to look after him, looking more than anything else like a madman who had escaped from his attendants. His leanness was quite beyond description. He had, one might almost say, no body left at all; he was skin and bones and nothing more. His eyes, large but dim and surrounded by deep bluish circles, stared constantly straight in front of him, undeviating. They never looked to the left or the right and never seemed to see anything. I am quite sure of that, for more than once I had noticed that he could stare straight at you and walk straight into you, just as though he had seen nothing but empty space before him.

He had lately begun to frequent Mueller's, he and his dog, but none of the regular customers had ever dared to speak to him and the old man had never said a word to any of them.

"Why does he come to Mueller's?" I thought to myself as I watched him from the other side of the street, unable to take my eyes off of him. "What does he come to do?" I was conscious of a sort of spiteful feeling against him developing in my heart, the consequence, most likely, of illness and fatigue. "What does he think about?" I wondered. "What ideas could he have inside that head? Does he still think at all?" There seemed to be no expression left in that ancient face of his. And where had he found this wretched old dog that appeared to be such an integral and inseparable extension of her master, whom she so closely resembled? This unfortunate animal seemed to be eighty years old, like her master, and looked like no other dog that had ever lived. I don't know why, but the very first time I saw her I imagined that this dog was a beast of some unique species; that she had within her some sort of sorcery; that she was a kind of Mephistopheles in canine form, and that her destiny was in some way or other linked with that of her master by a mysterious tie. She was as thin as a skeleton, or to put it better, as thin as her master. If you had seen this beast you would have thought, as I did, that she had not touched food for years. She was quite bald; her tail stuck to her body like a piece of wood and was pressed tight between her emaciated legs; and her long ears, along with the rest of her head, drooped sadly toward the pavement. In all my life I had never seen a more wretched-looking beast.

When the pair of them walked along the streets, the master in front followed by his dog, her nose glued to the skirts of his coat, their gait and appearance seemed to be crying out with every step, "Oh, but we're old, we're old, oh God, but we're old!"

One day the idea struck me that the old man and his dog had become detached from a page of *Hoffmann's Tales*, illustrated by Paul Gavarni, and that they toured the world as a sort of walking advertisement.

I crossed the road and went into the pastry shop. The old man's behavior inside was equally bizarre and Mueller, from behind his counter, always made an expression of disgust whenever this unwelcome visitor arrived. This singular customer never ordered anything but would go straight to a chair in the corner near the stove and sit. If this chair happened to be occupied, he would stand before the occupant and stare vacantly with a stupid, perplexed look for a few moments and then shuffle off with a disappointed air to the other side of the room near the window. There he would take a chair, seat himself slowly, take off his hat and put it near him on the floor. He would then place his cane alongside his hat, lean full length against the back of his chair and so remain, like a marble statue, for three or four hours at a time. No one had ever seen him with a newspaper in his hand or heard him say a word or even utter a sound.

He used to sit there staring fixedly before him with his dull, lusterless eyes, so that one would readily wager that he neither saw nor heard anything of what was going on around him. His dog, after turning around two or three times in place, would lie down at his feet, gloomy and dejected, push her nose tightly between her master's boots, give a profound sigh and then stretch out full-length on the floor where she would lie immovable, as though she had ceased to live, the whole evening. Anyone might well imagine that these two vampiric creatures, long since dead, were in the habit of resuscitating themselves at sunset solely in order to come to Mueller's shop to fulfill some mysterious obligation unknown to man.

When he had sat like this for some hours, the old man would get up, take his hat and cane, and start towards home. The old dog would get up too, head bent low and tail between her legs, and mechanically follow her aged master.

Most of Mueller's regular customers were Germans, owners of the various establishments on Voznesensky Prospect; a locksmith, a baker, a tailor. Mueller would often approach his guests at their tables and sit with them for a while. He greeted most visitors, including dogs and small children, with great warmth and high spirits. There was a most welcome feeling of camaraderie among the occupants of the shop and visitors were free to play cards, listen to the music, or simply read one of the German newspapers which Mueller kept on hand. I was in the habit of visiting Mueller's on the first day of each month to read the Russian magazines which he also made available. Without exception, everyone in the shop did their best to avoid the old man and they made every effort to sit anywhere but near him in order to show him their disapproval, but he never took the slightest notice of them.

When I went into the shop on this particular evening, I found the old man already installed near the window. His dog, as usual, was stretched out at his feet. I sat down quietly in a corner and wondered, "Why do I come here where I have absolutely nothing to do, especially now when I'm sick and would be much better off going straight home, having a cup of tea and crawling into bed? Have I come here with no other purpose than to study this old man?" A feeling of revulsion seemed to have taken possession of me. "What have I got to do with this old wretch, or he with me?" I remembered the feeling of uneasiness he had caused me in the street. What was this strange compulsion of mine that focused in on every little unimportant event that occurred, and yet kept me from actually observing what was going on around me? A compulsion which one critic who had reviewed my last novel (and who was himself a thinker) had observed and pointed out.

These uneasy thoughts continued to trouble me as I sat there, the weight of illness falling heavier and heavier upon me, until at last I felt that I could not leave this warm room without a greater risk to my health. So, I took up a French newspaper, read a few lines, and dozed off.

The Germans in the room, talking about Frankfurt or smoking or reading, did not disturb me, but after about thirty minutes I suddenly woke up, shivering. "I'd better get home," I thought. But a silent pantomime that was taking place in the shop at that moment prevented me from leaving.

I have already mentioned that the old man, as soon as he had settled himself in a chair, would fix his eyes upon some point or other and keep them thus fixed for the rest of the evening. It had been my misfortune, on several occasions, to have this stupidly obstinate gaze (which saw nothing) focused upon me. It was a very uncomfortable, even eerie sensation, and I would usually change my place as quickly as possible.

For the last quarter of an hour the victim of his gaze was a small, neat and plump German, whose red face was encircled by a stiffly starched collar. He was a merchant from Riga, staying in St. Petersburg, whose name, as I learned afterwards, was Adam Ivanich Schultz, and he was an intimate friend of Mueller's. Not yet knowing anything about the old man, he was drinking a toddy and reading *The Village Barber*, when suddenly, raising his head to take a sip of his punch, he observed the old man's gaze sharply focused upon him.

Adam Ivanich was a particularly sensitive man, as are all Germans of the "better" class, and he found it both offensive and insulting to be stared at in so rude a manner. With barely suppressed indignation, he turned his eyes away from this ill-mannered neighbor, muttered something under his breath, and hid behind his book.

Moments later he peered out again and was met by the same obstinate look in the old fellow's eyes and the same utter absence of intelligence in his stare. Adam Ivanich still kept quiet. But the third time his patience gave way and he felt he must stand up for his dignity and not permit the fair city of Riga (of which he no doubt felt himself the representative) to be compromised in the presence of such distinguished company. He slammed his book onto the table with a loud bang, after which, carried away by his sense of compromised dignity and diminished self-esteem, he fixed his tiny, inflamed eyes upon the cause of his displeasure. It looked like a contest as to which one would overcome the other by the magnetic force of his gaze, as though they were waiting to see who would cave in first and admit defeat.

The sound of Adam Ivanich's book hitting the table and the eccentric position in which he now had placed himself quickly focused the attention of everyone present upon the pair. They all stopped what they were doing and looked on with grave and silent curiosity at the two champions. The scene was becoming very comical, but the magnetic attack of Adam Ivanich's stare didn't last long. He turned absolutely crimson, while the old man continued to stare at the furious Mr. Schultz with no more awareness of the onlookers than if they had been on the moon.

Soon Adam Ivanich's patience was completely exhausted and he hollered in German, with a shrill, piercing voice and a threatening air, "Warum starren Sie mich weiterhin so an?" But his adversary seemed to have neither heard nor understood the question and remained silent. So, Adam Ivanich decided to speak to him in Russian.

"Why you further stare me in such way?" he screamed with increasing rage, and in very bad Russian, leaping up from his chair.

The old man never moved, and the audience murmured its disapproval. Mueller himself, attracted by the noise, entered the room. Upon learning of the circumstances, he judged that the old man was deaf and put his lips close to his ear.

"Herr Schultz has just asked you not to stare at him so obstinately," he said as loudly as he could. The old man slowly turned his gaze upon Mueller and his face, expressionless until this moment, suddenly assumed a look of fear and anxiety. Violently agitated, he stooped and grabbed for his hat and cane, stood up, and with a pitiful smile (the smile of humiliation which a poor man puts on when he has been caught occupying some seat to which he is not entitled and is about to be bodily removed), prepared to go.

There was something so pitiable about this meek and submissive old man's terrified look that touched the heart so deeply that all present, beginning with Adam Ivanich, immediately softened towards him. It was clear that not only was this old man quite incapable of insulting anyone, but that he quite understood that he could be turned out from any place he happened to be in, at any moment, like a beggar. Mueller was a good sort of man and compassionate.

"No, no," he said, patting the old man's shoulder gently to calm him. "Please, sit down again. Herr Schultz, who is an eminent gentleman, well known at Court, has only requested that you not stare at him so, that's all."

But the poor old man understood no more this time than he had before and his agitation only increased. He stooped to pick up a tattered old blue handkerchief that had just fallen out of his hat and called his dog, which was stretched out full length on the floor with her two forefeet pressed against her nose.

"Azor, Azor," he cried in a trembling, broken voice. "Azorka!" But Azorka did not move. She seemed to be asleep. "Azorka," he repeated anxiously, and he touched the dog with the end of his cane, but the dog did not budge. The hat and cane dropped from his grasp as he bent down, fell on his knees and with both hands raised Azor's nose, but there was not the slightest sign of life. Poor Azorka was dead! Dead at her master's feet; of old age, perhaps, or perhaps of starvation.

The old man looked at her for a moment in consternation, as though he did not realize that the dog was dead, and then he stooped quietly over his old servant, his old friend, and pressed his pale face against that of his dead dog. There was a moment of silence. We were all deeply affected. At last, the poor old man got up, his ghastly pallor even whiter than before, and shivered as though under the influence of a terrible fever.

"You could have it stuffed, you know," said Mueller sympathetically, anxious to console the poor old fellow. "It can be stuffed very easily. Fyodor Karlovich Krieger here is a maestro at stuffing animals." Mueller picked up the old man's hat and cane from the floor and returned them to their owner.

"Yes, I know how to stuff animals very well," said Mr. Krieger modestly, coming forward. He was a very tall, thin German, with disheveled red hair and a hooked nose which supported a pair of spectacles.

"Oh yes," added Mueller, growing more enthusiastic over his idea," Fyodor Karlovich Krieger has a wonderful talent for stuffing all sorts of animals."

"Yes, I must say I have some talent for stuffing all sorts of animals," repeated Krieger, "and I am most anxious to stuff your dog there. At no charge, you understand," he added in a surprising display of generosity.

Mr. Schultz's face was now redder than ever and he, undoubtedly considering himself the innocent cause of all this trouble, also let loose with an outpouring of generosity. "No, no," he cried. "I will pay for stuffing the dog!"

The old man evidently heard all of this without understanding a word and he continued to shiver with fear.

"Look here, you must drink this glass of brandy," said Mueller at last, seeing that his mysterious visitor was intent upon getting away at all costs.

Mueller gave him the glass, which the old fellow took mechanically, but his hand trembled and before he had time to lift the brandy to his lips, he had spilled more than half of it. He put the glass down again on the serving tray without having touched a drop. Then, with a strange laugh completely inappropriate under the circumstances, he unsteadily, but quickly, made his way out of the shop, leaving Azorka stretched out on the floor.

The others were astonished by this behavior and one of the Germans remarked, "Well, did you ever see the likes of that?"

"That's a nice sort of thing to happen!" remarked another German as they all stared blankly at each other.

As for me, I darted out in pursuit of the old man. A few paces from the shop there was a little street, narrow and dark, bordered by high houses, and I had a feeling that he must have turned in there. The second building on the right side of this street was a house in the process of construction, surrounded by scaffolding. This scaffolding stretched nearly into the middle of the road and I caught sight of the old man hiding in the shadows made by the scaffolding and the wall of the next house. He was sitting there on the curb, his elbows resting on his knees, and he held his head between his two hands. I sat down by his side.

"Come, come," I said, having no idea how to begin. "You mustn't feel so miserable about poor Azorka. Let me take you home. Here, I'll hire a cab and we'll drive there together. Where do you live?"

He made no answer. I didn't know what to do. The street was empty. Suddenly he seized my hand.

"I'm choking! I'm choking!" he said. His voice was feeble and hoarse.

"Well, I'll take you home. Come," I said, lifting him by force. "You must have a cup of tea and get to bed. I'll call a cab. I'll get you a doctor, one of my friends."

I don't remember what else I said to him. He tried to get up, but when he was half on his feet he fell down again and began to mutter once more with that dreadful choking voice of his. I bent over him again and listened.

"Vasilyevsky." The word rattled in the old man's throat. "Sixth Line... Six... Sixth Line." He said no more, and was silent again.

"You live on Vasilyevsky Island, do you?" I asked. "But you were not going in that direction. You should have turned left and not right. You must go this way! Come with me, I'll take you there!"

He did not budge. I took his hand, but it fell back lifeless. I looked at his face, then touched it. He was dead. It seemed to me that all this was happening in a dream.

Well, this adventure caused me a great deal of worry and trouble, but as a result of it my feverish attack passed by itself. As others began to gather in the street, I was eventually able to learn where the old man lived. It was not on Vasilyevsky Island, but a step or two from the very spot where he had breathed his last, on the fifth floor of Klugen's house, just below the roof. He had a small hallway and a large room with a very low ceiling and three little skylights to serve for windows. The old fellow had existed there in great poverty. For furniture he had nothing but a table, two chairs and an old bed as hard as stone and with fibers of some coarse stuffing sticking out all over it. I discovered later that even this miserable furniture did not belong to him, but to the landlord. I could see that the stove had not been heated for ages and there was not a single candle to be found. Quite probably, his one reason for going to Mueller's was to sit in a warm room with light.

On the table there was an earthenware jug with nothing in it and an old crust of bread, as dry as a board. There was not a single kopek to be found and not even a change of linen to be buried in. Someone came forward and provided a shirt.

It was clear that he could not have lived like this, absolutely alone, so isolated. Somebody must have come by to look after him, however rarely. His passport was in the drawer of the table. The dead man had been a foreigner but was a naturalized Russian subject. His name was Jeremiah Smith, his calling a mechanic, and his age 78. On the table were two books, an abridged geography and a New Testament in Russian, the margins of which were covered with pencil and fingernail marks. I took these two books for myself. I made inquiries of the other inhabitants of the house and of the landlord. They hardly knew anything about him. There were quite a few other lodgers in the house, mostly mechanics and German widows, who occupied furnished rooms with board and service. The landlord knew nothing of his late lodger other than that he used to pay six rubles per month for his room and that he had not settled for the last month, so the landlord had been obliged to give the old man notice to vacate.

I asked the neighbors whether anyone ever came to visit Mr. Smith, but nobody could give a satisfactory answer to my question. The house was a large one and so many people came in and out of the arched gateway that it was difficult to keep track of everyone. The porter who had manned the gate for the past five years could no doubt have given some information, but he had gone home to his village two weeks earlier and had left his nephew in charge, a young fellow who did not as yet know half the inhabitants of the house.

I'm not at all sure my inquiries had helped in any way, but the old man was buried at last. In spite of all sorts of other business which I had on hand, I went over to Vasilyevsky Island every day, to the Sixth Line. I almost laughed at myself for doing so. What could I find in the Sixth Line but a row of houses? But then I thought, "Why did the old man talk about the Sixth Line at the very moment of his death? Or could he have been simply raving?"

As soon as his apartment was made available, I took it for myself. I liked it, especially the size of the room, although the ceiling was so low that at first, I was afraid that I would bang my head, but I soon got used to it. In any event, one couldn't expect much better for six rubles a month, and I liked the absolute independence and isolation of the space. There was nothing to take care of now except to find someone to serve me, until which time the porter agreed to come in at least once a day to tidy up and to act as waiter on special occasions.

I hoped too that somebody would come and inquire about the old man, but he had been dead five days now and as yet no one had turned up.

Chapter Two

At this time, that is about a year ago, I was on the writing staff of several journals, contributing short articles to each, but I felt sure that I could develop into an author of more important works, and at the moment I was working on a novel. All of my many efforts ultimately led me to where I am today, stretched out in a hospital bed so sick that, as far as I can determine, I am on the straight road to death. But if the end is so near, why am I taking the time to write down these reminiscences?

No matter how I try to resist it, this last and most painful year of my life continues to invade my thoughts. I am going to write the whole thing down because I believe that unless I do so, I shall simply die of sorrow. All of these bitter memories torment me. At the point of my pen, perhaps they will settle down in an orderly fashion and appear much less like a ghastly dream or nightmare. Just the mechanical act of writing has a tranquilizing effect. It calms me and reawakens within me my old habits as a writer and transforms my nightmarish and delirious visions into palpable shape, into real work. Yes, this is a good idea! Now, if I die, at least my attendant shall inherit my memoirs. He can seal the double frames of his windows with my manuscript when winter comes.

I started my story in the middle, I don't know why. At any rate, I must write it all down, so let's begin again at the beginning. My autobiography shall, at least, not be a long one.

I was born, not in St. Petersburg, but a long way from this city. My parents were good enough people, I suppose, but they left me an orphan when I was very young and I grew up in the house of Nikolai Sergeich Ichmenyev, the landowner of a small estate who took me in out of pity. He had but one daughter, Natasha, three years younger than me, and she and I grew up together like brother and sister. Oh, what wonderful childhood days! What a tragic joke that all I have to look back on (and regret) at twenty-five years of age is you, Natasha. That at the hour of my death, you are all I can look back on with joy and love. The sun used to shine so brightly. It was so different from this St. Petersburg sun. Our young hearts used to beat so joyously then, when we were surrounded by green fields and woods and not by piles of inanimate stones. How marvelous were the park and garden at Vassilyevskoe, the property on which Nikolai Sergeich was steward. Natasha and I used to walk together in that garden and in the damp forest which stretched beyond it.

Such happy times. There, life first revealed its sweet mysteries to us as we explored them together. I used to think that some mysterious being, unknown and unfathomable, existed hidden beneath each tree, within each shrub. The world of fairy tales and the world of reality merged into one for us, and often when the mists of evening were thicker than usual over the dark valleys, Natasha and I would stand together, hand in hand, overlooking the whirlpool in the river, and would look in each other's faces in the darkness and wait, with a fearful curiosity, to see something stalking out of the mist, or to hear some voice speaking to us out of the depths of the canyon, and to find that our nurse's tales were about to prove to be pure truth.

Once, years later, I reminded Natasha of the day when they first gave us a book to read called *First Readings for Children*, and how we immediately ran off into the garden near the little pond where there was a grassy bank beneath an old maple, and how we settled down there and read Madame de Genlis' fairy story, *Alphonso and Dalinda*. To this moment, I cannot think of that tale without strange emotion, and only last year, when I repeated the first lines of it to Natasha ("Alphonso, the hero of my tale, was born in Portugal; Don Kamir, his father," etc.), the tears came to my eyes. I must have looked very foolish, for Natasha could not help smiling, which contrasted oddly with my serious demeanor. She saw my reaction, however, and to make amends she began to talk over the past with me, and while she spoke, she too had been moved.

Oh, those delightful evenings we spent together, reminiscing over the past. And on the day I left for boarding school, how she cried, and again when we next parted, when I left Vassilyevskoe to continue my studies at the University. I was seventeen years old and she was going on fifteen. She has since told me that I was at that time a gawky, awkward boy, so badly put together that no one could look at me without laughing. When the moment came for parting, I remember that I took her aside to tell her something of terrific importance, but my tongue refused to utter a sound; it was paralyzed, and we had no conversation at all. I did not know what to say and I knew that she would not have understood what I meant. Anyhow, I wept hot tears over her and went away without having said a word. We did not see each other again until two years later, after her father had moved with his family to St. Petersburg as a result of the lawsuit, just as I was beginning my literary career.

CHAPTER THREE

Nikolai Sergeich Ichmenyev belonged to an honorable, but no longer wealthy, family. Upon the death of his parents, he had inherited a sizable piece of property, along with a hundred and fifty serfs. When he was twenty, he joined the hussars and had already served for six years (advancing to the rank of lieutenant) when one unfortunate evening he lost all of his property in a card game. He did not sleep a wink that night, but the next day reappeared at the card table and bet his horse, which was all he had left, on a single card. That card happened to win. So did the next one, and a third one, and in less than an hour he had won back fifty of his one hundred and fifty serfs along with the little estate known as Ichmenyevka.

He then gave up card playing, applied for his discharge from the army, received it two months later, and returned to vegetate on his property. He never again mentioned the circumstances just described and undoubtedly would have quarreled with anyone who dared to remind him of them.

He studied rural economy assiduously after that and a few years later, at the age of thirty-five, he married a young lady who came from a good, but poor, family named Anna Andreyevna Shoumiloff. Although she had no dowry and brought not a single kopek to the marriage, Anna Andreyevna prided herself on her proper education at a high-class school run by a French refugee named Madame Reveche, although no one could ever determine of what this magnificent education consisted.

Nikolai Sergeich developed into a first-rate scientific farmer and his neighbors looked upon him as a role model.

He lived in this quiet fashion for some years, until one eventful day when Prince Peter Alexandrovich Valkovsky (a neighboring landowner whose estate, Vassilyevskoe, boasted nine hundred serfs) arrived from St. Petersburg.

His arrival made a great sensation in the neighborhood. Although not quite in the first bloom of youth, the prince was still in the prime of life. His position was good, he had influential relatives, and he was handsome, rich and a widower. This last fact rendered him particularly attractive to all of the girls and young marriageable women in the neighborhood. People spoke of the brilliant reception which had been accorded him by the governor (who was discovered to be a distant relative of the prince). In short, he was one of those brilliant representatives of the highest St. Petersburg society, so rarely seen in the provinces, who produce such an extraordinary effect when they do make an appearance there.

However, it appeared that Prince Valkovsky was not quite as sweet as honey to *everyone*, especially not to those who could not benefit him in some way, his inferiors. Nor did he consider it useful to make the acquaintance of the other landowners near his own estate, which fact alone made him many enemies. What then must have been the general astonishment when he decided to pay a visit to Nikolai Sergeich? It was true, however, that the latter certainly was his nearest neighbor.

The arrival of the prince was a major event in the Ichmenyevs' home. From the very first day, Nikolai Sergeich and Anna Andreyevna were noticeably charmed by him, especially the latter whose enthusiasm knew no bounds. After a very short while, the prince felt perfectly at home with them, would visit almost every day, invited them into his home, cracked jokes with them, and sang and played on their wretched old piano. The Ichmenyevs could never see enough of him. How could anyone accuse so amiable, so agreeable a man of being proud and egotistical, as some of his neighbors insisted? Nikolai Sergeich, simple, honest, noble, and disinterested fellow that he was, had certainly made a good impression on the prince, as was very soon made clear.

Valkovsky had come from St. Petersburg to dismiss his steward, a treacherous German with respectable white hair, a Roman nose and eyeglasses, who stole from his master shamelessly and who had been responsible for the death of several peasants whom he had cruelly mistreated. This miserable creature, caught in the act of pillaging the prince's finances, played the injured innocent and talked a great deal about German honesty, but Valkovsky fired him, nonetheless.

The prince needed a new steward and his choice fell upon Nikolai Sergeich, who was certainly a perfect manager and honest in the full sense and meaning of the term. Valkovsky would have liked Ichmenyev to offer himself as the new steward, but when he failed to do so the prince decided one morning to make the proposal himself in the friendliest possible manner and in the form of a humble request. Nikolai Sergeich declined the offer, but the financial inducements (which were considerable) were most seductive to Anna Andreyevna, and the amiability of the prince become so pronounced that Nikolai Sergeich changed his mind and the prince at last achieved his goal.

It is clear that Valkovsky excelled in his understanding of human nature. The short space of time in which he had known the Ichmenyevs was quite enough for him to recognize that Nikolai Sergeich must be won over by friendship, by attachment of the heart, without which the temptation of money would mean very little to him. What the prince required was a steward in whom he could put his complete confidence so that he would never need to return to Vassilyevskoe unless he so desired. The charm which he exercised on Ichmenyev was so great that the latter sincerely believed that they were friends.

Nikolai Sergeich was one of those naïve, trusting and romantic individuals, so common in Russia, who easily attach themselves to others who are quite often unworthy of them, who give themselves heart and soul to their friends, and sometimes carry their devotion to a point which approaches the absurd.

Years passed. Valkovsky's lands were flourishing and he and his steward never had the slightest disagreement, their interaction exclusively confined to business correspondence. The prince, who never interfered in the slightest degree with any of his steward's arrangements, sometimes gave Nikolai Sergeich advice which astonished the latter by its practical and intelligent character. It was obvious that the prince not only disliked needless expenditure, but also understood the art of making a profit.

Five years after his visit to Vassilyevskoe, Valkovsky sent Ichmenyev orders for the purchase of another estate in the same neighborhood. It was a magnificent property of four hundred serfs. Nikolai Sergeich admired the prince tremendously and was so wholeheartedly interested in the prince's successes, in the attainment of his objects, in his advancement, that he worked as hard for the prince as he would have for his own brother.

But his enthusiasm reached its utmost limits when, as I am about to relate, the prince placed in his steward an amount of confidence which was really extraordinary.

However, as the prince is one of the chief actors in my story, I think I had better give a few details of his life prior to the events to be related.

Chapter Four

I have already said that Valkovsky was a widower. While still young he had married money. His family, who had always lived in Moscow, was quite ruined. His father had left him nothing but the estate at Vassilyevskoe, burdened with debt and a mortgage, so that at the age of twenty-two he had found himself penniless and forced to enter into government service in an office in Moscow, beginning his working life as the wretched sprout of an ancient but withered family tree. His marriage to the mature daughter of a merchant farmer saved him. Although her dowry was considerably less than he had been expecting, it was enough for the prince to clear his paternal acreage of debt and to plant his foot once again upon his own soil.

The merchant's daughter was quite unattractive, could barely write her own name, could not read two words in sequence, and had but one admirable quality: she had a sweet, good-natured personality. Valkovsky knew precisely how best to take advantage of this characteristic. After a year of marriage, he left his wife and a newborn son with her father in Moscow and went off to accept a prominent government post in another province, a position he had obtained through an influential relative in St. Petersburg. He thirsted for distinction and was determined to advance in his career. Knowing that he could not live with his wife in either St. Petersburg or Moscow, he resolved to begin his career in the provinces and wait for better times.

He treated his wife with the greatest cruelty. It was said that during their first year of married life he had very nearly killed her. (These reports would later arouse the greatest indignation in Nikolai Sergeich, who firmly sided with the prince and declared his master to be utterly incapable of any sort of vile behavior.)

After seven years of marriage, the prince became a widower and moved to St. Petersburg.

His arrival created quite a sensation in the capital. Still young, handsome, rich and with a great many shining virtues (including taste, geniality and unending good humor), he made his entrance into society not as a man seeking fortune and advancement but as one who projected a remarkable air of independence. He had, it was said, a sort of aura about him which commanded admiration and respect. Women adored him and a scandal concerning his involvement with a certain woman of the world only benefited his reputation further. He spent his money freely (although in private life he remained astonishingly frugal), and when he lost at cards, he did so without betraying the slightest emotion no matter how large the sum lost.

One of his cousins, Count Nainsky, who would never have taken notice of the prince had he simply come forward as a vulgar fortune seeker, was delighted by his success in society. He thought it not only possible, but advantageous, to honor him with some attention, and he welcomed the prince's seven-year-old son, Alexey Petrovich Valkovsky, into his household to be educated.

It was just at this point in time that Valkovsky went to Vassilyevskoe and made himself known to the Ichmenyevs.

Through the influence of the count, the prince was appointed an attaché to one of the principal embassies and went abroad. There were countless tales (always cloaked in mystery and never naming names) that hinted at the prince's scandalous affairs and business dealings, but no one knew for sure exactly what the details were. All that was positively known was that the prince was suddenly able to afford to purchase an estate with more than four hundred serfs, the estate I mentioned earlier.

After several years, the prince (having attained a high rank in government service) returned to Russia and found an excellent appointment in St. Petersburg. Word soon reached Ichmenyevka that the prince was about to marry again into a rich and powerful family and Nikolai Sergeich was delighted.

I was in St. Petersburg at the time, studying at the University, and Nikolai Sergeich wrote to me inquiring about the rumors and wondering if the reports of the impending marriage were true. He also wrote a letter of recommendation to the prince concerning me, but never received an answer. For my part, all that I could determine was that Valkovsky's son had been educated in Count Nainsky's household, then at the Lyceum, and that at the age of nineteen he had completed his studies. I gave Ichmenyev these fragments of information and added that the prince was very fond of his son, spoiled him, and had already made plans for his future, all of which I learned from several other students at the University who knew the young prince.

Shortly after that, Ichmenyev received a letter from Valkovsky which greatly surprised him. Until that moment the prince had restricted his correspondence with his steward to formal business matters, but suddenly he wrote Ichmenyev a frank, cordial letter about his family affairs. He complained about his son, Alexey Petrovich, whose conduct was causing him a great deal of distress. While he did not want to attach more significance to his son's rebellious behavior than the usual indiscretions of youth (he evidently wanted to downplay the nature of his son's offenses), he had resolved to punish the boy and to frighten him, and therefore wished to send him to live in the country with the Ichmenyevs, who would act as his guardians. The prince put himself entirely in the hands of his "honorable and excellent friend," and of his wife, and begged them to take the foolish, wayward youth into their family; to make him listen to the voice of reason while in exile; to love him, if possible, but most importantly to instill in the boy an understanding of the "moral and ethical behavior necessary to succeed in life."

The young prince arrived and was welcomed into the family like a son. Nikolai Sergeich soon loved him as he did his daughter, Natasha, and sometime later when he quarreled with the boy's father, he often thought with joy of his dear Alyosha (as he used to call the young prince, Alexey Petrovich).

He was certainly a charming young man, as pretty and as delicate as a girl, cheerful and trusting, with a heart endowed with sincerity and an openness to the noblest sentiments, an affectionate personality, honest and sympathetic. He soon became the idol of the Ichmenyev family.

He was, in spite of his twenty years, still a child, and it was difficult to understand why his father, who was supposedly so fond of him, had sent him into exile. He had led, it was rumored, a troublesome, unruly life in St. Petersburg, and had refused to enter into government service, which had annoyed his father. Ichmenyev never asked any questions, because he gathered from Valkovsky's letter that he wished to say nothing about the real reasons for his son's exile. According to one rumor, the boy had been guilty of unpardonable wildness. Another talked of a love affair, another of a duel, and still another of huge gambling debts. But there were some people who attributed the prince's action to certain personal considerations of a secret nature, to a calculating and egotistical scheme of the prince's own.

Ichmenyev repudiated all of these rumors with indignation, especially as the young man was greatly attached to his father, whom he had hardly known during his childhood and youth, but of whom he never spoke except with enthusiasm, and whom he evidently regarded with unquestionable allegiance.

Occasionally, Prince Alexey spoke of some countess and of a rivalry between his father and himself. It appeared that he had come between his father and the countess which made his father furious. Alexey used to tell this story with great animation and a sort of childish glee, but Ichmenyev refused to listen and stopped the boy whenever he attempted to tell it. Alexey did confirm, however, the rumors that the prince had matrimonial plans for him.

He had now spent a year in exile, and wrote occasionally to his father, most respectful and reasonable letters. By this time, Alexey had grown so used to living at Ichmenyevka that when his father came down in the spring on business, Alexey begged his father to be allowed to stay on as long as possible, assuring his father that he felt a real affinity for country-life. Every action, every impulse of Alexey's proceeded from his excessive impressionability and nervousness, from his warmth of heart, from his extraordinary readiness to succumb to any exterior influence, and from his almost absurd inability to take any action or think any thought of his own.

The prince received his son's request with a considerable show of opposition. Ichmenyev had some difficulty in recognizing his old friend, who had completely changed. The prince had become mean and petty, and in examining financial matters had showed himself to be repugnant and disagreeably combative. This was a source of great sorrow to Ichmenyev, who could not acknowledge it at first. However, everything was exactly the opposite of what had happened during the prince's previous visit, fourteen years earlier. This time, the prince made the acquaintance of all of the surrounding neighbors (the most important ones, that is), but never set foot in the Ichmenyevs' home, treating them as inferiors.

One day, something inconceivable happened. Without any apparent cause, there was a stormy argument between Valkovsky and Ichmenyev during which violent words were exchanged, offensive epithets were tossed, and Ichmenyev left the house indignant and angry. But that was not the end of it. Odious stories began to circulate in the district that Ichmenyev had been studying the character of the young prince in order to take advantage of the boy's weaknesses; that his daughter, Natasha, had manipulated her way into the boy's heart; and that, while pretending to notice nothing of it, Ichmenyev and his wife had encouraged their artful and depraved daughter to bewitch the innocent young man. As a result of such cunning, during the entire year he had spent with the Ichmenyevs, Alexey had never even set eyes on any of the other young girls in the neighborhood, whose beauty and charms were ripening within the family seats of the neighboring gentry. People went so far as to suggest that the young couple had arranged to elope to the neighboring village of Grigorievo, all with the consent and active participation of the girl's scheming parents. In short, a thick book would not hold the volume of wretched gossip which the scandalmongers of the neighborhood, both men and women, succeeded in circulating.

What was most astonishing of all is that the prince believed every word of it. In fact, he had only come down to Vassilyevskoe in response to an anonymous letter sent to him in St. Petersburg. It would certainly seem that anyone with even the slightest knowledge of Ichmenyev's character would have refused to believe a word of all this, and yet, as often happens in such cases, everyone preoccupied themselves with the rumors, talked about them, blamed Ichmenyev, shook their heads, and passed judgment without question.

Ichmenyev had too much pride to justify his daughter to a troop of gossipers, and he solemnly forbade his wife to enter into any kind of explanation on the subject with her neighbors. Natasha, so cruelly maligned for the better part of a year, never heard a word of any of these trumped-up lies and continued to be as happy and innocent as a child.

Meanwhile, the quarrel grew more and more venomous. The gossipers and scandalmongers were relentless and witnesses turned up to denounce Ichmenyev, never failing to convince the prince that Ichmenyev's handling of his estate's affairs had been less than honest. They went so far as to "prove" that three years earlier, during the sale of a forest, Ichmenyev had embezzled twelve thousand rubles from the proceeds, an action made all the more suspicious because the prince had not requested that the timber be sold, but had been convinced by Ichmenyev of the necessity for the sale and, after it was all over, had received from his steward considerably less than had actually been received.

These were all pure fabrications, as was proven later, but the prince believed them at the time and in the presence of witnesses accused Ichmenyev of theft. The latter could not bear the affront and responded to the prince with equal fervor. A dreadful quarrel followed and a lawsuit was started.

Ichmenyev soon saw that his case would fail. He required certain papers and, above all, he needed guidance and advice. He had absolutely no experience in such matters and it looked like he would lose the case and have his property confiscated. The indignant old man determined to move his home to the capital in order to look after his legal interests in connection with the lawsuit. He left an agent in whom he had complete confidence in charge of Ichmenyevka and set off for St. Petersburg.

Valkovsky, more than likely, soon realized that he had unjustly defamed Ichmenyev, but the insults had flown so freely from both sides that it was now impossible to find a means of reconciliation, and the angry prince did all he could to turn the situation to his own profit, which simply meant taking the last bit of bread out of his old steward's mouth.

CHAPTER FIVE

So, the Ichmenyevs moved to St. Petersburg. I will not describe my meeting with Natasha, who during the four years of our separation had never for a moment been out of my thoughts, but I will confess that my first thought upon seeing her again was that Fate had finally awarded her to me. It seemed to me at first that she had not matured much, that she had remained very much the girl-child of the days before our separation, but as time went on, I began to see new wonders in her every day, things which I had not seen before, perhaps because she had concealed them from me on purpose, as if the girl had wanted to hide her perfections from my eyes. And, oh, the joy of those discoveries!

During the period of his stay in St. Petersburg, Nikolai Sergeich was peevish and irritable. His affairs were not going well. He used to get angry and bury himself in his papers and take no notice of us. Anna Andreyevna, his wife, was like one lost and did not know what to do with herself. St. Petersburg terrified her, and she would sigh and tremble and lament about the old haunts where she had passed her life up till then. She would complain that Natasha had arrived at a marriageable age and there was nobody who gave her a second thought. She began to confide her deepest feelings in me, probably because there was no one else around better qualified to receive her confidences.

I had just finished my first novel and as a beginner I did not know the first thing about getting it published. I decided not to tell the Ichmenyevs anything about it until it was sold, and they were nearly ready to quarrel with me for leading a life of indolence, without employment and without making any effort to find employment. My adopted father criticized me severely and, as I knew his arguments were prompted by his paternal affection for me, I felt ashamed of telling him how I actually spent my time. How could I, in good conscience, tell him straight out that I did not want to be a "functionary," and that my function was to write novels? Instead I told him that I had not yet found a job, but that I was doing all that I could to find one. He, however, had no time to bother about my affairs just then.

Natasha had been present during one of my conversations with her father and later took me aside and implored me, with tears in her eyes, to think of my future. She questioned me about how I spent my time, but I didn't tell her my secret either, so she made me swear not to make myself wretched by my sloth and idleness. I just couldn't tell her about my novel yet, even though I am quite sure that one word of encouragement from her would have given me far more joy than all the flattering judgments which I later received.

My novel appeared at last, but long before its publication it was talked about in the literary world and Belinsky, himself, had rejoiced like a child over my manuscript.

If ever I was happy, it was not during those first intoxicating moments of my success, but rather during that period when I had not yet read or shown my work to a single soul. It was during those long nights of dreaming and of hopeful anticipation, while I labored passionately and lived among the characters that I had created, as though they were family members, living and breathing and real. I loved them and shared their joys and sorrows. Indeed, I remember now and again being actually moved to tears by the stupidity of one of my heroes.

I cannot describe the joy felt by my adopted parents, the Ichmenyevs, when they first heard the whisper of my success. Their first sensation was stunned silence. Anna Andreyevna simply would not believe that this new writer whom all the world was praising was her very own Vanya, and she simply shook her head in wonder.

The old man took even longer to acknowledge the situation after he first heard the news. He was deeply concerned and warned me that I would lose all hope of making a career in government service and spoke to me of the uncertain life led by most authors. However, the favorable notices which appeared in the newspapers and a few words of praise on my behalf from men he respected soon changed his opinion. As soon as he saw that I had money too and understood how well literary work can be remunerated, his last scruples vanished. Quick to leap from doubt to absolute confidence, as happy as a child for my success, he abandoned himself all at once to the most foolish aspirations on my account, to daydreams of the most dazzling description as to my future. Every day he invented some new career for me or planned some new project. He even began to assume towards me a deferential demeanor which he had certainly never demonstrated before. Every once in a while, his doubts would return and interrupt him even in the midst of one of his most exuberant fantasies, baffling and confusing him. To be an author! A poet! What a foolish occupation! What poet ever made his way in the world or attained greatness? There was nothing to be made of all these scribblers; worthless crew, the whole lot of them!

These doubts and confusions generally assailed him at the twilight hour. It was during that period of the day especially when he was most impressionable, nervous and suspicious. Natasha and I recognized this and generally found his behavior amusing. I would try to make him take a less pessimistic view of the matter by telling him amusing stories about General Soumorokof, or about how Derjavine sent snuff boxes filled with gold pieces, or how the Empress Catherine had personally visited the University. I spoke of Pushkin and of Gogol.

"I know, my friend, I know all that," he would say, though likely enough he had never heard a word of these stories until then. "I know all that, but what comforts me a little in your case is that your cooking is not stewed in verse. Poetry, my dear boy, is simply absurd. Now, don't argue with me. Take this from an old man who wishes you well. Poetry is a waste of time. It's one thing for college professors to go in for rhyming, but for a young fellow of your age, my boy, it's the straight road to the lunatic asylum. Pushkin is a great man, no one can deny him that, but verses and nothing but verses, simply nonsense. Not that I've read much poetry, but prose, now that is another thing altogether. An author can instruct, can talk of patriotism and virtue. I'm not a good hand at explaining things, but you know what I mean. It's my love for you that makes me speak to you like this. But let's have a look at what you're going to read to us," he concluded in a patronizing tone on the day I at last brought them a copy of my book. We were all sitting together around the table after tea.

"Now then," he added, "read us a bit of what you've been scribbling all this time. You have managed to get yourself talked about a good deal, let's see what's in it!"

The novel had appeared that very day and as soon as I could get my hands on a copy, I ran with it to the Ichmenyevs. I was unhappy that I couldn't read it to them earlier, but the manuscript had been in the publisher's hands. Natasha scolded me about my allowing strangers to read my novel before her.

The family assembled, I opened my book to read. Nikolai Sergeich assumed an air of the utmost solemnity for he was prepared to bring the most severe criticism to bear upon my work. He wanted to form his own opinion and to convince himself as to its merits. Anna Andreyevna also assumed a far more serious air than she normally wore. She even put on a new bonnet expressly in honor of the reading. For a long time, she had been aware that I regarded her Natasha with infinite love, that my spirit was nourished on her image and that my eyes darkened when I spoke to her. Natasha's eyes too looked at me more brightly than before. The time was near, I felt, when success would finally fulfill my golden dreams and bring me the happiness I longed for.

Natasha's mother had also observed the tendency on her husband's part to praise me extravagantly and to look at me and his daughter with a new and peculiar expression on his face, and she suddenly took fright. I was not a count or a prince or a reigning duke. If only I were some fine young fellow just out of law school, full of wisdom and honors! But what is a writer?

CHAPTER SIX

I read them the whole novel in one sitting, beginning after tea and not finishing until two in the morning. Nikolai Sergeich, at first, frowned. He had envisioned something on some inexplicably higher level, something that he might not be able to understand, but that would be important. Instead, what he had heard seemed so commonplace, the events were no different from his own daily experiences, the characters just like people he met every day. He had been anticipating some lofty hero performing great deeds or, at the very least, some historical figure like Pushkin's Roslavlev or Zagoskin's Yuri Miloslavsky. But instead he had been presented with a common little clerk, obscure, foolish and so poor that his shabby coat was missing its buttons, and the language had been so simple, so straightforward, so much like ordinary conversation, that he had understood every word of it. It was most surprising to him, and I think he felt that he had been deprived of something special. Anna Andreyevna exchanged glances with her husband and with a shrug seemed to be saying, "Will people really pay money to read about such depressing, commonplace people?"

Natasha, however, had listened with rapt attention, holding my hand in hers, never taking her eyes off me, and seemed almost to be reading along with me as she watched my lips move. I had read little more than half of my novel when I noticed all three of them crying. Anna Andreyevna had been sincerely moved by my hero's plight and her tears and exclamations seemed to suggest that she would have gladly helped him if she could, anything to relieve his misery.

The old man, after a few moments, set aside his higher aspirations. "From the very beginning," he said, "it is evident that it is going to be a long journey from first to last, but it is a simple tale that seizes the heart. The actions that occur are understandable and it is quite memorable, really. It seems to be saying that even the most oppressed person on earth is also a man and deserves to be called my brother."

Natasha suddenly rose, her cheeks and eyes red with tears. She grasped my hand quickly, kissed it, and ran out of the room. Her father and mother exchanged surprised glances.

"Well," said the old man, trying to justify his daughter's odd behavior to both me and himself. "That is good! She has been moved by your story. It was a fine noble impulse! She is a good girl, Natasha, a very good girl." But Anna Andreyevna, despite having been clearly moved during the reading, looked upon me now in a disapproving manner, as if to say, "It may be true that your character, Alexander Makedonsky is a hero in his own way, but why does he have to break the chairs?"

Natasha soon returned, looking radiant and happy once again, and pinched me as she passed by me.

The old man returned once again to his critique of my novel, speaking at first in a very "serious" tone of voice, but soon revealing his enthusiasm. "Well, Vanya, it is good, quite good! Comforting. Not high art, not great, of course, that is clear. Not like Dmitriyev's *The Liberation of Moscow*, in which the spirit of man seems to soar like an eagle, but in its own way it seems, from the very first line, to speak for all men, so to speak. You understand, Vanya, that in your own simple language you have made it most intelligible. Yes, precisely that! I love that it is intelligible! The people seem to talk like me, the events are so much like my own life. Not high art, perhaps, but a simple style, easily understood. You have done very well, indeed, Vanya. And what else is there to say? It is printed, it is too late to change anything. Perhaps in the second edition? Ah, will you be paid again for a second edition?"

"Yes, they pay well for this sort of thing, do they?" asked Anna Andreyevna. "The more I think about it, the more unbelievable it all seems. My lord, the things people will spend their money on."

"You know, Vanya," the old man continued, growing more intrigued by the subject, "this occupation of writing may not be on the same level as government service, but there is still something honorable in it. Even high-ranking people will read your book and you have mentioned, I think, that Gogol receives a yearly pension and lives comfortably abroad. And that may happen to you! But, of course, it is too soon to talk about such things. You need to write more books, even better books. So write, brother, write faster, you mustn't rest on your laurels! Strike while the iron is hot!"

He spoke with such conviction and with such warmth of heart that I did not want to stop him or do anything to stifle his enthusiasm.

"They may even give you a snuff-box," he added. "Why not? They will want to encourage you. And, who knows, you may even be invited to court." He said this in a whisper, with a wink of his eye. "Or, perhaps, it is too soon to talk about being invited to court."

"And why shouldn't he be invited to court?" said the mother, a little offended.

"You're going to make me a general before I know it," I laughed heartily. The old man laughed too, feeling very happy now.

"Come, Your Excellency, don't you want to eat something?" said Natasha, who had prepared a late supper for us. She was laughing and bouncing around as friskily as a puppy and ran to her father and threw herself into his arms. "My darling, darling, papa!" She was overcome with emotion and her father was too.

"Yes, yes, my sweet daughter, it is all very funny, but general or no general, it's time for supper. You are such a sweet, sensitive child," he said, patting her cheeks with his large hands. "You know, Vanya, you may not be a general, oh no, far from a general, but you shall be someone important, nonetheless. An author!"

"People call them writers nowadays, papa, not authors," Natasha said.

"Writers, not authors? I didn't know that. But what I was about to say, Vanya, is that you may not be appointed chamberlain, but you are now someone of importance. You may be sent abroad to Italy as an attaché or for your health or to study your art. You may even be provided with a subsidy while you write more books. The money would be wonderful, of course, but your honor depends on your earning such money and not in simply accepting the patronage of others."

"And you mustn't get a swollen head, either, Ivan Petrovich," added Anna Andreyevna with a laugh.

"Yes, but let him at least have a small medal to wear on his chest, papa. He deserves so much more than to be just an attaché." Natasha again laughed and pinched me on the hand.

"Ah, there she goes making fun of me," cried the old man with delight. Natasha's eyes flashed merrily and shone like stars in the candlelight. "I may have gone a little too far, but it seems to me, Vanya, when I look at you and compare you to many of the great writers, you seem so simple."

"Oh my God, papa, what do you expect him to look like?"

"No, no, I didn't mean it like that. Maybe I phrased it wrong, Vanya, but when I look at your face, it is not... well... poetic. You know, they speak of poets as pale, with their hair such and in their eyes there is such and, well, when I look at you I do not see the face of a poet. You're not Goethe, for example. Of course, that is not a bad thing. But look, my friend, I am not a philosopher or a scientist. I only know what I feel. So if your face is not the face of a poet, so be it, but I must add that it pleases me very much that there is no great misfortune in your face, yours is a good face, indeed. But you must remain honest, Vanya, be an honest man, that is the main thing. Live honestly and the road is wide open before you! That is what I wanted to say, precisely what I wanted to say!"

What a marvelous evening that was. There were many more fine evenings I spent with the Ichmenyevs. Frequently, I would bring news of the literary world, a subject in which the old man had suddenly taken considerable interest. He even began to read critical essays and scholarly articles in journals which he praised enthusiastically, even though he barely understood a word, and he could pontificate for hours on writers, both good and bad.

The old woman kept a vigilant watch over Natasha and me, but we managed to elude her on occasion. Fortunately, she didn't follow us about the house! Natasha and I needed very few words to communicate for we both understood each other completely. The one word I had longed to hear for so long finally came late one afternoon when Natasha, after casting her eyes down and turning her head away from me, whispered, "Yes."

Our love for each was no secret to her parents, but they remained skeptical about my chosen profession. "Indeed, you have had a great success with your first book, Ivan Petrovich," Anna Andreyevna told me one day, "but what will you do if the next one is not so well received? You may not always be so successful, and what then? At least if you had some steady employment..."

"This is what I have to say to you, Vanya," added the old man after thinking it over for a moment. "I have seen, noticed and recognized that there is something very special between you and Natasha, and it gladdens my heart even as it gladdens your own. Yes, that is all very well. But you see, Vanya, the two of you are still very young, and Anna Andreyevna and I are agreed that it is best for you both to wait. You have, of course, talent, Vanya, perhaps even remarkable talent, and it will no doubt take you far in the world. It may not be genius, as they first shouted about you—I read, in fact, today a criticism of your work in the newspaper—so let us say, simply, talent. But talent cannot be taken to the pawnshop and exchanged for money. You are both poor. Let us wait then for a year or, at the very least, half a year. By then you should be well along in your career and, if so, Natasha will be yours. But if you do not succeed, well then, you shall judge for yourself what is best. You are an honest man, I think." He stopped at this.

So, we waited a year. In fact, it was almost exactly one year later when, on a clear September evening, I went to visit the Ichmenyevs with a great sadness in my heart. I was very ill and as I entered their home I almost fainted, falling into a chair, which alarmed them greatly. But if my head was dizzy and if my heart was palpitating, it was not because I had on ten recent occasions arrived at their door and then turned and gone back home again without entering, nor was it because I had so far failed to achieve any noticeable success as a writer (having earned neither fame nor financial reward), nor was it because I had not been appointed attaché to any government office, nor was it because I had not been sent by a grateful nation to Italy to recover my health. No. It was because I had come to recognize in the past year that two people, both Natasha and I, could live ten years in the space of just twelve months and that now an even greater abyss lay between us.

And here I sat before the old man and his wife. He settled silently into his chair, barely looking at me in my shabby suit which hung badly on my shrunken frame. My face too had grown thin and pale, though still not, I am sure, the old man's image of a poet. The old woman stared with undisguised pity at me, a look which saddened me for it seemed to say, "My lord, is this the man to whom we almost gave our Natasha?"

"Take a cup of tea, Ivan Petrovich," she said, pointing to the samovar on the table. "How are you feeling? Are you still under the weather?" The sadness in her voice still haunts me to this day. She turned her glance to her husband. It was clear that he too had been sick. The strain of the lawsuit had had a devastating effect on his health and he sat motionless, staring into space, a cup of tea sitting next to him cold and undisturbed.

The young prince, who had been the primary cause of the quarrel between his father and Ichmenyev, had started to visit the Ichmenyevs in their home some five months earlier. The old man, who loved Alexey like a son and mentioned him in conversation almost daily, was delighted by the visits. His wife said it reminded her of their years at Vassilyevskoe and tears came to her eyes. The young prince's visits soon grew more and more frequent and Ichmenyev, who personifies the virtues of honesty and openness, refused to take any precautionary measures. His pride kept him from accepting the idea that Valkovsky might respond negatively upon hearing of his son's repeated visits to their home, and, as a consequence, Alexey was soon visiting the family on a daily basis, often staying past midnight.

Word quickly reached Valkovsky, of course, and the resulting scandal gave rise to even worse gossip and scandal mongering than Ichmenyev had endured at Vassilyevskoe. The old prince sent Nikolai Sergeich an insulting letter and positively forbade his son to go near the Ichmenyevs. This had occurred just two weeks before my visit.

The old man was in a terrible state of depression. His sweet, innocent Natasha had once again become the object of distorted lies and outrageous accusations and he knew that the man responsible was the same villain who had slandered his own name so grossly, and there was little he could do to demand satisfaction.

The first few days were especially hard on him and he took to his bed in despair. I was able to keep up with the details of what transpired from my own sickbed at home and had not been near the Ichmenyevs for three weeks. During that time, I had had a presentiment of still worse things to come and dared not allow my thoughts to dwell upon them. It was anguish for me to sit there now before my friends, trying to avoid thinking about the impending storm, and knowing that there was nothing I could do to avoid the inevitable.

As difficult as it was for me to face the family, I knew that I had to be there for Natasha's sake. There was something that drew me to her side this particular evening.

"Well," said the old man, shaking himself awake from his stupor. "Have you been sick or what? We haven't seen you in weeks. I know it's my fault, I should have come to see you, but there always seemed to be something that prevented it." Again he returned to his private thoughts.

"I'm afraid I've been rather grubby lately," I said.

He didn't respond for nearly five minutes, then finally he said, "Ha! Grubby! Grubby. I've often told you to take better care of yourself, but you never listened. I suppose it is still necessary for artists to starve in garrets before the muse of inspiration will deign to visit them."

I knew that the old man must have been greatly distressed for him to talk to me like that, so I let it pass. I just looked at him. His face was yellow and his sad eyes had a puzzled look that seemed to ask a question that he was too tired or too confused to answer. He was more irritable than I had ever seen him.

His wife looked at him anxiously. When he wasn't looking, she took the opportunity to give me a glance that clearly told me that she was worried about him.

"How has Natasha been feeling," I asked her. "Is she at home?"

"Yes, she's home," she answered, looking surprisingly embarrassed by her response. "I'm sure she will be out to see you soon. It is no joke when I tell you that she has changed greatly in the three weeks since you last saw each other, and we can't understand it. I don't know whether she is sick or what. God help her," she added, looking at her husband.

"No, no, she's fine. There's nothing at all wrong with her," Ichmenyev responded angrily. "She's not sick. She's just growing up. All girls are like that at her age. Who can understand a young woman's sorrows and whims?"

"Whims," said the mother. "You call them whims?"

The old man did not respond, but sat and drummed his fingers on the table. "My God," I thought to myself, "what has happened between these two to bring them to this state of affairs?"

"So, tell me, Vanya, what has been happening with you?" the old man asked again. "What is Belinsky doing? Does he still write criticisms?"

"Yes," I said, "he still writes."

The old man sat quietly for a moment, "Ah, Vanya," he said, waving his hand in a sad gesture of defeat, "there is already so much criticism."

Suddenly, the door opened and Natasha entered.

Chapter Seven

Natasha was carrying her hat in her hand as she entered, moved to set it down on the piano, then came to me and held out her hand without a word. Her lips moved slightly as if she wanted to say something to me, some friendly greeting perhaps, but no words came. We had not seen each other for three weeks and I was astonished by the change that had taken place in her. Her cheeks were pale and hollow, her lips parched with fever, but behind her dark eyelashes there was a fiery look of passionate determination. My God, she was beautiful. I could not remember her ever having looked more breathtaking than on that fateful day.

Was this the same Natasha who just one year earlier had trembled in sympathy with me as I read my novel, who had laughed so gaily and chided her father so affectionately during supper? The same Natasha who, there, in the next room, had turned her head, lowered her eyes, and told me "yes?"

Suddenly, a nearby church bell sounded its call to Vespers. Natasha trembled and Anna Andreyevna crossed herself.

"You should go to Vespers, Natasha, I know you want to. Go and pray. It's not far, and the walk will do you good. You don't get out enough and you always look so pale. It's as if someone has cast a spell over you."

"I don't think I will go today," she replied slowly in a voice so quiet and hoarse that I could scarcely hear her. "I don't feel well." The blood drained from her face.

"Why don't you go, my darling? You were on your way a moment ago. You've even brought your hat with you. Go. Go and pray to God to give you back your health."

"Yes, yes, your mother's quite right," said the old man. "You should go. You'll get a little fresh air at the same time. Vanya will walk with you."

I thought I saw a bitter smile on Natasha's lips. Her hand was trembling as she picked up her hat and put it on. Her movements seemed oddly mechanical, as if some unconscious force were compelling her against her will. Her father and mother watched her with astonishment.

"Good-bye," she said, in a scarcely audible voice.

"Why good-bye, my darling?" asked the mother. "You won't be gone long. It's just a short walk, you'll get a little air, and that will do you good. Oh lord, I had forgotten something important—I'm always so forgetful. I've made a little case for you. A man in Kiev taught me how to do it last year. It's a lovely little case and I've stitched a prayer inside it. It's a very appropriate prayer, my angel. Take it with you and, perhaps, the good Lord will send you back your health. You are our only child," and she took from her workbox a small golden cross which Natasha often wore around her neck. Anna Andreyevna had attached the little case to the same piece of ribbon that held the cross.

"Wear it in good health," she said, as she put the ribbon around Natasha's neck and made the sign of the cross. "There was a time when I used to baptize you like this every evening," she sobbed. "I used to read you a prayer before you went to sleep and you would repeat it back to me. But things are not the same now, my darling. You no longer feel the same tranquil spirit of the Lord. Oh, Natasha, Natasha! All I can give you is a mother's prayers and they don't seem to help you, they don't do you any good!" and she cried bitterly.

Natasha silently kissed her mother's hand and started in the direction of the door, but turned suddenly and went to her father, falling on her knees in front of him.

"Father, you must bless me too. Bless your daughter," she cried in a breathless voice.

We all exchanged confused glances as we stood and watched this solemn act. After a few moments, the old man looked down at her, completely bewildered.

"Natasha, my darling, my little one, my own dear little daughter, what is the matter with you?" he cried at last and a lifetime of tears ran down his cheeks. "Tell me why you are so sad? Why do you cry day and night? I see it all, you know. I don't sleep at night any better than you do, and I hear you crying. Tell me, my Natasha, open your heart to me and let your father share your troubles and we..." He did not finish but lifted her into his arms and held her close. She pressed herself convulsively to her father's breast and buried her head in his shoulder.

"Nothing, it's nothing, I'm a bit under the weather, that's all," she said, her voice suffocated by a flood of tears that she could not suppress.

"May God bless you, even as I give you my blessing now, my darling, my precious child," said her father, "and may He send you peace from this time forward, and keep you from all harm! Pray to God, my darling, that my prayers may reach Him."

"And my blessing upon you too," added her mother, weeping.

"Good-bye," Natasha whispered.

As she reached the door, she stopped and looked once again at her parents as if she had something more to say, but couldn't, and ran quickly from the room. I rushed after her, with a presentiment of evil gaining strength within me.

Chapter Eight

Natasha was silent as we walked through the streets toward the River Neva. Her head was bowed low and she didn't look at me, but when we reached the embankment of the river she stopped suddenly and grabbed me by the hand.

"I'm suffocating," she said, "suffocating."

"Come back, Natasha," I cried in fright, "come back home."

"Don't you see, Vanya, that I've left them and that I can't ever return?" she said with the most sorrowful look imaginable.

My heart stopped. I had suspected that something like this would happen and yet her words struck me like a thunderbolt. As we walked along the embankment, I tried to think of something to say, but I felt entirely lost. My head was spinning. It all seemed so grotesque, so impossible!

"You blame me, Vanya," she said finally.

"No, but... I can't believe it, this just can't be!" I answered, not knowing what I was saying.

"And yet it's all true," she said. "I'm leaving and I don't know what will happen to them. I'm not even sure what will happen to me."

"You are going to him, aren't you?"

"Yes."

"But this is impossible, Natasha," I cried out angrily. "You know it's impossible! Oh, my poor Natasha, this is madness! It will kill *them* and destroy *you*. You know that, don't you?"

"Yes, I know it," she said, "but what can I do? I have no choice." I heard so much despair in her voice, it was as though she were about to climb the stairs of the scaffold to be hanged.

"Come back, Natasha, come back before it's too late!" I begged with all the passion I could muster, knowing the futility of my efforts and recognizing how utterly absurd this moment was. "Have you thought about what this will do to your father?" I fought with the only weapon I had available to me. "You know that your father and his father are bitter enemies because of the lies the prince told. He humiliated and degraded your father by accusing him of embezzlement, by calling your father a thief! You know that he is suing your father in a court of law at this very moment and that he... my God, you must know this, Natasha... that he has accused your parents of encouraging you to seduce Alexey while he was with you in the country! Remember how your poor father has suffered from these insults, his hair has turned white! I won't say a word of what it will cost them to lose you, their one treasure, you, who are all that remains to them in their old age. You know all that already, but think about this, Natasha. Your father believes you to be as innocent as a lamb, that all the malicious stories about you and Alexey are simply lies. But now this has all flared up again and the prince has again insulted your father. Understand, Natasha, that if you do this, if you go to Alexey, suddenly all of the prince's vile accusations about you will be proven true, will be justified by your conduct. Everyone who has heard the insinuations and accusations against you and your father will now be able to say that the prince was right all along. The humiliation will kill your father, Natasha, the degradation, the shame of it all will kill him, and you will be responsible! You, Natasha, his innocent-as-a-lamb, little darling daughter. And your mother, do you think she will survive the old man's death? Natasha, please, think of what you are doing and wake up. Wake to your own self again, Natasha, and come home!"

She was silent, but the look in her eyes was filled with so much pain, such intense sorrow, that I realized how difficult her decision had been, and I knew that my cruel words were only torturing her more. I wanted to stop, but I felt compelled to continue.

"A little while ago you told your mother that you didn't want to go out, to go to Vespers. I think, at that moment, you were undecided about leaving home. Maybe you still have doubts."

She smiled bitterly. I knew that nothing I could say would change her mind, that it was useless to try.

"Do you really love him that much?" I asked, with a sinking feeling in my heart. I didn't know what else to say.

"How should I answer you, Vanya?" she finally responded. "It's simple. He told me to meet him here. I have done as he asked. I am here, waiting for him."

"But listen, listen," I begged, clutching at straws that were beyond my reach. "You can still do this, but there are other ways, better ways, to deal with this. You don't have to leave home. I'll help you to make other arrangements. I'll carry letters for you, help you to meet him in private, anything to make this easier than simply leaving home. Natasha, my love, you know that I will do anything to keep you from destroying your life. Meet with him in secret for just a little while, at least until your fathers end this stupid quarrel. Then, when the fighting is over, you and he will be free to love each other any way you please. You'll be very happy, really you will, Natasha, you'll see, and you won't have to give up everything!"

"Vanya, please stop!" she interrupted, grabbing my hand and smiling through her tears. "My dear, dear, Vanya, what a loyal and honest friend you are. You haven't said one word about yourself. I've walked out on you too and yet you forgive me, you think only about my happiness. Would you really carry letters for us?" she said with wonder and cried even harder. "I know how much you have loved me, Vanya, and how much you love me even now. And yet you have never uttered a single reproachful word, not one bitter thought. My God, I am the one to blame for all this. You remember every beautiful moment we have ever spent together. It would have been so much easier if I had never known, never even met him! You and I could have been so happy together. But I am not worthy of you. Why do you continue to talk about past happiness, what good does it do you? For three weeks I didn't see you, and I swear to you that not once in all that time did I think that you hated me or cursed me. I knew that you didn't want to come between us or to reproach us for our love. You refused to be an obstacle to my possible happiness. It must have been so painful for you to see us, and yet I did so long to see you. I love Alyosha madly, even more than madly, and yet sometimes it seems to me that I love you still more, but as my friend. I could never live without you. You are essential to me, my Vanya, you and your heart of gold! Oh, Vanya, what a bitter, terrible future we have!"

And her tears continued to flow. Yes, it was hard for me to watch.

"Oh, how I wanted to see you," she continued, trying to hold back her tears. "You look so thin and pale, have you been sick, Vanya? I didn't even ask about you. I talked only of myself! How are you doing now, Vanya? How is your novel going?"

"To hell with my novel, Natasha! Tell me, did Alexey insist on your eloping with him?"

"No, it was more my idea. Of course, he did say yes, and I have very... wait, I want to tell you everything. His father wants him to woo a very rich and aristocratic girl. You know how conniving the prince can be. Well, he insists on Alyosha marrying this girl and he'll do anything to make sure it happens because, well, he may not get another chance. Imagine, social position, a huge fortune, and I'm told that the girl is actually very pretty, well educated, with a good heart. Alyosha himself is quite taken with her. Well, his father wants to get Alyosha off his hands as quickly as possible so that he will be free to marry again himself. Well, naturally, the prince is determined to separate us in any way he can, because he is afraid that I have influence over his son."

"But is Valkovsky aware that you two are already in love with each other?" I asked, interrupting her.

"He knows everything."

"But who told him?"

"Why, Alyosha, of course. He told him everything."

"My God, what was he thinking? How could he tell his father, and at such a moment?"

"Now don't blame him, Vanya, don't laugh at him! You can't judge him the way you would anyone else. He's a child. A child who has been brought up quite differently from us. He's not aware of what he's doing. He's very impressionable, you see, and he tends to fall under the influence of the person nearest to him. The first bit of influence exerted over him is quite enough to cause him to renounce everything he believed just moments before. He has absolutely no strength of character. He is yours one day and later that evening he belongs to someone else. It's just the way he is, and he'd be the first one to admit it. Why, he might do something perfectly dreadful and you wouldn't know whether to blame him or feel just perfectly awful for him. He is capable of great self-sacrifice, but only until the next impression, and then he forgets all about it. And he will forget me too if I'm not always with him!"

"It's very possible, Natasha, that this proposed marriage is just a rumor. Do you really want to marry such a child?"

"His father is quite capable of such scheming."

"And how do you know this girl is so wonderful and that Alexey is taken by her?"

"He told me so himself."

"What? He told you that he might fall in love with another girl and demands that you sacrifice everything to stop him?"

"No, no, you don't know him! You haven't been with him enough to understand. You have to spend more time with Alyosha before you can make judgments about him. There is no one alive who is more honest or has a purer heart. It would be so much easier for me if he were a liar. I wouldn't be so drawn to him. It's not at all surprising that he should be attracted to her. If he were to spend a week without seeing me, he would probably go and fall completely in love with her... or someone else. But just as soon as he saw me, he would be all mine again. You see it's a very good thing that I know this about him because, if I didn't, I would simply die of suspicion. That's why I have decided, Vanya, that I must be by his side always, constantly, every moment, or he will forget about me and leave me! I understand him, Vanya, and without me every woman he sees might try to seduce him, and then what would happen? I would die! And, of course, I would be happy to die because what would life be without him? Worse than death, worse than torture. Oh, Vanya, you must see now how deeply I love him if I'm willing to leave my father and mother for his sake. You can't persuade me with your words because I am quite determined. I must have him by my side every hour, every minute! I can't go back now or I am lost! I know that!"

She stopped suddenly, then cried, "Oh, Vanya, what if he really has stopped loving me? If what you've just said is really true, that he is simply deceiving me..."

I had not said anything of the kind.

"If he was only pretending to be honest and sincere but was really wicked and vain! And here I am defending him against your arguments when he may be with some other girl right now, laughing at me! While I, horrible, horrible creature that I am, have left everything behind and am searching about the streets looking for him. Oh, Vanya!"

Her agonizing moan was so painful that it saddened me to the depths of my soul. I could see now that Natasha was unable to control herself, that a blind, irrational jealousy had so taken hold of her that only the most insane, irrational solution was available to her. But another kind of jealousy, in my own heart, flared up and compelled me to say things that I knew would be hurtful. "I don't understand how you could continue to love him after what you've just told me. You have no respect for him, you don't believe he really loves you, and yet you are still willing to throw your family aside and run off with him. Your love has blinded you to reality; it has taken possession of you. I don't understand that kind of love."

"Yes, I love him insanely," she answered, as if in great pain. "You have never known such love, Vanya. I know that I'm crazy, that I've lost my mind, and that this may not be real love, but it doesn't matter, it's the only kind of love I have. I've known all along, even in my happiest moments with him, that this can't last, that it will only cause me pain, but what can I do if the pain caused by him is the only thing that gives me pleasure? I know what to expect and how much I will suffer. He's told me that he loves me, but I know I can't believe it, not after what he's put me through in the past. I have no faith in his promises; I don't trust his promises and never have, even though I know he has never lied to me and that he is incapable of telling a lie. I've even told him, Vanya, that I don't want to tie him down, that no one wants to be tied down, I'm the first to admit it, but I'd be happy to be his slave, a voluntary serf who'll do anything for him, if only I can have him with me, near me, and I can see him and look at him. It seems to me that even if he loved another, I could be happy knowing that he loves someone else, just as long as I could still be with him, by his side. How degrading is that, Vanya? How much further down can I go?" she cried, her eyes flaming with insane passion. "I know how demeaning this is and yet I know that if he abandoned me, I would run after him to the farthest reaches of the Earth, even if he hated me, and drove me away. You've tried to persuade me to change my mind and return, but I have no mind of my own. What if I did go back? I'd only run after him again tomorrow. He has only to snap his fingers, to whistle for me, and like his dog I would run after him at once. I'm not afraid of any torture, Vanya, as long as it comes from him. I just can't say it any other way!"

"And what about your father and mother, have you forgotten about them?" I thought to myself, but I only said, "Has he actually told you that he wants to marry you?"

"Yes, he promised, he has promised everything. He is coming to get me now and tomorrow we shall be married, quietly, somewhere outside the city, although he doesn't know where just yet. He doesn't understand these things, he's just as innocent as can be, but what an amazing husband he's going to be! It's funny, right? We'll be married tomorrow and, who knows, maybe the next day he will reproach me for it, but I don't want him ever to have anything to reproach me for. I don't ask anything from him. If his marrying me makes him unhappy afterwards, he is free to do what he wants."

"Natasha, you are delirious, you are so confused," I said. "Are you going to him right now?"

"No, he promised to meet me here and to take me away, we agreed." She looked eagerly along the street, but there was no one in sight.

"And yet he hasn't come. He's made you stand and wait for him," I cried with indignation. Natasha seemed shaken by the impact of my words and her face was painfully distorted.

"Maybe he's not coming at all," she said with a bitter smile. "He wrote to me three days ago and said that if I didn't promise to come tonight, he'd postpone our elopement to another day and that he would go with his father to visit his fiancée. Oh, Vanya, what if he really went to see her!"

I didn't answer. She held my hand firmly and her eyes sparkled.

"He is with her now," she said, so faintly that I could hardly hear her. "He hoped that I wouldn't come, so that he could go to her and say afterwards that it was my fault, since he had given me advance notice and I hadn't shown up. He's tired of me and is planning to leave me. Oh, God! I am so stupid! He told me the last time I saw him that I made him sick! Why am I waiting for him?"

"There he is!" I cried, suddenly jealous, as I saw him walking toward us along the embankment. Natasha trembled and cried out when she saw Alexey. Then she let go of my hand and ran to meet him. The street was nearly empty. They flew into each other's arms and kissed and laughed. Natasha was laughing and crying at the same time, as if they hadn't seen each other for years. Her pale cheeks had turned crimson in her ecstasy. Alexey noticed me and immediately came over to me.

Chapter Nine

I looked at him closely. Although I had seen Alexey many times before, I now searched his face with a greater intensity, trying to understand what it was about him that puzzled me so, how a silly child like this could cast so powerful a spell over Natasha that it drove her nearly insane with love; a love so intense that she would recklessly sacrifice everything to worship at his shrine.

With both hands, Alexey clasped my hand warmly, and his clear, gentle expression immediately softened my heart. I knew that jealousy could cause a man to view his rival with unwarranted suspicion and I wanted to be as fair as possible. But I didn't like him and, knowing all that I did about him, I couldn't understand how anyone could fall in love with him, and yet it was clear that everyone else seemed to adore him. I didn't even like the way he looked, perhaps because he always dressed so elegantly, with a grace that seemed effortless to him. Later, I realized that my judgment was biased, but at the time I stubbornly refused to see beneath the surface. He was tall and slim, with a pale, oval face and blonde hair. His big blue eyes were kind and thoughtful, and sometimes, like gusts of wind, playful and childlike fancies would burst forth. His full red lips were perfectly formed and usually wore a serious expression, but when he laughed in that naïve, innocent way of his, it was impossible not to laugh along with him.

There were, of course, some minor flaws common to members of society: self-righteousness, frivolity, and a kind of polite insolence, but he was such a simple soul that he would be the first to acknowledge his faults and to laugh at them. His childlike honesty was so extreme that I don't think he could have told a lie, even in jest, unless he were entirely unconscious of it. Even when he behaved selfishly there was something so open and honest about his demeanor, so lacking in guile, that he never offended.

He was, however, weak and timid of heart, with absolutely no will or defenses of his own. To insult or lie to him would be as sinful as hurting a child, and his utter lack of knowledge of the world would probably not change in forty years. He seemed a perpetual child. Natasha instinctively felt that he could easily fall under the influence of another person but if he were persuaded to perform a bad deed, I think he would die of remorse upon learning of the consequences of his actions. But Natasha also understood that if she were to become his wife or mistress, she would start out as the queen of his heart and end as his victim. We often hurt the person we love most in the world, and Natasha knew that the rapturous joys of loving him would lead to madness and torment but she was, nevertheless, anxious to be the first to sacrifice herself.

Alexey's eyes sparkled with love for her and Natasha smiled at me in triumph. She had forgotten everything, parents, farewells, suspicions. She was happy.

"Vanya," she said, "I am guilty for doubting him. I thought you would not come, Alyosha, I doubted your love. Please forgive me for being suspicious and for being so unworthy," she implored, looking into his eyes with infinite love. He merely smiled, kissed her hand and then held it tightly in his.

Alexey turned to me. "Vanya," he said, "please don't blame me. I have been so anxious to greet you as a brother. I have heard such wonderful things about you from Natasha, and yet you and I have barely had a chance to speak to each other. Please, forgive me and be my friend," he said in a quiet, unassuming voice, and the blush on his cheek and the warmth of his smile immediately softened my heart to him.

"Yes, yes, Alyosha," Natasha cried. "Vanya is our dear friend and brother forever. He has already forgiven us and without that forgiveness we could never be happy. I have already told him that. Oh, you and I have been such wicked children, Alyosha, but the three of us shall be inseparable."

"Oh, Vanya," she continued, her lower lip trembling, "Go back home to them and let them know that you have forgiven me. It may not be so easy for them, but they love you, Vanya, and trust you, and when they see that you have forgiven me, maybe it will soften their hearts a little. Tell them everything, from the depths of your heart. You will find the words to make them understand. Be my defender and champion, protect me, save me! Why, do you know, Vanya, that I might never have had the courage to leave today if you had not stopped by? When I saw you, I felt in my heart that you would be able to soften the shock of my leaving them. You are my salvation. Go and tell them, Vanya, that I understand it won't be easy for them to forgive me, but at least convince them not to curse me, or God Himself will never forgive me. But if they do curse me, Vanya, let them know that I will continue to bless them and pray for them the rest of my life. They will have my love forever, even if I'm not with them. Oh God, why can't we all be happy?" she cried, suddenly, awakening to the truth of the situation. "After all, what have I done that is so terrible?" She buried her face in her hands.

Alexey quietly took her in his arms and held her tightly. There was silence for a few minutes.

I looked at Alexey reproachfully. "And you can allow yourself to make her your victim like this?"

"Don't blame me," he responded. "I can promise you that these troubles, as terrible as they may seem, will only last a minute, I'm sure of that. We just need to be strong for a little while to get through this ordeal. Natasha agrees with me. You know that it's just foolish pride, the family quarrel, the litigation, that are causing all the problems. But I've thought about it, and I'm convinced that this will all end soon. Our parents will see how happy we are together and they will forgive us and each other. We will all be one big, happy family. Who knows? Maybe our marriage will be the start of their reconciliation. I don't see how it can be any other way. What do you think?"

"You talk about marriage, but when are the two of you planning to marry?" I asked, looking at Natasha.

"Tomorrow or the day after tomorrow. At least by the day after tomorrow. Maybe. You see, I haven't made any actual plans yet. I wasn't sure that Natasha would show up today and, besides, my father wants to take me to see my fiancée this evening. Natasha has told you, I hope, that he wants me to marry this girl, but that I don't want to. So, I really couldn't be sure of anything happening today. In any case, it'll happen by the day after tomorrow, I'm sure of that, because things won't be the same otherwise. Tomorrow we'll head down the Pskov Road and stop in this village where a friend of mine from the University lives, a terrific fellow, you may know him. Well, at any rate, we'll find a priest in the village. I'm assuming there is a priest there, I probably should have checked on that first, but I didn't have the time. But this is all just detail. I'm sure we'll find a priest there, or in a village nearby. There's bound to be a priest around there somewhere, don't you think? I really should have taken the time to write my friend a letter and tell him that we're coming. He may not be home. Oh, but what does that matter? If we're determined to make this happen, it'll happen. In the meantime, Natasha will stay with me. I've rented a house for us to live in when we get back. I'm determined not to live with my father. You'll come and visit us, and our friends from the University will come, and it'll be like a reunion."

I think I must have looked a bit bewildered and sad, because Natasha gave me a glance that seemed to beg me to be tolerant. She had listened to his words with a sad smile, but with a look of proud admiration in her eyes, much as one might admire a little child's cheerful but nonsensical ramblings. I couldn't help but shake my head at him, though. It was very difficult to hold my temper.

"But are you really certain that your father will forgive you?" I asked.

"Of course, what else can he do? Except, maybe, curse me at first, he'll probably do that. He can be quite severe at times. He might even try to assert his legal power over me, as my father, but it won't be as bad as it sounds. He'll come around eventually, he loves me, and when he forgives me, Natasha's father will forgive her, and we'll all be happy again."

"But what if your father doesn't forgive you? Have you given any thought to that?"

"Oh, he'll forgive me. Maybe not right away, but I'll show him that I have character. He's often said that I have no character, that I'm too superficial, but I'll show him that I can take care of myself. And my wife, of course. Starting a family is no laughing matter, and I don't want to be thought of as a little boy anymore. He'll see that I have grown into a man and can support my family. Natasha tells me that that's much better than living at someone else's expense. She has a lot of practical ideas like that, things I've never thought of before. But I wasn't brought up to think... about things like that, I mean. But I did have an idea a few days ago, let me tell you about it, and Natasha should hear this too. I've decided to write stories and sell them to magazines the way you do. You can introduce me to publishers, can't you? And just last night I had an idea for a novel. I borrowed the idea from a comedy by Eugène Skrib. I think it could turn out splendidly. But I'll tell you about it later. The important thing is that my writing will bring in a lot of money. They do pay you, right?"

I couldn't help but laugh.

"You laugh," he said, and he laughed too, "but there is more to me than meets the eye. I have very astute powers of observation, you will see. You can test me yourself." He said this with the utmost sincerity. "Natasha is always telling me that I have so little understanding of the world, which is true, so I thought to myself, if I know nothing about real life, why not be a writer and just make things up."

Both Natasha and I were laughing now.

"Laugh," he said, "go ahead and laugh, but you'll see. And you'll help me, for her sake, because I know you love her too. I'll tell you the truth, Vanya, I know that I'm not worthy of her and I can't, for the life of me, understand what she sees in me, but I love her and would gladly give my life for her. Up till now, I haven't really thought about the consequences of her loving me, and I wasn't afraid of anything, but now I see that I am going to have to make some firm decisions and devote myself to taking care of her. But isn't it true, after all, that if a man is truly determined to do his duty, that he will find the strength and knowledge within himself to accomplish that task? And besides, I will have you to help me, as a loyal friend, and you know that I know nothing about anything, so there will be plenty for you to do. I hope you will forgive me for leaning on you in this way, but you are a much better man than I am, with a noble heart, and with your help I know that I can become worthy of both you and Natasha."

He clasped my hand again in both of his and the look in his eyes was brimming with such hope and assurance that I saw, clearly, that he believed me to be his friend.

"Natasha will help, too, and I know I will improve, so please don't think too harshly about me, and don't lose faith in us. I am confident that we'll have no money worries. If my being a writer doesn't work out—and to tell you the truth I think it's a silly idea and only suggested it to see what you thought of the idea—I can always give music lessons. You didn't know that I was musical, did you? And I'm not ashamed to work for a living, if necessary. I'm open to all possibilities. I also have a lot of trinkets, knick-knacks, that I can sell, and that will provide us with living expenses for a while. And if all else fails, I can go into government service. My father would like that, he's been encouraging me for years, but I've always said my health is too unreliable for that kind of work. But when he sees that my marriage has made me so much stronger and more dependable, and that I am working for the State, he will be so proud that he will forgive us immediately."

"But Alexey Petrovich, have you taken even a second to consider what happened this evening in her home and how her parents will react to this?" I asked. Natasha was overwhelmed with grief by my comment, but I continued. "Have you thought about what is going on between *her* father and *your* father?"

"Yes, you're right, it's terrible. I have been thinking about that and I am devastated, but what can I do about it? I love her parents very much; they took me into their home and loved me like a son, and look how I am repaying their kindness. I can only pray that they will forgive us. And this quarrel, this lawsuit, you cannot imagine how terribly we both feel. We love each other so much and yet our fathers fight. If only they would resolve their dispute and become friends again. They really should, you know, and then everything will be all right. But I must say that you're really making me think about this. Natasha, what we're doing really is a terrible thing. I tried to tell you that before, but you insisted on going through with it. But tell me, Ivan Petrovich, there must be some way to resolve this conflict, isn't there? If we love each other, why shouldn't we be able to convince them to care about each other? How can they resist our love? You would be surprised to learn that my father is really a very kind-hearted man. He spoke so tenderly to me this morning about my future, and now here I am betraying him, all because of a little misunderstanding. It's all so stupid, really. If he took the time to get to know Natasha, within half an hour he would consent to anything she asked." He looked again at Natasha with a tender, compassionate gaze.

"I've told him a thousand times," he continued, rambling on incessantly, "that he would love Natasha if he really knew her—after all, no one has ever seen such a girl—but he is convinced that she is some sort of seductress, and my first obligation is to clear her name of such misconceptions, and I will, I promise you. Oh, my Natasha," he cried excitedly, "the whole world will soon know you and love you as I do, and what more do we need to find happiness? Beginning today, with God's blessing, we will bring peace, happiness and reconciliation to everyone, right Natasha? But what's the matter with you, are you all right?"

Natasha was as pale as death. She had been following his words attentively but had been growing paler and paler and her eyes had clouded over until she had drifted into a form of trance from which Alexey had suddenly awakened her with his question. She looked around and then, quite unexpectedly, rushed into my arms. She pulled from her pocket a letter which she was careful to conceal from Alexey. It was a note to her parents she had written the night before. She gave it to me with such a look of despair on her face that the image of it will haunt me forever. I was made terrifyingly aware that only now, at this precise moment, had she finally awakened to the inescapable horror of her decision. She tried to say something to me, but no words came, and she fainted. I only just managed to catch her. Alexey too had turned pale from fright. He took a flask of whiskey from his pocket and gave her a sip, then he kissed her lips and fingertips. Within two minutes she had regained consciousness. Alexey hailed a nearby cab and I lifted Natasha into the carriage. She grabbed frantically for my hand, her feverish tears burning my fingers. The carriage started off and I stood there for a long while, watching as my happiness vanished in the distance, severing my soul in two. Then, slowly, I retraced my steps along the road to her parents' house. I have no memory of what I said to them, it was all such a blur.

So ends the history of my happiness and my love. I will now return to my interrupted story.

Chapter Ten

Five days after Smith died, I moved into his apartment. All that day I was unbearably sad. The weather was miserably cold, alternating between rain and snow. Only briefly in the early evening did the sun show its face, and a stray beam of light found its way through my skylight windows, peaking in like a curious visitor.

I was beginning to regret my decision to move here. The room was wonderfully large, but the low-hanging ceiling, the sooty, musty odor, and the vast emptiness of the space (in spite of the woeful furniture supplied by the landlord) required some getting used to. I thought that surely this room had contributed to Smith's poor health and I feared for my own.

The next morning, I set to work organizing my papers. Having no briefcase, I was forced to use a pillowcase to transport them and as a result they were badly crumpled and out of order. I settled down to work on my novel, but my head was filled with so many other things that the pen soon fell from my hand.

I moved to the window. It was dark and dreary outside, which only served to depress me even more. My head was filled with sad, morbid thoughts, and it occurred to me that I would die here in St. Petersburg. Maybe in the spring, I thought, things would improve. When the sunlight returns, life will bloom again and a visit to the fresh fields and forests of my childhood will draw me out of my shell. If only there were some spell or magic potion that would enable me to erase the memory of the past few years from my mind, I might be able to start anew. Perhaps, I thought, I should take up residence in some lunatic asylum where my mind could be flushed clean of its debris and I would awaken with a whole new brain filled with life, confidence and hope for a brighter future. But then I laughed. What would I do when I left the asylum and returned home, write more novels?

I occupied myself for the rest of the day with similar bleak and dismal thoughts. Natasha had sent me a note the day before and I had promised to visit her late this evening. When the time arrived for the appointment, I quickly pulled myself out of my melancholy mood and gathered my things together. Even with the rain and slush, I thought, getting out of the apartment could only serve to brighten my spirits.

When darkness fell, my apartment seemed to expand and grow even more spacious. The previous night I had imagined that I could see Jeremiah Smith in a corner of the room, sitting and staring at me as he had so many times in Mueller's shop, and at his feet was Azorka. But something happened this evening that greatly surpassed that nightmare. I must preface this story by acknowledging that my senses had been greatly altered by the nervous strain of the past few days and, in my depressed state of mind, strange images and bizarre thoughts combined to create what I would call a mystic horror, a petrifying fear of some indefinable and nonexistent terror that made a mockery of all the sane and reasonable arguments against it. That fear was growing stronger and stronger, becoming an irresistible fact, dreadful, monstrous and inescapable, and any attempt to reason it away was useless. The mind, in such moments, acquires a greater clarity and sharpness and the fearful melancholy that takes possession of the senses resembles that terror experienced by people who fear the resurrection of corpses in graveyards. Such was the state of my mind when the event in question occurred.

I remember that I was standing at the table with my back to the door. I picked up my hat and suddenly felt a creeping sensation up my spine. I felt with certainty that if I turned, I would see Smith standing in the darkness with his hollow eyes and that toothless grin, silently laughing at me, his long, skeletal frame quaking from that laughter. The image of this ghost was vividly and distinctly drawn in my imagination and I had the overpowering conviction that this inescapable experience was really happening. At this moment, I thought I heard the door creaking open. I turned quickly and stared into the darkness. Indeed, the door was open, just as I had imagined it. I let out a cry. For a long moment the threshold was empty and silent. There was a slight movement and I was suddenly aware of a strange being whose eyes, gradually discernible in the darkness, were examining me closely and steadily. An icy chill ran through my body. The creature moved slowly in toward the light and I recognized the figure of a child, a young girl, and had the apparition been Smith himself it could not have been more frightening or strange than the appearance of this unexpected stranger at this late hour.

She had opened the door so slowly and quietly that it was clear she was afraid to enter. She took a few steps toward me without making a sound. I could see now that the girl was about twelve or thirteen, small, very thin, and so pale that she looked like she had only recently recovered from a serious illness. Her dark eyes flickered brightly in the candlelight. In her left hand she held a tattered shawl which she clutched tightly over her chest. Her dress was little more than rags and her thick black hair, soaked from the rain, clung to her face and shoulders. We both stood for several minutes examining each other.

"Where is Grandpa?" she asked finally, her voice hoarse and barely audible.

With this question, my terror instantly vanished. Upon closer examination I could see her resemblance to Smith. "Your grandpa?" I asked. "He's dead."

I instantly regretted the hastiness of my answer, but before I could say anything the girl began to tremble. Within seconds her shaking became so convulsive that I was afraid she would injure herself. I ran forward and grabbed her before she collapsed to the floor, holding her tightly for several minutes until her seizure had passed. As soon as she recovered, she made an unnatural effort to toss off the incident as a minor concern and pulled away from me.

"Forgive me, please, little girl, I'm so sorry. I didn't mean to... to announce it so abruptly, to shock you in that way. But maybe... maybe I'm wrong. Who are you looking for? The old man who lived here?"

"Y-y-yes," she whispered with considerable effort.

"Was his last name Smith?" I asked.

"Y-yes."

"Oh, well, then I'm afraid it's true," I said. "He died a few days ago. But please, don't be sad, don't cry. Why didn't you come sooner? Where have you come from? They buried him yesterday. He died suddenly, quite unexpectedly. So, you're his granddaughter?"

The girl did not respond to my barrage of questions but turned in silence and quickly moved toward the door. I was so surprised by this I didn't know what else to say.

She stopped in the doorway and without turning to me asked, "Azorka is dead too?"

"Yes, Azorka is also dead," I answered. It then occurred to me that this was a strange question, as if the girl were somehow confident that Azorka would just naturally die at the same time as the old man.

After hearing my answer, the girl quietly closed the door behind her and moved down the hallway to the staircase. After a moment I ran after her, upset with myself for letting her get away. I stopped at the top of the spiral staircase and listened for the sound of her footsteps, but hearing nothing I darted down after her. I had neglected to bring a candle with me and as the stairs were always dark and dirty, quite common in old buildings with small apartments, I had to grope my way carefully down the curving staircase to the fourth floor. From there the stairs descended to the ground floor in a straight line and I could see no one below me. I stopped to catch my breath and instinctively felt a presence behind me in the dark. I felt around in the blackness with my hands and came upon the girl, cowering against the wall in a corner of the stairwell. She turned her face to the wall and began to cry.

"Look, what are you afraid of?" I asked. "I didn't mean to scare you. It's all *my* fault. Your grandfather, when he was dying, mentioned you. They were his last words. I have a book he left behind, I think it's yours. What's your name? Where do you live? He mentioned the Sixth Line on..."

But I didn't get to finish my thought. She cried out in terror (perhaps because I knew where she lived) and pushed me aside with her tiny, bony hand, then rushed down the staircase. I hurried after her and heard the sound of her feet on the steps. Suddenly the sound stopped. When I reach the bottom of the stairs I rushed out into the street, but there was no sign of her. I ran up to Voznesensky Prospect where Mueller had his shop and searched both directions in vain. She had disappeared. She was probably hiding on the stairs when I ran past, I thought, and left the building after me.

Chapter Eleven

This was to be an evening of most unexpected encounters. The pavement on Voznesensky Prospect was wet with black slush and I had to dart quickly out of the way of a passer-by as he hurried down the street, his head bent down, apparently deep in thought and quite unaware of my presence. I caught a brief glimpse of his face as he passed and was astonished to recognize Nicolai Sergeich. The old man had taken to his bed three days earlier, seriously ill, so meeting him on the street in such damp, miserable weather was a great surprise, made even more so by that fact that he rarely left his home in the evening. Moreover, since Natasha had left home nearly six months earlier, he had become a virtual recluse.

When I called his name, he stopped and seemed delighted to see me, taking my hand in his strong grip. Without asking where I was headed, he steered me in the direction he was going and hurriedly pulled me along with him.

"Where is he off to?" I wondered to myself. Asking him, I knew, would be a wasted effort because he had grown so irritable in recent months that I was sure he would regard my innocent question as an insult or some shaded hint that he was doing something he shouldn't. As we hurried along the street, I stole a glance at him. He had lost a great deal of weight and his beard was shaggy and untrimmed. The hair sticking out from under his crumpled hat and hanging down over the collar of his worn-out overcoat had turned surprisingly grey. I have noted before that the old man had grown quite absent-minded and forgetful and would sometimes sit alone in his room and talk out loud and gesticulate with his hands as if in conversation with another person. It was difficult for me to witness his declining mental health.

"Where are you off to, Vanya?" he asked. "I've been taking care of some business. How are you feeling?"

"I should be asking you that," I responded. "You were terribly sick just a few days ago and here you are up and about in this terrible weather."

As I expected, the old man did not answer me.

"How is Anna Andreyevna feeling?" I asked.

"Fine, fine," he responded, "although she's a little under the weather too. She's been feeling a bit low. She often speaks about you and wonders why you don't come to visit us anymore. Maybe you were on your way there right now, perhaps?" He looked at me suspiciously. "Or maybe I'm keeping you from something else, you have other plans?" He had suddenly grown irritable and distrustful and I attempted to avoid an argument by telling him that I was, indeed, on my way to visit Anna Andreyevna (although I knew this would make it too late for me to keep my appointment with Natasha).

"Well, that's good, very good, Vanya," he responded, evidently much relieved by my answer. He calmed down and continued our walk in silence.

A few minutes later he mechanically repeated, "Yes, that's very good," as though waking from a deep thought. "You see, Vanya, God did not bless us with a son and Anna Andreyevna and I have long felt that He sent you to us. I have always considered you my son and the old woman feels the same way. You have always been most respectful and tender towards us, never ungrateful, and we bless you for that, Vanya, and pray that God will bless you and love you as we do." His voice was shaky and he took a moment before continuing.

"Have you been sick, Vanya?" he continued. "Why haven't you been to see us for so long?"

I told him the story of my encounter with Jeremiah Smith and explained that his death and my subsequent illness had prevented me from paying them a visit. I almost mentioned that I had visited Natasha during that period but, fortunately, caught myself in time.

The old man was greatly impressed with my story about Smith and he listened with great interest. But when he learned that my new apartment was even damper than my previous one and that I was paying six rubles for it, he grew angry again. When he was in an irritable mood, his patience was extremely thin, and Anna Andreyevna was usually the only person who could calm his temper (and even she was not always successful).

"It's that literature of yours," he said. "It's brought you to the garret and will eventually lead you to the cemetery. I told you it would, I predicted it. Is Belinsky still writing criticisms?"

"He died of tuberculosis. It seems to me that I mentioned that to you some time ago."

"Dead, is he? Dead! Well, that was bound to happen. Did he leave anything to his wife and children? I think you once said he was married. I don't understand why these people marry."

"No, he left her nothing." I said.

"Well, there you have it," he said dramatically, as if closing the subject. His concern for the deceased literary critic seemed as genuine as it would have been had he been discussing his own brother. "Nothing! How can there be nothing? But you know, Vanya, I predicted something like this would happen. He may have earned his place in history, perhaps even immortal fame, but such glory can't put food on the table. Like me, this man praised you and saw glowing things in your future, and then he died. But then, who doesn't have to die? And life is good and the world is a beautiful place and... Look there!"

With a suddenly unconscious gesture of his arm he pointed to a dim, fog-bound street illuminated by flickering gas-lamps, to the dirty houses, to the shining rain-soaked pavement, to the grim, angry and wet passers-by, all crowned by a solemn St. Petersburg sky, the totality of which created a vivid landscape as if drawn in India ink.

We walked on and soon arrived at St. Isaac's Square at the base of the recently completed cathedral, dark and ominous and barely discernible silhouetted against the somber sky. Towering above us was Montferrand's statue of Tsar Nicholas, rearing up on a magnificent steed.

"You have said to me, Vanya," the old man continued, "that this critic was a good man, magnanimous, personable, sympathetic, but let me tell you that there are many such men in the world and all they really know how to do is create more orphans. And yet I suppose that one should be content to die, anything to get out of this. Go anywhere, even to Siberia. It's bound to be an improvement. What is it you want, child?" he said abruptly, coming upon a little girl begging in the street.

She was tiny, perhaps seven or eight, dressed in tattered rags, with no stockings and battered old shoes on her dirty feet. Her dress, which she had clearly outgrown, was insufficient to protect her from the cold night air, but she did her best to hide the fact that she was shivering. Her pale, sick and emaciated face was turned up towards us and as she reached out her trembling hand her look was a timid, silent plea for kindness, mixed with an anticipation of rejection.

Ichmenyev immediately began to shake and he turned towards her with so sudden a movement that she stepped back in fear.

"What is it you want, little girl, don't be afraid. You want money?" he asked her. "Yes, well just a moment, this is for you, here, here, take it." He was quaking with emotion as he hurriedly explored his pockets in search of money. The few coins he drew forth were evidently insufficient to satisfy his generous spirit, for he pulled open his purse and handed her a ruble note, which was all he had with him.

"May the good Lord Jesus watch over you and bless you, my child, and may God's angels protect you!" He made the sign of the cross several times over the girl's head, but stopped suddenly when he realized that I was standing next to him. His mood changed abruptly and he frowned before quickly resuming his walk. I hurried after him.

"You see, Vanya," he said after a long, angry silence, "I cannot stand to see such tiny, innocent little children trembling from the cold in the street because of their cursed mothers and fathers. Could any mother send her child out to beg in the streets if she herself were not living in an equally wretched state? There may well be more future orphans huddled in a corner somewhere, with this one being the eldest, and the mother may be too sick to beg herself and..." He cut himself off abruptly. "Well, they are not princely children, Vanya, that is certain. There are many children in this world who are not the children of princes."

He was silent again and appeared reluctant to continue. When he spoke again he seemed embarrassed and a little confused.

"You see, Vanya, I have made a promise to Anna Andreyevna and we have both agreed that if the opportunity presents itself we will take an orphan, some small, helpless little girl, into our home and care for her. Life can get pretty boring for an old couple like us, living all alone, and lately Anna Andreyevna has grown restless and irritable. So, I was hoping that you might have a little conversation with her. Don't say that I asked you to, of course, but make it sound like it's your own idea. Talk to her, feel her out on the subject. I've been meaning to bring this up for a while, but I haven't had the opportunity. It's just too painful for me to discuss it with her myself and, well, why should I? What's an orphan child to me, I don't need to deal with children at my age. It might be pleasant to have a child's voice in the house again, of course, but it's really to give Anna Andreyevna something to do, someone to take care of other than just me, and I think it would cheer her up a bit. Of course, it doesn't make a difference to me one way or the other, you understand, but, look, it's getting late, and the old woman is probably tired of waiting, so why don't we take a carriage?"

It was half past eight when we reached the Ichmenyev's home.

CHAPTER TWELVE

The old husband and wife were very fond of each other, and love and long-term routine had created an inseparable link between them. But Nikolai Sergeich, not only now but in earlier, happier times, often found it difficult to express his feelings and would treat Anna Andreyevna in a manner that was, at least in the eyes of other people, downright unkind. In many respects he was tender and sensitive, but like others with similar temperaments, he found it difficult to express his gentler emotions and found it easier to mask these feelings behind an outwardly stern exterior, not only in public but in more private moments as well. Such was the case with Ichmenyev in his relations with his wife. He respected her and regarded her with the highest esteem (despite the fact that her only noticeable characteristic seemed to be that she was a good person and nothing more), and she in turn knew almost nothing about anything except how to love him, which she did simply and, perhaps, a bit too demonstrably.

If anything, their affection for each other had grown even stronger since Natasha had left home, and their awareness that they had no one in the world except each other for company made their bond even stronger. And while it is true that Nikolai Sergeich could become remarkably moody and irritable on occasion, the two were rarely ever apart and a separation for even as little as two hours could result in pain and depression for both of them.

There was an unspoken agreement between them not to speak about Natasha, and Anna Andreyevna was afraid to even hint at the existence of her daughter in front of her husband, although this was very difficult for her. She had forgiven Natasha in her heart long before and she and I would have private conversations about her lovely, unforgettable daughter whenever her husband was not in the room. She became positively ill if she didn't receive news from me and, when I did visit, her insatiable curiosity for every little detail was never satisfied. She became extremely agitated and fearful when I told her once that Natasha was sick (although not seriously) and very nearly rushed out to attend to her personally. But this was an extreme case. She wanted more than anything to go to her daughter but feared her husband's angry reaction and suppressed these feelings when in his company. In private conversation with me, however, she spoke of Natasha in the warmest possible terms and always used affectionate pet names for her. She complained about her husband's bitter feelings toward his daughter and his stubborn unwillingness to forgive her. On occasion, when her grief became almost unbearable, she would find the courage to confront him directly and declare that God would never forgive his cruel and unconscionable lack of mercy, but that was as close as she ever came to dealing with the situation.

On such occasions, the old man became either sullen and quiet, retreating into himself, or aggressive and hostile, rising in anger and storming out of the room. Leaving the room, I soon came to realize, was really his way of giving his wife an opportunity to vent her feelings to me—which she never failed to do—and for me to fill her in on the latest news about Natasha. Immediately after our arrival this particular night, he declared, "I'm soaking wet! Why don't you sit down, Vanya, and tell Anna Andreyevna about your new apartment? I'm going to change my clothes," and without so much as a glance at either one of us, he hurried into the other room.

"There he goes again," his wife said. "He pretends he has something to do, but he's really ashamed to express his feelings. He knows that you and I will talk about Natasha and he's purposely giving us the time to do that, but when he comes out again, he'll pretend that nothing has been said. And it's so silly because he knows that I know what he's doing, so why does he pretend otherwise? There should be no secrets between us. He still loves Natasha and I know he wants to forgive her, but he is too stubborn to admit it. I hear him crying at night, but the next morning his pride takes hold of him again and he hides his feelings. But tell me, Vanya, where did he walk to?"

"I was just going to ask you that," I responded. "I have no idea."

"I was so stunned when he left. On a cold, wet night like this, he never goes out unless it's for something very important, but what could be so important now? I'm afraid to ask. I keep hoping that he'll go to her, forgive her. He hears all the latest news about her and seems to know her every move, don't ask me how, but he never lets on, and he was very sad all day yesterday and this morning too. But Ivan Petrovich, have you nothing to say to me? I've been waiting for your return like the second coming and yet your eyes tell me nothing. What is that villainous man of mine planning? To disown Natasha?"

I immediately described to Anna Andreyevna everything I knew about the situation. As always, I was completely frank with her. There was something happening that might lead to a major rupture concerning Natasha's relationship with the young prince, Alexey Petrovich. Natasha had written begging me to come to her that very evening at nine o'clock, but I had been waylaid by Nicolai Sergeich just as I was leaving to visit her.

Prince Valkovsky, I explained, had returned two weeks earlier from a trip abroad and had immediately set to work solidifying his son's wedding plans. Alexey had been spending considerable time with his future bride and, from all reports, was beginning to fall in love with her. Natasha was extremely upset when she wrote the note and said that everything would be decided tonight, but failed to provide any further details. It was *imperative*, however, that she see me tonight.

"Go, Vanya, by all means, go. But first, have a cup of tea before he returns. Matroyna, where is the samovar? Matroyna! That girl is so slow.

Yes, you'll have a cup of tea and then make some plausible excuse and go. And tomorrow, early, you'll come here and tell me everything. My lord, we don't have enough troubles already, what could be worse? He knows, I'm sure of it. Nikolai Sergeich knows everything that is going on. I think he gets the news from Matroyna. She has a goddaughter, Agasha, who works in the prince's house. You know how servants hear things. Well, Nikolai Sergeich was terribly angry this morning. He was screaming at Matroyna about money, and about this and about that, and you know when he is like that my feet go numb and my heart pounds. After lunch, he skipped tea and went in to take a nap, and I looked in on him—there is small crack in the door he doesn't know about—and saw him praying on his knees for a full hour. When he came out at five o'clock, he grabbed his hat and coat and went for a walk. What does Natasha say in her note, may I read it?"

I showed her the note. For many years, Anna Andreyevna had held one cherished dream (which she confided only in me) that the young prince, whom she often referred to as a villainous, insensitive and foolish boy, would finally marry Natasha and that Prince Valkovsky would consent to the marriage and end the feud between the families. On no account would she dare to express such a thought openly while her husband was alive, although she knew that he suspected that she held such feelings and would reproach her in an indirect manner. Her greatest fear was that if he learned of the possibility of such a marriage, he would curse Natasha and cast her from his heart forever. We all held this belief and knew that if Nikolai Sergeich were ever to forgive Natasha it would be on the condition that she return home, repentant and having severed her relationship with Alexey completely.

"He's a cowardly, spineless boy," Anna Andreyevna said. "I have always thought so. He's like a weathervane that spins this way and that, depending on how the wind blows. I'm not surprised to hear that he is now enthralled by another woman."

"I have heard, Anna Andreyevna," I objected, "that his fiancée is a very charming girl. Yes, even Natasha has said very nice things about her."

"And you believe that?" she cried. "Charming? You writers think any pretty young girl who flips her skirt in your direction is 'charming.' And if Natasha says so, it's only because she is a sweet, noble soul who will readily forgive the sins of others while she herself suffers. Oh, these villains with their arrogant pride. Look how much Natasha has given up for him and he blithely moves on to the next girl. If only my husband would forgive her and bring her home. Has she lost weight?"

"Quite a bit, yes."

"My poor little girl. And we have such new troubles of our own, Vanya, I spent last night and all of today crying. I'll tell you about it some other time, but let me tell you how often I have been on the brink of begging Nikolai Sergeich to forgive our little girl, but I am so afraid he might curse her. Curse her! God himself is unforgiving to children whose parents curse them, so I live each day in terror of what he might do. And you, Vanya, who grew up in our home, you know that he was never unkind to you for a moment, and you come here and tell me that this other woman is 'charming?' But Matroyna knows better. She knows the inside story. Prince Valkovsky, she says, is involved with a countess who for many years, even when her husband was still alive, behaved appallingly while living abroad. After she became a widow, she scandalized Europe. The Italians and Frenchmen were practically fighting her off and there were several barons who were pursuing her, but she hooked onto the prince. Well, she went through her share of the family estate in no time, but the countess has a stepdaughter by her first husband who received two million rubles when her father died. Through proper investments, her fortune is said to be worth over three million now.

"The prince is no fool," she continued, "and he's not one to let such an opportunity pass him by, so he decides to marry this heiress off to his son Alyosha. Another of his relations, a count who helped educate the boy, agreed that three million rubles is no laughing matter and suggested that the prince go to the countess and make the proper arrangements. But the countess will have none of it and fights tooth and nail against such a proposal. 'You are free to marry me,' the countess said to the prince, 'but my stepdaughter will most definitely not marry your son.' The stepdaughter is said to be an angel, a devout and obedient child, and will not go against her stepmother's wishes. So, the prince tells the countess, 'Do not worry. You have exhausted your own fortune and have many debts, but if you convince your innocent and wealthy stepdaughter to marry my foolish but obedient son, we will be their guardians and will have legal control of the money. What good does your marrying me do without a source of income?' The prince is a clever man, indeed, and he convinced the countess to consider his plan. For the past six months she has refused to change her mind, but she and the prince recently went to Warsaw together and came away with an agreement. That is what I was told by Matroyna, who received the information, in the strictest confidence, from her source in the prince's house. Three million rubles. Yes, charming, indeed."

I was amazed by Anna Andreyevna's story. It was in complete agreement with the version I had heard recently from Alexey himself, who claimed that he was not interested in Katerina Fedorovna's money. But the young heiress was attracted to Alexey and became enthusiastic about the idea of marrying him. Alexey also told me that his father was planning to marry the countess, although the prince denied this publicly in order to avoid provoking the countess. I have already written that Alexey was very fond of his father, whom he admired and praised and believed in like an oracle.

Anna Andreyevna had been extremely irritated by my praise of the young prince's future bride and said, pointedly, "This 'charming' girl is not a countess, you know. Natasha would be a much better match. She is from a long and noble family and this other girl is merely the daughter of a brandy dealer. I had forgotten to tell you that yesterday the old man was rummaging through some old papers in his desk. He was sitting there, very serious, and I thought it best to keep quiet. But then he got irritated with me for not saying anything and called me over to join him. He showed me some documents and explained to me about our family histories. The Ichmenyev family can boast noblemen dating back to the reign of Ivan the Terrible and the Shoumiloffs were around in the time of Alexei Mikhailovich Romanov and are even mentioned in Karamzin's *History of the Russian State*. So, you see, Vanya, we are in no way inferior to others. I'm not sure why he chose to tell me all this now, but I think he was offended by the insulting comments made about Natasha. They have nothing over us except their money, and that greedy bastard of a prince runs after it like the thief he is. Everybody knows this. Is it true that he became a Jesuit while he was in Warsaw?"

"Foolish rumor," I answered, although I was struck by how pervasive this rumor had become. But hearing about Nikolai Sergeich exploring his family history interested me greatly. He had never before boasted about his pedigree.

"They are all villains and thieves," continued Anna Andreyevna. "But tell me about my Natasha, my dear friend, is she grieving, does she cry? Ah, but it is time for you to go to her! Matroyna! Matroyna! She's an unreliable girl. But say something, Vanya."

What was there for me to say? The old woman began to cry. "You mentioned some new troubles before. May I ask what they are?"

"Oh, Vanya, my cup of troubles is not yet empty," she cried. "I had a locket with a childhood portrait of Natasha in it. We had met an artist while traveling once, a very fine painter, and Nikolai Sergeich paid him to create a portrait of our little girl, she was just eight years old at the time. The artist painted her as a little Cupid, with curly blonde hair, and a lovely little see-through muslin dress. She was so pretty, so very pretty, and I asked him to draw in little wings, but he refused to change it. Well, Vanya, after all these misfortunes began, I took the locket from its box and attached it to the same ribbon that holds my cross so I could wear it next to my heart. I was so afraid that Nikolai Sergeich would see it and throw it away or burn it like he has with so many of her other things. There is nothing left of Natasha in the house but this one little souvenir, and I used to take it out and look at it, yes, and even talk to it, when he wasn't around. I would bless it at night and when I spoke to it, I seemed to hear Natasha speaking back to me. It's difficult for me to tell you this, but that locket was the one thing in my life that comforted me, and I was so glad that my husband didn't know about it. And then, yesterday morning, it wasn't there! It had disappeared. I thought maybe I had dropped it and I searched and searched for it. I tore off the bedcovers, I looked everywhere, everywhere. And then I thought, maybe *he* found it! Or Matroyna. I knew it couldn't have been Matroyna because she would have returned it to me. She is devoted to me with her entire soul. Matroyna! When are you bringing in the tea? And then I worried, 'what will happen if *he* finds it?' I became very depressed and would sit by myself and cry and cry, the tears wouldn't stop. But then Nikolai Sergeich began acting so much more affectionate, yes, more affectionate, with me. He would look at me, sadly, as if he knew very well what I was crying about, and he pitied me. And I started thinking, what does he know? Maybe he found the locket and threw it out and is feeling guilty about that. I had already searched outside the window and I had Matroyna search again but she found nothing. Maybe he threw it in the river, I thought, and cried all night long. It was the first night I was not able to bless it, and I feared that this was a sign of some great calamity, some great harm. It was clearly a bad omen and I have been crying ever since, crying and waiting for you, my angel of God, to come and comfort me and ease my heart."

The old woman continued to cry.

"Oh, yes, Vanya, I forgot to ask you. When you spoke to Nikolai Sergeich, did he say anything about an orphan?"

"Why, yes, Anna Andreyevna," I responded, "he mentioned it to me on our walk here. He said that you had both agreed to take in an orphan girl and educate her."

"I did not decide, Vanya, he decided. Nor did I agree. What do I want with an orphan? She will only remind me of my Natasha. I have a daughter already and she will remain my daughter forever. Where does he come up with such an idea? If he thinks it will comfort me, he is wrong, or perhaps he thinks it's a way to banish memories of Natasha from his mind, by attaching himself to some new child. What did he say to you earlier? What was his mood like, did he seem angry? Wait, I hear him coming, you can tell me some other time, but remember you must come back tomorrow!"

Chapter Thirteen

The old man came in and looked at us curiously as he sat at the table.

"Where is the samovar? Is the tea not ready yet?"

The moment Matroyna saw Nikolai Sergeich enter the room she hurried in with the tea, just as if she had been holding off until his return. She was an old, tested, and loyal servant, but had an obstinate, stubborn personality, and was the most relentless complainer of any maid in the world. Although she was a little afraid of the old man and always spoke to him in the most respectful manner, Matroyna dearly loved the old woman but clearly held the dominant position in *that* relationship.

"Hmm, it's bad enough to come in soaking wet, but to have a servant who doesn't wish to serve the tea," he grumbled.

Anna Andreyevna immediately winked at me. Her husband could not tolerate these mysterious glances between us and pretended not to notice, but his eyes clearly acknowledged what had happened.

"The lawsuit is going very badly," he said suddenly. "I am going to lose the case. Because I don't have access to some very important papers I need and our inquiries haven't been properly filed. The charges against me are all lies but the prince knows how to manipulate the law to his advantage."

I didn't know how to respond to this statement, so I kept quiet. He looked at me suspiciously.

"Well, what's to be done about it?" he asked with a new surge of anger, irritated by our silence. "It's better it happens now than later. I'm not a thief, but if the court decides that I must pay, I will pay. My conscience is clear, so let it be on their heads. When I have lost everything, I will sell what property we have remaining and move to Siberia."

"My God, why there?" his wife cried. "Why so far away?"

"What have we got closer that is better?" he responded rudely, welcoming the objection and, perhaps, hoping for an argument.

"Well, there are people," she began, looking at me for support.

"What people?" he shouted, his face turning red. "Thieves, liars, traitors? You'll find plenty of them in Siberia too, so you needn't worry there. But if you don't want to go with me, that's up to you, I'm not forcing you!"

"Nikolai Sergeich, how can you say such a thing?" she responded with great emotion. "I will go wherever you go. I have no one in the world but you except..." She broke off and looked at me again, imploring me to intercede, but I knew that when the old man was in this mood, anything I said to him would only anger him more.

Instead, I said to her, "Calm yourself, Anna Andreyevna, Siberia is not as bad as it may seem. If the worst happens and you need to sell Ichmenyevka, Nikolai Sergeich may be right about moving to Siberia. There you'll be able to find a good private home and..."

"Well, at least someone has something supportive to say," the old man roared. "We'll sell off everything and be on our way!"

"I never expected to hear such a thing from you!" she said to her husband, wringing her hands together. "And from you too, Vanya! You've had nothing but love and kindness from us, and now you..."

"Well, what else are we to do?" he interrupted. "When we have no money left, no home? Shall I go to Prince Peter and beg him to forgive me?"

When she heard the prince's name, the old woman began to tremble with fear. The teaspoon fell from her hand and landed on her saucer with a jangling sound.

"No, in fact that's an excellent idea!" he continued, taking a stubborn, malicious joy in taunting his wife. "Don't you agree, Vanya? Why should I pack up and move to Siberia? Tomorrow, I'll put on my best clothes with a nice clean shirt, trim my hair and beard, I must look my best for such an important man. I may even buy a new pair of gloves, very stylish ones, and pay court to his highness. 'My lord,' I'll say, 'father of us all, please have mercy on your humble servants and forgive us. Give me a piece of bread. I have a wife and small children!' Is that what you want, Anna Andreyevna? Do you want that?"

"No, my dear, I don't want that. Please forgive me for speaking so foolishly, for making a nuisance of myself, and please don't make me cry," she pleaded, trembling more and more with fear.

I am sure that at that moment the old man's soul was struck a near fatal blow as he witnessed his wife trembling with uncontrollable grief, and I believe that his pain may have been even greater than hers. But he had been unable to resist. So it is with some tender-hearted people when their own grief and anger become unbearable, they must lash out at someone, often the very person they would least want to hurt. They find a strange sort of solace in their own misery. Women, for example, sometimes feel misery and resentment even when there is no cause for resentment or unhappiness. There are also many men, as in the case of Ichmenyev, who occasionally display this characteristic even though they are in no way weak or feminine in their outward appearance. The old man felt the need to quarrel as a way to relieve his own suffering.

The idea occurred to me at that moment that Anna Andreyevna may have been right when she suggested that he had made an effort to reconcile with Natasha. Under the influence of some heavenly guidance, perhaps he had set out to visit his daughter but had been diverted by some event or circumstance. Thus thwarted, he had returned home angry and ashamed of his weakness and vented his feelings by attacking the person whom he suspected of sharing his desires and of influencing his feelings. By failing to provide Anna Andreyevna with the delight and joy of his noble intentions, he made her the victim of his wrath instead.

Whatever his state of mind a moment before, the sight of his wife trembling before him instantly shamed the anger out of him. He stood silently for a good minute and I tried not to look at her. As the silence stretched on, I feared that the tension in him was building again and would eventually have to explode, perhaps even in a curse.

"You see, Vanya," he said suddenly, "I didn't mean to say that, but the time has come, I think, to speak frankly, you know what I mean? I'm glad you're here because I want to say out loud, so you both can hear, that I have had it with all of this nonsense, the tears, the sighing. The fact is that what I have torn out of my heart, with blood and pain, will never again find a home in my heart. It is over and done. That was six months ago, Vanya! I am saying this openly and precisely so that there can be no misunderstanding," he added, keeping his angry glance focused on me and avoiding his wife.

"I repeat," he continued, "I have had it, I am through with it. There are people who think I'm a fool, a coward. They say I'm weak and the lowest form of scoundrel, that I have gone insane with grief. That's all rubbish! I have taken all of my sentimental feelings and wiped them from my memory. Yes! Yes! Yes! I have no memories!"

He leaped from his chair and banged the table with his fist, rattling his teacup.

"Nicolai Sergeich! Have you no pity for Anna Andreyevna? Look at what you've done to her," I said indignantly, unable to resist. But I was only adding fuel to the fire.

"Pity?" he screamed. "I have no pity because she has no pity for me! Do you think I am blind to the plotting that goes on behind my back, in my own home, in favor of some slut of a daughter who is deserving of all the punishment and curses that could be inflicted upon her?"

"No, Nikolai, no," Anna Andreyevna pleaded. "Say anything you want, but don't curse your only daughter!"

"Curse? Curse?" he repeated, his voice growing louder and louder. "Yes, I do curse her, because I am the one who has been abused by her." He turned to me and pointed at his wife as he spoke. "Every day, day and night, I must endure her resentful scolding, her demands, her subtle hints that I should go and beg for forgiveness... yes, yes, that's what she expects of me. She tries to soften my heart so I'll show a little pity! Look here, Vanya! Here is what that sinful daughter of mine has done to me! I am called a thief, a swindler!" He pulled a bundle of papers from the side pocket of his coat and tore through them looking for one particular page. Not finding it, he grabbed more sheets of paper from his other pockets, tossing them on the table one after another. In his haste, another item was caught up with the papers and fell hard upon the table. Anna Andreyevna let out a cry. It was the lost locket!

I could hardly believe my eyes. The blood rushed to the old man's cheeks and he gasped audibly as he realized what he had done. Anna Andreyevna stood, hands clasped in front of her, and looked imploringly at her husband. There was a glow in her eyes that radiated hope and joy. The blush on the old man's face told her everything. She had not been mistaken; the mystery of the missing locket had been solved!

She realized that he had found it, was delighted by his discovery, and had jealously secreted it away so that he could look, with undying love, upon the face of his beloved daughter. Like her, he had hidden it away and taken it out only when alone to talk to, ask questions of, and even imagine responses from. And in moments of excruciating sadness, he had fondled it and kissed the angelic image of his darling child, she to whom he had publicly denied forgiveness but instead cursed in front of everyone.

"My darling Nikolai, you still love her," she cried, forgetting that he had cursed her just moments before.

But immediately upon hearing her words, he grabbed the locket and with a look of insane fury in his eyes threw it on the floor and stamped upon it with his boot.

"Forever! Forever I curse you!" he screamed hoarsely. "I curse you forever!"

"My Natasha!" the old woman cried. "My baby girl, he is crushing her, crushing her with his boot! You tyrant! You unfeeling bastard!"

But when he heard his wife scream, the insane old man stopped, horrified by what he had done. He quickly reached down, retrieved the locket from the floor, and rushed toward the door, but before he had taken two steps, he fell to his knees and grabbed hold of the arm of the sofa for support. He wept like a child, like a woman, relentless sobs that nearly suffocated him as he gasped for air, inexorable tears that vibrated in his chest. This seemingly cruel old man had become a child in the blink of an eye.

No longer a man capable of curses, Ichmenyev was unashamed to reveal his feelings as his imprisoned emotions broke free. His rapturous love for his daughter became evident as he kissed her portrait over and over again, clutching to his lips the locket that only seconds before he had nearly crushed under his foot.

"Forgive her! Forgive her!" his wife cried as she bent over and embraced him. "Forgive her and bring her home! God will rejoice in your humility and mercy and welcome you on the Day of Judgment."

"No! No! Never!" he rasped. "Never, never!"

CHAPTER FOURTEEN

I was an hour late for my nine o'clock appointment with Natasha. She was living then on the fourth floor of a dirty merchant house near the Semenovskaya Bridge over the Fontanka River. Originally, after leaving her parent's house, she had lived with Alexey in a small, but beautiful and comfortable third floor apartment near the Foundry, but the young prince had quickly depleted his capital. As a music teacher he was a dismal failure and he soon began to build up large debts. His initial funds went to furnish the apartment and to buy presents for Natasha, although she implored him, often with tears, to be more prudent with his money. But Alexey had a simple and sensitive heart that delighted in giving Natasha pleasure, in making each day with her a holiday. Sometimes he would spend an entire week planning and building up to some new surprise, teasing her and providing hints that would increase her anticipation. But such efforts were usually met by bitter recriminations from the object of his generosity and the result would be arguments and fighting.

Alexey was also spending money in ways that Natasha did not know about at the time. His school chums proved a bad influence on him and he would join them on excursions with a Minna or Josephine and he would fall in love for a night and then return to Natasha with the dawn, as much in love with her as ever. But such love carried an element of self-loathing as well. He would often come to me, depressed and tortured, and protest that he was unworthy of Natasha's love, that he was useless and evil. He couldn't understand why she loved him when he was such a child. He was partially right, of course. They were a badly matched couple. He behaved like a child and she treated him like one.

With tears in his eyes, Alexey would tell me about his various sexual escapades and beg me not to tell Natasha. On such occasions, Alexey would go to Natasha (dragging me along with the hope that my presence would soften her heart) and make some timid effort to confess, but she would immediately see through him. Although clearly jealous, Natasha would forgive what she called "his little eccentricities." This was not any kind of pretense on her part, for this exquisite creature truly delighted in forgiving and pardoning her Alyosha and she felt there was something subtly charming about her act of forgiveness.

There was one instance when Alexey, upon receiving Natasha's unqualified forgiveness, burst forth like a fountain with joy and rapture, and with tears of happiness, hugged and kissed her, and then proceeded to narrate his recent adventures in the arms of Josephine in the minutest detail and with such childish frankness, that Natasha ended up laughing along with him. The evening ended quite happily with the two entwined in each other's arms.

When Alexey ran out of money, he began to sell things. Natasha insisted that they move to a smaller, less expensive, apartment on the Fontanka and once there they continued to sell off their possessions. Natasha even sold some of her dresses and began to look for work. When Alexey found out, his despair knew no limits. He cursed himself, swore that he hated himself, and then proceeded to do nothing whatever to improve the situation. Soon it became clear that Natasha's meager earnings would prove their only reliable financial resource.

When they first began living together, Alexey had a major fight with his father. The prince's plan to marry his son to Katerina Fedorovna Filimonova, the stepdaughter of the countess, was still in its infancy, but he was determined to carry through with it. He had taken Alexey to visit his proposed bride and encouraged the boy, with considerable cunning and not a little bullying, to woo Katya and win her heart. When this effort was thwarted by the countess, Valkovsky decided to ignore his son's relationship with Natasha for the time being and direct his efforts to charming and pleasing the boy in order to maintain his love and loyalty. Alexey's infatuation for Natasha, he decided, would soon dissipate on its own, long before any marriage could take place. The young couple would not leap into marriage without first securing his own consent and their own financial solvency. And Natasha showed no inclination toward even discussing the subject.

Alexey, in private conversation with me, assured me that his father was actually quite happy with the situation and enjoyed the fact that it upset Natasha's father. But in reality, the prince continued to show his dissatisfaction with Alexey and proceeded to reduce his son's already scant allowance even more (he had never been particularly generous to begin with), and threatened to cut the boy off entirely. However, about this time, the prince traveled to Poland with the countess, determined in his own sly way to pursue his pet project. Alexey was too young for marriage, perhaps, but his future bride was very wealthy, and to overlook such an enviable virtue was unthinkable. Valkovsky soon decided to speed things along. Rumors began to spread that Alexey was engaged to marry the young heiress and when the prince returned to St. Petersburg, he greeted his son most warmly. But when he discovered that Alexey was still intent on marrying Natasha, he was shocked and soon ordered his son to break off the relationship.

Valkovsky quickly came up with an even better plan, however, and took Alexey with him to visit the countess. Her stepdaughter was almost beautiful and almost still a child, but she had a warm, generous heart, a pure, unblemished soul, and a cheery, witty and tender disposition. After six months with Natasha, Alexey's passion for her will surely have lost its novelty, the prince decided, and Katya, seen through fresh eyes, will most certainly seem all the more attractive.

The prince was only partially correct. Alexey was attracted to the girl, but he saw that his father's unusually engaging personality was feigned and only served to camouflage his cold and calculating manipulations. But the value of this information was offset by the charms of Katya, whom he was now seeing every day.

When I headed for Natasha's apartment, I knew that she had not seen Alexey for five days. I was very concerned about what she would have to say to me. Even from afar, I was able to distinguish the candle burning in her window. Some months before we had agreed that if there was a candle in her window, it meant she wanted to see me. That way, if I were walking by (which I did nearly every night) and saw the signal in the window, I would know that she was waiting for me and that I was needed. Recently, the candle had been on display quite often.

Chapter Fifteen

I found Natasha alone. She was quietly pacing back and forth across the room, deep in thought, with one hand on her chest. The samovar was boiling on the table; she had prepared the tea for me much earlier. When she saw me, she smiled silently and held out her hand. Her face was pale and in her expression I saw a tender, patient kind of anguish. Her clear blue eyes seemed even larger than usual and her hair appeared thicker, perhaps because she had lost so much weight.

"I was beginning to think you weren't coming," she said, taking my hand in hers. "I was about to have Mavra go and look for you. I was afraid you were sick again."

"No, I'm not sick. I was delayed. I'll tell you about it later. But what's happened with you, what is it?"

"Nothing," she answered calmly, as if surprised by my question. "What do you mean?"

"You wrote to me yesterday and asked me to come see you. You begged me to arrive precisely at nine o'clock, not one minute earlier, not one minute later. That's not your typical invitation to tea."

"Oh, yes. I was expecting him yesterday."

"And did he show up?" I asked.

"No," she said. She took a moment before continuing. "And I thought, if he doesn't show up, I'll have something to discuss with you."

"Are you expecting him tonight?" I asked.

"No, he spends his evenings there."

"What are you saying, Natasha? Do you think he may never return?"

"Of course he will," she said, with a very serious expression. The speed with which my questions were assaulting her made her uncomfortable.

She was quiet again and we walked about the room in silence. After a few minutes, she stopped and smiled. "I've been waiting for you a long time. Do you know what I've been doing to pass the time? I've been pacing about the room reading poetry. Do you remember the poem 'Sleigh Bells?' We used to read it together, remember?

"The storm has passed, the sky is clear,
I await the sound of his sleigh.
When the sleigh bells ring, my love will appear
And I'll welcome the light of the day.
The frosted glass on the windowpane
Is aglow like a twinkling star.
The room is warmed by the morning sun
And the steam of the samovar.

"Such lovely verses, Vanya. What a pretty picture they paint, like an embroidered tapestry. I can picture the house in my head, very much like the one we grew up in, with the cotton curtains and the roughhewn log beams. The woman waits with such patience and tenderness for her lover. It all seems so comforting, and yet, so sad at the same time."

She became silent for a moment. Her hand went to her throat, as if suppressing a sigh.

"You are such a good friend, Vanya," she said after a moment and then became quiet again. Clearly, she had something to say, but had either lost her train of thought or couldn't find the right words. Meanwhile, we continued to pace about the room. In one corner there was a lamp illuminating a portrait of Jesus, which struck me as odd since Natasha had not been particularly devout lately.

"Is tomorrow a holiday?" I asked.

"No," she answered sharply. Then, more calmly, she continued, "No, it's not a holiday. You must be tired, Vanya. Sit down. You haven't had your tea, have you?"

"Yes, I've had tea," I said. "But let's both sit down."

"You had tea before? Where have you just come from?"

"From them," I said. We always referred to her parents as "them" and to their house as "there."

"From them? What time did you go there? Did you just happen to stop by or did they ask you to come?" She bombarded me with more questions and her face grew paler the more agitated she became.

I described every detail of my encounter with her father, my conversation with her mother, the scene with the locket, everything in the greatest of detail. I kept nothing from her. She listened intently, devouring my every word, and tears sparkled in her eyes. She was particularly agitated when I told her about the incident with the locket.

"Wait, wait," she cried frequently, interrupting my story and imploring me to recall even greater details about what had happened and what was said. I went over many of the details a second and third time until she was finally satisfied that there was nothing more to learn. "And do you really think he was coming to visit me?" she asked when I had finished.

"I don't know, Natasha, I can't even begin to guess. What's clear is that he misses you very much and is miserable without you. But whether or not he was on his way here is..."

"And did he really kiss my portrait in the locket?" she interrupted. "Did he say anything when he kissed it?"

"I don't know, Natasha, most of it was just incoherent mumbling, but he did use many affectionate pet names for you."

"Pet names? Affectionate?"

"Yes." I said, and she began to cry softly.

"My dear papa," she said, and after a few seconds added, "He knows about everything, you know, so I'm not all surprised. He knows all about

Alyosha, where he goes and whom he sees."

"Natasha," I said timidly, "Let's go to him..."

She instantly started to rise from her chair but stopped herself. "When?" she asked. She must have thought I meant immediately.

"No, Vanya," she added, clasping me by the shoulders with both hands. "We've talked about this many times. Let's have no more of it."

"But do you really mean to say that you won't make any attempt to end this silly feud?" I asked, feeling very discouraged. "You can't be so pig-headed that you won't even consider making the first move! That's probably all the excuse your father needs to give in and forgive you. He's your father, Natasha, he loves you. But he was very hurt and you have to pamper his pride a little. It's your duty as his daughter, and it's the right thing to do. Just make an effort and he'll forgive you unconditionally."

"Unconditionally, that's not possible! And don't reproach me, Vanya, it's not necessary. I have thought about it, day and night. In fact, there hasn't been a day since I left home that I haven't thought about it. You know very well that we've talked about this many times, but you also know, as well as I do, that it's just impossible."

"At least try."

"No, my friend, I can't. Even if I did try it would only anger him more. We can't turn back the clock, Vanya. We'll never be able to relive those blissful days when we were children together. Even if he were able to forgive me and allow me to come home, he wouldn't know me anymore. He loved another girl, a large child. He delighted in my childlike innocence, and when he hugged me and patted me on my head it was like I was still a seven-year-old sitting on his knee and reciting nursery rhymes. From my earliest childhood to the day before I left home, he would come into my room at night and bless me. A month before I left, he bought me a pair of earrings and made a big show about keeping them a secret from me, but I found out about them anyway. He was like a little boy imagining how delighted I would be when he gave me the earrings, and then, when he found out that I already knew about them, he became so outrageously angry. And just three days before I left, he saw how depressed I was. What do you think his solution was? He bought tickets to the theater! My God, he thought that theater tickets would instantly cure me! I say it to you again, Vanya, he knew and loved a little girl, and never thought for a moment that I might actually grow up to be a woman. It never even occurred to him. So what good would it do for me to go home? He wouldn't know me.

"And if he *did* forgive," she continued, "who would he be forgiving? Not the person he would greet when I returned. I'm not a child; I have lived through too much to be called a child. Even if he liked the person he met, he would forever be lamenting the loss of the happy child he had known. The past always seems so much rosier until you really think about it, then it becomes torturous." She caught herself and added, "Oh, but I didn't mean our past, Vanya," but she left a pain in my heart, nonetheless.

"Everything you say is true, Natasha," I said. "But it just means he'll have to get to know the *new* you, and he'll fall in love with you all over again. You really can't believe that a good man like your father wouldn't be able to observe and understand you, in his heart."

"Oh, Vanya, you're being difficult. There's nothing special about me to understand, that's not what I'm saying. My father is a jealous man. He is offended that my affair began and, perhaps, ended without his knowledge. Alyosha was there every day and he never saw our love grow. He didn't see it coming. I never went to him and told him how I felt, but kept everything from him. So when I ran away, he blamed it on my secrecy and saw it as a betrayal of his trust. I assure you, Vanya, it was the secrecy that offended him, not my love for Alyosha. When I ran off with my lover, he saw it as my deserting *him*! Even if he could take me back, that seed of resentment would remain in his heart and by the second day, by the third day, his dissatisfaction would grow into hostility and the quarreling would begin again.

"Let us assume, Vanya, that I do go to him and beg his forgiveness. I tell him, from the bottom of my heart, that I was wrong, that I understand exactly how much I have offended him and that I truly regret it. What if I tell him how much genuine suffering my 'happiness' with Alyosha has caused me, how miserably unhappy I have been, that I am almost choking on my pain. Even that would not be enough for him. He would demand more. He would require me to curse my past, curse Alyosha, and repent for the sin of falling in love. He would demand the impossible, that I wipe away the past six months and erase all memories from our minds. But I can't do that, Vanya. I will not curse anyone and I cannot repent. What happened is what happened and nothing can change that. No, Vanya, the time is not yet right."

"But will it ever be right?"

"I don't know. Maybe it'll be necessary to suffer even more before we can realize our future happiness. Suffering cures all. Oh, Vanya, there is so much pain in the world!"

I was silent and looked at her thoughtfully.

"Why are you looking at me like that, Alyosha?" she asked and then corrected herself with a laugh. "I mean, Vanya!"

"I'm looking at your smile, Natasha. Where did it come from? You've never smiled like that before."

"Why, what's different about my smile?" she asked.

"There is still a trace of your old innocence, but when you smile, I seem to see something pulling at your heart. You've lost so much weight and your hair seems so much thicker, is that possible? And that dress you're wearing, it must have been made for you when you were living with them."

"Ah, you still love me, don't you?" she answered. There was a tender, affectionate look in her eyes. "Tell me how you are, Vanya. What have you been doing?"

"Nothing's changed," I said. "I'm still working on my novel, but it's not easy. Inspiration is elusive and ideas are difficult to pin down. But I'm still writing for a magazine, and I have to submit a specific number of pages every week without fail, so that keeps me busy. I'm considering giving up writing novels and dedicating myself to lighter material, something without a trace of gloom, no tears. Everyone seems to want to laugh and be cheerful!"

"Poor, Vanya, forever with your nose to the grindstone. But what about Smith?"

"Smith? He died a week ago."

"Yes, but hasn't he appeared to you in nightmares? I'm serious, Vanya. When you were sick, your nerves were frayed and I thought you might be having strange visions. It occurred to me when you told me about the new apartment you were renting. Is it still damp? It sounds like a dreadful, dreadful room."

"Well, yes. Actually, something did happen there this evening. But I'll tell you about it later."

She wasn't listening anymore. She seemed preoccupied with other thoughts.

"I don't understand how I could have left them like that," she said finally. "I was in such a fever." Her expression told me that she wasn't expecting an answer and she probably wouldn't have heard me if I had given one.

"Vanya," she said, her voice barely audible. "I asked you here for a reason."

"Which was?" I asked.

"I'm leaving him."

"You *have* left him or you *intend* to leave him?"

"I can't live like this anymore. I asked you here to tell you that, and to tell you about everything that has happened, even what I've kept hidden from you until now."

She often started like that, intent on revealing secrets to me, only to discover that I already knew them.

"Ah, Natasha, you've said that a thousand times. Of course, you can't continue to live together. You have nothing in common. You're much too different. But do you have the strength to leave him?"

"Until now it was just a thought, but now I've definitely made up my mind. I love him beyond measure, but I'm his worst enemy. I stand in the way of his future and I must let him go. He can't marry me and go against his father's wishes. I don't want to tie him down. I'm glad that he's fallen in love with another woman. It'll be easier for him to let me go. I see this as my duty. If I truly love him, then I must prove it by freeing him. It's my duty. Isn't that true?"

"But you've never done anything to force him to stay."

"No and I never will, that's not going to change. If he walked into the room right now, I would act just the same as always. But I have to find a way to make it easier for him to leave me with a clear conscience. That's what tortures me. Help me, Vanya, please, what should I do?"

"The simplest way is for you to fall out of love with him and in love with someone else. But even then, you can't be sure it'll work. You know how he is. He left you five days ago and may well have deserted you, but if you were to write him a letter and tell him you wanted out, he'd come running back immediately."

"Why do you hate him so?"

"Me?"

"Yes, you! You! You're his enemy, both secretly and openly. You can't even mention his name without sounding vengeful. I've seen it a thousand times; you enjoy degrading and insulting him. It's true."

"Well, if, as you say, I've done that a thousand times, there's no need to mention his name ever again. Let's change the subject."

After a moment of silence, she said, "I'd like to move to another apartment. Now don't get angry, Vanya."

"He'll find you no matter where you move," I said. "And damn it, I'm not angry!"

"Love is strong. Maybe his new love can hold him. Even if he did come back to me, it would only be for a minute, don't you think?"

"I don't know, Natasha, he doesn't seem capable of doing anything in a normal way. I think he wants to marry *her* and continue to love *you,* and in his mind, that's quite reasonable."

"If I could only know for sure that he really loves her, it would be so easy to make up my mind. Vanya, don't lie to me. Are you hiding anything from me that I should know about?" She looked at me imploringly.

"There's nothing, my friend, really. I give you my word. I'm always honest with you. But what I think is that he may not have fallen in love with the stepdaughter of the countess as strongly as it appears. So, keep your spirits up."

"Oh my God, Vanya, do you really believe that? If I could only know for sure. I just wish he were here this minute so I could look in his eyes, then I'd know. He can't hide anything from me. But he's not here, he may never be here!"

"And yet you're here waiting for him, aren't you?"

"No, he's with her. I know because I sent someone to check on him. And, you know, Vanya, it may be foolish, but I'd really like to see her too. Is that possible, do you think? That we could meet somewhere?"

I had an uneasy feeling as I said, "Of course, you could see her. But just getting a look at her isn't going to do you much good."

"It would be enough for now. I could guess the rest. Listen, Vanya, I've been acting like an idiot, pacing up and down, up and down, just thinking about them, my brain is ready to explode. But here's a thought. You could meet her, couldn't you? The countess praised your novel, you told me so yourself, and you've been to a few of Prince Rudolph's society parties. You're sure to run into the countess there one night and she could introduce you to her stepdaughter. Then you could come back here and tell me all about her."

"Natasha, my dear, can we please talk about this later? Right now I want to ask you, do you really think you're strong enough to break up with Alyosha? Look at yourself, you look like death itself."

"I can take it," she said, barely audible. "It's for him. Everything I do is for him! But you know, Vanya, the one thing I can't stand is the thought of him sitting there with her right now, laughing and telling stories the way he used to here, and completely forgetting about me. He's staring into her eyes, the way he did with me, and not a single thought of me enters his head. He's not even thinking about me sitting here with you," she cried in despair.

"But, Natasha, only a minute ago you said..."

"We need to do it together," she announced, with a sudden burst of inspiration. "We have to break up at the same time! He'll have my complete blessing, of course, but it's just too difficult, Vanya, to imagine him just forgetting about me! Oh, I'm such a mess, I don't know what I'm saying. I *think* I'm being so calm and rational, but it's really not true. What's going to happen with me?"

"You'll be fine, fine, Natasha, calm yourself!"

"It's been five days, five days!" she continued. "Asleep or awake, all I do is think about him. It's always about him, about him. Oh, Vanya, let's go there now, take me there!"

"Calm down, Natasha," I begged her.

"No, let's go now!" she insisted. "I've been waiting for you for three days, so I've had plenty of time to think about this. That's what I was writing to you about. You must take me to him and you cannot refuse me. I've been waiting for you! Three days! There's a party at Prince Rudolph's tonight. He'll be there!"

She was delirious. At that moment, I heard a commotion in the hallway. Mavra was arguing with someone.

"Wait a second, Natasha, who's that? Listen!" She stopped to listen but there was a smirk on her face as if she doubted I was telling the truth. Then, suddenly, she turned pale.

"Oh, my God! Who's there?" she whispered.

She tried to hold on to me, but I hurried into the hall to see what was happening. As I feared, it was Alyosha, and Mavra was doing her best to prevent him from coming in.

"Oh, so now you show up," Mavra was saying. "Where have you been off to? If you want to wander, go wander, go! What have you got to say for yourself?"

"I'm not afraid of you or anyone! I'm going in there!" Alyosha sounded considerably more confident than he looked.

"I'm going to hurt you if you don't stop!" Mavra announced.

"Ah, there you are," he said as I came through the door. "I'm so glad you're here! Well, I'm here too, now. But how am I going to..."

"Well, come in," I said. "What are you afraid of?"

"I'm not afraid of anything, I can assure you. By God, I have nothing to feel guilty for," he declared, then added, "Do you think I should feel guilty? Well, you'll see how I explain myself to Natasha!"

He stood his ground and called out, "May I come in?" But there was no answer.

"What's the matter?" he asked me, his confidence quickly fading.

"Nothing," I said, and moved aside to let him enter.

Alyosha carefully stepped into the room and looked about timidly. There was no one there. Suddenly I spotted Natasha hiding between the cabinet and the window. She seemed neither living nor dead. When I think back on this scene, even now, I can't help laughing. Alyosha quietly slithered past me and toward her.

"Natasha! What's the matter? How are you? What's new?"

"Well," she answered, "nothing much." She seemed quite embarrassed and a bit guilty when she realized she was hiding in the corner. "Have some tea?"

Alyosha was confused and frightened. "Oh, Natasha! Maybe you're thinking that I'm to blame for something? Well, I am blameless, I am innocent! You'll agree when you hear what I have to say."

"But... Oh, what's the use?" Natasha whispered. She held out her hand to Alyosha, who took it. "Whatever you have to say, I'm going to forgive you, and things will end up pretty much the way they always do." The blush was beginning to return to her cheeks as she moved back into the center of the room. She kept her eyes on the floor, rather than looking at Alyosha.

"Oh, my God!" he yelled with enthusiasm. "If only I had been guilty of something, I wouldn't have the nerve to look you in the face again!" He turned to me. "But look here, she won't look at me. She thinks I did something wrong, just because of the visible evidence against me. Five days I was gone! She hears rumors that I am engaged to another woman, and yet she reaches out her hand to me and tells me that all is forgiven. Oh, Natasha, my dear, sweet angel, I am not guilty, and you know it! Quite the contrary. I am innocent. But you should be there! Right now. They have invited you to the party. What time is it?" He retrieved the gold pocket watch from his vest pocket. "It's half-past-ten. I've been there all evening," he continued, returning the watch to his pocket, "but I told them I wasn't feeling well and needed some fresh air. It's the very first moment I've had in five days to get away from them, and here I am running to you! I could have gotten here sooner, Natasha, but I purposely didn't come. I'll tell you why later, but you need to know that I am blameless. Completely!"

Natasha raised her head and looked at him. The expression on his face was so open and honest, so enthusiastic and caring, that it was impossible for her not to believe him. I half expected them to fly into each other's arms as usual, but Natasha seemed so emotionally overcome by her joy that she lowered her head again and began to sob quietly.

Alyosha would have none of it. He quickly kneeled before her and in a frenzy of passion kissed her hands and feet. Natasha's legs began to tremble visibly. I pushed a chair towards her and she fell back into it.

Chapter Sixteen

Within a minute or two the three of us were laughing like lunatics.

Alexey's voice rang out, "Please let me tell you my story! It's not at all like my other tales; this one is really interesting!" His words only prompted greater laughter from Natasha and me. "Aren't you ever going to stop laughing?" he cried. Clearly, he was determined to tell his story, but his comic indignation only added to our amusement. Natasha made an attempt to suppress her glee, but one look at Alyosha's childish pout set her off again. Like Gogol's Nozdrev, we had reached the point where Alyosha only needed to raise a finger to stretch our cheeks to their limits and set our stomachs to quaking.

Mavra, who had been working in the kitchen, came to the doorway and stood there with a sour expression. She had been expecting Natasha to give the young prince a severe scolding and was dismayed to discover that five days of separation had resulted in little more than unrestrained merriment.

Natasha at last realized that her high spirits were making Alyosha unhappy and she stopped laughing. "What is it you want to tell us?" she asked.

"Do you want me to bring out the tea?" interrupted Mavra, who had no respect whatsoever for the sullen young man.

Alyosha waved his arms and shouted, "Go away, Mavra! Get out!"

Mavra shook her head and retreated to her kitchen.

"I will tell you everything that has happened, and everything that is going to happen, because I know all about it. I imagine that you both want to know where I've been for the last five days. I will tell you, if you let me. Well, first of all, Natasha, I want you to know that I have been deceiving you. Not just this week, but before that."

"Deceiving me?"

"Yes, deceiving you, for an entire month, even before my father came home. The time has come for me to be completely honest. About a month ago, I received a long letter from my father that I kept a secret from both of you. In the letter he told me straight out, and in such a serious tone that it frightened me, that his matchmaking campaign for me had been successful and that he had found me a perfect bride. I was unworthy of her, he pointed out, but we were to be married anyway, so I had better accept that fact and clear my head of all the nonsense, and so forth and so on. Well, of course, we all know what 'nonsense' he's referring to, right? So, that's the letter I hid from you."

"Hid from me?" Natasha said. "That's ridiculous. The moment you received it you came here and told me everything. I still remember how you became such a sweet little boy, tender and obedient, like a puppy who had misbehaved. You wouldn't leave my side until you had revealed every fragment of the letter."

"That can't be!" Alyosha looked genuinely surprised. "Well, I probably didn't tell you the most important thing. You may have both guessed it, that's not my concern, but I know I didn't tell you. And I've been feeling terribly guilty about keeping it from you."

"I remember too, Alyosha," I said. "You came to us and described the whole letter in detail. I certainly didn't have to guess at anything." I looked at Natasha.

"You told us everything," Natasha added. "So stop bragging about your great skill at keeping secrets. Even Mavra knows about the letter, don't you, Mavra."

"What's not to know?" Mavra replied, sticking her head back through the door where she had apparently been standing the whole time. "You told all three of us. Sly as a fox you're not."

"Oh, you're so aggravating! She's just trying to annoy me, Natasha. She wasn't even here when I told you. Don't you remember, Mavra, we didn't have any money then and I sent you to pawn my silver cigarette case? So you couldn't possibly have heard me. And even if you were here, you usually fall asleep when I'm speaking anyway! Natasha, you've done a fine job of training her, I must say. But let us all assume, just for the sake of argument, that I actually did describe my father's letter. What I didn't convey to you was the tone of the letter."

"Well, what about the tone?" Natasha asked, barely able to suppress a smile.

"Now look, Natasha, you may think this is all a joke, but it's no joke I can assure you! This is very important. My father had never before spoken to me in such a tone, a tone that stunned me, as if the whole city were collapsing around me. That's the kind of tone!"

"Well, go on then. Why did you feel that you had to hide the tone from me?"

"Oh my God, I didn't want to frighten you! I was hoping it would all settle down on its own. But soon after my father returned, we had dinner together. I was fully prepared to respond to each of his demands, clearly, solidly and seriously, but it didn't quite work out that way. He never even brought up the subject! He's very clever. Instead, he behaved like there was nothing to talk about, as if the whole matter was settled and there couldn't possibly be any room for discussion. Not even a chance to discuss it! Can you believe such arrogance? And then he became so friendly and affectionate toward me, I was shocked. Oh, yes, he's a very clever man, my father, if you only knew. He reads everything and knows everything. He only has to look at you once and he can read your every thought. Maybe that's why he's been called a Jesuit. Natasha doesn't like it when I praise him. Please don't be mad at me, Natasha. And another thing: he never used to give me money, but yesterday he did! Natasha, my angel, our money worries are over. Here, look! Everything he held back when he was punishing me, a full six months' allowance, he's made up for!"

He took from his pocket a huge bundle of fifteen hundred rubles and tossed it on the table.

"Look how much!" he said. "I haven't counted it yet. So you see, Mavra, you won't need to pawn any more spoons or cuff-links for us!"

Mavra looked surprised and delighted by this news and regarded Alyosha with newfound respect.

Natasha urged him to continue his story. "Well," he said, "what am I going to do now? How can I go against his wishes? I swear to you both that if he had come out and given me orders, I would have stood up to him like a man and refused him. But now, what can I say? I can see you're unhappy with me, Natasha. From the way you two are looking at each other, I can see you think I've been trod upon and there is not an ounce of strength in me. There is strength in me and it's even more than you think. And to prove it, I said to myself, 'I have a duty to my father and I should tell him everything.' So I did. I expressed myself and he listened."

"Yes, well, what exactly did you express to him?" Natasha asked with a sense of foreboding.

"That I do not want another fiancée, that I already have a fiancée, and it is you. I didn't exactly say it in those words, but I was preparing him and I plan to tell him tomorrow. So I've solved that problem. But what I did tell him is that marrying for money is shameful and ignoble and that it was silly for us to consider ourselves aristocrats. I was very frank with him, you see, and spoke to him man to man. There are different levels of aristocracy, I said, and using his own measuring standards, we are no different from anyone else, and I am proud to be like everyone else. I spoke with great fire and passion. I even surprised myself. I proved to him, from his point of view, that we are princes in name only. First of all, I said, 'What makes a prince? Wealth. Wealth is the main thing, the principal thing that makes a prince. Nowadays, Rothschild is a prince among princes.' Then I said, 'A prince's place in society is also essential. High society has forgotten about our family long ago. They rarely think about us today.' Uncle Semyon was renowned in Moscow for having frivolously squandered away his estate and more than 300 serfs, and my father might well have been forced to become a ploughman, like so many other princes, had he not married my mother. So I proved to him, clearly and eloquently, that there really is no reputation for us to maintain. He never objected to anything I said, but he did suggest that I continue to call on Count Nainsky to keep in good with him, and that I must be pleasant to Princess K., my godmother, because she has influence in the world and can introduce me to the proper people. I tell you all this, Natasha, to show you just how much I gave up when I fell in love with you; such was the effect of your influence. Until now, my father has avoided speaking about you directly. He and I are both cunning, waiting for the right moment to spring, and you can be sure there is great sport to be had when that happens!"

"Yes, but enough of that. What was the result? Is anything resolved? That's the important thing, Alyosha. You do prattle on so!"

"Oh, good Lord, Natasha, it's impossible to know what he's decided. As for my prattling, it's not true. I don't prattle. Father hasn't decided upon anything, but he did listen to all of my arguments and he smiled at me, as if he pitied me, which may not be the ideal response, but it shows he cares. And he did say, 'I understand and I quite agree with you.' Then he added, 'When we go to Count Nainsky's home it may be best to say nothing about this, as they may not understand as well as I do.' It seems they don't entirely understand him either, because they're angry with him about something. I don't think they like him very much. When I first went there, the count was very arrogant and condescending to me; as if he had totally forgotten that I had grown up in his household. I think he was angry at me because of my ingratitude, but really there is no ingratitude whatever. It's just so boring in his house, so I stopped visiting.

"The count has treated my father very cavalierly too; so haughty and proud, in fact, that it's a wonder my father continues to go there. I know he only puts up with them for my benefit, but I never asked him too. I thought about confronting my father about the count but I held my tongue; I knew it would only make him angrier. So I came up with a plan that was quite ingenious. I determined to make the count respect me and like me. And I succeeded perfectly. Everything changed in a single day."

"Listen, Alyosha," Natasha interrupted. "I thought you were going to tell me something that concerned *us*. I don't care about how you ingratiated yourself to the count. I couldn't care less about the count."

"Couldn't care less? Do you hear her, Ivan Petrovich? She says she couldn't care less. The count is the most important part of my story and you will care when you hear the rest. Just let me finish. The two of you, let's be honest, often treat me like a fool. Well, maybe I do say or do foolish things on occasion, but I can be very clever when I want to be, and this is one of those times. When you hear what I've done, I know you will both agree that I'm not at all stupid."

"That's silly, my darling, no one considers you stupid." Natasha refused to accept the idea that Alyosha might be a little slow-witted, and on those occasions when I pointed out this fact, she became very angry with me. She hated to see him humiliated in any way. Although she was certainly aware of his limitations, she never gave a hint of her feelings to him for fear of hurting his pride. Alyosha, however, was acutely sensitive to such insults and always knew what Natasha was thinking. Natasha would then try to placate him with excessive flattery and soothing words. That is why Alyosha's current rant was creating conflicting emotions in her heart. "You shouldn't put yourself down like that, Alyosha. You're just a little frivolous, that's all."

"Exactly," he responded. "So I'll prove to you I know what I am doing. After the reception at the count's, I knew father was angry with me, but I thought to myself, 'Hold off, don't say anything yet.' Then we went to visit the princess. I had heard that she was quite old and senile and almost completely deaf, but that she loves dogs. She has a whole flock and adores them all. In spite of her frailties, she has such an enormous influence in society that even a proud man like the count bows down to her. Isn't that a charming image? So during the carriage ride with my father, I came up with a plan of action, and what do you think I based it on? Simply the fact that dogs *love* me! I don't know why, but I seem to have a magnetic attraction to them, or maybe it's just because I love all animals so much. Oh, Natasha, speaking of magnetic attractions, we had a séance the other day. It's terribly interesting, Ivan Petrovich. Amazing! I called up Julius Caesar."

"Oh, my God, why would you want to speak to Julius Caesar?" Natasha cried. She was once again convulsed by laughter. "That's all that was missing!"

"Yes, well I... Wait, why shouldn't I want to speak to Julius Caesar? I don't see what's so funny?"

"Nothing, nothing," she said, trying to resume her serious demeanor. "What did Julius Caesar have to say to you?"

"Well, he didn't say anything to me," he responded, looking quite offended by the suggestion. "I simply held a pencil and he moved it around on the paper. At least, they said it was Julius Caesar doing the writing, but, of course, I'm not sure I believed them."

"Well then, what did Julius Caesar write?" Natasha asked.

"I couldn't tell. It ended up looking something like 'moisten it,' like in Gogol. Completely illegible."

Growing more frustrated, Natasha prompted him, "Yes, well, tell us about the princess now."

"Well, you keep interrupting me! We arrived at the princess's home and I began flirting immediately with Mimi. Mimi is the nastiest, most contemptible and obstinate little dog, and a biter, but the princess is crazy about her. I think they may be the same age. I started by giving candy to Mimi and within ten minutes, she learned how to give me her paw, something she had never done before in her entire life! The princess was absolutely thrilled and almost crying from happiness. 'Oh, Mimi," she cries, 'you gave me your paw, you gave me your paw.' Then someone walked in the room and she said, 'Mimi, give him your paw!' and Mimi did so and she cried, 'Oh, she shook your hand! She shook your hand! My godson taught her that trick!' And then the count came in and the princess said, 'Mimi can shake hands!' and she looked at me with such tender emotion; she's really a very sweet old lady, I almost pity her. Well, then I needed to come up with something else to do. Fortunately, she dropped her snuff box. I saw immediately that there was a portrait painted on it of her as a bride sixty years ago, so I pretended I didn't know it was her and said, "What a charming picture, this is an ideal beauty!" Well, the princess just melted completely. She asked me about this and about that, and where had I studied, and who do I visit, and told me what glorious hair I have, and it was all so boring and predictable, but she absolutely adores me. I made her laugh by telling her a risqué story. She loves that sort of thing. Of course, she shook her bony old finger at me, but laughed anyway. When she finally permitted me to leave, she kissed me and blessed me and made me promise to come every day to entertain her. The count took my hand and his eyes oozed steel. My father, one of the most noble and honest of human beings, whether you believe it or not, nearly cried from happiness during our carriage ride, and when we arrived at his home he embraced me and became mysteriously frank and open about my career, connections, money, marriages. I couldn't follow most of what he had to say, but that's when he gave me the money. That was yesterday. Tomorrow I'm going to see the princess again, but don't ever doubt that my father is an honorable man, even if he does want me to break up with you. He's just blinded by the millions that Katya has and you don't. He wants them for me and it's just his ignorance that makes him behave unjustly towards you. What father doesn't want happiness for his son? It's not his fault that he thinks money and happiness go hand in hand. They all think like that. But when you see things from his standpoint, you can easily see that he's right. I hurried over here immediately to assure you that any prejudices you may have against him are unfounded since he is, it goes without saying, completely innocent. I don't blame you at all."

"So, all that's really happened is that you've set yourself up with the princess. Is that the cunning plan you spoke of?" Natasha asked.

"What? No. What are you saying? That's just the beginning. I only told you about the princess so you could see how I plan to control my father. But that part of the story hasn't started yet."

"Well, say something," Natasha pleaded.

"Today, something else happened that was so extraordinary that I am still astonished by it. I've already mentioned that my father and the countess have been playing matchmaker, but until now there's been no official announcement, so it's not too late to break it off without creating a scandal. Count Nainsky is the only other person who knows and he is, after all, a relative and patron. And even though Katya and I have grown very close over the past two weeks, we have never said a word about the future. Or of marriage. Or even love. Before anything like that could happen, we would need to obtain the consent of Princess K., from whom all good fortune and influence flow. If she approves, the world will approve, that's how influential she is. And the countess, Katya's stepmother, is very anxious for me to be accepted into society. It's very important to her. You see, her reputation abroad has followed her home and the princess absolutely refuses to receive her. That's why the countess has changed her mind about me. She thinks that my marriage to Katya would be her entrée into society, so she was particularly delighted by my success with the princess. But none of that is important. The main thing is that even though I've known Katerina

Fedorovna most of my life, even last year I was still just a boy and didn't know anything about women. So I never thought much about her."

"The fact is that you were in love with me a year ago," interrupted Natasha. "That's why you didn't think about her, but now..."

"Not another word, Natasha!" Alyosha exclaimed hotly. "You are mistaken and you wound me! I won't bother to contradict you, but you should listen and you'll learn everything! Oh, if only you knew Katya, what a tender, gentle and open-hearted creature she is. But listen and you'll know everything. Two weeks ago, when my father took me to see Katya, I decided to study her very closely. And then I noticed that she was studying me closely too. Well, of course, that aroused my curiosity, and her interest in me, combined with my father's letter, prompted me to double my efforts to get to know her better. I'm not going to shower you with her praises, but I will say one thing. She is the one bright exception to her whole dreary circle. She has such a strong, straightforward spirit and a pure and honest soul that she makes me feel like a little boy in her presence, like a little brother, despite the fact that she is only seventeen years old.

"I also noticed," he continued, "that there is something secretly melancholy about her. She rarely says anything when she's at home and seems intimidated and frightened about something. She's clearly afraid of my father and has no love for her stepmother, although for some reason the countess pretends Katya just adores her, which isn't true. Katya obeys her, of course, but nothing more. So, four days ago, after all my observations, I decided to proceed with my plan, which I successfully carried out today. And that was to tell Katya everything, confess the truth, and get her on our side once and for all."

"What do you mean?" Natasha asked uneasily. "What is there to tell her, what is there to confess?"

"Everything. Absolutely everything," Alyosha responded. "And I thank God for inspiring me to do it, but listen to the rest. Listen. Four days ago, I decided to stay away from you until I had brought this business to an end. I knew that if I were with you, I would just follow your advice and never be able to build up my strength and resolve. So that's what I did, and I was brave and I did precisely what I set out to do, which was to come back to you with a solution. And I have."

"Well, what is it? Tell us faster!"

"It's very simple! I approached her boldly and honestly and... but wait. Before that I need to tell you one other thing that surprised me very much. My father received a letter this morning. I was about to enter his office and saw him standing there staring at this letter and he seemed quite surprised by its contents. At first, he said nothing, but then he started to smile and move about excitedly, and then he was laughing like a madman. I was afraid to enter the room until he calmed down. When I did go in, he spoke to me in a vague, hazy sort of way and told me to be quick and prepare for a visit to Katya. I thought it was pretty early in the day for a visit, but I did as I was told. You know, Natasha, you must have been misinformed about there being a party there today because there was no one else there."

"Oh, Alyosha, don't be distracted. Just tell me, please, what did you say to Katya?"

"Well, fortunately, we had two full hours to ourselves. I simply told her that in spite of any plans being made for us to marry, it wasn't going to happen, and that in my heart I felt great sympathy for her, but she was the only one who could save me. Then I told her everything. Can you believe it, Natasha? She knew absolutely nothing about you and me. If only you could have seen how touched she was by our story. At first, she turned pale and seemed a little frightened. But when I told her how you had run away from your home, and how we had been living, and how we had suffered, and that we were now coming to her for help—told her I was speaking for you too, Natasha—and that we needed her to intercede for us by going to her stepmother and telling her that she refused to marry me. That was our only hope I told her and only she could rescue us. Katya listened with such sweet, sympathetic eyes. You can't imagine how lovely her eyes looked at that moment. I think her entire soul passed through those sparkling, blue eyes. She thanked me for being honest with her and promised to help us. Then she started asking questions about you and told me she wanted to meet you and get to know you, and that she wanted you to know that she already loved you like a sister and she hoped you would love *her* like a sister. Then when I told her I hadn't seen you in five days, she chased me away and insisted I go directly to you."

Natasha was touched. "And you wasted so much time telling us about some old princess and her nasty dog, when you had this to reveal? Oh, Alyosha, Alyosha," Natasha said reproachfully. "How did Katya behave when she released you? Was she pleased and happy or did it seem unimportant to her?"

"Yes, she was very pleased that she could act in so noble a manner, but she cried nevertheless, because she loves me too, Natasha. She admitted that she's come to love me; that she doesn't see anyone else, and that she has liked me for a long time. She was especially attracted to me because she is surrounded by craftiness and lies. Compared to the others, I am sincere and honest. Then she stood up and started to say, 'God be with you, Alexey Petrovich, I wish you…' but before she could finish, she burst into tears and ran out of the room. We did agree, however, that she will talk to her stepmother tomorrow and tell her that she won't marry me, and I'm to have an equally serious conversation with my father informing him of our decision. She criticized me for not having told him before and said, 'An honest person has nothing to fear.'

"She is so noble," Alyosha continued. "She doesn't like my father because she thinks he is too devious and money-hungry. I tried to defend him, but she didn't believe me. She said if I can't convince him to call off the wedding—and she doesn't think I'll succeed—then I will have to resort to the patronage of Princess K., because my father wouldn't dare go against her wishes. We both gave each other our word to be like brother and sister. Oh, Natasha, if only you knew her history and how unhappy she is living with the countess and her friends. She hates them all. Of course, she didn't tell me that directly, but I could see what was in her heart. She would love you so much, Natasha, and once you saw what a good heart she has, you would feel the same way about her. You two were born to be sisters. I was thinking that I'd like to get you two together and then just stand back and admire you both. I hope you don't mind my talking about her like this, Natasha. I wouldn't want you to misunderstand. I love talking about her to you and about you to her. You know very well that I love you more than anyone, you're my all!"

Natasha looked silently at him. There was great affection in her eyes but sadness too, somehow. It was as if his words had both caressed and tortured her at the same time.

"I started to admire Katya more than two weeks ago," Alyosha said. "I would drive there every night and then come home and think of the two of you, comparing each of your qualities."

"And who came out on top?" Natasha asked with a smile.

"Sometimes you and sometimes her, but you always won out in the end. Whenever I speak with her, I always feel so much better about myself afterwards, more clever and manly and noble. Well, tomorrow all will be decided."

"Don't you feel a little sorry for her, Alyosha? You said she loves you; you noticed that yourself."

"Yes, of course, I feel sorry. But the three of us shall love each other and then..."

"And then good-bye," Natasha said quietly, almost to herself.

Alyosha looked puzzled by this remark, but before he could comment, the conversation was interrupted in a most unexpected manner. There was a sudden noise in the kitchen, which also served as the entryway to the apartment. Mavra poked her head in the doorway and beckoned to Alyosha.

"There is someone asking for you," Mavra said in a mysterious whisper.

"Who could be asking about me *here*?" Alyosha said, turning to us with a bewildered look. "I'll go see."

In the kitchen stood Prince Valkovsky's uniformed valet. The prince had been passing Natasha's building in his carriage and stopped to inquire if Alyosha was there with her. After speaking with Alyosha, the valet left.

"That's very odd," Alyosha said, looking very confused. "He's never done that before."

Natasha too looked most uneasy.

Suddenly the door opened again and Mavra hurried in. "The prince is coming up," she whispered, then ducked out again.

Natasha turned pale and stood up. Suddenly, her eyes caught fire and she leaned against the table as she stared at the door through which her uninvited guest was about to appear.

"Natasha, don't be frightened, I'm with you. I won't let him bully you," Alyosha said, attempting to suppress any fear that he may have been feeling.

The door opened and, on the threshold, stood Prince Valkovsky, in person.

Chapter Seventeen

As Valkovsky's steely glance darted quickly around the room, taking in each of us, I found it difficult to determine his attitude—was he enemy or friend? I'll take a moment to provide a more detailed description of his appearance.

I had seen him before when I was a boy. Now he was a man of about 45, no more, with strong, extremely attractive features. His expression could change instantly, depending on the circumstances, from pleasant charm to sullen anger. His ideally formed oval face featured a dark complexion that set off his excellent teeth, small, thin lips, straight but slightly hooked nose, broad, wrinkle-free forehead and suitably large, gray eyes, the totality of which represented a handsome man but, nevertheless, did not elicit an agreeable response. One always had the sensation that his expression was a facade, deliberately created, borrowed from others for a particular purpose, and that you were not seeing his true feelings. If you studied him more intently, however, you would begin to notice something malicious, devious and decidedly selfish behind the mask. What drew your attention most prominently were his gray eyes. They seemed to have a will of their own. When he wanted to gaze gently and affectionately, his eyes would often reflect a rigid, distrustful and even malevolent ray. The rest of him was decidedly elegant. He was reasonably thin, with soft, dark brown hair which had yet to turn gray, giving him an appearance younger than his actual years. His ears, hands and feet were also remarkably good. He was, in total, a thoroughbred. His one lapse may have been his sense of fashion, which tended to favor the styles of much younger men. He seemed more like a big brother to Alyosha, making it difficult for a stranger to accept him as the father of an adult son.

Valkovsky approached Natasha directly and said to her, "My arrival at your home at this hour without advance notice is certainly unusual and outside the rules of proper etiquette, but I hope you will believe that I am, at least, fully aware of the eccentricity of my behavior. I also understand with whom I am dealing. I know that you are an insightful and generous woman. If you will permit me just ten minutes of your time, I believe I will be able to justify my surprise visit."

He said all of this politely, but with an air of forceful determination.

"Won't you sit?" said Natasha, who had not yet fully recovered from her initial surprise and fright.

The prince bowed and sat down.

"First of all, permit me to say a few words to you," he said, indicating his son. "Alyosha, you left earlier without waiting for me and without even saying good-bye to the countess or providing any excuse for your behavior. Shortly after you rushed out, we were informed that Katerina Fedorovna had fainted. The countess was about to go to her when Katya hurried in on her own. She told us straight out that she cannot be your wife and intended to join a convent. She said that you had asked for her help by acknowledging that you were in love with another woman, Natalia Nikolayevna. Katya was clearly devastated by this information and her announcement, it goes without saying, was completely unexpected and both surprised and frightened me. Traveling past your house just now, I noticed a light in your window," he continued, turning to Natasha. "An idea which I have been considering for some time took hold of me and I felt a strong determination to convey it to you. You will, I hope, excuse the sharp manner in which I express myself, but this has come upon me so suddenly..."

"I'm sure I will consider whatever you have to say," Natasha said hesitatingly.

The prince stared intently into her eyes, perhaps trying to read her thoughts.

"I look forward to your insight," he continued, "and hope you understand that even though I may have arrived here unexpectedly, I understand precisely with whom I am dealing. We have known each other a long time and I realize that my behavior towards you in the past may have appeared very troubling and unjust. But you are aware of the unpleasantness that exists between your father and me. I don't try to justify myself. Perhaps I am more to blame than I realized until recently. If that's true, it's because I was deceived by information that was presented to me. I often leap to negative conclusions, I admit. I tend to suspect the worst before seeing the best, an unfortunate characteristic of a bitter heart. But I don't try to hide my faults. I believed the rumors about you, and when you ran off with Alyosha I was very worried about him. But I didn't really know you at the time. The information that I have since gathered about you, little by little, comforted me and as I continued to observe Alyosha's behavior, I grew more and more encouraged until finally I realized that my suspicions about you were groundless. I learned that you had thrown off your ties with your parents and that your father was dead set against you marrying my son. I also realized that you were not using your influence over Alyosha to coerce him into marriage. That fact alone clearly demonstrated that you are an admirable young woman."

The prince bowed his head courteously to Natasha.

"Nevertheless," he continued, "I fully admit that I have used every power within my means to prevent any possibility of your marrying my son. I know I may be expressing myself too bluntly, but I believe that it's important for me to be brutally honest with you and hope that you will listen, understand, and agree with me. Shortly after you left your home, I left St. Petersburg, but I was no longer afraid for Alyosha's well-being. I knew that your pride would not permit you to marry him until after our family troubles had ended, nor would you stand between Alyosha and his obligations to me, knowing that I would never forgive him for marrying you. You also didn't want it said about you that you had set your sights on finding the son of a prince for a fiancé just so you could enter into his family. On the contrary, you showed very little interest in us and may well have been waiting for me to approach you to request the honor of your marrying my son. But whatever the circumstances, I continued to be your enemy. I'm not trying to justify my behavior, but I will provide you with an explanation. It's really very simple. You are unknown in society and you are not rich. Although I do have some money, our family name is on the decline. Money and connections are very important to us. The countess's stepdaughter has no connections, but she is very rich. If we delay much longer, there are bound to be other suitors and Katya will find another bridegroom. It's very important that that not happen, and although Alyosha is still very young, I am determined that he shall marry Katya. You see, I am very honest with you, I'm hiding nothing.

"You may well look with contempt upon a father who admits to pushing his son into marriage solely for his own self-interest and enhancement. It's certainly a reprehensible act to expect the son to cast aside a wonderful girl who has sacrificed everything for him. But I make no apologies. There is a second reason why I want my son to marry the stepdaughter of Countess Zinaida Filimonova. Katya is a girl worthy of the highest respect and love. She has been beautifully brought up, has a sweet and gentle nature and is very bright, although in some respects still a child. Alyosha has none of these qualities. He is frivolous, obstinate and, at twenty-two, still a complete child. He has, perhaps, one positive virtue, a good heart, but even that can be a dangerous attribute when combined with his other deficiencies. I realized a long time ago that my influence over him is on the decline. His youthful enthusiasm has pushed aside his sense of responsibility. I'm very fond of the boy, but there is very little I can do to control him. But it's important for him to be under the influence of someone with a high moral character. Alyosha has a weak and submissive nature and is easily influenced by others. It's far simpler for him to be loved and controlled by someone else than to try to be a leader himself. He'll be that way the rest of his life. So you can imagine how delighted I was to discover in Katerina Fedorovna the ideal wife for my son. But that delight soon vanished when I realized that there was an even greater influence exerting its pull on Alyosha. And that's you. When I returned to St. Petersburg, I noticed a remarkable change in Alyosha. True, he was still childish and flighty, but I saw some nobler qualities emerging. He thought less about toys and more about honor and higher aspirations, for example. Some of his ideas were rather strange and unsound, of course, sometimes even absurd, but his inclinations and desires were better and stronger. He seemed to be building upon a stronger foundation and I credit that change entirely to you," the prince said, nodding his head toward Natasha. "You have, in a sense, re-educated him. I acknowledge that. There was, in fact, a moment when I thought you might actually be the right woman to make Alyosha happy. But I quickly pushed that idea out of my head. I needed to find a way to distract him away from you at any cost. So I put my plan into action and I thought I was close to achieving my goal. Until an hour ago, I thought victory was mine. But then that incident at the countess's house cast aside all those assumptions, and the simple fact occurred to me that Alyosha is truly serious about his attachment to you. Moreover, the tenacity and strength of that attachment is remarkable. I say it again, you have re-educated him, and the degree to which you have accomplished that task is greater even than I had imagined.

"Today he demonstrated to me an intelligence which I had, by no means, suspected, and at the same time a remarkable grace and level-headedness. He chose the most efficient route possible to maneuver himself out of a difficult situation. He accomplished this by appealing to the noblest instincts of the human heart, the ability to pardon and repay an unkind act with generosity. He went to the very person creating the obstruction and requested her involvement and assistance. He instilled pride in a woman who already loved him while at the same time admitting that she had a rival, by creating sympathy for that rival by a promise of sisterly friendship. To attain his goal without insult or offense is something not even the most adroit of wise men could accomplish, but only someone with a fresh, unblemished and focused heart. I am confident that you, Natalia Nikolayevna, had no hand in Alyosha's act today either by suggestion or advice. In fact, you've probably just learned about it from him a little while ago, if I'm not mistaken. Am I?"

"No, you're not mistaken," Natasha answered. Her entire face and eyes glowed with a lustrous light, much like that of inspiration. The prince's words were already having an effect on her. "I haven't seen Alyosha in five days," she added. "He thought of it and carried it out all by himself."

"That may be true," the prince said, "but clearly this unexpected ingenuity, this determination, this noble fortitude, are all the result of your influence on him. I came to that realization during my ride here and, as a result of that, have come to a decision. My matchmaking plans with the countess have been irreparably destroyed, but if it's not to be, it's not to be. But I have determined that you alone can make Alyosha happy and serve as his guide. In fact, you've already set off on the road to his future happiness. I've kept nothing from you and I'm not hiding anything from you now. I make no secret of my love for money, connections, nobility, even rank. I know this is prejudice, but I love my prejudices and it's difficult to cast them aside. But there are circumstances when other considerations must take precedence. For one thing, I love my son, and I've reached the conclusion that he must either remain with you or perish without you. I admit that I probably reached that conclusion a month ago, but it's only today that I can fully acknowledge it. I could have visited you tomorrow to tell you all this, instead of imposing on you at this late hour, but perhaps my eagerness to speak to you tonight will convince you of my passion and sincerity. I'm not a child. I certainly wouldn't rush to make such an important decision without considering all sides of the issue. When I entered your home this evening I was already resolved, but I feel it may take a while before I can satisfactorily convince you of my sincerity. But on to the business at hand! Let me tell you why I came here. I came to offer you my sincerest gratitude and most solemn respect, and to ask you, please, to do me the honor of accepting my son's hand in marriage. Do not think that I stand here as a terrible father who has finally decided to forgive his children and graciously agree to their happiness. No, no, you would be giving me too much credit by assuming me capable of such sentiments. Nor should you think that I came here confident of your answer, knowing how much you have sacrificed for him. Again no! I'll be the first to admit that he doesn't deserve you. He's a good boy and he himself can confirm this, but that is insignificant. I came here to beg you," he said, standing with a great show of solemnity and respect, "to accept me as your friend. I know I have no right to expect this of you, but please give me some hope that you will allow me to earn that right. May I hope?"

The prince bowed respectfully and awaited Natasha's reply.

The whole time he had been speaking, I had been watching him carefully. He was aware of this.

I later realized that his speech had been quite inconsistent in a number of respects. His tone did not, at first, correspond to the alleged impulse that drew him to us at that awkward hour. Some of his comments seemed noticeably rehearsed and in other places he seemed to be affecting an artificial joviality to hide his feelings with careless humor and jokes. These thoughts occurred to me later, but my perception at the time was quite different. His final words were conveyed with such emotion and sincere respect for Natasha, and the sparkle of teardrops on his eyelashes was so convincing, that he easily conquered Natasha's noble heart. She, like him, rose and stood silently before him for a moment. Then she raised her hand and extended it to him. The prince accepted her hand and kissed it tenderly. Alyosha reacted enthusiastically.

"Didn't I tell you, Natasha?" he said with great excitement. "You didn't believe me! You wouldn't believe me when I told you that he was the noblest person in the world! But now you can see for yourself!" Alyosha rushed to his father and embraced him warmly. Valkovsky returned his embrace but hurriedly pulled away, clearly embarrassed to express his feelings openly.

"Enough," he said, picking up his hat, "I have to go. I asked for ten minutes of your time and have taken a full hour. Before I go, however, I would like to ask if you will permit me to call again as soon as possible, and as often as possible?"

"Yes, yes!" Natasha answered, "As often as possible. I would like to learn how to love you," she added with some confusion.

"You are so straight-forward, so honest!" the prince said, smiling at her. "You refuse to be insincere even out of courtesy. I like that. It's so much more refreshing than the false politeness of most of the people I know. Yes, I realize more than ever how hard I will have to work to deserve your love!"

"Please, you flatter me too much!" she said shyly, looking especially endearing at that moment.

"As you wish," Valkovsky said, "but permit me two additional words. Regrettably, I am unable to visit you tomorrow or the day after. I received a letter today that demands my immediate attention. I leave tomorrow morning. But I wouldn't want you to think that I stopped in this evening merely because I was unavailable tomorrow or the next day. I know you'd never think of such a thing, but I am overly concerned about such matters. It's my suspicious nature; the same suspicious nature that has caused so many problems in my life and resulted in the unfortunate misunderstanding with your father. Let's see, today is Tuesday. Wednesday, Thursday and Friday I shall be away from St. Petersburg, returning on Saturday. Without fail, I shall visit you on Saturday. May I count on your company for the entire evening?"

"Without fail, without fail!" Natasha was almost giddy with excitement. "I'll expect you on Saturday evening. I can't wait!"

"You make me very happy," Valkovsky said. "I look forward to getting to know you better." He turned suddenly to me and extended his hand. "But I can't leave without taking a moment to shake your hand. I hope you will excuse the informal nature of our conversation. I know we've met before and have even been formally introduced, but I'd like to tell you how pleasant it is to renew your acquaintance."

"Yes, we have met before," I said, "but I honestly can't recall our having been introduced."

"It was at Prince Rudolph's, last year."

"Oh, I'm sorry, I had forgotten," I said. "But I promise you that this time I will not forget. This evening will be especially memorable."

"Yes, to me also. I have known for some time what a sincere, honest friend you have been to Natalia Nikolayevna and my son. I hope you will permit me to be a fourth to your threesome. Is that possible?" he added, turning to Natasha.

"Yes, Vanya has been our dear friend, and I would love it if we could all be together," she said.

Poor Natasha. She was glowing with happiness when she saw the prince engage me in conversation. She loved me!

"I've met many people who admire your talent," the prince continued. "I know in particular two such worshippers who would be delighted to meet you. They are my dear friend, the countess, and her stepdaughter, Katerina Fedorovna. I trust you will not refuse me the pleasure of presenting you to these two ladies."

"I'm flattered and would be delighted to meet them. I know so few people."

"Well, give me your address. Where do you live? It would be a pleasure to..."

"I really don't receive visitors, Prince, at least not at present."

"Of course, I wouldn't presume to make myself an exception, but..."

"No, please, you're most welcome to stop in, if you'd like. I live in an alley off Voznesensky Prospect in Klugen's building."

"Klugen's building!" he exclaimed, as if startled by the news. "When... Have you lived their long?"

"No, just a short time," I answered, aware that he was scrutinizing me closely. "I live in apartment forty-four."

"Forty-four? Do you live alone?"

"Yes, quite alone."

"Ah, yes... then... It seems I know this house. So much better. I will, without fail, visit you. I have so much to tell you and I expect to hear a great deal from you. You, in a great many ways, can be of assistance to me. But, you see, I begin by asking you a favor. Before I've even visited! Again, your hand!"

He shook my hand and Alyosha's, then kissed Natasha's, and left, without asking Alyosha to follow him.

The three of us were very confused. All of this had happened so unexpectedly that we were quite unprepared. It seemed to each of us that a great deal had changed, in one moment, and that we were on the brink of something new and unknown.

Alyosha squatted next to Natasha and quietly kissed her hands. He barely looked at her, perhaps afraid of what she might say.

"Alyosha, my dear," she said at last, "I want you to go to Katarina Fedorovna tomorrow."

"I was just thinking that myself," he said. "I'll go."

"But it might be difficult for her to see you. What should we do?"

"I don't know, my darling, I was thinking that too. Let me think on it. I'll see... I'll figure out something." Unable to restrain his excitement, Alyosha added, "Everything has certainly changed for us now, Natasha!"

She smiled and looked at him tenderly.

"And how diplomatic he was," Alyosha said to me. "He knew about your poor apartment and said nothing."

"Nothing of what?" I asked.

"Well... of your moving... or anything," he said, his cheeks turning red.

"That's ridiculous, Alyosha, why should he have said anything?" I asked.

"Well, that's what I'm saying. He was very discreet. But he did praise you! I told you he would... I told you. He's very understanding and caring. But he treated me like a child. They all do. But, in a way, I guess I really am."

"You are a child," Natasha said, "but you're more perceptive than all of us. You're a good person, Alyosha."

"But he said that my good heart would get me in trouble. What did he mean? I don't understand. But, Natasha, shouldn't I hurry after him? I can come see you in the morning."

"Yes, go my darling, that's a good idea. Go see him immediately, do you hear? But come back tomorrow as early as possible. You're not going to disappear for another five days, are you?" she added slyly, caressing him with her eyes.

We were all feeling a quiet, complete contentment.

"Are you coming with me, Vanya?" Alyosha shouted as he left the room.

"No, he'll stay with me a little longer. I have something else to say to Vanya. But be here early tomorrow."

"First thing! Goodnight, Mavra."

Mavra was very excited. She had listened to the prince's speech, had overheard everything, but she didn't understand it all. She could guess some of it but wanted to question us about the rest. But meanwhile, she looked very serious, even proud. She too realized that much had changed.

At last we were alone. Natasha took my hand but remained silent for a while, as if searching for the words.

"I'm tired," she said finally in a weak voice. "Listen, are you going to see *them* tomorrow?"

"Of course."

"Tell Mama, but don't tell him."

"Yes. I never speak to him about you."

"Well, he'll hear about it anyway. But pay attention to what he says, his state of mind. My God, Vanya, would he really curse me for this marriage? No, he couldn't."

"The prince will have to fix this," I said hurriedly. "He'll have to reconcile with them, and then everything will be settled."

"Oh my God, I hope that happens. I pray it happens."

"Don't worry, Natasha, it'll happen. All signs point to it."

She stared at me a moment.

"What do you think of the prince?"

"Well, if he meant what he said, then, in my opinion, he is a very decent man."

"If he meant what he said? What do you mean by that? He couldn't possibly have been deceiving us!"

"I'm sure you're right," I answered. Then a thought flashed through my mind. "It was strange."

"You were staring at him so intently."

"Yes, there was something strange about him, it seems to me."

"I thought so too. He said so many things... Oh, my dear Vanya, I'm tired. You should be going. But tomorrow, come see me as early as possible after seeing them. And one last thing. You don't think I was insulting when I said I'd like to learn how to love him, do you?"

"No, why insulting?"

"Or foolish? It seemed like I was saying that I didn't like him now."

"Quite the opposite. It was wonderful, and sweet, and spontaneous. You looked so wonderful at that moment. If he didn't understand that, then he's a fool."

"I thought you looked angry at me, Vanya. That's wrong of me. I'm very suspicious and vain. Now don't laugh at me. I never hide anything from you. Ah, Vanya, you are my dearest friend, my guide. If ever I'm unhappy, I know you'll always be there to comfort me. You may even be the only one. What can I ever do to repay you? Don't ever curse me, Vanya!"

As soon as I got home, I undressed and got into bed. My room was as dark and damp as a cellar. Many strange thoughts and sensations were crowding my mind and it was a long time before I could fall asleep.

But there was one man who was probably laughing at us that very minute as he lay in his comfortable bed, if he even thought of us at all. Which I doubted.

CHAPTER EIGHTEEN

At 10 o'clock the next morning, I was rushing out of my apartment to visit the Ichmenyevs on Vasilyevsky Island, to be followed by a visit to Natasha, when I ran into my tiny visitor from the previous evening, Jeremiah Smith's granddaughter. I don't know why, but I was delighted to see her. It had been impossible to get a good look at her in the shadows of dusk, but in the morning light I was even more astonished by her appearance. It would be difficult to imagine a stranger, more unique creature.

Small, with large, black, non-Russian eyes and long, thick and tangled black hair, her silent and mysterious stare would have attracted the attention of anyone in the street. Indeed, the most striking aspect of her face was the perpetual gaze of mistrust, even suspicion.

Her tattered and filthy dress looked more like a pile of discarded rags in the daylight. She seemed to me the victim of some slow, lingering and fatal illness that was gradually sapping the life out of her. Her thin face was deathly pale with a yellowish tint, but in spite of her fading health, the dirt and the rags, she had a haunting kind of beauty. Her eyebrows were sharp, thin and very beautiful, her broad, low forehead was unusually striking, and her lips, although nearly colorless, were perfectly formed and suggested a bold and proud character.

"Oh, you're here again," I said. "I had a feeling you'd show up again."

She stepped into the room slowly and cautiously, just as she had the night before, and looked around. She seemed to be inspecting each detail of the room, as if taking inventory of each of the changes that had occurred since her grandfather had lived there. "Like grandfather, like granddaughter," I thought. For a moment, I worried that she might be insane. She stood silently for the longest time.

"The books," she whispered finally, staring at the floor.

"Yes, your books, I have them. I was holding onto them for you."

She looked at me curiously and I recognized a hint of a smile, but she caught herself and returned to her former haughty and mysterious expression.

"Did Grandpa mention me to you?" she asked, surveying me from head to toe.

"No, he didn't, but he..."

"Then how did you know that I would show up again?" she asked sharply. "Who told you?"

"Because it seemed to me that your grandfather couldn't have lived all alone, without help. He was very old, weak, and I thought there must be someone who looked in on him. Here are your books. Are you learning from them?"

"No."

"Then why do you have them?"

"Grandpa taught me out of them when I used to visit."

"Then why did you stop visiting?"

"I didn't. I got sick," she offered as an excuse.

"What family do you have? A father and a mother?"

She lowered her eyebrows and frowned at me with a scared look in her eyes. Suddenly and quietly, she turned and headed for the door just as she had the night before. I followed her with my eyes, but she stopped on the threshold.

Turning slightly toward me, as she had when she asked about Azorka, she asked, "What did he die of?"

I went to her and began to recount the incidents leading up to her grandfather's death. She listened quietly but carefully, her back still towards me. I mentioned that her grandfather had spoken about the Sixth Line just before his death. I had assumed that someone near to him lived there and that they would come to inquire about him.

"He must have loved you very much," I said, "to think of you at the moment of his death."

"No," she said, almost involuntarily. "He didn't love me."

She was clearly agitated. As I was telling her my story, she had struggled mightily to avoid revealing her anxiety, too proud to show her true feelings. She had grown even paler and chewed on her lower lip. But the most astonishing thing was the rapid beat of her heart which was clearly audible some two or three steps away, as is the case with an aneurysm. I thought for sure she would burst into tears at any moment but she managed to hold them in.

"Where is the scaffolding?" she said.

"What scaffolding?"

"Where he died."

"If you'd like to see it, I can take you there on our way out. But listen, what is your name?"

"It doesn't matter."

"What doesn't matter?"

"Nothing. I have no name!" she said sharply and made a move toward the door again.

"Wait a moment," I called to her. "You are certainly a strange little girl! I wish you only the best. I've been worrying about you ever since I saw you crying on the stairs yesterday. Your grandfather died in my arms and when he mentioned the Sixth Line with his last breath, I felt as if he were entrusting me with your care. I had a dream about him. I even held onto your books for you. And yet you're still so timid with me, so afraid. You're obviously very poor, and probably an orphan, perhaps even living with strangers. That's true, isn't it?"

I pleaded with her as gently as I could, not knowing why I cared so deeply about her feelings. I was oddly attracted to her, not just out of pity, but something else. Maybe it was her connection to Smith or my own curious fascination with her state of mind, but she had touched my feelings in a way that was impossible to resist. My words seemed to touch her and she looked at me with a new, softer expression, her eyes meeting mine for a long time. Then she lowered her head again in thought.

"Elena," she whispered suddenly.

"Your name is Elena?"

"Yes."

"Will you come and visit me sometimes?"

"I can't," she stammered. "I don't know." She stopped to think it over. Just then the chimes of a neighborhood clock began to sound. Her agitation returned instantly and she asked in a frightened voice, "What time is it?"

"It should be half past ten," I replied.

She let out a cry of terror and turned to go, but I stopped her again. "I can't just let you run off like this. What are you afraid of? Are you late for something?"

"Yes, yes, you have to let me go! I ran off. She'll beat me!" Her voice trembled as she struggled to break free from my grasp.

"Listen to me and stop struggling. I'm going to Vasilyevsky Island right now, to the Thirteenth Line. I'm late too so I'm going to take a carriage. Come along with me and you'll get there much faster than on foot."

"But you can't go where I live!" she cried with a look of terror that disfigured her features, just from the sheer thought of my seeing where she lived.

"Look, I told you I was going to the Thirteenth Line, not to where you live. Come with me, it'll be faster."

We hurried down the stairs and I hailed the first cab that appeared, a wretched affair, but Elena was evidently in such a hurry that she climbed in beside me. I made the mistake of asking her who it was that she was frightened of and she became so panicked that she nearly fell out of the carriage. After that I kept my questions to myself. It was certainly a mystery.

The carriage seats were extremely awkward to sit in and with each bump Elena grabbed hold of my coat with her dirty, freckled left hand to steady herself. With her other hand she held tightly to her books as if they were priceless treasures. After one particularly large bump, Elena suddenly exposed one leg and I was greatly surprised to discover that she wore nothing but a pair of torn old boots, with no stockings at all. Although it may have been an inappropriate remark given her anxious state, I couldn't resist commenting.

"You have no stockings on! How could you go out in such cold, damp weather with no stockings?"

"I don't have any," she answered abruptly.

"But surely you live with someone who could have found a pair of stockings for you to go out in!"

"This is the way I like it."

"But you could get sick. You could die!"

"So I'll die then."

She clearly did not want to answer my questions.

"That is where *he* died," I said, pointing to the street curb where the old man had taken his last breath.

She studied the area for a moment and turned to me suddenly. "For God's sake, don't follow me! I promise I'll come back and visit you as soon as I can, but please don't follow me!"

"Well, I've already told you I wouldn't and I won't. But what are you so afraid of? It hurts me to see you so frightened."

"I'm not afraid of anyone," she responded indignantly.

"But you said a little while ago that she would beat you."

"So, let her beat me," she said defiantly with an astonishing mix of both arrogance and fear. "I don't care!"

Finally, we crossed the bridge and arrived on Vasilyevsky Island. Elena told the driver to let her out at the corner of the Sixth Line and she jumped out before the carriage had come to a stop. She looked around fearfully.

"Drive away! Drive away!" she hollered to the driver and then looked at me.

"Don't come after me!" she implored and quickly darted around the corner.

I told the driver to go ahead, but after the carriage had gone a short distance, I told him to stop, paid him, and jumped down onto the pavement. I quickly walked back to the Sixth Line and caught a glimpse of Elena hurrying along the other side of the street. She stopped and looked back several times to make sure she was not being followed, but I was able to duck into a doorway and remain out of sight.

I debated with myself whether or not I should follow her and decided that I must. Hiding behind gates and lampposts, I was able to avoid being seen as she continued along the other side of the street. I resolved not to follow her into any house, but felt that I must discover in which house she lived. I was feeling as depressed as I had been when the old man's dog, Azorka, had died at his feet at Mueller's.

Chapter Nineteen

We walked a long distance until we reached Maly Prospect. Elena was practically running. Finally, she stopped and went into a small grocery shop.

I stopped and waited. "Surely this girl doesn't live in that shop," I thought. A moment later she came out again, but instead of her books, she was carrying a small ceramic mug.

After walking a short distance more, she entered the gate of a nondescript stone building, a small, two-storied house painted a dingy yellow. In one of the three windows on the lower floor there was a miniature red coffin which indicated that an undertaker had his shop there. The second-floor windows were very small and completely square-shaped, with dismal green frames and pink cotton curtains barely visible behind the dirty glass.

I crossed the street and approached the house in order to read a small sign which bore the words, "Madame Bubnova." I barely had time to register this information when a caustic female voice reverberated from inside the courtyard screaming curses at someone. I glanced through the slats of the gate and saw a large, lower class peasant woman wearing a kerchief on her head and a green shawl. Her face was an appalling purplish color, and her bloodshot eyes had a fierce look in them. In spite of the early hour it was clear that she was already intoxicated and she was scolding Elena, who cowered beneath her clutching the ceramic mug in front of her.

A thickly rouged and powdered woman stood watching from the stairs behind them and a moment later other faces began to appear. One, a pleasant but disheveled looking woman in a modest dress, appeared through a basement door, and from another door came an old man and a young girl. A tall, heavyset man carrying a broom stopped his work in the yard and turned his attention to the scene before him.

"Oh, you bloodsucking little shit," the purple woman screamed, releasing a stream of obscene curses that poured from her vile mouth without a single pause for breath.

Finally, gagging for air, the woman turned to her neighbors and cried, "I sent her to the shop for cucumbers and she ran away! I yanked her hair out yesterday for pulling the same stunt and she does it again today. She rips my heart out when she disappears." She turned again to the tiny girl and continued. "Where do you go? Who are you seeing? Tell me, you venomous little snake, you monstrous mediocrity, or I'll kill you!"

The woman threw herself angrily on the girl and lashed out at her with her fists. When it looked as if one of her neighbors might intervene, the woman stopped and waved her hands frantically, as if giving testimony in her own defense. "You've seen it for yourselves," she screamed at the growing crowd. "This ungrateful little monster repays my saintly kindness with lies and deception. Me, who took her in off the streets when her mother died. None of you lifted a finger to help. You've barely enough to eat for yourselves. But I took her into my home and you see how she repays me. Sucking me dry like a blood-thirsty mosquito. For two months she's been like a rabid animal, vermin feeding on my flesh."

She turned again to the girl and screeched, "Leech! Parasite! You stubborn little bastard! Silence. That's all I get from you, even when I beat you. Not a single word. Silence! My heart breaks. Silence! Why do you treat me like this, with such contempt? Without me, you'd be living on the streets, dying of starvation. You should be bathing my feet with kisses, you thankless creature."

"Why are you so angry, Anna Trifonovna?" the rouged woman on the stairs asked cautiously. "What has she done to get you so worked up?"

"What has she done you ask? My dear friend, you know what a good woman I am. I don't bother other people with my troubles. But this ungrateful orphan will send me to an early grave. I sent her to the shop for cucumbers and she returned three hours later! Can you imagine how worried I was? My heart ached, it ached! Ached! Ached!" She turned again to the girl. "Where have you been? Who are you seeing? What new friend have you found? Am I not friend enough? Didn't I forgive your mother's debt of fourteen rubles and even pay to have her buried at my own expense?" She turned to the woman in the basement doorway. "My dear, you are a woman, you understand, you know! Doesn't such benevolence deserve some kindness in return? But she disobeys me. I've tried to make her happy. Didn't I clothe this scrawny scarecrow in a muslin dress and give her shoes fit for a holiday? And see what she's done, dear people. Within two days, the dress was torn to shreds and she ran off again. And didn't I catch her tearing the dress on purpose with her own two hands? 'I want to wear cotton,' she tells me, 'not muslin!' For that I made her scrub the floors, but she ran off again. I beat her something fierce when she returned and took away her stockings and shoes. 'She can't go out in bare feet,' I thought, but off she runs again and returns in these scruffy boots she stole from someone's trash. Where have you been sneaking off to, you evil spawn of Satan? Speak, you putrid pile of dung."

The harpy suddenly grabbed Elena's hair and drew her closer. The mug crashed to the ground, scattering the cucumbers across the yard, infuriating the woman even more. With a frenzied passion, the woman lashed out at the girl, beating her about the face and head, but Elena remained stubbornly silent, making no cry or complaint and making no effort to evade the woman's flailing fists.

I rushed through the gate and charged at the drunken woman. "What are you doing?" I screamed. "How dare you treat a defenseless child like that?" I grabbed for the woman's arm and pulled her off the girl.

"What's that?" the woman squawked, letting go of Elena and standing with her fists on her hips. "Who the hell are you? This is my house!"

"That doesn't give you the right to bully a poor orphan. She's not even yours. I heard you say that she was only staying with you!"

"Lord Jesus!" she screamed. "What the... did you come here with her? Are you the one she goes to see? You have no right to come to my house and attack me. I'll have the law on you! Help! Help me, I'm being attacked!"

Suddenly, she rushed at me with her fists flying. At that moment there was a shrill, inhuman wail and I turned to see Elena, who a moment before had been standing like a statue, fall to the ground and begin to writhe in a fit of epileptic convulsions. The disheveled looking woman, followed by another young girl, hurried to Elena, lifted her in her arms and carried her down the steps and into the building.

"Go ahead and shake, damn you," the crone shrieked as Elena disappeared into the house. "That's the third attack this month. She does it to irritate me!" The woman turned again and rushed at me. As I tried to hold her off, she called to the man with the broom. "Why are you standing there, you idler? I pay you good money! Help me!"

The lazy porter made a half-hearted attempt to earn his pay by calling out to me, "See here now, go away. Don't poke your nose around here!" He waved his broom in the air. "If you don't want a beating, just bow and take your leave."

There seemed to be nothing else for me to do, so I went to the gate and opened it. My outburst had been completely useless and yet fury still raged within me as I made my way to the sidewalk.

As I passed through the gate, I turned and looked back into the yard. The woman hurried up the stairs and into the house and the man with the broom, having earned his day's wages, disappeared around the corner of the building.

A moment later, the woman who had carried Elena into the basement apartment came up the steps. Seeing me, she stopped and looked at me curiously. Her kind and quiet demeanor encouraged me to venture back into the yard and address her directly. "May I ask you," I said, "who that little girl is and how she came to be living with that cruel woman? Please don't think I ask out of mere curiosity. I've met this child before and her living conditions are of great interest to me."

"Well, if you're interested in her well-being," the woman said quietly, as if afraid to be heard by others, "you'd better take her home with you and get her out of this place, that's for sure." She turned and started back down the steps.

"But if you won't answer my questions, how can I help her? I don't know anything about her. Am I right that that woman was Madame Bubnova herself, the mistress of the house?"

"Yes."

"But how did that little girl end up in her clutches. Did her mother die here?"

"I don't want to say anything. It's none of my business." She started to walk away again.

"Please," I called to her. "Help me. I'd like to do something for the girl, but I need to know who she is. Who was her mother? Do you know?"

"She was a foreigner, I think. Spoke with an accent. She was living downstairs with us, but she was very sick and died of consumption."

"Then she must have been very poor, sharing a room in a basement..."

"Oh, yes, poor thing! Our hearts went out to her. We're struggling ourselves and she owed us six rubles for the five months she stayed with us. But we paid for her funeral and my husband made the coffin they buried her in."

"But that Bubnova woman said she paid for the funeral."

"Humph," the woman snorted with indignation.

"What was the mother's last name?" I asked.

"Oh, I can't pronounce it, sir. It was German, I think."

"Smith?"

"No, that's not it. Anna Trifonovna insisted on taking the child in to live with *her*, but it's just not right. Not right at all."

"But she must have had some reason to adopt the girl..."

"For no good reason, that's for sure," the woman said. She looked around nervously, afraid she might have been overheard. "We are outsiders, sir. It's none of our business."

"You'd better watch your tongue, woman," I heard a man behind her say. He was wearing a full coat over a dressing gown and looked like a craftsman, the woman's husband.

"She has no right speaking to you about something that's none of our business," the man said to me, glancing in the direction of Madame Bubnova's door. "We're coffin makers and if you ever have need of our services, I'm sure we can satisfy your requirements. But until then, we have nothing to say. Good day, sir."

I turned and walked away from the house in deep thought, angry with myself for being unable to help the girl. Something the coffin-maker's wife had said made me very uneasy and fearful for the child's safety.

As I started down the sidewalk, I heard a man's voice call my name. I turned and saw a rowdy-looking drunk staggering towards me. Although he was dressed neatly, his coat was ragged and his cap was greasy. In spite of my initial revulsion, there was something about him that seemed familiar. He winked at me and grinned broadly.

"Don't you recognize me?"

Chapter Twenty

"Yes, it's you, Masloboyev!" I cried, suddenly recognizing my old classmate from our provincial high school. "This is a surprise meeting."

"A surprise meeting indeed. Six years we haven't met. Although we've actually met several times, but your excellency did not deign to glance in my direction. After all, you are a general, sir. At least, a literary general, that is."

Saying this, he smiled ironically.

"Well, my friend, Masloboyev," I said, "that is not true. First of all, if there are literary generals, I am no more than a foot soldier, and second, let me tell you that I recall several times seeing you on the street, but you yourself seemed to be ignoring me. Why should I acknowledge a man who is trying to avoid me? And you know what I think? If you were not drunk right now, you probably wouldn't have called out to me as you did. I'm right, aren't I? Well, either way, hello! I'm very happy to see you again."

"Really? You mean you're not embarrassed to be seen in the company of a man dressed as I am? Well, you needn't answer that, it doesn't matter. You were always a very pleasant fellow, as I recall. You even got into a fight once defending me, but instead of thanking you I made fun of you for being such a fool. You were such an innocent soul! But hello, my dear friend, hello!"

He embraced me and kissed my cheek.

"All these years I've been thinking about you, dear Vanya, pining away, day and night, night and day. You're not an easy man to forget! But tell me, what have you been up to all this time?"

"Oh, well, I've been pining away too."

He gazed at me with a look of strong affection, clearly under the influence of too much wine, but he had always been a pleasant fellow even when sober.

"No, Vanya," he said in a surprisingly somber tone. "Your situation is nothing like mine!" A moment later, he brightened and announced, "By the way, Vanya, I read it. I read it. We should have a long talk. Are you in a hurry?"

"I am in a hurry, I must confess," I said, "and should tell you that I'm terribly upset about something. But I've got a better plan. Where do you live?"

"I'd be happy to tell you but that's certainly *not* a better plan. But can I tell you something that *would* be better?"

"Of course, what?"

"Look there, see?" He pointed to a sign about ten paces from where we were standing. "See? A confectioner's and restaurant. It's really just a simple café, but the atmosphere is warm and pleasant, decent food, and the vodka is unspeakably good! It's traveled all the way from Kiev on foot! I've sampled it many, many times and they wouldn't dare try to push anything inferior on me. They know Philip Philippich! I'm Philip Philippich! What? Why are you grinning? No, let me tell you what I propose. It's a quarter past eleven now—I've just checked—and at exactly 11:35, I'll let you go. Meanwhile, we'll raise a few glasses. Twenty minutes for an old friend, that's fair, isn't it?"

"If it really is only twenty minutes, I'll join you, but I swear to you, I really am very busy."

"Ah, so we have a plan! But first, a few words. You do not look at all happy. Has something happened just recently to upset you?"

"Yes."

"That's what I thought. I have been learning Physiognomy, the science of reading facial characteristics and body language and I have been practicing on you! So, let's go, let's talk. In twenty minutes, I'll have time to throw back some birch wine, a cocktail with orange bitters, a parfait d'amour, and maybe something of my own invention. I drink, old man, I drink, on holidays and on Sunday mornings before Mass. You needn't join me, of course, but if you do drink, I believe you would display a special nobility of the soul. But come! A word or two and then we'll part for another ten years. For I am not a worthy companion for you, my friend!"

"Well then, let us go quickly. Twenty minutes of conversation and then I must run."

To reach the restaurant we had to climb a long wooden staircase leading to the second floor, but halfway up we came upon two inebriated men who staggered to one side to let us pass. One of them was a beardless young man with just the hint of a mustache that did little to disguise his intensely stupid face. He was dressed like a dandy, but in such comic fashion that it seemed he was wearing someone else's clothes. He wore expensive rings on his fingers and a fancy stickpin in his tie and his hair was combed in a ludicrous style that pointed straight up. He kept smiling and giggling.

His companion was easily fifty years of age, short, fat and balding, with a flabby, drunken, pock-marked face and a pair of spectacles on a miniscule nose which resembled a ruby red button. He also wore an expensive-looking stickpin and his expression was immoral and malevolent as he gazed at us through eyes that were little more than slits. Apparently, they both knew Masloboyev, but the fat man, upon seeing my companion, screwed up his face in a nasty grimace, while the younger man offered some kind of fawning, sickeningly sweet smile. He even took off his cap.

"Excuse me, Philip Philippich," he muttered, gazing fondly at Masloboyev.

"What?"

"Excuse me, sir," he said again as he flicked at his collar. "Mitroshka is sitting up there. It seems, Philip Philippich, sir, that he is a scoundrel."

"Why do you say that?"

"It's because, sir, last week Mitroshka smeared my friend's face with sour cream in a very indecent way." He suddenly hiccupped loudly.

The other man angrily poked him with his elbow.

"Come join us, Philip Philippich, and we'll down another half-dozen drinks in your honor. What do you say?"

"No, sir, that I cannot do," Masloboyev replied. "I have business."

The young man hiccupped again. "And I have business which concerns you." His fat friend once again nudged him with his elbow and he responded angrily. "Later! Later!"

Masloboyev did his best to avoid looking at the two men as we eased past them on the staircase. We entered the first room and discovered a long counter heavily laden with cakes, pies, pastries and succulent treats of every variety accompanied by glass decanters of multi-colored liqueurs. Masloboyev grabbed me and quickly pulled me into a corner.

"That young man is the son of Sizobryukhov who made a fortune raising meadowsweet. The boy inherited half-a-million rubles when his father died and he's been carousing ever since. He returned after months in Paris with almost nothing left in his pocket and then turned around and inherited another fortune from his uncle. So here he is, trying to squander the rest. A year from now, he'll be passing the hat around. He's as stupid as a goose but is seen in the finest restaurants, cellars and taverns with actresses on his arm, and he recently applied for a commission in the mounted cavalry. The older man is Arkhipov, a merchant or manager or, perhaps, a government procurer, but he is most certainly a rogue and a rascal and presently Sizobryukhov's closest friend. He is Falstaff and Judas combined, twice bankrupt, and a degenerate, licentious creature with perverse tastes. I know of at least one criminal incident in which he was implicated, but he bought his way out of it. I'm actually very glad that we have run into Arkhipov as I've got a bone to pick with him. He is, of course, robbing Sizobryukhov blind. He knows every little corner in the city where foolish young men like to congregate. That's why he's so useful to the boy. Mitroshka is that dashing young man with the Gypsy face and the expensive velvet tunic standing over there by the window. He buys and sells horses but he is also a master con artist who could forge a note right before your eyes and still pass it on to you in a legitimate transaction. He's a true Slavophile, and I have to admit he pulls it off admirably, but dress him up in a proper dress coat and you could take him to the finest English club and pass him off as Count Barabanov. No one would see through the ruse. But he's likely to end up badly. His kind usually do. But as I was saying, Mitroshka dislikes the fat man even more than I do. Mitroshka and Sizobryukhov were very close until Arkhipov seduced the boy away before Mitroshka could fleece him. If the three of them met here in the restaurant, there must be something up. I even know what it is because Mitroshka himself told me that Arkhipov and Sizobryukhov would be hanging around here today. I came to take advantage of Mitroshka's hatred for Arkhipov because I have my own good reasons to feel the same way. I don't want Mitroshka to suspect, and don't keep staring at him, but when we leave here, I expect Mitroshka to come running after us to tell me what I want to know. And now let us go, Vanya, into the other room."

As we walked, Masloboyev turned to a waiter and said, "Well now, Stephan, you understand what I need you to do?"

"Yes, sir, I do."

"And you'll take care of it?"

"Yes, sir."

"Wonderful. Come, Vanya, let's sit down. Why are you looking at me like that? I see you staring at me. Are you surprised? Don't be. Anything can happen to a man that he's never even dreamed of, even in the days when... Well, yes, when we crammed Latin together in school. Look, Vanya, believe in one thing. Masloboyev may have indeed strayed from the path, but his heart remains the same, only the circumstances have changed. Though I may be covered in soot, I'm no dirtier than the next man. I had planned to be a doctor and later a professor of Russian literature. I even wrote an article about Gogol. I was set to marry—every soul seeks sustenance in another—and she agreed, even though I was so poor I couldn't tempt a cat to live with me. I was preparing for the wedding ceremony and even borrowed a pair of boots to substitute for my own which had been in tatters for more than a year, but we never went through with the wedding. She married a teacher and I took a job as a clerk. Not even in a business office. It was... well, just an office. But then the music changed for me and I began to thrive. I may not be in government service but I have found it easy to amass money. I take a bribe now and then, but I am an honest man. I feed with the sheep but run with the wolves. And I have learned the rules. For example, there is safety in numbers but keep your secrets to yourself. I deal in matters of confidentiality. Do you understand?"

"I think so. Are you some kind of detective?"

"No, not really a detective, but I do take on some cases, more as an avocation than vocation. And yet I am a professional. You see, Vanya, I drink vodka. Never so much that I lose my senses and throw away my future. But *my* day is past. You can't decorate an egg once it's broken. One thing I will say is this, if there were not still a little of the old me rattling around inside, I should never have approached you on the street. It's true, I have seen you before, many times, and have wanted to say hello but I didn't dare. I kept putting it off because I am not worthy of you. You were right before, Vanya, when you said I wouldn't have spoken to you if I weren't drunk. But I'm just prattling on about nonsense. I'd much rather talk about you. Well, my dear soul, I've read it. Read it! I am referring, of course, to your first born. As I read it, I almost felt myself becoming a better person! Almost, yes, but I thought better of it and preferred to stay a dishonorable man. So there you have it."

As he prattled on, he grew progressively drunker and began to weep at his own maudlin tales. Masloboyev had always been a nice enough fellow in school but he had a sly and cunning mind that developed early. He had a good heart but he was a lost man. There are a great many other Russian people like him. They are more than capable, but live their lives in a chaotic, confused state, consciously fighting against their conscience, either out of weakness or misguided determination, and always ending up in wreckage, even though they knew beforehand they were heading down the path to ruin. Masloboyev, for example, had chosen to drown himself in vodka.

"Now, my friend," Masloboyev continued, "only one word more. I heard the thunder that greeted your newfound fame and then I read your critics. Yes, I know you imagine that I read nothing. Then I saw you in the street wearing a battered hat and shabby boots, traipsing through the mud without galoshes, and I drew my own conclusions. You've taken up journalism as a trade now, am I right?"

"Yes, Masloboyev."

"So, you've joined the literary hacks."

"Looks like it."

"Well, my boy, here's what I say: drink is better! Here I can lie down on a sofa—and I have a nice couch with springs—and imagine myself to be Homer or Dante or a Roman Emperor. One can imagine whatever one wishes. But you cannot imagine yourself Homer or Dante or a Roman Emperor, firstly because you want to be yourself and secondly because all you desire is forbidden to you as a literary hack. I have a good imagination and you have only reality. Tell me openly and honestly as a brother—and if you won't speak as a brother, you will offend and humiliate me for ten years—you like money, don't you? I have more than enough. Stop making faces at me. Take a little money and pay off the debtors. Get rid of the burden and when you put aside enough to last a year, sit down with your favorite idea and write a great book! Eh? What do you think?"

"Listen, Masloboyev! I appreciate your brotherly offer, but I can't give you my answer right now. The reason why is a long story. There are circumstances. However, I promise I will tell you later and we will speak like brothers. Thank you for the advice. I promise that I will come to you and come many times. But here's the thing. You are frank with me and therefore I dare ask your advice on a matter about which you are quite knowledgeable."

And I told him the whole story of Smith and his granddaughter, starting with the scene in Mueller's pastry shop. Oddly enough, as I told him my story a look in his eyes told me that he already knew something. I asked him about it.

"No, no, it's nothing really," he answered. "Although I had heard *something* about Smith, about an old man dying outside a pastry shop. It's really this Madame Bubnova that I know something about. Just two months ago I managed to get some money out of her. *Je prends mon bien partout où je le trouve*, which is probably the only thing I have in common with Molière. But even though I squeezed a hundred rubles out of her, I promised myself I wouldn't settle for less than another five hundred. Nasty woman! She runs a most unsavory kind of business. Normally that wouldn't matter to me, but she takes it to extremes. Don't imagine me a Don Quixote. The point is that I can take advantage of circumstances and when, half an hour ago, I ran into Sizobryukhov, I was very pleased. Sizobryukhov apparently was brought here, and brought here by the fat man, and as I know the kind of profession the fat man trades in, I drew my own conclusions. Well, yes, I really have this covered! I am very glad you told me about this young girl, it puts me on the right track. I am engaged in a variety of private commissions for some very peculiar people. I was recently looking into a matter for a prince, and let me tell you that this is not the sort of thing one would expect from a prince. And then, do you want to hear another story about a married woman? You come visit me some time, brother, and I'll tell you some stories that you would not believe."

"And what was the name of this prince?" I interrupted him, with an uncomfortable premonition.

"Why do you need to know? Oh, very well. His name is Valkovsky."

"Peter?"

"Yes. Do you know him?"

"Yes, but not very well," I said, getting to my feet. "Well, Masloboyev, I shall ask you more about this gentleman very soon. You have definitely aroused my interest."

"Well, old friend, you may visit me as often as you want. I have many interesting stories to tell, but within certain limits, you understand? I can't afford to be indiscreet and lose my honor. It's not good for business."

"Of course. Only as far as your *honor* will allow."

I was very excited and he noticed it.

"But what about the story I've just told you. Has it made you think of something?"

"About your story?"

"Yes. But wait two minutes for me. I will pay."

He walked over to the buffet and, as if by accident, suddenly found himself standing near the man in the velvet tunic whom he had so unceremoniously called Mitroshka. It seemed to me that Masloboyev knew him a little more intimately than he had admitted to me. It was evident, at least, that they were not meeting for the first time.

Mitroshka was an uncommonly distinct-looking young man. In his tunic and red silk shirt, with sharp well-formed features and a still youthful, dark-skinned complexion and bold flashing eyes, he made a curious but not unappealing impression. His gestures suggested a restless, nervous personality, but at that moment he seemed to be restraining himself, perhaps anxious to project an image of extreme efficiency and reliability.

"Look, Vanya," Masloboyev said when he returned to me. "Come see me at seven o'clock this evening and I may have something to tell you. On my own, as you can see, I have nothing to offer you. In the old days, maybe, but now I am nothing but a drunk. But I still have connections who can be most useful. A little piece of information from one, a bit more from another, and that is how I survive. In my free time, you see, I investigate certain matters. But that's enough for now. Here's my address on Shestilavochnaya Street. Right now, brother, I am too drunk. I'll have one more and then head on home. You come by this evening and I'll introduce you to Alexandra Semyonovna and we can talk about poetry."

"But what about that other matter?"

"Well, yes, that too, perhaps."

"Then, perhaps, I will come. Yes, I will come."

CHAPTER TWENTY-ONE

Anna Andreyevna had been expecting me for a long time. Ever since I had told her about Natasha's note the day before, she was eager to learn more. She had been waiting for me since ten o'clock that morning, so by the time I arrived at two o'clock, the poor woman's anxiety had reached a fever pitch. In addition, she wanted to tell me about her budding hopes since yesterday and that Nikolai Sergeich was sick and feeling gloomy, and yet he was also being particularly gentle with her. When I arrived, she was clearly unhappy with me. Her teeth were clenched and her cold and indifferent expression seemed to be saying, "Why do you come here every day?" She was clearly angry at my late arrival. But I was in a hurry and without further delay I described yesterday's scene with Natasha. As soon as the old woman heard about the older prince's visit and his solemn proposal, she immediately dropped her feigned displeasure. I can't find words to describe how happy she was, barely able to contain herself. She wept and crossed herself, bowed to me on her knees, hugged me, and wanted to rush to Nikolai Sergeich and tell him of her joy.

"Have mercy, sir, he has been made ill from the humiliation and insults he has endured, but when he finds out that Natasha has been exonerated, he will forget it all at once."

I had a difficult time dissuading her. The dear old woman had lived with her husband for twenty-five years and yet knew so little about him. She was anxious, as well, to go with me immediately to Natasha. I convinced her that not only might Nikolai Sergeich disapprove of her actions, she might also damage the situation by going. With difficulty, she changed her mind, but kept me half an hour extra and kept on talking the whole time.

"How can I just sit here alone in four walls with such joy in my heart?"

Finally, I persuaded her to let me go alone, reminding her that Natasha had been waiting impatiently for me. The old woman crossed herself several more times to bless my journey and sent a special blessing with me to Natasha. I told her I would absolutely not return again that evening unless there was something new to report about Natasha. I didn't see Nicolai Sergeich at all on that visit. He had not slept the previous night, complaining of a headache and chills, and was now asleep in his study.

Natasha had also been waiting for me all morning. When I entered the room she was, as usual, pacing up and down, anxiously rubbing her hands together as though in meditation. Even now, when I think back on it, I can see her in that poor room, dreamy, deserted, waiting with folded hands and downcast eyes, walking aimlessly back and forth.

As she continued to pace, she asked me quietly why I was so late? I told her briefly of my many adventures, but she didn't seem to be listening. It was clear that she was very concerned about something.

"Anything new?" I asked.

"Nothing new," she replied, but I could see immediately from her expression that she had new information she was eager to reveal but, as usual, she would not tell me until I was just about to leave. That's the way she was and I was used to it.

We began, of course, to talk about yesterday. I was particularly struck by the fact that we agreed completely with each other in our impression of Prince Valkovsky. She positively disliked him, even more than she had yesterday. As we discussed his visit, Natasha suddenly said, "Listen, Vanya, it always happens that when people meet someone they don't like at first, that it's really a sign that they *will* like them later. At least, that's the way it usually works with me."

"God willing, Natasha. And that's my opinion, and it's the final one. I've been thinking about the prince and he seems devoutly religious, so perhaps he was quite serious when he agreed to your marriage."

Natasha stopped in the middle of the room and looked at me sternly. Her face changed, her lips quivered slightly.

"But in a case like this," she said with astonishment, "how could he have been deceiving... lying?"

"Yes, of course, that's right!" I agreed quickly.

"Of course he wasn't lying. There is nothing to even think about. There could be no excuse for such deception. How could he look me in the eyes as he did and be mocking me? Could any man be capable of such an insult?"

"No, of course not," I confirmed, and thought to myself: "You poor girl, you can't think of anything else as you pace back and forth and, perhaps, you're even more in doubt than I am."

"Oh, how I wish he would return soon!" she said. "He wanted to spend the whole evening with me, and then... He must have important business to do or he wouldn't have gone away. Do you know what it is, Vanya? Have you heard anything?"

"God only knows. After all, the prince is always making money. I've heard he's taken a share in some contract in St. Petersburg. The affairs of business mean nothing to us, Natasha."

"Of course, nothing at all. Alyosha mentioned some letter yesterday."

"News of some sort. Has Alexey been here?"

"Yes."

"Early?"

"At noon. He likes to sleep late. He sat for a while and then I chased him to Katerina Fedorovna. That was the right thing to do, wasn't it, Vanya?"

"Why, wasn't he planning to go there anyway?"

"Yes, he was going..."

She wanted to say something else but stopped. I looked at her and waited. Her face was sad. I would have asked her, but she sometimes disliked being questioned.

"He's a strange boy," she said finally, her mouth twisted slightly as if trying not to look at me.

"Why do you say that? Have you heard something?"

"No, nothing, but... He was very sweet, I thought. Only I..."

"Now all of his troubles and worries are over," I said.

Natasha looked intently and searchingly at me. She may have been tempted to reply, "He had very few sorrows and cares before," but it seemed to her that my words conveyed the same idea. She pouted.

A moment later, however, she was gracious and polite again. This time she was exceptionally gentle. I stayed with her for over an hour. She was very worried. Valkovsky had frightened her. I noticed from some of her questions that she wanted to know if she had made a favorable impression on him yesterday. How had she behaved? Had she expressed too much joy? Was she too ill-tempered? Or, conversely, too appeasing? She didn't want him to misjudge her. Or to laugh at her. Or to feel contempt for her. Her cheeks flushed like fire at the thought.

"How can you get so upset by what you imagine some evil man might think of you? Let him think what he wants," I said.

"Why is he evil?" she asked.

Natasha was apprehensive, but her heart was pure and honest. Any mistrust on her part came from a clear conscience. She was proud and noble, and her pride could not endure having someone she thought superior made to look ridiculous in her own eyes. Contempt from an inferior, of course, would have been met with her own contempt, but her heart ached at the thought of mockery of something or someone she considered holy, no matter who was doing the laughing. It wasn't from a lack of firmness on her part. It arose from too little knowledge of the world and being unaccustomed to other people, having been closed up in her own little world. She had spent her life in the safety of her own corner. And finally, that trait present in most good-natured people, perhaps inherited from her father, of stubbornly believing that people are better than they are, exaggerating their positive qualities, was strongly developed in her. It is difficult for such individuals to deal with later disappointments, even more so when they feel somehow guilty. Why expect more from people than they can give? But disappointment is always awaiting these people. It is best to sit quietly in their corners and not venture into the light. I have even noticed that they come to love their corners and grow increasingly unsociable. Natasha, however, had suffered many misfortunes, many insults. She was a wounded creature and could not be blamed, if any of my words sounded accusatory.

But I was in a hurry and got up to go. She gasped and almost started crying at the thought of my leaving, even though all the time I had been sitting there she had shown me no special tenderness; quite the contrary, in fact, she had seemed colder than usual. She kissed me and then looked into my eyes for a long time.

"Listen," she said. "Alyosha was quite bizarre today and even surprised me. He was very nice, very happy, but he flew in like a butterfly, so self-possessed, spinning around and admiring himself in the mirror. He's a little too brusque now... Yes, and he stayed only a short time. Imagine. He brought me candy."

"Candy? Well, that's very sweet and simple-minded. Oh, the two of you! You've started watching and spying on each other, trying to read each other's secret thoughts, and understanding nothing. He hasn't changed. He's just as cheerful and schoolboyish as ever. But you... there's something different about you... something!"

As always, when Natasha changed her tone and approached me to complain about Alyosha or to confer about an embarrassing misunderstanding or reveal some secret, always expecting me to understand her with half a word, she would look at me with a grin, as if begging me to say something that would immediately set her heart at rest. But I remember, too, in those instances, how I always took on a stern and harsh tone, as if scolding her, and (although I did it quite unintentionally) it always worked. The severity and importance of my words were effective; they seemed more authoritative, and sometimes a person just feels an irresistible need to be scolded. Natasha was often quite comforted.

"No, Vanya," she said, staring into my eyes with one of her little hands on my shoulder and the other clutching my own hand. "I thought he seemed somehow more... you know, affected. As though we'd been married ten years, but he was still being polite to his wife. Am I reading too much into this? He laughed and spun around, but somehow it seemed to be only partly about me, not like it was before. He was in a hurry to see Katerina Fedorovna. I spoke to him but he wasn't listening and started talking about something else; you know, that grand, nasty habit aristocrats have that we've both worked so hard to wean out of him. In short, he was... he seemed indifferent... But look what I'm doing! Starting in again! Ah, we are so demanding, Vanya, such capricious despots! Only now I see it! I can't accept even the slightest change in his face when only God knows why his face has changed! You were right, Vanya, to reproach me just now! This is all my fault! I create my own bitterness and then complain about it. Thank you, Vanya, you have comforted me completely. Ah, if only he would come again today! But maybe he would be angry about what happened this morning."

"But you didn't really quarrel, did you?" I asked in amazement.

"No, I revealed nothing! But I was a little sad, and although he acted so cheerful and thoughtful, I thought his good-bye was a bit cold. Yes, I will send for him. And you will come, too, Vanya. Today!"

"Certainly, unless something delays me."

"Why, what something is that?"

"Oh, it's just something I've imposed on myself! At any rate, it seems that I must come!"

CHAPTER TWENTY-TWO

At seven o'clock I was at Masloboyev's. He lived in a small house on Shestilavochnaya Street in a rather untidy, though not poorly furnished, apartment made up of three rooms. There were some signs of prosperity but an overall look of disarray. The door was opened by a very pretty girl of nineteen, very simple, but very nicely dressed, neat, and with friendly, welcoming eyes. I immediately realized that this was Alexandra Semyonovna, the young wife he had mentioned in passing that morning, hinting that I would be delighted to meet her. She asked who I was and upon hearing my name told me Masloboyev was waiting for me, but that he was sleeping in his room. She led me there and I found Masloboyev asleep on a beautiful, soft sofa, covered with his dirty overcoat, his head on a leather bag. Just as we entered, he awoke from a light sleep and called me by name.

"Ah, Vanya, is that you? I've been waiting for you. Just now in my dream you came and woke me. So, it's time. Let's go."

"Go? Where to?"

"To see a lady."

"What lady? Why?"

"To Madame Bubnova, to break up her little party. Ah, such a beauty," he said, turning to Alexandra Semyonovna and kissing his fingertips at the thought of Madame Bubnova.

"Oh, you're making that up!" the girl said, as if it was her duty to pretend to be angry.

"Have you two met? Alexandra Semyonovna, I'm honored to present Ivan Petrovich, a literary general. It is only once a year you can inspect him for nothing. Any other time you would have to pay."

"There, he's playing the fool again," she said to me. "Please don't listen to him. He's always making fun of me. What kind of a general could this man be?"

"I'm trying to tell you," Masloboyev said, "He's a very special kind. And you, your Excellency, do not imagine that we are foolish. We are much smarter than we seem at first glance."

"Don't listen to him! He's always trying to embarrass me in front of other people. He's shameless. If only he would take me to the theater once in a while!"

"No, Alexandra Semyonovna, love your home. Do not forget that you must love... something. Have you forgotten the word I taught you?"

"Of course I haven't forgotten. It means... some nonsense."

"Well, what was the word then?"

"I'm not going to embarrass myself in front of a guest. It's probably something naughty. I'm not going to say it."

"So, you *have* forgotten the word."

"No, I haven't! Penates... love your Penates. Why should I love them? It's all lies!"

"Yes, Penates. Love your hearth and home. But at Madame Bubnova's..."

"Damn you and your Bubnova!" she said and ran from the room with great indignation.

"It's time to go! Farewell, Alexandra Semyonovna," he called to her as we left.

"See here, Vanya, first let's grab this cab. There now. And secondly, I learned something after I said good-bye earlier; it's no longer just a hunch, but a certainty. I stayed on Vasilyevsky Island for another hour. That fat man is a terrible scoundrel, filthy, ugly, and with vile and perverse tastes. I've known for a long time that he and Bubnova were in business together. She recently got hold of a girl from a respectable family. That muslin dress you mentioned this morning when you spoke about the orphan made me very uneasy because I had already heard something about it before. I've just now learned something else, quite by accident, but it seems likely. How old is this girl?"

"From how she looks, I'd say thirteen."

"But small for her age. That sounds about right. If necessary, she'll say she's eleven; another time, fifteen. And since the poor thing has no protection, no family, then..."

"Do you mean...?"

"What do you think? Yes. Madame Bubnova would never have taken in an orphan out of compassion. And if the fat man is involved in this, it's definitely true. He visited Bubnova this morning. He promised that blockhead Sizobryukhov a beautiful married woman today, the wife of an official at headquarters. These rich boys are always inclined to prefer a higher class. It's like in Latin grammar, remember, where prominence takes precedence?" Masloboyev paused a moment. "I think I'm still drunk from this morning. Bubnova doesn't usually involve herself in such nasty business, but she thinks she can fool the police by claiming she's adopted the girl, but I'm on to her! I can throw a scare into her because she remembers me well... And that's the story. Do you understand?"

I was quite shaken up by these revelations and feared that we would be too late, so I urged the cabman to hurry.

"Don't worry, Vanya," Masloboyev assured me, "measures have been taken. Mitroshka is there already. Sizobryukhov will pay with cash, but that pot-bellied scoundrel will pay with his skin. That was decided this morning. And I'll take care of Bubnova... Because she doesn't dare to..."

We arrived at the restaurant and stopped, but the man called Mitroshka was not there. We ordered the coachman to wait at the restaurant and hurried to Madame Bubnova's on foot. Mitroshka was waiting for us at the gate. Bright light streamed from the windows of the house and we could hear the sound of Sizobryukhov's drunken laughter.

"They've been up there for a quarter of an hour," Mitroshka told us. "It's time."

"But how can we get in?" I asked.

"As guests," Masloboyev said. "She knows me and she knows Mitroshka, as well. The doors may be locked, but not to us."

He knocked quietly on the gate and it was opened immediately by the porter, who exchanged winks with Mitroshka. We walked quietly so we would not be heard inside. The porter took us up the steps and knocked. His name was called from within and he answered, "There is someone here to see you!"

The door opened and we all went in at once. The porter disappeared.

"Yes?" Madame Bubnova whined. "Who is it?" She was drunk and unkempt and stood before us with a tiny candle in her hands.

"Who is it? How can you ask such a thing, Anna Trifonovna? Don't you recognize your honored guest? Who, if not me? Philip Philippich!"

"Ah, Philip Philippich! It is you. But who are your...? Why are you...? Please come in, sir."

She was quite flustered.

"Where?" Masloboyev asked. "In here? But there is a partition... No, we would prefer the next room. Are there no lovelies to welcome us?"

The hostess instantly collected herself.

"Yes, for such honored guests, I would dig all the way to China for them."

"Three words, my dear Anna Trifonovna. Is Sizobryukhov here?"

"Yes. In there."

"Ah, just the man I'm looking for. How dare that scalawag run off on a drunken spree without inviting me?"

"I don't think he's forgotten. He's been expecting someone. It must be you."

Masloboyev pushed open the door and we found ourselves in a small room with two windows decorated with geraniums, several wicker chairs and a battered old upright piano; just the sort of atmosphere one would expect from such an establishment. But even before we entered, even while we were still talking in the hall, Mitroshka had vanished. I learned later why he had not joined us, but had been met at another door by the thickly rouged woman I had seen behind Bubnova that morning. They were, apparently, very good friends.

Sizobryukhov was sitting on a slender mahogany sofa in front of a round table covered with a cloth. On the table were two bottles of warm champagne and a cheap bottle of rum. There were plates of baked sweets, cakes and nuts of three varieties. Sitting at the table, opposite Sizobryukhov, was a disgusting, pockmarked creature of some forty years in a black taffeta dress with bronze bracelets and brooches. She was, all too obviously, the fake "officer's wife," but Sizobryukhov was drunk and seemed perfectly content. His fat companion was not with him.

"So, this is the way I find you!" Masloboyev roared with laughter. "And after you invited us to Dussot's!"

"Philip Philippich, what a pleasure!" Sizobryukhov muttered, standing to greet us with a blissful expression.

"Have you been drinking?" Masloboyev asked.

"Excuse me, sir."

"No need to apologize, but you could invite your guests to join you. We may have to catch up. I've brought another guest, a friend!"

Masloboyev pointed to me.

"Pleased, sir, to make your... it's my pleasure to... Hic! Hey, you call this champagne? It tastes like sour cabbage soup."

"You offend me," said the officer's wife.

"So, you didn't dare show your face at Dussot's," Masloboyev bellowed. "And after inviting me!"

"He's been telling me that he's been to Paris," the woman said. "But I think he's lying!"

"Theodosia Titishna," Sizobryukhov whimpered. "You wound me. I was there. We went."

"But what would a peasant like him be doing in Paris?"

"We have! We could! I was there with Karp Vasilich. Do you know Karp Vasilich?"

"And why would I want to know Karp Vasilich?"

"Well, it's just... it could be beneficial to you. We were there in Paris, at Madame Joubert's. He broke a glass."

"He broke what?"

"A glass mirror. It stretched almost from floor to ceiling. Karp Vasilich was so drunk and he was prattling on in Russian with Madame Joubert and he leans his elbow against this big mirror. Madame Joubert shouted at him in her own language, 'Be careful! That glass cost me seven hundred francs!' That's four hundred rubles. 'You'll break it!' He just looked at me and grinned. I was sitting on a sofa across from him with a real beauty next to me; not a mutt like you, but a real knockout, that's the only word for her. And he called to me, 'Stephan Terentyevich. Shall we go halves?' And I said, 'Done!' So, he took his fist and smashes it against the mirror. Bang! Splinters of glass flew everywhere. Joubert screamed and confronted him face to face. 'What are you, a hooligan?' In her own language, of course. And he told her: 'You, Madame, may have the money. I am no criminal.' And he immediately handed over six hundred and fifty francs. He disputed the other fifty."

At that moment, a terrible, piercing scream rang out two or three rooms from where we were. I shuddered and cried out as well because I recognized Elena's voice. Immediately after her plaintive cry, we heard more screams, curses, scuffling, and finally the clear, crisp sound of a palm slapping a face.

It was probably Mitroshka resolving the situation in his own way. Suddenly the door flew open and Elena ran in, her face pale and eyes dim, wearing a torn and crumpled muslin dress. Her hair had been carefully brushed, but it now appeared tousled as if from a fight. I stood just inside the door and she ran straight to me and threw her arms around me. Everyone jumped up with alarm. There were more screams and cries from the other room. Suddenly, Mitroshka appeared in the doorway dragging by the hair his fat nemesis, who was now utterly disheveled. Mitroshka pushed Archipov across the threshold and flung him into the room.

"Here he is! Take him!" Mitroshka said with a look of complete satisfaction.

"Look," Masloboyev said, quietly coming up to me and tapping me on the shoulder. "Take our cab and take the girl to your home. There is nothing else for you to do here. We will settle the rest tomorrow."

I did not need to be told twice. I grabbed Elena's hand and took her out of that den. I still don't know how things ended there. No one tried to stop us. Madame Bubnova was struck with horror. It all happened so quickly that she didn't know what to do. The cab was still waiting and in twenty minutes we were at my apartment.

Elena was half-dead. I undid the hooks on her dress, sprinkled her face with water, and laid her on my bed. She had become feverish and was delirious. I looked at her pale face, her colorless lips, her dark, tangled hair which had earlier been brushed and pomaded, but was now hanging down on one side, her entire getup with pink ribbons still attached here and there to her dress, and finally understood the whole ugly truth. Poor little thing! She was getting worse and worse. I did not want to leave her and decided not to go to Natasha's that evening. Occasionally, Elena opened her long, dark eyelashes and looked long and hard at me, as if she recognized me. It was past midnight when she finally dozed off. I fell asleep beside her on the floor.

Chapter Twenty-Three

During the night I kept waking up almost every half-hour. Each time I did, I went to my poor guest and watched carefully over her. She still had a fever and was slightly delirious. But toward morning, she fell into a sound sleep. A good sign, I thought, but decided to run for a doctor while she was still sleeping. I knew a doctor, a good-natured old man who from time immemorial had lived alone with his German housekeeper near Vladimir Square. I arrived at his door around eight and he promised to be at my room by ten o'clock. I wanted to stop to see Masloboyev on my way home, but I thought better of it. I knew that Elena could wake up at any time and be frightened by her unfamiliar surroundings. In her depressed state of mind, she might not even remember how and when she had arrived at my apartment.

She opened her eyes at the very moment I entered the room. I approached her and gently asked how she felt. She did not answer, but for a long time stared at me with her large, expressive black eyes. It seemed to me from her gaze that she understood and was fully conscious but, as was her usual habit, she didn't answer me. Since her very first visit to my room she had displayed an obstinate pride whenever I questioned her, and she would stare at me with a mixture of both scorn and curiosity. I tried to put my hand on her forehead to see if she had a fever, but she silently and firmly removed my hand and turned her face to the wall. I moved away so I wouldn't disturb her.

I had a big copper kettle that I used instead of a samovar to boil water and, as usual, the building's porter had furnished me with enough wood to last for five days. I lit the stove, went to fetch some water and filled the kettle. As I prepared the table for tea service, Elena turned her head and watched me with curiosity. I asked her if she wanted anything, but she immediately turned her face away again and said nothing.

"Why is she so angry?" I wondered. "Such a strange girl!"

As promised, my old doctor friend arrived at ten o'clock. He examined the patient with a German's attention for detail and reassured me that, although she still had a fever, Elena was in no particular danger. He did point out, however, that she seemed to have a chronic condition, something about an irregular heartbeat, that would require special observation. He wrote out a prescription for some medicine, more out of custom than necessity, and then immediately started asking me who she was and how she had come to be in my apartment. The old man was a chronic snoop.

Elena had had a striking effect on him. She had pulled her hand away from his when he attempted to take her pulse and refused to show him her tongue. She answered none of his questions but gazed fixedly the entire time at the large Order of Saint Stanislaus pendant swinging from his neck. "Her head probably aches," the old man said, "and, my heaven, how she stares!"

I didn't think it was necessary to tell him much about Elena and assured him that it was a very long story.

"Let me know if you need me again," he said as he left. "At any rate, she is in no danger."

I decided to stay with Elena the whole day and remain close by her side as much as possible until she recovered. But knowing that Natasha and Anna Andreyevna would be upset if they waited all day in vain for me to show up, I decided to send a letter to Natasha telling her that I could not come that day. I could not write directly to her mother because Anna Andreyevna had told me not to send her any more letters after I had once sent her the news of Natasha's illness.

"The old man frowns when he sees a letter from you," she had told me. "He really wants to know what is in it but is too stubborn to ask, so he ends up cranky and upset the whole day. And besides, Vanya, a letter from you is such a tease. What can I learn from ten lines? I want to ask more but you're not here to ask!"

So I wrote only the one letter to Natasha and posted it on my way to the apothecary.

Meanwhile, Elena fell asleep again. In a dream, she moaned and shuddered slightly. The doctor had guessed correctly. She had a very bad headache. Occasionally, she cried out and woke up briefly. She glanced at me with great annoyance, as if it were especially difficult for her to be in my presence. I must confess, this was very painful to me.

Masloboyev came at eleven o'clock. He was preoccupied and seemed absent-minded and left in a hurry after only a minute.

"Well, my brother, I didn't expect to find you living in luxury," he said, looking around, "but this place is really little more than a trunk. It's a packing case, not an apartment. How can you write with all these outside distractions? I thought about it yesterday when we went to Bubnova's. I belong to a class of people who rarely do anything worthwhile, but you are different. Listen, I may come to visit you tomorrow or the next day, but you must certainly visit me on Sunday morning. By that time, we may have a solution to this girl's case. I told you yesterday—well only hinted at it—but we will talk seriously, because you need to take this seriously. And finally, would it be too great a dishonor for you to accept a little money from me as a loan?"

"Don't worry about me," I interrupted him. "Just tell me what happened at Bubnova's last night after we left."

"Oh, that. Yes, that ended quite well, our goal was achieved. But I have no time now. I just came to see how you want to handle the situation with the girl."

"I don't know. I must confess I've been waiting to talk it over with you!"

"Oh. Well, have you considered keeping her here, as a servant?"

"Please keep your voice down," I said to him. "She's very ill but she *does* know what's going on around her. She looked startled when you arrived because I think it reminded her of what happened yesterday."

I proceeded to tell him what I knew about Elena's background and how I perceived her character. Masloboyev seemed very interested. I also told him I was hoping to find a house where Elena could live and mentioned the Ichmenyev family. To my great surprise, he was already partially acquainted with Natasha's history and I questioned how he knew.

"I've been hearing passing comments about her situation for some time," Masloboyev said. "I've already mentioned to you that I know about Prince Valkovsky. That's a good idea about setting her up with the old couple. She'll only cause you trouble here. Oh, and one more thing. She'll need proper papers, but don't worry about that, I'll take care of it. Farewell, come see me more often. Is she sleeping now?"

"I think so," I answered.

But as soon as he left, Elena immediately called to me.

"Who was that?" she asked. Her voice trembled, but she looked at me with that same intent and haughty expression. Other than that, she said nothing.

I told her Masloboyev's name and added that he had been responsible for helping me get her away from Madame Bubnova and that Bubnova was afraid of him. Elena's cheeks suddenly glowed red at the memory of the night before.

"And she will never come here?" Elena asked, looking at me keenly.

I hastened to reassure her. She paused and started to take my hand in her burning fingers, but immediately pushed it away as if coming to her senses.

"It can't be that she really finds me disgusting," I thought. "She's just being cautious, or... or perhaps the poor child has been so badly mistreated that she's afraid to trust anyone in the world."

At the appointed time, I went to fetch the medicine and stopped in at a restaurant where I was well known and could pay on credit. I had brought with me a small pot from home and had the restaurant fill it with chicken soup for Elena. But she refused to eat any, so I left the soup warming on the stove.

After giving her the medicine, I sat down to work. I thought she was asleep, but inadvertently glanced over and saw that she had raised her head and was watching me intently as I wrote. I pretended not to notice her.

Finally, Elena did fall asleep and, to my great delight, slept quietly without delirium and without groans. I was suddenly struck by the thought that Natasha, unaware of what was happening with Elena, might be very angry with me for not coming to see her that day. She might be doubly disappointed by my lack of attention at a time when she seemed to need me most, to have something important to tell me. My failure to show up could appear to her to be a deliberate snub.

As for Anna Andreyevna, I had no idea what excuse I could give for arriving a day late. I thought and thought and then suddenly decided to run to see both of them. I would only be absent about two hours and Elena was asleep and would not hear me go. I jumped up, threw on my coat, grabbed my cap, and was about to leave, when Elena suddenly called to me. I wondered instantly if she had only been pretending to be asleep.

I should point out that even though Elena's outward behavior clearly demonstrated that she did not want to talk with me, her regular need to make contact with me demonstrated quite the opposite objective and, I confess, I found this reassuring.

"Where are you planning to send me?" she asked as I approached her. In general, her infrequent questions came so unexpectedly that I was never prepared for them. This time it took a moment for me to understand what she was asking.

"Just now you were talking with your friend about sending me to work in some house. I don't want to go."

I bent down and could feel the heat emanating from her. She was once again burning with fever. I tried to comfort and assure her that if she wanted to stay with me, I wouldn't send her anywhere. As I said this, I took off my coat and cap. I wasn't going to leave her alone in her present condition.

"No, go!" she said, immediately sensing that I was planning to stay. "I'm tired. I need to sleep. I promise I'll go to sleep right away."

"But how will you get along alone?" I asked, uncertainly. "Although I shouldn't be gone for more than two hours."

"Well, go then. What'll happen if I'm sick for a year? You can't just sit around the house staring at me." She tried to smile and looked at me strangely, as though struggling with some sympathetic feeling stirring in her heart. Poor little thing! Her gentle, tender heart was revealing itself in spite of her remoteness and evident mistrust.

I decided to run to Anna Andreyevna first. She was waiting for me with great impatience and reproached me right away; she was terribly anxious. Nikolai Sergeich had gone out immediately after dinner and she had no idea where he was. I sensed that the old woman would not be able to resist telling him everything, as usual, in tiny little hints. She couldn't help it, she admitted, wanting to share her joy with him, but Nikolai Sergeich was, in her own words, blacker than the storm clouds. "He says nothing. Won't answer my questions. And suddenly after dinner, he just gets up and walks out."

As she told me this, she was practically trembling with fear and begged me to wait with her until Nikolai Sergeich returned. I pleaded and told her flat out that I would come the next day. I had, in fact, run there precisely to tell her just that. This time we almost quarreled. She cried and sharply and bitterly reproached me, and only when I started for the door did she suddenly throw herself on my neck, hug me with both arms, and tell me that she wasn't angry with her "little orphan," and that I shouldn't take offense at her words.

Natasha, contrary to my expectations, did not seem as happy to see me as she had been the day before and on other occasions. It was as if I were, in some way, intruding on her. When I asked her if Alyosha had been there that day, she replied, "Of course he was, but he only stayed a short time. He promised to look in on me tonight," she added, distractedly.

"And was he here last night, too?"

"N-no! He was detained!" she added quickly. "Well, Vanya, how are things going with you?"

I saw that for some reason she wanted to end the conversation and turn to another subject. I looked at her closely. She was obviously upset. When she saw that I was studying her closely, she suddenly grew angry and looked at me with such force that her eyes seemed to burn into me. "She's very unhappy about something," I thought, "but she does *not* want to talk about it with me."

In response to her question about my work, I told her about Elena, leaving out none of the details. She seemed extremely interested and even impressed with my story.

"Oh, my God!" she cried. "And you left her all alone... sick!"

I explained to Natasha that I hadn't planned on coming to see her at all that day, but that I was afraid she was angry with me and needed me for something.

"Need you," she said to herself, thinking about something. "Perhaps I do need you, Vanya, but it will have to wait until next time. Have you been to see my family?"

I told her about my visit with her mother.

"Yes, God knows how my father will react to this latest development. And yet, what is there to react to?"

"What do you mean, 'what is there to react to?'" I asked. "A crisis like this?"

"Yes, so... Where do you suppose he went this time? The last time this happened, you thought he came to see *me*. Look, Vanya, if you can, come see me tomorrow. Maybe I'll have something to tell you then. I'm so ashamed to have to bother you. But now you should get home to your guest. I suppose it's been a couple of hours since you left her?"

"Yes, about that. Good-bye, Natasha. But what happened with you and Alyosha today?"

"What? Alyosha? Oh, nothing. I'm surprised you're so curious."

"Good-bye, my friend."

"Good-bye." She gave me her hand clumsily and turned away to avoid my final farewell glance. I left feeling quite puzzled. "And yet," I thought, "she has a lot on her mind. It's no laughing matter. By tomorrow she'll be anxious to tell me everything."

I returned home, depressed, and was shocked when I walked through my door. It was already dark. I could see Elena sitting on the sofa with her head on her chest, as if deep in thought. She didn't look up at me, but as I approached her, I heard her mumble something. "I wonder if she's delirious?" I thought.

"Elena, my dear, what's the matter?" I asked, sitting down beside her and covering her hand with mine.

"I want to go... I'd rather be with her," she said, without raising her head to me.

"Where? To whom?" I asked in surprise.

"To her... Bubnova. She says that I owe her a lot of money because she paid to have Mama buried. I don't want her to say nasty things about Mama. I want to work for her and pay her back what I owe. Then, I can leave on my own. I'm going back to her."

"Elena," I said, "Calm down. You can't go back to her. She'll torment you. She'll destroy you!"

"Let her destroy me, let her torment me!" Elena repeated my words excitedly. "I won't be the first. Others, much better than me, have suffered. There was a beggar woman on the street who told me I was poor and that I wanted to be poor. All my life, I'll be poor. My mother told me *that* when she was dying. I'm going to work... I don't want to wear this dress..."

"I'll buy you another one tomorrow. And I'll bring you your books, too. You'll live with me. I won't let anyone take you away from me if you don't want to go. Take it easy..."

"I'll be a servant girl!"

"All right, all right! Just relax now. Lie down and go to sleep!"

But the poor child burst into tears. Little by little, her tears turned to sobs. I didn't know what to do, so I brought her water and dabbed her temples, her forehead. Finally, she fell back on the sofa in complete exhaustion and began to shiver again with feverish chills. I wrapped her up in whatever I could find and she fell into a restless sleep, constantly trembling and waking up frequently. I'd had an exhausting day and was determined to go to bed as soon as possible. Dreadful thoughts consumed my brain. I sensed that I would have a lot of trouble with this girl, but I was more concerned about Natasha and *her* situation. As I look back on that moment, I realize that I've rarely been as depressed as I was when I fell asleep on that unfortunate night.

Chapter Twenty-Four

I woke up late, about ten o'clock in the morning, feeling dreadful. My head was spinning and I had a terrible headache. I looked at Elena's bed and saw that it was empty. At the same moment, I heard a sound from the other room of someone sweeping the floor with a broom. I went to look. Elena was standing there holding a broom in one hand and holding up the hem of her elegant dress (which she had not yet removed from the evening before) to keep it from dragging on the dirty floor. There was firewood for the stove piled in a corner, the table had been cleared, and the kettle scrubbed. Simply put, Elena was doing the housework.

"Look, Elena," I called to her, "who asked you to clean the floor? I don't want you making yourself sicker than you already are. Do you think I brought you here to be my housemaid?"

"Who's going to tidy up, then?" she said, straightening up and looking at me haughtily. "I'm not sick now."

"But I didn't bring you here to work, Elena. Are you afraid that I might reproach you like Madame Bubnova; that you have to repay me for letting you live here? And where did you get that disgusting broom? I don't have a broom," I added, looking at her in surprise.

"This is my broom. I brought it here myself. I used to clean up for Grandpa. The broom has been here, under the stove, right where I left it."

I returned to the other room, deep in thought. Was I wrong to think that she could accept my hospitality without doing something to repay me, to avoid being in my debt? Did my kindness make her resentful? Two minutes later she came in and sat down on the couch and stared at me in silence, just as she had the evening before. Meanwhile, I boiled water in the kettle and made tea, poured her a cup, and handed it to her with a piece of white bread. She ate in silence and without comment. She hadn't eaten anything in nearly twenty-four hours.

"You've stained your nice dress with that filthy broom," I said, noticing the big dirty band at the hem of her skirt.

She looked around and suddenly, to my great surprise, put down her teacup, grabbed the front of her muslin dress in both hands and ripped it open in one pull from top to bottom. As the cloth settled around her waist, she looked up at me silently with a cold, hard expression. Her face was pale.

"What are you doing, Elena?" I cried, thinking that she had suddenly gone insane.

"This is an evil dress," she said, almost breathless with excitement. "Why do you call this a nice dress? I don't want to wear it!" She suddenly jumped up, letting the torn garment fall to the floor. She was now wearing only her undergarment. "I didn't want it. She forced me to wear it for that man. I already tore one dress, ripped it to shreds. Tore it! Ripped it!"

She then reached down and grabbed it off the floor, tearing furiously at the unfortunate dress. In a moment there remained little more than tattered strips of cloth. When she finished, she was pale white and so agitated that she could hardly stand still. I was surprised to see such bitterness. She looked at me with a defiant scowl, as if I were guilty of something too. But I already knew what I had to do.

I would go immediately, that morning, to buy her a new dress. This wild, fierce creature could only be tamed in one way: through kindness. She looked to me like someone who had never known even a single kind person. In spite of having been severely punished for tearing one dress, she had done it again with even greater ferocity this time, as if recalling the terrible memory of that earlier event.

In Tolkutchy Market, one could buy a plain, simple dress for very little money. Unfortunately, at that moment, I had almost no money at all. I had decided the night before that I would go in the morning to a place near Tolkutchy where I could get some money. I grabbed my cap. As I headed toward the door, Elena followed me with her eyes, as if waiting for something.

"Are you going to lock me in?" she asked, as I picked up the key to my apartment door, just as I had done the night before and on every other occasion when I went out.

"My dear friend," I said, walking up to her. "Don't be upset with me for that. I lock my door because someone might try to get in. You're sick and I don't want you to be frightened. Who knows? Bubnova herself might take it into her head to come here..."

I told her this quite deliberately. I really was locking the door because I didn't trust her. It seemed to me that she might suddenly decide to run away from me at any time. Until she could convince me otherwise, I decided to be cautious. Elena said nothing and I locked her in again.

I knew an entrepreneur who had recently published the third volume of a multi-volume compilation of articles. He occasionally gave me work and paid regularly. I went to him and managed to get an advance of twenty-five rubles upon my promise to deliver a new article to him within a week. I had been hoping to find some time to work on my novel, but he was a reliable resource if I wanted to avoid complete destitution.

Having obtained the money, I went to Tolkutchy. There I soon found a familiar old peddler woman who sold old clothes. I pantomimed Elena's size and she instantly found for me a simple dress made of a light-colored cotton, very strong and only washed once, for a very low price. I also took a kerchief for Elena's neck and as I was paying, I realized that Elena would need a coat or shawl or something like that. The weather was cold and she had absolutely nothing. But I put off that purchase for another day. Elena was so sensitive and proud. God alone knew how she was going to react to the dress, despite the fact that I had deliberately chosen one as simple and unpretentious as possible. Nevertheless, I still bought her two pairs of cotton stockings and one pair of woolen. I would give them to her on the pretext that she was sick and the room was cold. She would also need new undergarments, but I decided to hold off until Elena was more comfortable with me. I also bought some inexpensive curtains for the bed, something I thought was necessary under the circumstances, and I hoped would give her a little pleasure.

I returned home with my purchases around one o'clock. I had unlocked the door as inaudibly as possible, so Elena did not realize I had returned. She was standing at the table looking through my books and papers but when she heard me, she quickly shut the book she was reading and walked away from the table, blushing. I looked at the book and discovered that it was my first novel, published in book form, and on the title page of which was printed my name.

"Do you always break in on someone without knocking," she said in a teasing tone. "Someone came by while you were gone but the door was locked."

"It might have been the doctor," I said. "Did you call out to him?"

"No."

I said nothing but took the bundle, untied it and took out the dress.

"Here, my dear Elena," I said, approaching her, "you can't go out dressed in those rags. I bought you a dress. It's very simple and the cheapest one I could find, so you have nothing to worry about. It was just one ruble twenty kopecks. Wear it in good health."

I put the dress beside her. She blushed and looked at me with wide eyes. She was extremely surprised, and a little ashamed, I thought. There was something soft and gentle in her eyes that lit up her face. When she said nothing, I turned back to the table. My act of kindness seemed to have moved her, but her willpower prevailed and she sat down without taking her eyes off the floor.

My head still ached and was spinning more and more. The fresh air had not brought me the slightest relief. Meanwhile, I had to go to Natasha. My concern about her had not decreased since the previous day. On the contrary, it had grown more and more. Suddenly, I had the feeling that Elena wanted to say something to me and turned to her.

"When you leave, don't lock me in," she said, looking away and moving her finger along a seam on the armrest of the couch as if completely fascinated by its stitching. "I have nowhere else to go."

"Well, Elena, I agree. But if a stranger comes? Perhaps... God knows who."

"So leave me the key and I'll lock the door from inside. And if someone knocks, I'll just call out, "There's no one home!" And she looked at me with a shrug that seemed to say, "That's how easy it is!"

Before I could respond, she suddenly asked, "Who washes your clothes?"

"There is a woman, here in thi s house."

"I know how to wash clothes. Where did you get that food you brought me yesterday?"

"At the inn."

"I know how to cook. I'll cook for you."

"Come on now, Elena, what do you know about cooking? Let's not discuss it."

Elena paused and looked down. She seemed quite upset by my comment. At least ten minutes went by before she spoke again.

"Soup," she said suddenly, without looking up.

"What about soup? What kind of soup?" I asked, surprised.

"I know how to cook soup. I made soup for Mama when she was sick. I even went to the market."

"Elena, you're very proud," I said, going to her and sitting next to her on the couch. "I understand how you feel. I understand in my heart. You're all alone now, without family, unhappy. I want to help you. You'd do the same for me, if I were sick. But you won't admit that, so it's hard for you to accept my gift of friendship. You immediately want to pay me back because you're afraid I'll be angry, like Bubnova. If that is what you're feeling, you don't have to be embarrassed, Elena."

She did not answer, but her lips were quivering. It seemed that she wanted to tell me something, but she refrained and kept silent. I got up to go to Natasha. This time I left the key for Elena. "Lock the door when I leave," I told her. "And if anyone knocks, be sure to call out, 'Who is it?'"

I was absolutely convinced that something bad had happened to Natasha and that she was keeping it from me, as she had often done in the past. At any rate, I was determined to stay for only a moment so as not to annoy her with my insistence.

And that's exactly what happened. She once again met me with that same hard, unhappy look. I wanted to retreat immediately, but my legs gave way.

"I just came to see you for a minute, Natasha," I said. "For advice. What should I do about my guest?" I quickly began to tell her more about Elena. Natasha listened to me silently.

"I don't know what to suggest, Vanya," she answered. "From what you've told me, I'd say she's a very strange creature. Maybe she's been hurt, scared. Give her a little time to recover. Are you thinking of having her live with my family?"

"She says she won't leave me. And God knows what it would be like with your parents, so I don't know. But tell me, my dear friend, how are you? Yesterday, you didn't seem at all well," I said timidly.

"Yes. I still have something of a headache today," she answered absently. "Have you been to see my folks?"

"No. Tomorrow I'll go. After all, tomorrow is Saturday."

"What has that got to do with anything?"

"The prince is coming in the evening."

"So what? I haven't forgotten."

"No, I was just..."

She stood in front of me for a long time staring at me. In her eyes was a kind of determination, a doggedness; something intense, feverish.

"You know what, Vanya," she said. "Be kind enough to leave me. You're really disturbing me."

I rose from my chair, unable to hide my look of inexpressible astonishment.

"My dear, Natasha! What is it? What's happened?" I cried in fright.

"Nothing has happened! All... you will know all tomorrow, but for now I want to be alone. Listen, Vanya, leave now. It's so hard... so hard to look at you!"

"But tell me at least..."

"Tomorrow! All will be known tomorrow! Oh, my God! Please, go away!"

I went out. I was so disturbed that I barely knew where I was going. Mavra ran down the hall after me.

"Why is she so angry?" she asked me. "I'm afraid to go anywhere near her."

"But what's the matter with her?" I asked.

"It's been three days since he last showed his face here."

"Three days?" I asked in amazement. "But she told me just yesterday that Alyosha was here yesterday morning, and that she was expecting him last night."

"Last night? No. And he wasn't here in the morning either! I tell you, we haven't laid eyes on him in three days. Did she really tell you he was here yesterday morning?"

"That's what she told me."

"Well," Mavra said, deep in thought, "she must really be hurting if she won't even admit it to *you*. A fine gentleman *he* is!"

"What does it all mean?" I cried.

"The truth is I don't know what to do with her," Mavra cried, waving her hands. "Yesterday, she started to send me to fetch him, but twice stopped me on the street and made me return. And today she won't say a word to me. I wish you would go to see him. I don't dare leave her alone."

I rushed outside and down the stairs.

"We'll see you this evening, won't we?" Mavra shouted after me.

"We shall see," I called back to her. "I may just run up to ask you how she is! If I'm still alive!"

I really felt as if I had been struck in the heart.

CHAPTER TWENTY-FIVE

I went straight to Alyosha. He lived with his father on Malaya Morskaya near Saint Isaac's Square. The prince had a very large apartment, despite the fact that he usually lived alone. Alyosha was currently occupying two beautifully furnished rooms. I very rarely visited him there. In fact, this would be only my second visit. He came to see *me* more often, especially at first, during the early stages of his courtship of Natasha.

He was not at home. I went straight up to his rooms and wrote him the following note:

"Alyosha, you seem to have gone completely mad. Considering that on Tuesday evening your father personally asked Natasha to do you the honor of being your wife, and you were glad to have this request (which I witnessed) made for you, you must admit that your behavior in this situation is somewhat strange. Do you know what you're doing to Natasha? I write to remind you that your conduct toward your future wife has been unworthy of you and frivolous to the highest degree. I know very well that I have no right to preach to you, but I choose to disregard that fact.

"P. S. Natasha knows nothing about this letter and she was not the one who told me about you."

I folded the note and left it on the table. When I spoke to the servant, I was told that Alexey was hardly ever at home and that he wasn't expected back until nearly dawn.

I went straight home. My head was swimming and my legs were weak and trembling. The door was already unlocked. As I entered, I saw Nikolai Sergeich Ichmenyev waiting for me. He was sitting at the table in silence, staring in amazement at Elena, who was sitting on the couch and staring back at him with an expression of equal surprise, although stubbornly silent. "It's clear," I thought, "that she must seem very strange to him."

"Ah, my friend," the old man said, "I have been waiting an hour for you and, frankly, did not expect... to find you living like..." He looked around the room, seemingly paying no mind to Elena. I could see his astonishment clearly reflected in his eyes. But looking at him closer, he also appeared apprehensive and depressed. His face was paler than usual.

"Sit down, sit down," he continued, with an anxious wave of his hand. "I hurried here to see you but... but what's wrong with you? You look terrible."

"I'm not feeling at all well. I've felt dizzy since this morning."

"Well, look, that's not something you should ignore. Have you a cold or what?"

"No, it's just a kind of nervous condition. I have it sometimes. But what about you? Is there something troubling you?"

"No, nothing, nothing! There is the lawsuit, of course. Sit down."

I pulled up a chair and sat facing him at the table. The old man leaned slightly toward me and whispered.

"Now don't look at her and pretend we're talking about something else. What have you got to say about this little visitor of yours?"

"I'll tell you all about her later," I said. "This poor girl, a complete orphan, is the granddaughter of the very Smith who lived here and died outside of the pastry shop."

"Ah, so it's his granddaughter! Well, brother, she's a bit peculiar, isn't she? See how she just stares at me? If you hadn't shown up in the next five minutes, I would have left! It took forever to convince her to unlock the door and she hasn't said a word since 'Who is it?' Why is she here? I supposed she came to see her grandfather, not knowing he was dead?"

"Yes. She was devastated when I told her. When the old man died, his last few words were about her."

"Hmmm! The grandfather sounds a lot like the granddaughter. But you can tell me more about them both later. If she's as poor as you say, maybe we can do something to help her out a little. But for now, do you think you can send her on her way? I've got some serious matters to discuss with you."

"No, I can't send her away. She lives here... with me. She has no one else in the world. But you're free to talk in front of her. After all, she's just a child and, as you can see, she doesn't talk much."

"Well, yes, of course, a child. But I'm really quite stunned. You say she's living with you? Good God in heaven!"

The old man looked at her in amazement again. Elena, sensing that we were talking about her, sat silently, her head down and her fingers once again following the stitches on the armrest of the sofa. She was wearing her new dress, which fit her perfectly, and her hair was neatly combed, perhaps in honor of the dress. Truth be told, were it not for the strange, wild look in her eyes, she would have appeared to be a perfectly lovely young girl.

"Short and sweet, that's what I have to tell you, brother," the old man began again. "It's very complicated, a most important matter..."

He sat with downcast eyes that clearly reflected the importance of his message, but in spite of his haste and his promise of "short and sweet," he couldn't seem to find the words to begin. "I wonder what's happened," I thought.

"You see, Vanya, I've come to ask you for a favor. But first... I should probably explain to you the circumstances... extremely delicate circumstances..."

He cleared his throat and stole a glance at me, then looked away and blushed, red-faced with rage at his own awkwardness. He was angry but resolved to continue.

"Well, how should I put this? It's really quite simple. I plan to challenge the prince to a duel and would like you to arrange the matter and be my second."

I fell back in my chair and stared at him in amazement.

"Why do you look at me like that?" he asked. "I'm not crazy."

"But excuse me, Nikolai Sergeich, what reason... on what pretext? And, ultimately, why would you want to?"

"Pretext! Reason!" the old man cried. "That's rich!"

"All right, all right, I know what you're going to say, but how can this help your situation? What could you possibly gain from a duel? I confess, I don't understand."

"I didn't suppose you *would* understand. Listen, son, our lawsuit is over, or practically. There are just one or two formalities to take care of. I've lost. The Court says I have to pay him ten thousand rubles. And Ichmenyevka is all I have for security. So this vile man, who has all the money he needs, takes title to Ichmenyevka, I'm all paid up, and once again I'm a free man. I'll be able to hold my head up and say to this... so and so... this *worthy* prince, 'You have insulted me for the past two years. You've disgraced my name and the honor of my family and I've had to endure all of this! You wouldn't allow me to challenge you to a duel before this because you told me outright, "You're a clever man, you want to kill me so you won't have to pay me the money you know will be awarded to me sooner or later! No, first let's see how the litigation is resolved and we'll see." Well now, my dear Prince, the case is resolved, you have my land, so there is no longer any barrier to our meeting on the field of honor. What, did you imagine that I wouldn't want to avenge myself eventually for everything, for everything you did to me?'"

His eyes sparkled. I stared at him in silence. I tried to probe his secret thoughts.

"Listen, Nikolai Sergeich," I finally said, determined to tell him what had to be said, the key point, without which we could not understand each other. "May I be totally honest with you?"

"You may," he answered firmly.

"Tell me straight. Is this idea of yours prompted solely by your desire for revenge or have you another objective in mind?"

"Ivan Petrovich," he answered, "you know that I do not discuss certain matters in conversation, matters that I keep close to the vest, so to speak. But I will make an exception with you this one time, because you have a clear, sharp mind and have at once seen through my plan. Yes, I have another purpose. My objective is to save my lost daughter and to steer her away from the path to destruction that past circumstances have now led her to."

"But how can you save Natasha by dueling with the prince, that's my question?"

"To stop in its tracks a plot that is now afoot. Listen. Do not imagine for one second that this is all sparked by some kind of paternal affection or similar weakness. All that is nonsense! I do not reveal the inside of my heart to anyone. Not even to you. My daughter deserted me, walked out of my house with her lover, and on that night I cast her out of my life, tore her from my heart forever, you remember? Just because you saw me sobbing over her portrait does not mean that I am willing to forgive her. I do not forgive her. I wept for lost happiness, for a vanquished dream, but not about her, as she is today. I may, on occasion, but not often, cry, and I'm not ashamed to admit it, just as I am not ashamed to admit that until that day I loved my daughter more than anything else on Earth. All of this may seem to contradict my current outburst. You may ask, if I am so indifferent to the fate of someone I no longer consider my daughter, why am I so concerned with thwarting a plot to lead her astray? I answer: first, I do not want to see that loathsome, treacherous man triumph in any way and, secondly, from the most basic feelings of humanity. Even if she is no longer my daughter, she is still a weak, insecure and easily deceived creature who does not deserve to be utterly destroyed. I cannot get involved in this matter directly, but indirectly, by way of a duel, I can. If he kills me or sheds my blood, do you think she would step over my dead body and stand before the altar with my murderer's son, as cruelly, say, as the daughter of Servius Tullius—remember that book I gave you from which you learned to read?—when she drove a chariot over the corpse of her father? And finally, if I should come out victorious, the other princes will certainly not permit the wedding to go forward. In short, I do not want this marriage and I will do anything in my power to prevent it. Do you understand me now?"

"No. If you wish to honor Natasha, how can you interfere with her marriage, which is exactly what is needed to restore her good name? After all, if she is to live happily on Earth for many years, she needs her good name."

"She can spit on the opinion of these contemptible people! Do you think I care what *they* think of me or of her? The greatest shame of all would be for her to enter into such a marriage, to be attached in any way to that despicable crowd. A noble pride, that is the answer to a disdainful world. Then, maybe then, I would be willing to extend my hand to her, and woe to anyone who dares to dishonor my daughter!"

Such a desperate and naïve idealism amazed me. But I quickly realized that he was speaking out of anger and had not yet considered the full impact of what he was proposing.

"You're asking too much of her," I said, "callously demanding a strength from her, a force, which you did not provide for her at birth. Do you think she has agreed to the marriage because she wants to be a princess? No, she is in love, it's passion, it's fate. And finally, you have so much contempt for public opinion and yet you bow down before it yourself. The prince has offended you; you have been publicly accused of trying to marry your daughter into a princely house through fraud and deceit, and here you are, reasoning that if she refuses the marriage *now*, after a formal proposal on their part, then, of course, this will be the most thorough and obvious refutation of the old slander. This is what you are hoping for. And yet you will only feed his low opinion of you by trying to force him to confess his mistake. You want to make him appear foolish and for that you would sacrifice the happiness of your daughter. All to satisfy your own ego!"

The old man frowned and did not speak for a while.

"You're being unfair to me, Vanya," he said to me at last, and tears shone on his eyelashes. "I swear to you, unfair. But let's leave it! I cannot turn my heart inside out for you." He stood and picked up his hat. "One thing I will say. You have been talking about the happiness of my daughter. I absolutely and unquestionably do not believe that this will be a happy marriage. And more than that, without my intervention, this marriage will never take place."

"What do you mean? Why do say that? Do you know something you haven't told me?" I asked anxiously.

"No, I don't know anything special. But that damned fox could never have decided on such a path. It's all nonsense, some kind of trap. I'm sure of that, and mark my words, the truth will come out. Second, if the marriage actually does take place, it will happen only because that scoundrel has some mysterious, secret plan by which this marriage will benefit him in some way, some financial advantage which I do not yet understand. And finally, decide for yourself. Can you honestly say, from your heart, that she will be happy in this marriage? There will be reproaches, humiliations, from a foolish boy who is already tiring of her love, and who, once the vows have been exchanged, will begin to disrespect her, hurt and humiliate her. As her passion for him grows stronger, his for her will begin to cool, the result being jealousy, pain, living hell, a divorce, maybe even crime itself. No, Vanya! If you are still assisting them to make this happen, I predict that you will have to answer to God, but it will be too late! Good-bye!"

I stopped him.

"Listen, Nikolai Sergeich, we can work this out. Be patient. Be assured that there are more than one pair of eyes watching this unfold, and maybe it can be resolved in the best way possible, on its own, without the intervention of force or artificial means, such as this duel. Time is the best peacemaker! And finally, let me tell you that your entire scheme is completely impossible. Surely you can't believe for one minute that Prince Valkovsky will accept your challenge?"

"Not accept? Why do you say that?"

"I swear to you, he will not accept. And believe me when I say that he will find some perfectly legitimate excuse, something that will make him appear dignified and stately, while you will be completely ridiculed..."

"My boy, have mercy! You have wounded me with that! But how can he refuse? No, Vanya, you're just a poet, a romantic! Do you imagine that it would be indecent for him to fight me? I'm as good a man as he is. I am an old man, an injured father, and you are a Russian writer, and therefore also a respectable person who can serve as my second and... and... I really don't understand why you still need more..."

"You'll see. He will make some excuse and you will discover for yourself that your entire plan is impossible."

"Hmm... well, my friend, we'll try it your way. I will wait a respectable amount of time, of course. We'll see what time alone can do. But there's one thing more, Vanya. You must give me your word of honor that you'll never repeat a word of this conversation to anyone, especially Anna Andreyevna!"

"Of course."

"And one more favor, Vanya. Let *us* not ever talk about this matter again either."

"All right, I give you my word."

"And finally, please, I know that you probably find your visits boring, but do come by and see us more often, if you can. My poor Anna Andreyevna loves you so... and... she becomes so miserable without you... do you understand, Vanya?"

He squeezed my hand.

"I heartily promise to visit more often," I said.

"And now, Vanya, one last, delicate matter. Have you any money?"

"Money?" I repeated in amazement.

"Yes." The old man blushed and lowered his eyes. "I look around at your apartment... at your circumstances... and when I think that you must now have other... extra expenses..." He nodded toward Elena and reached into his pocket. "Here, my boy, one hundred and fifty rubles for a first installment."

"One hundred and fifty! A first installment! But you've just lost your lawsuit!"

"Vanya, you really don't understand, do you? You may have some urgent need in the future. Or you can use the money to help you make an independent decision, free from outside influence. Perhaps you don't need it now, but with the Mademoiselle... there may be a time in the future... Anyway, I'll leave it with you. That's all I could come up with. If you don't spend it, you can always return it. But for now, farewell! My God, how pale you are! You look terrible..."

I did not argue and took the money. It was all too clear why he left it with me.

"I can hardly stand on my feet," I answered him.

"Do not ignore it, Vanya, my boy, take care of yourself! Do not go out today. I will tell Anna Andreyevna about your condition. Do you need a doctor? I'll visit again tomorrow; at least I'll try, if my legs will carry me. Now, you should lie down. Well, good-bye. Good-bye, little girl. Look, see how she turns her back on me?" He spoke quietly in my ear. "Listen, my friend, here are five more rubles, for the girl. But you mustn't say I left them for her. Just buy her something. Get her some new shoes, underwear... she'll need a lot of things. Farewell, my friend!"

I accompanied him to the gate. After he left, I asked the porter to fetch some food at the inn. Elena had not had lunch.

Chapter Twenty-Six

But as soon as I returned upstairs, I felt dizzy and collapsed in the middle of the room. I remember Elena screaming and rushing to grab me before I hit the floor. I remember nothing after that.

When I awoke, I found myself already in bed. Elena told me later that she, along with the porter who had brought her lunch, had moved me there. I woke up several times and each time I saw Elena's sweet, caring face staring down at me. But all of that I remember as if in a dream, obscured by a dense fog, the sweet image of a lovely young girl appearing in flashes out of the haze like a vision. She brought me things to drink and sat beside me on the bed with a sad, frightened look, running her soft, tiny fingers through my hair. One time, I remember her gentle kiss on my face. On another occasion, waking suddenly in the night with just the light of a candle standing on the table next to the bed, I saw the silhouette of Elena's face lying next to me on the pillow. She was sleeping quietly, her pale lips half parted, with one hand cupped under her cheek. It wasn't until the following morning that I was fully conscious. The candle had burned down to a small puddle of wax and the bright pink rays of dawn were already playing on the wall. Elena was sitting in a chair next to the table, her head bowed low and her chin resting on her left hand. She was fast asleep. I remember gazing a long time at her sweet, innocent face, which even in dreams bore a sad, unchildlike expression and a strange, deathly beauty, pale, with long lashes on thin cheeks, framed by jet-black hair, thick and flowing, tied carelessly on the side. Her other hand lay on my pillow. I softly kissed her thin little hand and even though the child was not awake, I thought I caught the glimmer of a smile dance on her pale lips. I continued looking at her until, finally, I drifted quietly into a deep, healing sleep. This time, I slept until almost noon. Waking up, I felt almost fully recovered. Only a general weakness and a heaviness in my limbs bore witness to my recent illness. I had had similar nervous attacks before and I had grown used to them. The illness rarely lasted more than a day, but inflicted mayhem on my mind and body before subsiding into oblivion.

It was almost noon. The first thing I noticed was a heavy string stretched across one corner of the room. The curtains I had purchased the day before were attached and partially hid the sofa, which Elena had pushed into the corner, providing herself with a small private bedroom of her own.

She was sitting before the stove boiling the kettle. When she saw that I was awake, she smiled cheerfully and immediately came over to me.

"My dear friend," I said, taking her hand, "You have been up all night looking after me. I didn't know you could be so caring."

"And how do you know that I was looking after you? Maybe I just went to bed and slept through the night," she said, looking at me with a sly, good-natured playfulness, but at the same time blushing shyly at her own words.

"I woke up and saw everything. You fell asleep just before dawn."

"Would you like some tea?" she interrupted, as if having difficulty continuing this line of conversation, a trait all too common among modest, open-hearted people who are uncomfortable accepting praise.

"I would love some," I answered. "But did you ever get anything to eat yesterday?"

"I didn't have supper, but I did have a late lunch. The porter brought it. You, however, should not be speaking. Get some rest. You're still not completely well."

She brought me my tea and sat down next to me on the bed.

"Rest, I will... for now," I told her. "But before nightfall, I must get up and go see someone. I really have to, my little darling."

"Oh, is that right? Who do you have to see? Was it that man who was here yesterday?"

"No, not him."

"That's good, I didn't like him. He's the one who got you all upset yesterday. To see his daughter, then?"

"And what do you know about his daughter?"

"I heard everything yesterday," she said, looking down at me, her face darkening and her eyebrows shifting down over her eyes. "He's a horrible old man," she added.

"You don't know anything about him. He's actually a very good man."

"No, no, he was nasty! I heard him," she said with fervor.

"What did you hear?"

"He refuses to forgive his daughter..."

"But he loves her. She behaved very badly towards him, and yet he feels tormented because he's so worried about her."

"Why doesn't he just forgive her then? But even if he did forgive his daughter, she shouldn't come back to him."

"But why? Why shouldn't she?"

"Because he doesn't deserve her kindness," she answered eagerly. "She should stay away and become a beggar on the streets, and then let him *see* her begging on the streets and that will make him suffer even more."

Her eyes sparkled and her cheeks glowed.

She may actually be right, I thought to myself.

"Was he the man whose home you wanted to send me to?" she added after a moment.

"Yes, Elena."

"No, I'd rather take a job as a servant."

"Oh, but that doesn't make any sense, my darling. It's silly. Who would hire you as a servant?"

"Any man," she answered quickly, looking more and more downcast. She was visibly irritated.

"Yes, but what peasant or working man is going to hire a girl like you as a servant?" I asked, grinning.

"Well, then a nobleman."

"A girl with your temperament living in the home of a nobleman?"

"I can change!" The more annoyed she became, the more snappish were her replies.

"Maybe, but you couldn't stand to be mistreated."

"I can! They could scold me all they want, I would purposely remain silent. They could beat me, I would be silent, completely silent, even *as* they were beating me. And I wouldn't cry. That would annoy them even more if I didn't cry."

"What happened to you, Elena? To be so angry, and yet so proud? You must have known so much unhappiness."

I got up and walked over to my dining table. Elena stayed on the couch, gazing distractedly at the armrest, her fingers scratching at the stitching. She said nothing.

"She's probably mad at me for what I said," I thought.

Standing at the table, I automatically opened the book I had brought home the day before to research my article, and little by little I started reading. That's often the case with me. I open up a book to check on something and before I know it I'm engrossed in reading.

"What do you write about?" Elena said, with a timid smile, as she quietly approached the table.

"Oh, all sorts of things. That's how I earn my money."

"Solicitations?"

"No, not solicitations. They're short articles about a lot of different things. But I also write stories about different people and places. And sometimes I put them all together into what is called a novel." She listened with great curiosity.

"Is it all true, what you write?"

"Well, no, I make up most of it."

"Why would you make up things that aren't true?"

"Because people like to read it. Here, you were looking at this yesterday. Do you know how to read?"

"I know how."

"Well then, see for yourself. I wrote this book."

"You? I'll read it."

There was clearly something she wanted to say but was having difficulty getting it out. Was there some hidden message behind her questions?

"Do you get paid a lot for what you write?" she finally asked.

"Well, it depends. Sometimes a lot, and sometimes nothing at all, because the end result doesn't come out right. Writing is very hard work, Elena."

"So you're not rich?"

"No. No, I'm not rich."

"So I will work and help you."

She stared at me and then lowered her eyes and blushed. Suddenly, she rushed towards me in two quick steps, grabbed both of my hands and pressed her face tightly against my chest. I looked down at her in astonishment.

"I love you! I'm not proud," she said. "You said yesterday that I was proud. No, no... I'm not like that. I love you. And you're the only one who loves me!"

She began to weep and a moment later her chest was heaving with sobs with the same intensity as her anger from the day before. She fell to her knees in front of me and kissed my hands, my feet…

"You do love me!" she repeated. "You're the only one… the only one who cares about me."

She grabbed tightly around my knees with her arms. All of the emotions that she had so long suppressed had suddenly burst forth in one gigantic, irresistible impulse, and I understood how the coldness of a heart locked tightly from the world can suddenly melt, and the more tightly sealed the blockage, the greater the need to break through the barrier and flow free. Elena's words cascaded forth in an inevitable rush of emotion, combining love, gratitude and affection, mixed with an astounding flood of tears.

She sobbed to the point of near hysteria. With difficulty, I pulled her to her feet and lifted her in my arms. I carried her to the sofa and sat next to her as she continued to sob, clinging to me and burying her face in my chest, as if ashamed to look at me.

Little by little the tears subsided and briefly, once or twice, she pulled back and let her eyes slide up my face, her gaze soft and timid, not quite ready to reveal everything. Finally, she blushed and smiled.

"Are you feeling any better?" I asked. "My sweet tender-hearted little child, my sweet Elena?"

"No, don't call me Elena," she whispered, once again hiding her face from me.

"Not Elena? What then?"

"Nellie."

"Nellie? Why Nellie? It's a very pretty name, so I'll call you that if that's what you want."

"That's what my mother called me. And no one else. Just her. And I would never want anyone else to call me that… Except you. I want you to call me Nellie. And I will always love you. Always."

"Such a loving and generous heart," I thought to myself. "But what you have put me through to earn the privilege of calling you Nellie. But now I know that I have won your heart forever."

"Nellie, listen," I said, as soon as she had calmed down. "You say that your mother was the only one who really loved you and no one else. Didn't your grandfather love you?"

"No, he didn't!"

"And yet you cried over him when he died. Remember? Here, on the stairs."

She thought for a moment.

"No, he didn't love me. He was an evil man." A disgusted look contorted her face.

"He wasn't entirely to blame, Nellie. He seems to have been completely out of his mind. He died like a madman. Remember, I told you how he died."

"Yes, but he only became forgetful in the last month before he died. He used to sit here all day waiting for me, and if I didn't show up, he would just sit here another day, and then a third day, without ever taking a drink or a bite to eat. He was much better before."

"What do you mean before? Before what?"

"Before my mother died."

"So you were the one who brought him food and drink then?"

"Yes, that was me."

"Where did you get them? From Madame Bubnova?"

"No, I never took anything from Bubnova," she insisted, her voice rising in volume.

"Then where did you get them if you had no money?"

Nellie paused and turned pale. She looked at me for a long, long time.

"I went into the streets and begged. When I had five kopecks, I would buy him bread and tobacco."

"And he *allowed* you to do that, Nellie? Nellie?"

"When I first started, I didn't tell him. But then, when he found out, he used to take me out himself and make me beg. I would stand on the bridge asking passers-by for coins, and he walked around nearby, watching and waiting, and when he saw someone give me a coin, he would throw himself at me and grab the money away, afraid that I might hide it from him, not save it for him."

Saying this, she smiled a sarcastic, bitter smile.

"It was when Mama died," she added, "that he started going funny in the head."

"So he must have been very fond of your mother. He didn't want to live without her."

"No, he didn't like her. He was angry and wouldn't forgive her... just like that evil old man from yesterday," she added, softly, almost in a whisper, as her face grew paler.

I shuddered. The plot of a novel suddenly flashed in my mind. This poor woman dying in a cellar at the undertaker's, her orphan daughter visiting from time to time her grandfather, a crazy, eccentric old man who had once cursed her mother and now dies in a pastry shop shortly after the death of his dog!

"Azorka was Mama's dog once," said Nellie suddenly, smiling at the remembrance. "Grandpa was very fond of Mama at first, and when Mama ran away, she left Azorka with him. That's why he loved Azorka so much. But he never forgave Mama for leaving, and when the dog died, so did he." As she said this, the smile vanished from her face.

"Nellie, what did he do before?" I asked, after a brief pause.

"He used to be rich. I don't know what he did," she answered. "He had a factory. So Mama told me. At first she thought I was too young and didn't speak about him. She would just kiss me and say, 'You'll know everything when the time comes, my poor, unhappy child!' She was always calling me poor and unhappy. And at night, when she used to think I was asleep—and I was purposely pretending to be asleep—she would stand crying over me and kiss me and say 'poor, unhappy!'"

"What did your mother die from?"

"From consumption. It's been six weeks now."

"Do you remember when your grandfather was rich?"

"No, that was back before I was born. Mama even left Grandpa before I was born."

"Who was the man she left with?"

"I don't know," Nellie answered, quietly, as if thinking. "She went abroad and I was born there."

"Abroad? Where was that?"

"In Switzerland. I've traveled all over. Italy, Paris."

I was surprised.

"And do you remember any of that, Nellie?"

"I remember a lot."

"How is it you speak Russian so well?"

"Mama used to teach Russian even then. She was a Russian because her mother was Russian, and my Grandpa was an American, but also Russian. And when Mama came back to Russia a year-and-a-half ago, I learned the language properly. Mama was already sick. Then we got poorer and poorer and Mama was always crying. She spent a long time when we arrived in St. Petersburg searching for Grandpa, and she kept saying all the time that she was to blame, and she was always crying. Crying, crying! And when she learned that Grandpa was poor now, too, she cried even more. She tried to contact him and wrote letter after letter, but he never answered any of them."

"Why did your mother come back here? Just to find her father?"

"I don't know. But before that we lived very well." Nellie's eyes sparkled. "Mama and I lived alone together. She had a friend, a very nice man, like you. They had known each other before she ran away. But he died there, and Mama and I came back here."

"Was he the man your mother ran away with when she deserted your grandfather?"

"No, not with him. Mama went with another man... but he ended up leaving her."

"What was *his* name, Nellie?"

Nellie looked at me and said nothing. She undoubtedly knew the identity of the man who had deserted her mother, and who was probably her father. It was difficult for me to even dignify the scoundrel with a name.

I did not want to torment her with any more questions. She was an extraordinary little character, tough and passionate on the outside, but also emotionally bottled-up and afraid of being hurt; sweet, but also proud and inaccessible. In the short time I had known her, despite her professed love for me (a love that until then she had reserved only for her mother), Nellie had been careful not to expose her fragile emotions or unhappy past. But on that one day, in the course of several hours of anguished confession, interrupted frequently by convulsive sobs, she revealed her true feelings and provided me with a tale of such appalling remembrances that I shall never forget it, although her most important story was yet to come.

Chapter Twenty-Seven

The sun had already set when I realized that it was time to put aside the nightmare of the past few days and think about the present.

"Nellie," I said, "I know you're still upset and in pain, but I have to leave you alone with your grief and tears for a little while. Another friend of mine also has a father who refuses forgiveness and she too is unhappy, wounded and abandoned. She is waiting for me now. After listening to your sad story, I cannot bear to make her wait another minute."

I don't know if Nellie understood what I had just told her, but my nerves were on edge from both her story and my recent illness, so I rushed to Natasha. It was already nine o'clock by the time I reached the house where she was lodging.

From across the street I saw a carriage drawn up in front of Natasha's gate which I immediately suspected belonged to the prince. As I started up the staircase, I heard above me the sound of someone groping cautiously up the same stairs, obviously unfamiliar with the house. I imagined at first that it must be the prince, but soon changed my opinion when I heard the stranger fumbling his way up the dark staircase, grumbling and cursing at each misplaced step, and growing angrier the higher he rose. Of course, the staircase was narrow, muddy and steep, but such foul language could hardly be attributed to a prince. This man swore like a Cossack. But on the third-floor landing, a small lamp burning inside Natasha's room illuminated the face of the stranger and I discovered, to my astonishment, that it *was* the prince. He seemed very disturbed by my unexpected appearance on the stairs behind him. He did not, at first, recognize me, but suddenly his face was transformed. The spiteful and hateful look in his eyes suddenly became friendly and cheerful, and he gave me an extraordinarily pleasant handshake.

"Oh, it's you! And I was about to fall on my knees and pray to God to spare my life. Did you hear how I was cursing?"

He laughed lightly, but a moment later his face assumed a serious and thoughtful expression.

"Alyosha and Anna Nikolayevna are living in this house!" he said, shaking his head. "It is these so-called little things that reveal the true measure of a man. I am afraid for him. He is kind, he has a noble heart, but he is not yet a man. He claims to be passionately in love and yet he houses the object of that love in a pigsty like this. I have even heard that *sometimes* there is not even enough food to eat," he added in a whisper, searching for the bell handle. "My head is ready to explode when I think about his future and, most importantly, about the future of Anna Nikolayevna when she marries him."

This was the second time he had misstated Natasha's name, but he failed to recognize the error in his vexation over not finding a bell. I tugged on the door handle and Mavra immediately opened the door and greeted us anxiously. The kitchen was separated from the main room by a small wooden screen, and through the open door I could see that both areas had changed noticeably. Everything had been wiped and cleaned, there was a fire in the stove, and the table was set with new dishes. It was obvious that we were expected. Mavra rushed to remove our coats.

"Is Alyosha here?" I asked her.

"He hasn't shown up," she whispered to me, mysteriously.

We went in to greet Natasha. There were no special preparations in her room; it was much the same as always. However, her room was always so clean and well-ordered, there was nothing to clean up. Natasha met us standing next to her door. I was struck by how painfully thin and pale she looked, although there was a brief moment when color flashed on her cheeks. Her eyes were feverish. Without a word, she quickly took the prince's hand. Clearly confused and visibly agitated, she did not seem to notice me, so I waited patiently in silence.

"Well, here I am," the prince said in a cordial, friendly tone. "I've only just returned a few hours ago. And all this time you have never been out of my thoughts." He kissed her hand. "I am so happy that my initial impression of you has changed so much and I can't wait to engage you in conversation. But first of all, I notice that my wayward son is not present."

"Excuse me, Prince," Natasha interrupted him, looking embarrassed and confused. "I have a few words to exchange with Ivan Petrovich. Vanya, come with me... just two words."

She grabbed me by the hand and led me behind the screen.

"Vanya," she said in a whisper, having pulled me into the darkest corner. "Will you forgive me or not?"

"Natasha, what are you talking about?"

"No, Vanya, you are always so forgiving of me, but there comes a point when patience ends. You have never ceased to love me, I know that, but you must think me terribly ungrateful, and I *was* ungrateful yesterday and ungrateful the day before; selfish, cruel..."

She suddenly burst into tears and pressed her face against my shoulder.

"No, Natasha," I hastened to reassure her. "It's because I was very sick all night, and even now can barely stand on my feet, that I didn't come by yesterday evening or today. And you have been thinking that I was angry. You are my dearest friend. Do you imagine that I can't see the pain you're feeling in your soul?"

"Well then... that means you have forgiven me again, as always," she said, smiling through her tears and clutching my arm until it hurt. "The rest we can talk about later. I have so much to say to you, Vanya. But now we must return to him."

"Quick, Natasha, we left him so suddenly."

"I want you to see, to see what happens," she whispered to me hurriedly. "I understand everything now. I've figured it all out. It's all his doing. This evening will answer a lot of questions. Let's go!"

I did not understand, but there was no time to ask. Natasha returned to the prince with a bright smile. He was still standing with his hat in his hands. She cheerfully apologized, took his hat, and pulled him to a chair. The three of us were now seated around her table.

"I was about to say when I came in," continued the prince, "that I have only seen my wandering boy *once* for less than a minute. He was getting into a carriage to visit the Countess Zinaida Filimonova. He was in an awful hurry and, can you imagine, he was too busy to even stop and visit with his father after four days of separation. And it seems that *I* am responsible, Natalia Nikolayevna, that he is not here with you and that we have arrived ahead of him, for I took the opportunity, since I would not be able to visit the countess today myself, to have him carry my greetings to her. But he should be here any minute."

"And did you make him promise to come today?" Natasha asked calmly with a steady glance at the prince.

"Oh, my God, he would have come under any circumstances, how can you ask?" he exclaimed in surprise, returning her stare. "However, I do understand why you are angry with him. Indeed, it is rude of him to be the last to arrive. But, again, I am to blame. Do not be angry with him. He can be flighty and foolish and, believe me, I do not defend such behavior, but there are special circumstances which require his presence at the home of the countess and her relations that make it imperative that he visit her as often as possible. And as he is probably never far from your side, forgetting everyone else but you, I do hope you'll not be angry and pardon his taking a couple of hours, and no more, to attend to my request. I am sure he hasn't been to see Princess K. since that evening, and I'm quite upset that I didn't have an opportunity this morning to ask him!"

I glanced at Natasha. She listened to the prince with a slight smirk, but his remarks were so straightforward, so natural, that it seemed impossible to suspect him of anything.

"And you really don't know that he hasn't been with me in several days?" Natasha asked in a quiet and calm voice, as if speaking about the most commonplace matters.

"What? Not been…? What are you saying?" asked the prince, apparently in complete astonishment.

"The two of you were with me on Tuesday, late in the evening. The next morning, he stopped by for half an hour, and since that visit I have not seen him even once."

"But this is incredible," the prince said, looking even more astonished. "I thought he never left your side. I'm sorry, this is so strange... so inexplicable."

"But completely true, I'm sorry to say. I was especially looking forward to seeing you this evening to find out where he's been."

"Oh, my God! He should be here right now! But what you are telling me is a complete shock. I confess, I'm used to his being late, but this is something I never expected!"

"How surprised you seem! And yet I would have thought this was something for which you'd be fully prepared, even knowing in advance that he would not be here."

"Knowing in advance… But I assure you, Natalia, that I have seen him for only that one brief moment today and I have discussed his activities with no one else. I find it strange that you do not seem to believe me," he continued, looking at both of us.

"God forbid," interrupted Natasha. "I'm absolutely convinced that what you tell me is the truth!"

And she laughed again, right in the prince's face, causing him to flinch.

"Explain yourself," he said in confusion.

"But there is nothing to explain. I say it in very simple words. You know how flighty and forgetful he is. Now that you have provided him with unlimited freedom, he has become reckless and wild."

"But it is impossible for him to behave in such a fashion. There must be some more reasonable explanation and when he returns, I shall have to question him about this matter. But above all else, I am surprised that you think I am guilty of something, that you are accusing me in some way when—as you can plainly see—I am here and not there. I understand, Natalia, that you are very angry with him, and you have every right to be and... and, of course, I'm the first one to blame," he continued, "since I'm the first to arrive here, am I not?" He turned to me with an angry smirk.

Natasha looked livid.

"Excuse me, Natalia Nikolayevna," he went on with dignity, "for while I may have been guilty of going away so soon after our first meeting, I see in you a suspiciousness that has caused you to change your opinion of me, exacerbated undoubtedly by the circumstances. Had I not gone away, you would now know me better, and Alyosha would have behaved more appropriately under my supervision. When he arrives, you shall hear for yourself how I reprimand him."

"And after receiving such a reprimand, he will certainly begin to resent me," Natasha said. "It cannot be possible for you to imagine that your actions would benefit me in any way."

"Are you hinting that I would intentionally do something to turn him against you? You insult me, Natalia."

"I prefer not to use hints when I speak," she responded. "Quite the contrary, I always try to be as direct as possible, as you will undoubtedly discover this evening. I seriously doubt that I have insulted you because you would have to *care* about my opinion to be truly insulted. I understand our relationship completely and recognize that you do not take my words seriously. But if, by any chance, I truly have offended you, then I apologize if I have not demonstrated the proper… hospitality."

Despite the light and even humorous tone with which Natasha offered this last phrase, with a smile on her lips, never have I seen her so thoroughly angry. At once I recognized the heartache she had been suppressing these past three days. Her mysterious suggestion that she knew and understood everything frightened me, especially as it clearly referred to Prince Valkovsky. She had obviously changed her opinion of him and looked upon him now as her enemy. She seemed to think that all of her recent difficulties with Alyosha could be directly attributed to the influence of the prince and, apparently, had evidence to back up her suspicions. I feared that there might be a scene between them at any moment. Natasha's derisive tone, her remark that the prince did not take her words seriously, her mocking apology for a lack of hospitality, and her promise, which seemed more like a threat, that she would speak plainly that evening, were so blatantly obvious it was not possible that the prince did not understand everything. I saw that his face had changed, but he managed to control himself. He acted as though he did not understand her words, did not understand their true meaning, and, of course, he made a joke of it.

"God forbid I should demand an apology from *you*!" he said with an exaggerated laugh. "I would never ask for and, indeed, it is quite against my rules to ask a lady for an apology. Even on our first meeting I warned you about my character, so I trust you will not be angry with me if I make one observation, something which applies, perhaps, to all women and with which I think you may agree." He turned to me and continued, courteously. "I have noticed in the female character a trait that if, for example, a woman is at fault in any way, she would much prefer to make amends with a thousand caresses at a later date, than acknowledge her mistake and ask for forgiveness at the moment she is confronted with evidence of her misconduct. So, even if you are correct in believing that you have offended me, I would certainly not ask for an apology at this moment. I would much prefer to wait for a more advantageous time when you realize your mistake and attempt to make amends with... a thousand caresses. And you are so kind, so pure, so fresh, I am sure that when you finally realize your error, your plea for forgiveness will be most charming. So rather than an apology, I would prefer that you illuminate how I can prove that my honesty and directness are more genuine at this moment than you seem to believe?"

Natasha blushed. I, too, felt that there was something in the tone of the prince's response which seemed too glib, too casual, and even a bit facetious.

"You want to *prove* that you are being honest and direct with me?" asked Natasha, looking at him with defiance.

"Yes."

"If that's true, you will fulfill my request."

"I give you my word in advance."

"Then here it is. You will not distress Alyosha either today or tomorrow with even a single word or hint about me that will cause him concern. No reproach or reprimand for his having forgotten me or our plans today. I just want to meet him when he arrives as if nothing has happened, so that he sees no tension between us. I need that. Will you give me that promise?"

"With the greatest pleasure," replied the prince, "and may I add with all my heart that I have rarely met anyone with a more sensible and clear-headed view of such matters. But here, it seems, is Alyosha now."

Indeed, there was a noise in the front alcove. Natasha started and seemed to prepare herself for what was to come. Prince Valkovsky sat with a serious expression, awaiting his son's appearance. He kept a close eye on Natasha as the door opened and his son rushed into the room.

Chapter Twenty-Eight

Alyosha sailed into the room, his face shining with happiness and cheer. It was evident that he had also spent the previous four days cheerfully and happily. I could see from his expression that he eagerly wanted to tell us something.

"Here I am!" he proclaimed to the whole room. "I, who should have arrived before anyone else. But you will soon know everything! Everything! Even you, Papa! I didn't have time to exchange two words with you this morning but now I have so much to tell you! He usually doesn't like me to call him Papa except in moments of extreme giddiness like this," he confided, turning to me. "At any other time, God forbid! And he usually calls me by my full name. But from this day forward, I want him to always feel as giddy as I do! Actually, I have completely changed in these past four days, completely, completely changed, and I will tell you all about it. But that's for later. Right now, the important thing is that she is here. She is here! Again. Natasha, my darling, hello, my angel!" he said, sitting down beside her and greedily kissing her hand. "Oh, how I've missed you! But that's how it is. I couldn't help it. You are so dear to me! But you look a little thinner, you're so pale…"

He excitedly covered her hands with kisses, hungrily watching her with his beautiful eyes, as though he could not get enough of her. I looked at Natasha and her expression told me that we were of one mind: Alyosha was completely innocent. When, in fact, could this *innocent* ever be guilty? The bright color suddenly surged to Natasha's pale cheeks, as if all the blood that had gathered in her heart had suddenly rushed to her head. Her eyes flashed and she looked proudly at the prince.

"But where in the world… where have you been for… for so many days?" she said in a faltering and restrained voice. Her breath came hard and unevenly. My God, how she loved him!

"You must think that I am to blame, at least it must seem that way. But, of course, I was to blame, I know that, and I come to you knowing that. Katya told me yesterday and today that a woman cannot forgive such negligence. She knows everything that happened here on Tuesday, I told her the other day. But I argued with her, insisting that there *was* one such woman named Natasha, and that in all the world there was, perhaps, only one other woman her equal, and that was Katya. And I came here, of course, knowing that I'd won the dispute. Could an angel like you refuse to forgive me? When I hadn't arrived yet, you must have thought, 'Ah, something has obviously delayed him.' Never! 'Ah, he doesn't love me anymore!' My Natasha would never think such a thing! As if I or anyone could stop loving you! It's not possible! My heart has been aching for you all this time. But that doesn't excuse my guilt! But when you hear everything I have to say, you will agree that I was completely justified. And I have so much to tell you; I need to pour out my soul to you all, and so I am here. I had wanted to rush to you today, but I didn't have a minute free, even for a kiss on the fly, and so I failed. Katya had an important errand for me to run—That's when you saw me in the carriage, Papa—I had received another note from Katya! All day long she has messengers running back and forth between houses. Vanya, I only had a moment to read your note last night, and you are absolutely right about everything you wrote. But what could I do? It's physically impossible! And so I thought, 'Tomorrow night, I'll explain everything,' because, my dear Natasha, it was impossible for me to *not* come to you this evening."

"What note?" Natasha asked.

"Vanya went to my rooms when I was out and left it for me. He was very angry with me for not coming around to see you. And, of course, he was absolutely right! That was yesterday."

Natasha looked at me.

"But if you had the time to visit all day long with Katerina Fedorovna…" began the prince.

"I know! I know what you're going to say," Alyosha interrupted. "'If you have time for Katya, then you should have twice the reason to be here.' I absolutely agree with you and will add that it is not twice the reasons, but a million times more reasons! But first you must understand that there are strange, unexpected events in my life which have me confused and have turned my life upside down. Well, that's what keeps happening to me, such events. And I tell you that I have completely changed from end to end, so they must have been important events!"

"Oh, my God, what's happened already? Don't keep us in suspense, please!" exclaimed Natasha, smiling at Alyosha's feverish energy.

In fact, he was a bit ridiculous, chattering so quickly that his words flew from his mouth without reason or rhyme. He just kept saying that he wanted to talk, talk, talk, but he held tightly to Natasha's hands and kept raising them to his lips, as if he could not kiss them enough.

"But that's what has happened to me," Alyosha went on. "Ah, my friends! What I have seen and done, the people that I have met! First, Katya, she is perfection! I really, really had no idea until now! And then, on Tuesday, when I told you about her, Natasha—you remember how I talked with such enthusiasm? Well, even then I had no idea. She hid herself from me until today. But now we know each other perfectly! We couldn't be closer. But first, let me start at the beginning. Natasha, if you could have only heard what I told her about you when I saw her the next day, on Wednesday; told her everything that there was between us. And by the way, I know how foolish I seemed when I came to see you on Wednesday! You met me with such enthusiasm, you were so excited about this new state of ours, you wanted to talk to me about all of it. You were sad and, at the same time, mischievous and playful with me, while I was trying to behave so respectably! A fool! Such a fool I was! Because really, well, I just wanted to show off, boast that I was soon to be your husband, a solid, respectable man, and here I was boasting in front of you! Oh, you must have been laughing at me inside and I absolutely deserved your mockery!"

The prince sat in silence with a triumphant, ironic smile as he watched Alyosha. He seemed delighted that his son was behaving in such a frivolous and even ridiculous manner. All that evening I watched him carefully, and I became completely convinced that he did not like his son, notwithstanding his frequent claims of fatherly devotion.

"After you, I went to Katya," Alyosha prattled on. "I have already said that we have only just this morning totally gotten to know each other. It was odd how it happened—I can't even remember—a few warm words, some feelings expressed, thoughts frankly revealed, and we were best friends forever. You must, must get to know her, Natasha! As she spoke, Katya told me *about you*! She explained to me what a treasure you are! Little by little, she told me all her own ideas and her outlook on life. She is so serious and yet such a delightful girl! She spoke of our duty to help others; how we all need to serve humanity, and as we came to know each other perfectly, after five or six hours of intimate conversation, we ended up swearing eternal friendship and to work together our whole lives!"

"Work? At what?" his surprised father asked.

"I've changed so much, Papa, that's all there is to it. I know this must surprise you, given all of your earlier objections," Alyosha replied solemnly. "People like you are so practical; you have so many restrictive rules, serious, severe, and to you all of our young and fresh ideas seem suspicious, threatening, even bizarre. But I am no longer the boy you knew me to be a few days ago. I am a man! I boldly look everything and everyone in the face. If I believe what I know to be true, then I will pursue it to the utmost, and if I do not veer from my course, I am an honest man. That's all I need. Say what you want, I believe in myself!"

"I see," said the prince scornfully.

Natasha looked at us with concern. She was afraid for Alyosha. He was often at a disadvantage when it came to clever conversation, and she knew it. She did not want Alyosha to make a fool of himself in front of us, especially his father.

"What are you trying to say, Alyosha?" she asked. "It sounds like some kind of philosophy which someone has put into your mouth. Maybe you should just tell us in your own words."

"But I *am* telling you!" cried Alyosha. "You see, Katya has two distant relatives, cousins, I think, named Levenka and Borenka. One is a student and the other is... just a young man. She's on good terms with both and they're just extraordinary men! They rarely visit the countess, on principle. Katya and I were discussing the destiny of man, our mission in life, and she mentioned them to me and gave me a letter of introduction, which I immediately took to them to make their acquaintance. That evening, the three of us gathered together with many of their friends, a dozen different people, students, officers, artists, even a writer! They *all* know you, Vanya! That is, they have read your writings, and many are expecting great things from you in the future. They told me so themselves. When I said that I knew you and promised to introduce them to you, they all accepted me with open arms as a brother. Almost at once, I told them that I will soon be a married man, so they regarded me as a married man. Levenka and Borenka live on the fifth floor, right under the roof, and they meet with their friends as often as possible, but mostly on Wednesdays when they all gather at Levenka and Borenka's room. They're all young and fresh, and filled with a fervent love for all mankind. We talked about our present and future, of science and literature, and they spoke so well, so simply and directly. There was also a high-school student who's part of their group. They all treat each other with such decency and respect! I've never seen men like these! Where have I been all my life? What have I seen? What ideas have I grown up with? You're the only one, Natasha, who has ever spoken to me like that. Oh, Natasha, you definitely must get to know these people. Katya is already on friendly terms with them all, and they speak of her almost with reverence. Katya told Levenka and Borenka that when she comes into her inheritance, she will immediately donate a million rubles for the common good."

"And who will manage this million? Levenka and Borenka and their cronies?" asked the prince.

"Not true, not true, Papa, shame on you!" Alyosha cried angrily. "I know what you're thinking! We've talked a great deal about this million and finally came to the conclusion that it should be used primarily on public enlightenment..."

"Yes, it seems that I do not yet know very much about Katerina Fedorovna," said the prince, almost to himself, with the same mocking smile. "I was expecting a great deal from her, but… this..."

"This is what?" Alyosha interrupted. "Why does this seem strange to you? Because it is outside your usual routine? Because no one has ever donated a million rubles before and she will? Is that it? Perhaps she does not choose to live at the expense of others, because living like a millionaire means living at the expense of others. I've just recently learned that. Katya wants to be useful to her country and make a meaningful contribution. I used to read about such generosity in my schoolbooks, but when *you* learn that it may cost a million, you think there is something wrong. But where does this vaunted wisdom, which I believe in so whole-heartedly, come from? Father, why are you looking at me like that? Like you think I'm a fool, a buffoon! Well, what if I am a fool? Natasha, you should hear what Katya says about that: 'The mind is not the main thing; it's what guides that mind, the character, the heart, the noble spirit.' But better still is something Bezmygin said. Bezmygin is a friend of Levenka and Borenka and, just between us, he is a genius! Only yesterday in conversation he said: 'A fool who confesses to being a fool is no fool at all!' How true is that? Bezmygin has a brilliant mind and sprinkles truth wherever he goes."

"A definite sign of genius," said the prince.

"You laugh at everything! But I have never heard anything like that from you, or from any of your friends, either. On the contrary, you and your crowd hide everything, keeping your noses to the ground, afraid to go against any of the acceptable rules, as if that were possible! As if that were not a thousand times more *impossible* than what we say and what we think. And yet you call us Utopian! You should have heard what they said to me yesterday..."

"But what exactly *is it* that you say and think?" Natasha asked. "Tell me, Alyosha. I still, somehow, do not understand."

"In general, everything that leads to progress for humanity, to love, and it's all connected to contemporary issues. We were talking about governmental transparency and a free press, about social reforms, the love of humanity, contemporary thinkers whose work we read and criticize. But most importantly, we give each other the freedom to be completely candid with each other and just talk to each other about ourselves, with no hesitation. Only through such frankness and honesty can we achieve our goal. That is especially what Bezmygin is striving for. I mentioned this to Katya and she is in complete sympathy with Bezmygin. And because we are all under the guidance of Bezmygin, we have all pledged to live honest and straightforward lives, and no matter what anyone says about us, no matter how we may be judged, we will not be embarrassed or ashamed of our enthusiasm, our interests or our mistakes. If you want to be respected by others, first and foremost you must respect yourself. That's what Bezmygin says and Katya totally agrees with him. We are currently discoursing on our common beliefs and assembling these ideas into a unified whole to reach a collective interpretation."

"What a lot of nonsense!" cried the prince, anxiously. "Who is this Bezmygin? No, this cannot be left to..."

"What cannot be left?" Alyosha interrupted. "Understand, Father, why I am saying all this to you now. It's because I hope and wish that you, too, will join our circle. I have already pledged your name on your behalf. You laugh. Well, I *knew* you would laugh! But hear me out! You are a kind and considerate man, so you will understand. You do not know them. Perhaps if you would *listen* to their ideas and *study* them, you will become an expert on them, but for now, you have never actually seen them or heard them speak, so how can you judge them? You only *imagine* that you know them. No, you must come with me and listen to what they have to say directly, and then... then, I give you my word, you will be one of us! And most importantly, I want to use every means available to rescue you from this venomous crowd of predators you have become attached to, and to save you from your warped convictions."

Prince Valkovsky listened to this verbal assault in silence with a malignant sneer. There was venom in his eyes. Natasha watched him with unconcealed revulsion. He saw it but pretended not to notice. But as soon as Alyosha had finished, his father suddenly burst out laughing. He even fell back in his chair as if he were unable to contain himself. But the laughter was certainly not sincere. He was quite clearly laughing for the sole purpose of hurting and humiliating his son. Alyosha was indeed wounded, and his face revealed extreme sorrow. But he waited patiently for his father's feigned joviality to subside.

"My father," he said sadly, "why are you laughing at me? I came to you openly and honestly. If, in your opinion, what I say is nonsense, then help me to understand *why* you feel that way, and don't just laugh at me. Besides, what do you have to laugh at? Principles that are, to me, now holy and honorable? Well, suppose that I *am* wrong, completely wrong, and that I *am* a fool, as you have called me several times, but if I *am* mistaken, it is a sincere, honest mistake. It doesn't diminish my honorable intentions. I admire lofty ideals. Even if they are misguided, the basis for them is sacred. I've told you that you and all of your friends have never told me *anything* that could guide me through life, something I could take away with me. Refute what I have said. Tell me something better, and I'll follow you. But don't laugh, because it's very distressing to me."

Alyosha said what he had to say with great sincerity and astonishing dignity. Natasha watched him sympathetically. The prince listened to his son with genuine amazement and immediately changed his tone.

"I did not mean to offend you, my boy," he answered. "On the contrary, I feel sorry for you. You are getting ready to take a sizable step forward in life, and it is a good time for you to stop being a feather-headed child. That's what I was thinking about. I laughed involuntarily and did not mean to hurt you."

"Then why does it feel that way?" Alyosha asked with bitterness. "Why has it seemed for so long that you look at me with antagonism, with an unsympathetic sneer, and not as a father should look at his son? Why do I feel that if I were in *your* shoes, I would not have ridiculed and insulted *my* son as you did me? Listen, let us speak frankly, now, once and forever, so that there can be no misunderstanding. I want you to tell me the truth. When I came here, I felt that you had some surprise for me that I was not expecting. Am I right? If so, isn't it better for all of us to reveal our true feelings? How much evil could be eliminated by a little honesty!"

"Speak, speak, Alyosha," said the prince. "What you suggest is very sensible. Perhaps you should start with her," he added, looking at Natasha.

"Don't get angry with me for being completely frank," Alyosha began. "You agreed that we should both be honest, so hear me out. You approved my marriage to Natasha. You made us both happy when you overcame your early objections. You were generous, and we both appreciated your noble deed. But now you seem to take joy in insinuating that I am a foolish boy and not fit to be Natasha's husband. What's more, you find pleasure in ridiculing, humiliating and denigrating me in Natasha's eyes. You're always happiest when you can make me look absurd. I've noticed that for some time now. As if you're trying to prove something to us, that our marriage is ridiculous, absurd, and that we are not a suitable couple. It's as if you really didn't believe in what you intended for us. As if you look at it all as a joke, a comic farce. It's not just what you said today that makes me feel this way. On that same Tuesday when you showed up here, you said some strange things that astonished and even upset me. And on Wednesday, too, when you were leaving, you gave some none-too-subtle hints about our present situation and said some things about Natasha, not offensive, quite the contrary, but somehow not quite what I'd like to hear from you. A little too flippant, somehow, without affection, without respect for her. It's hard to describe, but the tone was clear. One senses it in one's heart. Tell me I'm wrong. Reassure me, encourage me—and *her*. Because you've upset *her*, as well. I recognized it the moment I arrived here this evening."

Alyosha said this eagerly, with great strength. Natasha listened with obvious pride and a burning sense of excitement, twice saying quietly to herself: "Yes, that's true."

The prince seemed almost embarrassed. "My friend," he began, "I certainly cannot remember everything I said, but I find it very strange that you could misinterpret me so. I'm ready to reassure you all I can. If I laugh now, it's understandable; it's only to cover up my bitter feeling. When I think about you soon becoming a husband, it seems to me completely unimaginable, comical and, excuse me, even ridiculous. You reproach me for my laughter, but I tell you that it is all *your* doing. Oh, I am to blame, too. Perhaps I haven't been paying close enough attention to you lately, but it is only this evening that I have discovered precisely of what you are capable. Now I tremble when I think about your future with Natalia Nikolayevna. I was in too great a rush. I see now the disparity between the two of you. Love passes, but incompatibility remains forever. I cannot predict the future, but if your intentions are honest, consider this, you will be the ruin of Natalia Nikolayevna, the absolute ruin! You've been talking now for an hour about your great love of humanity, the integrity of your convictions, the noble people you've met. Ask Ivan Petrovich what I told him this morning after we climbed those disgusting stairs to the fourth floor and were standing together outside this door, thanking God for sparing our lives and legs. Do you know what involuntary thought came immediately to mind? I wondered how you could, with such love for Natalia Nikolayevna, accept her living in this wretched apartment? Can you not understand that if you have no money, if you cannot fulfill your obligations, you have no right to be a husband, no right to take on any such responsibilities? Love alone is a small thing. Love reveals itself through deeds. And yet you proclaim, 'Come live with me and suffer with me!' It's not humane, it's not noble! You talk about love for humanity, admire universal goals, and yet betray love through your own willful blindness. It's incomprehensible! Do not interrupt me, Natalia, let me finish. I may sound bitter, but I have to speak. You've been telling us, Alyosha, how you recently came to appreciate all that is noble and good and honest, and you have reproached me and my friends, suggesting that we have no such aspirations, merely judicious common sense. But consider this: while you have been admiring all that is lofty and fine since what happened here on Tuesday, you have been neglecting for four days the woman I would have thought you regarded as the most precious treasure in the world! You've admitted that you argued with Katerina Fedorovna, insisting that Natalia loves you with so much generosity she would forgive your every transgression. But what right have you to rely on such forgiveness and even make bet on it? Have you really given no consideration to the bitter thoughts, the doubts, the suspicions you have created in Natalia Nikolayevna these past few days? Do you really think that your fascination with all these new ideas gives you the right to neglect your most important duty? Excuse me, Natalia, for breaking my word, but this serious situation is more important than any promise, you will understand. Do you know, Alyosha, that I found Natalia Nikolayevna agonizingly distressed when I arrived, completely understandable given the hell you have put her through these past four days, a period that should have been the happiest of her life. Such appalling behavior on one hand, weighed against words, words, words on the other! Am I not right? And you then blame *me* for what is entirely your fault?"

Prince Valkovsky finished. He was so carried away by his own eloquence, he could not hide his triumph from us. When Alyosha heard about Natasha's suffering, he gave her the most painful of looks, but Natasha had already made a decision.

"Don't distress yourself, Alyosha," she said, "there are others more to blame than you. Sit down and listen to what I have to say to your father. It's time to end this!"

"Explain yourself, Natalia!" the prince cried. "I implore you! For two hours I have puzzled over your mysterious little hints. This is getting unbearable, and I confess I did not expect to be greeted in such a fashion."

"Maybe you thought you could fascinate us so with your words that we would not notice your secret intentions. What explanation do you need? You already know everything and understand everything! Alyosha is right. Your number one thought is to separate us. You knew in advance, almost by heart, everything that would happen here this evening, ever since last Tuesday, and you've calculated it all on your fingers. I've already told you that you don't take us or our wedding plans seriously. You are toying with us; playing a game with your own preconceived goal. And you are winning. Alyosha was right when he reproached you. You see all of this as a farce. Well, you should be very happy and not blame Alyosha, for he had no idea what you were planning and yet performed exactly as you had anticipated. Maybe even better!"

I was petrified with astonishment. I had expected the evening to be a complete disaster, but Natasha's unforgiving frankness and overtly contemptuous tone amazed me. So, she really did know something, I thought, and had decided to make a clean break. She may have even been looking forward to confronting the prince face-to-face. Prince Valkovsky turned a little pale. Alyosha's innocent face betrayed his fear and agonizing uncertainty.

"Consider what you are accusing me of," cried the prince, "and the words you are saying! I do not understand."

"Ah, so you do not wish to understand *my* words," Natasha said. "Even Alyosha understood *you* as well as I did, and we did not discuss this; we haven't even seen each other! Even he saw that you were playing a demeaning, offensive game with us, and he loves you and looks on you as a god. You didn't think it necessary to be careful or cunning with him, assuming he'd never see through you, but he has a sensitive, tender and impressionable soul, and your words, your tone, as he said before, he senses it in his heart."

"I do not understand a word of it, not a word!" repeated the prince with amazement. He turned to me to witness his confusion, annoyed and angry, then turned back to Natasha. "You are suspicious, you are confused. You are clearly jealous of Katerina Fedorovna and ready to blame the whole world... me first, apparently, and... and all I can say is you have given me a strange opinion of your character. I'm not used to such scenes. I would leave here immediately were it not for the interests of my son. I am still waiting for a gracious explanation."

"So, you still stubbornly refuse to understand my words, even though you know all of this by heart? Do you really insist that I say what I have to say?"

"With the greatest anticipation."

"Very well then, listen," Natasha cried, her eyes flashing with anger. "I will tell you everything, everything!"

CHAPTER TWENTY-NINE

Natasha stood up and started to speak while standing, not noticing in her excitement that she *was* standing. As the prince listened, he too stood. The whole scene became very solemn.

"Do you remember what you said to me on Tuesday?" Natasha began. "You said you wanted money, connections and a high-ranking position in the world. Do you remember?"

"I remember."

"Well, in order to obtain the money to achieve those goals that were just beyond your reach, you came here on Tuesday and invented a match between your son and me, calculating that your little joke would steer you on the right path."

"Natasha!" I cried. "Think of what you're saying!"

"Little joke? Calculating?" repeated the prince with an air of outraged dignity.

Alyosha sat and watched, grief-stricken, comprehending almost nothing.

"Yes, yes, do *not* interrupt me! I have promised I would say everything," Natasha continued, irritated. "Do you remember how Alyosha refused to listen to you? For six months you did all you could to distract him from me, but he paid no attention. And then the moment came when you could no longer tolerate his behavior. Any further delay and the bride, the money—most importantly the money, as much as three million rubles—would slip through your fingers. There was only one solution. To get Alyosha to fall in love with the girl *you* had chosen for his bride, assuming that if he fell in love with *her*, he would fall out of love with *me*..."

"Natasha, Natasha!" Alyosha cried with anguish. "What are you saying?"

"You forged ahead with your scheme," she went on, without stopping to comfort Alyosha. "But once again, it was the same old story! Everything should have worked out perfectly, except... I was in the way again! There was still hope, of course. A clever man of your experience and cunning could see that Alyosha was growing weary of his former affection. You could not help but notice that he was beginning to neglect me, staying away for five days. Perhaps you thought he would just grow bored and give up, when suddenly, on Tuesday, Alyosha's decisive action shocked you. What were you to do?"

"Excuse me," cried the prince. "On the contrary, the fact is..."

"I suggest," Natasha once again interrupted, "that you asked yourself that very evening, 'What do I do now?' and decided to *permit* him to marry me. Not really, of course, you just said that to calm him down. The date of the wedding, you thought, could be postponed indefinitely, and his feelings for Katya were starting to grow, which you were quick to notice. So, it was on this new love you pinned all your hopes."

"Novels, novels," said the prince softly, as if to himself. "You spend too much time alone, brooding, and reading novels."

"Yes, on this new love you pinned your hopes," Natasha repeated, not hearing and not paying attention to the prince's words, consumed by a feverish excitement. "And what were the odds of this new love succeeding? Their friendship began *before* he had learned of the girl's many perfections! But at the very moment he was telling this girl he could not love her, because duty and a prior love forbid him, she suddenly revealed so much generosity, so much sympathy for him and her rival, and displayed a heart so full of forgiveness that, even though he knew her to be attractive, he had never until that moment realized just how *remarkable* she was! He then came to visit me and did nothing but talk about the favorable impression she had made on him. So, of course, he felt compelled to pay a return visit to this magnificent creature the very next day, if only to express his gratitude. And why shouldn't he go? After all, his previous love was happy now that her future had been resolved, assured that he would dedicate his life to her, while the other girl would have only a few minutes of his time. How ungrateful would Natasha appear, to be jealous of such a brief meeting. But then he quietly robs Natasha not of mere minutes, but one day, two days, three… And during this time the other girl presents herself to him in a completely new and unexpected form. She is so noble, so enthusiastic, and yet such a sweet, naive child that she seems a mirror image of him. They swear to each other eternal friendship, like siblings who never wish to be separated. In five or six hours of conversation his soul is opened to new experiences and his heart is surrendered to her. Finally, the time will come when he stops to compare his old love to these new, fresh sensations. With the former, everything is familiar and predictable. It's so serious and demanding, filled with jealousy and reproaches… and tears. And if he attempts to lighten the moment, he is treated as a child, not an equal. And worst of all, it is so unendingly monotonous."

Natasha took a moment to choke back tears and a twinge of bitterness.

"What's next? Time, of course. A date for the wedding with Natasha has not yet been chosen, so there is still time to encourage a change. And so began your words, insinuations, interpretations, eloquence. You might even dream up a story about this annoying Natasha which will cast her in a negative light and... the precise method is unknown, but the victory will be yours! Alyosha, do not blame me, my darling! Do not say that I don't understand your love or appreciate you enough. I know that you love me, even now, and that you may not, at this moment, understand my complaint. I know that I've behaved badly saying these things, but what can I do if I understand everything so clearly and yet love you more and more... beyond sanity?"

She covered her face with her hands, fell back into her chair and sobbed like a child. Alyosha cried out and ran to her. He never could see her cry without crying himself.

Her sobs, I think, were very helpful to the prince. Natasha's vehemence during this long explanation, the sharpness of her outbursts against him (for which he had every right to be offended) could obviously be attributed to an insane rush of jealousy, to wounded love, even to illness. It was entirely appropriate for him to express sympathy.

"Calm down, Natalia Nikolayevna, don't distress yourself," the prince said. "All these frenzied hallucinations stem from solitude... You were so infuriated by his thoughtless behavior—it *was* only thoughtlessness on his part, you know. The most important fact upon which you base your distress was the incident on Tuesday, which really should have proven the immensity of his attachment to you, rather than the opposite, which you seem to think."

"Oh, do not speak to me, do not torment me even now!" interrupted Natasha, weeping bitterly. "My heart has told me everything. It has known for a long time! Do you think I cannot recognize that our old love has ended... here in this room? When he left me, forgot about me. I went through all that. Made up my mind... Well, what else could I do? I don't blame Alyosha, but I know he is deceiving me. Don't you think I've tried to deceive myself? So many times, so many times! Haven't I listened to every tone of his voice? Haven't I learned to read his every expression, his eyes? All is lost… lost. It is all buried. Oh, I'm so miserable!"

Alyosha cried in front of her on his knees.

"Yes, yes, it's my fault! All mine!" he repeated through his sobs.

"No, Alyosha, don't blame yourself! It is their fault… our enemies. They are to blame!"

"But let me ask," the prince began with some impatience, "on what evidence you ascribe to me all these... crimes? It's nothing but a supposition on your part. You have no proof!"

"Proof!" exclaimed Natasha, quickly rising from her chair. "You want evidence, you devious creature? You could not… could not have had any other motive when you came here with your *proposal*. You had to reassure your son, to ease his pain, so that he could, in good conscience, freely surrender himself to Katya. Without that, he would remember me and never give in to you, and you are tired of waiting. That's true, isn't it?"

"I confess," the prince replied with a sarcastic smile, "if I *had* wanted to deceive you, I would certainly have done so in such a calculated manner. You are very… clever, but you should be able to *prove* what you say before rebuking someone in such an offensive manner."

"Prove? After all the times you've tried so desperately to break us apart? A man who teaches his son to neglect his duties in pursuit of position and money is corrupting him! What you said before about the disgusting staircase and this wretched apartment. Did you not take away the very allowance you had previously provided in order to force us into poverty and hunger? To then chide him about the apartment and the staircase is disingenuous! Why did you suddenly come to us that evening with a fevered pitch about new ideas and attitude, and why was *I* suddenly so important? I have paced the floor here for four days thinking about it, weighing your every word, remembering each expression on your face, and I've come to the conclusion that it was all an invention, a joke, a mean-spirited and offensive farce, not at all out of character for you. Don't forget that I've known you for a very long time! Whenever Alyosha came from visiting you, I could guess from his face all that you had told him, trying to exert your influence on him. No, you don't fool me! Maybe you have some further calculations I haven't foreseen, maybe I haven't seen the worst yet, but it's all the same! You have deceived me, that's the main thing! I wanted to say that to your face!"

"Is that all? Is that all the evidence you have? But think, you crazed woman, with that *comic farce*—as you refer to my proposal on Tuesday—I bound myself, too. It would be rather careless on my part."

"What, to what are you bound? What does it mean in your eyes to deceive me? To insult a girl in my lowly position, a wretched, unhappy fugitive, cast out by her father, disgraced, of low moral character! But why concern yourself if this joke can bring at least some, though very little, benefit?"

"Think about the position you're putting yourself in, Natalia! You insist that I have insulted you, but such an insult is so extreme, so humiliating, I can't understand how anyone could even imagine such a thing, let alone believe it. What kind of upbringing must you have had to conceive of such a scheme. I have a right to be upset with you for turning my son against me. Even if he doesn't attack me now on your behalf, his heart is still against me."

"No, father, no!" cried Alyosha. "If I haven't attacked you it's because I can't believe you are capable of such an insult!"

"Do you hear?" cried the prince.

"Natasha, it's my fault!" Alyosha insisted. "He is not to blame, I am. To accuse him is sinful and appalling!"

"Do you hear him, Vanya?" Natasha asked. "He has already turned against me!"

"Enough!" said the prince. "We must put an end to this painful episode. This blind and furious attack of jealousy exposes a side of your personality entirely new to me. I understand now. We were in too great a rush. You don't even realize how terribly you've offended me, but that is nothing to you. We rushed into this decision. Rushed. It is appropriate that he considers my word sacred. I am his father and I wish only the best for my son.

"Your word means nothing!" Natasha cried, beside herself. "This should be a happy occasion for you! But you should know that I decided two days ago, here by myself, to release him from his promise, and I repeat it now in front of you all. I give him up!"

"Or perhaps you want to increase his anxieties again, revive his sense of duty, as you suggested before, so he feels bound to you as before. This, I think, describes your own *scheme*, but only time will tell. I'll wait for a calmer moment to discuss this with you. I hope you do not sever our relationship completely. I hope, too, that you will learn to better appreciate me. I had wanted to tell you about my plans for your family which would prove that I... But enough! Ivan Petrovich," he added, turning to me, "I have always wanted to get to know you better and I feel that now more than ever. I look forward to it. I trust you understand me. I will pay a visit to you within a few days, if you will permit me."

I bowed. I realized, too, that I could no longer avoid his acquaintance. He shook my hand, bowed to Natasha, and left with an air of affronted dignity.

Chapter Thirty

For several minutes, none of us said a word. Natasha sat thinking, sad and exhausted. All her energy had suddenly left her. She stared straight ahead, lost in thought and seeing nothing, her hand clasped in Alyosha's.

Alyosha was quietly dealing with his own grief by weeping and glancing occasionally at Natasha with timid curiosity. Finally, he made an effort to comfort her, begging her not to be angry and blaming himself. He clearly wanted to defend his father and made several half-hearted attempts to do so, but he didn't dare bring up the subject directly for fear of reigniting Natasha's wrath. He swore his undying love for Natasha and warmly defended his affection for Katya by insisting that he loved her only as a sister, a dear, sweet sister, whom he could not simply abandon. It would be unseemly behavior and cruel, as well. He assured Natasha that if she got to know Katya, the two would become inseparable friends immediately and never quarrel about anything. This idea pleased him tremendously. He was being completely honest, he insisted, and could not understand Natasha's fear or pretty much any of the things she had said earlier to his father. He only knew that Natasha and his father had had a falling out, and *that* fact lay like a stone on his heart.

"Are you blaming me for the fight with your father?" Natasha asked.

"No! How could I blame you," he asserted, "when it was entirely my fault? I drove you to anger and in your fury you accused him in order to defend me! You always stand up for me and I don't deserve it. But someone had to be at fault, so you blamed *him*, and that's just not right. I am entirely to blame!" cried Alyosha, growing more and more excited. "He was trying to be so supportive and you shocked him!"

Natasha's angry, reproachful look made him pull back quickly.

"But I'm not blaming *you*! I'm not!" he said. "I'm entirely at fault!"

"Yes, Alyosha," she went on, bitterly. "Now your father has come between us and destroyed our world… forever. You always believed in me more than anyone, but now he has poured into your heart suspicion and distrust of me. You blame me, and he has robbed me of half your heart. A black cat has run between us."

"Don't say that, Natasha! Why do you talk about a black cat?" He was hurt by the expression.

"His feigned kindness and generosity have drawn you in," Natasha continued. "And now, more and more, he will turn you against me."

"I swear to you that's not true!" Alyosha cried with renewed anguish. "He was angry when he said we had rushed into this decision. You'll see tomorrow… or the next day… he'll change his mind. And if he's still too angry to approve our marriage, I swear I won't obey him. I should have the strength for that... I think. And do you know who will help us?" he suddenly announced, delighted with his idea. "Katya will help us! And you will see what a wonderful creature she is! You will see for yourself if she is your rival and wants to separate us! And how unfair you were just now when you said I would fall out of love with you the day after our wedding! You hurt me when you said that. No, I'm not like that, and if I went often to visit Katya..."

"Hush, Alyosha, go see her whenever you like. That's not what I meant earlier. You misunderstood. Be with whomever makes you happy. I can't demand more of your heart than it can give me."

Mavra came in.

"Well, should I serve the tea now or what? It's no joke to keep the samovar boiling for two hours. It's eleven o'clock."

She spoke rudely and heatedly, evidently in a foul mood and angry with Natasha. The fact was that since Tuesday, Mavra had been excited that her young lady (of whom she was very fond) was getting married, and she had managed to spread the news throughout the house, the neighborhood, the shops, and to the porter. She had boasted about it and triumphantly told people that the prince—an important man, a general and extremely rich—had come to beg her young lady's consent and she, Mavra, had heard it all with her own ears, but now, suddenly, the plans had gone up in smoke. The prince had stormed out angrily and the tea had not been served, and, of course, it was all her young lady's fault. Mavra had heard her speaking disrespectfully to him.

"Oh... yes," Natasha replied.

"And the appetizers... shall I serve them?"

"Yes, bring them, too." Natasha was distracted.

"We've been preparing things, making plans," Mavra continued. "I've been running all over town. I ran all the way to the Neva to buy the wine... and back..." She then hurried out, slamming the door angrily.

Natasha blushed and looked strangely at me. Meanwhile, tea was served along with the appetizers. There was game, and fish of some sort, and two bottles of excellent wine from Grigory Eliseyev. "What were all these preparations for?" I wondered.

"It's all my doing, you see, Vanya," Natasha said, moving to the table, too embarrassed to face me. "I had a presentiment about everything that happened today, although I had hoped that it might end differently; that Alyosha might return and make peace and we would reconcile. All my suspicions would prove to be unfounded, and I would be convinced... and... just in case, I prepared a snack. Well, I thought we would be talking late into the night."

Poor Natasha! She blushed as she said this. Alyosha was delighted.

"You see, Natasha?" Alyosha cried. "You didn't believe it yourself. Just two hours ago you thought you might be wrong! So it can still be set right! I am to blame. I take full responsibility and I will fix this. Natasha, let me go immediately to my father! I've got to see him. He is hurt. He has been offended and needs to be comforted. I will tell him everything, speaking only for myself, I will leave you out of it. And I'll fix things. Don't be mad at me for wanting to leave you and go to him. It's not that at all. I feel sorry for him, but he will justify his behavior to you, you will see. I will be with you tomorrow as soon as it is light and I will spend the whole day with you, and I won't go to Katya's..."

Natasha did not try to stop him. She even encouraged him to go. She was terribly afraid that Alyosha would now force himself to stay with her from morning to night and soon grow bored of her. She asked only that he not speak for her, and she tried to smile a little brighter as she bid him goodbye. He was about to leave, but suddenly came to her, took both of her hands in his, and sat down beside her. He looked at her with inexpressible tenderness.

"Natasha, my darling, my angel, please don't be angry with me and let's never quarrel again. And give me your word that you will always believe me, and I will believe you. I'll tell you truthfully, my angel, there was one time when we quarreled with each other. I don't remember about what, but it was my fault. We wouldn't speak to each other. I didn't want to be the first to apologize and I was terribly miserable. So I walked around the city, wandered everywhere, went to see my friends, and my heart was so heavy, so heavy. And then I had a thought. What if you were to, let's say, fall ill and die? And as I imagined that, I suddenly felt such despair, as if I had really lost you forever. My thoughts grew more and more oppressive, more terrible. And little by little, I began to imagine myself visiting your grave and falling on it in despair, hugging your tombstone and collapsing in anguish. I imagined myself kissing the stone and calling out to you, if only for a moment, and praying to God for a miracle, that in that moment you might rise up before me. I imagined how I would have rushed to embrace you, smother you in my arms, kiss you, and then die myself in a state of bliss, having once again been able to embrace you if only for a brief moment. And as I imagined all that, I suddenly thought, why should I have to pray to God for a brief moment with you when we've been together for six months, and during those six months how many times have we quarreled, how many days did we not speak to one another? For days on end we were on bad terms and despised our happiness, so why should I be praying for you to return to me for one brief moment and be willing to give up my whole life for that moment? And as I imagined all that, I couldn't stop myself from rushing to see you as fast as I could. I ran here and you were expecting me, and as we embraced each other after that quarrel, I remember feeling like I really was losing you. Oh, Natasha, let's never quarrel again! It's always so painful for me! And, my God, how could you ever imagine that I would leave you?"

Natasha was crying. They embraced each other warmly and Alyosha once again vowed never to leave her. Then he flew off to see his father. He firmly believed that everything would soon be settled, that he would fix everything.

"It's over! All is lost!" Natasha said, pressing my hand convulsively. "He loves me and will never cease to love me, but he loves Katya, too, and in a little while he will love her more than me. And that viper, the prince, will not rest until he..."

"Natasha! I, too, believe that the prince is insincere, but..."

"You didn't believe everything that I said to him! I could see that in your face. But wait a bit and you'll see for yourself whether or not I'm right. And I was only speaking generally. God knows what else he has on his mind! He is a horrible person! I've spent four days pacing the floor here and understand everything. He had to let Alyosha follow his heart in order to relieve his son of the grief that is weighing him down, the guilt he feels for not loving me fully. He invented this proposed marriage in order to insinuate himself between us, to influence and charm Alyosha with his generosity and magnanimity. It's true, very true, Vanya! Alyosha is just such a character. He would have relaxed his anxiety about me, his unease would have been put to rest. He would think that because I was going to be his wife forever, he was free to pay more attention to Katya. The prince evidently studied Katya and realized that she and his son would make a perfect couple, that she would appeal to him more than I would. Oh, Vanya, you are my only hope now. He wants to get together with you, to become better acquainted. For God's sake, do not refuse him. Try to arrange to meet the countess. Then get to know Katya thoroughly and tell me what she is like. I trust your opinion. Nobody understands me like you do, and you will understand what I want. Find out how close their friendship really is and what they talk about. It is Katya, Katya above all, that you should study. Show me one more time, my dear, my beloved Vanya, what a good friend you are! You are my hope, my only hope now!"

By the time I returned home it was past midnight. Nellie opened the door to me with a sleepy face. She smiled and looked at me. The poor thing was really annoyed with herself for having fallen asleep. She had tried to wait up for me. She told me that someone had stopped by to see me, had sat with her awhile, and then left a note on the table. The note was from Masloboyev. He wanted me to call on him the next day at one o'clock. I wanted to ask Nellie more about Masloboyev's visit, but I postponed the conversation until morning, insisting that she should go right to sleep. The poor child had exhausted herself waiting up for me and had only just fallen asleep a half hour before my arrival.

Chapter Thirty-One

The next morning, Nellie told me some strange things about Masloboyev's visit of the night before. It had seemed odd to me that Masloboyev would call in the evening when he knew that I would not be at home (I had told him that during our most recent conversation). At first, Nellie told me, she had been afraid to unlock the door and admit him, but he had pleaded, assuring her that if he did not leave a note for me, the consequences would be very bad for me the next day. When she finally let him in, he immediately wrote a note, went up to her and sat down beside her on the couch.

"I got up and did not want to talk to him," Nellie said. "He scared me. Then he started talking about the Bubnova, how angry she was, and that she daren't try to take me back now. He began to praise you, Vanya, and said that you two were great friends. That he had known you when you were a boy. When I started talking to him, he brought out some candy and offered it to me, but I didn't want to take it. He kept assuring me that he was a good man and that he knew how to sing and dance. Then he jumped up and started to dance. It made me laugh. Then he said he would sit with me a while longer. 'I'll wait for Vanya,' he said. 'Maybe he'll come back soon.' He told me I shouldn't be afraid and asked me to sit down next to him. I sat down, but I still didn't feel like talking. Then he told me that he used to know my mother and my grandfather, and then... then I started to speak... and he stayed a long time."

"And what did you talk about?"

"Oh... about Mama... the Bubnova... and my grandfather. He stayed for two hours.

Nellie didn't seem to want to tell me what they had discussed, so I didn't push her, hoping to learn everything later from Masloboyev, although it seemed obvious that he had deliberately stopped by when I wouldn't be home in order to catch Nellie alone. I wondered why.

Nellie showed me three candies he had given her. They were wrapped in small pieces of red and green paper. "They smelled nasty," she laughed. "He probably bought them at a greengrocer's."

"Why haven't you eaten them?" I asked.

"I don't want to," she answered with an exaggerated frown. "I didn't take them. He left them on the couch."

That day I had a lot of running around to do, so I started to say goodbye to Nellie.

"Are you going to be bored here all alone?" I asked on my way to the door.

"Bored, but not bored. I'll only be bored because you'll be gone a long time."

She looked at me with so much love as she said this. In fact, all that morning she had stared at me with the same fond, gentle glance, cheerful and friendly, but at the same time, there was something almost bashful, even timid, about her, as if she were afraid she might do or say something to annoy me and perhaps diminish my affection for her. And she seemed too embarrassed to say anything.

"And why *not* bored, then?" I asked. "After all, you said that you would be 'bored but not bored.'" I could not help smiling at her as she gave me a sweet and playful look.

"Oh, I know why," she said, grinning and looking embarrassed again. We talked in the doorway with the door open. Nellie was standing in front of me, her eyes downcast, one hand clutching my shoulder and the other pinching the sleeve of my coat.

"What? Is it a secret?" I asked.

"No... nothing... I... I have begun reading your book while you're away," she said softly and looked up at me with a gentle, penetrating gaze. Her cheeks were turning red.

"Aah, so that's it! Well, do you like it?" I was a self-conscious author seeking praise, and would have given, God knows what, if I could have kissed her at that moment. But I knew, somehow, that with Nellie that was not possible. She stood silently.

"Why… why did he die?" Nellie asked finally with a look of deep sadness. She looked at me again briefly and then lowered her eyes.

"Who?"

"The young man in your book… with consumption."

"What could I do, Nellie? It was inevitable."

"It was not inevitable," she answered softly, almost in a whisper, but a moment later she suddenly and angrily pouted her lips and stared indignantly at the floor.

Another minute passed.

"And she… well, will they… the girl and the old man," she whispered, still pinching from time to time at my sleeve. "Will they live together? And not be poor anymore?"

"No, Nellie, she will go away and marry a country gentleman, and he will be left alone." I answered with the utmost regret, truly sorry that I could not tell her something more comforting.

"Well, that's… that's terrible! Yech! I don't want to read it now!"

She angrily pushed my hand away and turned her back. She then moved to the desk and stared into the corner of the room, her eyes on the floor. She was flushed and breathing irregularly, as if by some terrible disappointment.

"Come on, Nellie, don't be angry!" I started toward her. "It's not true, you know… the things I write. It's just fiction. There's no reason to be angry! You're such a sensitive little girl!"

"I'm not angry," she said shyly, looking up at me with such a sweet, tender expression. Suddenly, she grabbed my hand and pressed her face against my chest. Then, for some reason, she began to cry.

But at that same moment, she started laughing. She was crying and laughing at the same time. I, too, started laughing, thinking it funny but, at the same time, somehow sweet. But she would not allow me to lift her head, and when I tried to pull her little face from my chest, she pressed it against me more firmly, still unable to stop laughing.

Finally, this tender moment ended and we said good-bye. I was in a hurry. Nellie was flushed and in her embarrassment her eyes shone like stars. She ran after me on the stairs and implored me to come back soon. I promised to be back in time for dinner and as early as possible.

My first visit was to the Ichmenyevs. Anna Andreyevna was very sick. Nikolai Sergeich was locked away in his office and although he had heard me arrive, I knew it would be a quarter of an hour before he would join us, giving his wife and me time to talk. I didn't want to upset Anna Andreyevna, so I softened as much as possible my story about the previous night, but I told her the truth. To my surprise, while the old woman was disappointed, she was not at all startled to learn of the possible break-up.

"Well, Vanya, it is just what I expected," she said. "After your last visit, I thought about it and came to the conclusion that it would never happen. We do not deserve such a blessing. And he is such an evil man, who could expect anything good from him? He is taking ten thousand rubles from us for nothing. He knows it's for nothing, but he'll take it anyway. He'll grab the last piece of bread from our mouths and force us to sell Ichmenyevka. Natasha is smart and absolutely right to distrust him. But you know, my poor, poor husband," she continued, lowering her voice, "he has been opposed to the wedding. He doesn't want to admit it. At first, I thought he was just being foolish, but he means it. Well then, what will happen to my little darling? He has already cursed her. And what about Alyosha? What does he say?"

She questioned me for a long time and, as usual, sighed and moaned over each of my answers. Recently, I had noticed that she seemed more and more off balance. Any news shocked her. Her anxiety over Natasha was breaking her heart and destroying her health.

The old man came in wearing a bathrobe and slippers. He complained of feeling feverish, but greeted his wife warmly, and while I was with them, he looked after her like a nurse, looking into her eyes and smiling almost timidly. There was a great deal of tenderness in the way he looked at her. He was terrified of her illness, knowing he would be lost if she were to die.

I stayed with them for an hour. When I got up to leave, he came with me to the front door and started talking about Nellie. He was seriously thinking of taking her into his house as a substitute for his daughter, Natasha. He wanted my advice on how to win Anna Andreyevna's approval. With special curiosity he asked me about Nellie and if I had learned anything new about her. I filled him in briefly and my story seemed to make an impression on him.

"We'll talk about it," he said firmly, "but for the time being... Well, I will come and see you when my health is a little better. Then we'll decide."

Exactly at one o'clock I was at Masloboyev's. To my great surprise, the first person I encountered was the prince! He was standing in the doorway putting on his coat while Masloboyev hurriedly helped him and handed him his walking stick. Masloboyev had already told me he was acquainted with the prince, but this meeting astonished me greatly.

The prince seemed confused when he saw me.

"Oh, it's you!" he cried with feigned enthusiasm. "Imagine running into you. But I have just now learned from Mr. Masloboyev that he is familiar with you. I am glad, very glad to have met you and I would very much like to speak with you. I hope you will allow me to call on you as soon as possible. I have a favor to ask. Help me to explain our present situation. You understand, of course, that I am referring to what happened yesterday. You are a close friend and have been following the whole course of this affair. You have influence. I'm terribly sorry I can't stop to talk with you now. Business! But in a few days, perhaps even sooner, I'll have the pleasure of meeting with you. For now..."

He shook hands with me enthusiastically, exchanged glances with Masloboyev, and hurried away.

"Tell me, for God's sake..." I began as I entered the room.

"I can't tell you anything right now," Masloboyev interrupted, hurriedly grabbing his hat and heading for the front door. "Important business! I must run, my boy, I'm late!"

"But you wrote me to come at one o'clock."

"So what if I wrote you? That was yesterday, and today I've learned something that has my head spinning. Such news! They're waiting for me. Forgive me, Vanya. If you want satisfaction for my wasting your time, you can punch me in the head. If that will please you, go ahead and punch me, but do it quickly for Christ's sake! I can't be late, they're waiting!"

"Why should I punch you? If unexpected things happen, plans change. But tell me..."

"No, that's all I can say for now," he interrupted, rushing past me as he put on his overcoat. I followed his action and put my own coat back on. "I have something very important to tell you," he continued. "Something that concerns you and your interests. But it will take more than a minute so, for God's sake, come back later, around seven o'clock; a little earlier or a little later, I'll be home."

"This evening," I said, with confusion, "I was planning to go to..."

"So, my boy, go now where you wanted to go this evening and in the evening come to see me! Vanya, you cannot imagine the things I have to tell you!"

"Yes, all right, but can't you give me a hint? I admit, you've piqued my curiosity."

By this time, we had reached the gates of the house and were standing on the pavement.

"So you'll come?" he asked insistently.

"I said I would."

"No, give me your word of honor."

"Oy, what a fellow! You have my word of honor."

"Excellent and noble. Which way are you going?"

"There," I answered, pointing to the right.

"Well, I'm going that way," he said, pointing to the left. "Farewell, Vanya! Remember, seven o'clock!"

"Strange," I thought, looking after him.

I had intended to visit Natasha that evening, but as I was now committed to Masloboyev, I decided to go to her now. I was sure I'd find Alyosha with Natasha and, indeed, he was there and very glad to see me.

He was very sweet and gentle with Natasha and brightened up when I came in. Natasha tried to appear cheerful, but it was evident that she was greatly distressed. Her face was pale and sick, and she had not slept. She was extremely affectionate with Alyosha.

Alyosha spoke almost non-stop, clearly trying to cheer up Natasha, whose expression remained grimly serious, and he was obviously avoiding any mention of either Katya or his father. Evidently his efforts at reconciliation had failed.

"Do you know what?" Natasha whispered to me quickly when he stepped out to give some order to Mavra, "He wants badly to get away from me. But he's afraid. And I'm afraid to tell him that it's all right, because he might then decide to stay on purpose. But most of all I'm afraid he will get bored with me and grow cold. What am I to do?"

"My God, what a position you two have put yourselves in! And how suspicious and watchful you are of one another. Just explain to him how you feel and get it over with. He may be just as frustrated with the situation as you."

"But what can I do?" she cried, frightened.

"Wait, I'll settle this." And I went into the kitchen under the pretext of asking Mavra to clean one of my overshoes which had mud on it.

"Be careful, Vanya!" she shouted after me. As soon as I went to Mavra, Alyosha rushed toward me as if he had been waiting for me.

"Ivan Petrovich, my dear fellow, what am I to do? Advise me. Yesterday I gave my word to Katya I would visit her today, right about now. I cannot disappoint her! I love Natasha beyond words. I would walk through fire for her, but you must agree that I can't just ignore my obligations over there..."

"Well, then go."

"But what shall I do about Natasha? After all, I don't want to grieve her. Dear Ivan Petrovich, help me..."

"In my opinion, you should just go. You know how much she loves you. If you stay, it will seem like you are bored and being forced to sit with her. Do what's best for you. But follow my lead. I'll help you."

"My dear Ivan Petrovich, how good you are!"

We went back. After a minute, I said to him, "By the way, I have seen your father."

"Where?" he cried, frightened.

"On the street, by chance. He stopped to speak with me for a moment, and again suggested that he wanted to get to know me better. He asked about you, and if I knew where you were now. He seemed anxious to find you, to tell you something."

"Ah, Alyosha, you should go and see him," Natasha said, following my lead.

"But... where will I find him now? Is he at home?"

"No, I remember, he said he would be at the countess's."

"But what about...?" Alyosha asked naively, looking sadly at Natasha.

"What's wrong, Alyosha?" she asked. "Do you really think you have to give up your friends in order to placate me? That's silly. First of all, it's not possible, and second, you're being ungrateful to Katya. You two are friends and it is rude to just cut her off. Finally, you insult me if you think that I'm so jealous of you. Go immediately, I beg you, and calm your father down."

"Natasha, you're such an angel and I'm not worthy of you!" Alyosha cried with both delight and remorse. "You are so good, while I... I... Well, let me tell you! In the kitchen, I asked Ivan Petrovich to help me get away from you and this was his plan. But don't judge me, Natasha, my angel! I'm not entirely to blame, because I love you a thousand times more than anyone else, so I've invented a new plan—to open up to Katya and tell her all about our present situation and about what happened yesterday. She'll think of some way to save us, she's devoted to us with all her heart and soul..."

"Well, go then," Natasha answered with a smile, "and tell Katya that I would love to get to know her as a friend. How can we arrange that?"

Alyosha was delighted. He immediately launched into a hypothetical plan to bring the two together. It would be so easy, he thought. He grew more and more excited at the idea. He promised to bring back an answer that very day, in less than two hours, and then he would spend the rest of the evening with Natasha.

"Will you really come?" Natasha asked, following him to the door.

"Do you doubt it? Farewell, Natasha, my dear, my eternal love! And good-bye, Vanya! Oh, my God, I accidentally called you Vanya! Listen, Ivan Petrovich, I love you. Let me call you Vanya. Let's drop formalities."

"Yes, let us," I said.

"Oh, thank goodness! Because I've thought of it a hundred times but didn't dare to ask you. Thank you, Ivan Petrovich. Wait, I've done it again. But it is very difficult to say Vanya all of a sudden. I remember Tolstoy wrote something about two people who promise to call each other by their pet names but can't quite manage it so they use no names at all. Oh, Natasha, someday you must re-read *Childhood, Adolescence, Youth*."

"Yes, I will, but go, go, go," Natasha laughed, pushing him toward the door. "He's chattering away with such joy..."

"Good-bye! I'll see you in two hours!"

He kissed her hand and hurried away.

"You see, you see, Vanya!" she said and burst into tears.

I sat with her for two hours, attempting to comfort her, and succeeding at last. She was right about everything, of course—all her fears and apprehensions. My heart ached when I thought of her present situation. I was afraid for her, but what could I do?

Alyosha seemed strange to me, too. He loved Natasha no less than before, perhaps even more—stronger, but more painfully—out of remorse and gratitude. But at the same time, a new love had invaded his heart. How it would end, it was impossible to foresee. I, too, was looking forward to meeting Katya. I promised Natasha again that I would.

In the end, she seemed much happier. Meanwhile, I told her all about Nellie, Masloboyev and Madame Bubnova, about my unexpected meeting today with the prince, and my designated date with Masloboyev at seven o'clock. All of this seemed to interest her greatly. I spoke briefly about her parents but did not mention her father's visit to my apartment or his desire for a duel with Prince Valkovsky, as I knew that might scare her. She seemed puzzled by the prince's connection to Masloboyev and his great desire to befriend me, although the latter made some sense given the present situation.

At three o'clock, I went back home. Nellie greeted me with her bright little face.

CHAPTER THIRTY-TWO

At exactly seven o'clock I was at Masloboyev's. He greeted me with loud cries and open arms. Needless to say, he was half drunk. But most of all, I was surprised by the extraordinary preparation for our meeting. It was evident that I was expected. An attractive brass samovar was boiling on a small round table covered by a beautiful tablecloth. The tea service glittered with crystal, silver and porcelain. On another table, covered with a different but no less luxurious cloth, stood plates of delectable sweets, fruit preserves (both dried and liquid) from Kiev and France, jellies, candy, oranges, apples, and three or four varieties of nuts. In effect, a virtual fruit shop. On a third table, covered with a snow-white cloth, stood a variety of snacks: caviar, cheese, a pie, sausages, smoked ham, fish, and a row of fine crystal decanters filled with spirits in a variety of colors—green, ruby, brown and gold. Finally, off to the side stood a small table covered with a white cloth, with two bottles of champagne. On the table before the sofa stood three bottles—Sauterne, Lafitte and Cognac—all expensive labels from Eliseyev's. At the tea table sat Alexandra Semyonovna wearing a simple dress, but one apparently chosen with thought and deliberation. She knew what looked good on her and took pride in her appearance. She stood up to greet me with a subdued grace. Her fresh little face beamed with enchantment and pleasure. Masloboyev was wearing beautiful Chinese slippers, an expensive dressing-gown, and fresh, elegant linen garments. On his shirt and anywhere else that had attachments, he wore fashionable cufflinks and buttons. His hair was combed, pomaded and fashionably parted on the side.

I was so taken aback that I stopped in the middle of the room and stared, open-mouthed, first at Masloboyev, and then at Alexandra Semyonovna, who glowed with blissful satisfaction.

"What is the meaning of all this, Masloboyev? Are you having a party here tonight?" I finally asked, uneasily.

"No, only you," he answered solemnly.

"But why?" I asked, pointing at the savories. "You have enough food here for a regiment!"

"And drink. Don't ignore the main attraction—drink!" added Masloboyev.

"And this is all for me alone?"

"And for Alexandra Semyonovna. It was her pleasure to arrange it."

"Well, it's just as I expected," Alexandra Semyonovna said, flushing, but not without satisfaction. "Either I can't receive a visitor properly or I'm accused of overdoing it!"

"Ever since this morning when she learned that you were joining us tonight, she has been bustling about in the throes of a..."

"And that's a lie! It's not since this morning I've been planning, but since last night when you told me the gentleman was coming this evening..."

"She misunderstood me."

"I did not misunderstand! That's exactly what you said! I never lie. And why shouldn't I prepare for a guest? We go on and on, day after day, and no one ever comes to visit. I want our friends to see that we can entertain them as well as anyone."

"And, most importantly," added Masloboyev, "to see what a beautiful mistress and hostess you are. Imagine, my friend, I was caught up in the middle of all this, too. She stuffed me into this linen shirt, covered me in cufflinks and studs, added Chinese slippers and a dressing-gown, then she combed and pomaded my hair with bergamot oil. She tried to sprinkle me with perfume—crème brûlée—but *that* I simply could not allow. I had to take a stand and assert my conjugal authority!"

"It was not bergamot! It was the best French pomatum in a painted porcelain jar!" Alexandra Semyonovna retorted, her face turning crimson. "Judge for yourself, Ivan Petrovich, he never lets me go to a theater or a dance. He gives me only dresses, more and more dresses. I put them on and all I can do is parade around this room. The other day, I finally persuaded him to take me to the theater, and just as I turned to fasten my brooch, he went to the cupboard and drank one glass after another until he could barely stand. And so we stayed at home. The fact is that no one, absolutely no one, ever comes to visit. In the morning, he sometimes has people stop in to discuss business, but he always chases me out. Yet we have samovars and a dinner service and fine cups. We've everything—all gifts. We rarely buy anything but the spirits… and the pomade. All those goodies—the pie, the ham, the fish, and the sweets—those we bought for *you*. If only others could see how we live. For a year I thought, if we ever have a guest, any guest, we would show them all this and entertain them. And they would compliment us and it would feel nice. As for my pomading him, the fool, he's not worth the effort. He'd be happy in dirty rags. Look at that beautiful dressing-gown. It was a present. But why give him such a robe when he would much rather just get drunk? You'll see, he'll offer you vodka before we take tea."

"What? But, of course, I'll offer him a drink. Come, Vanya, join me in a glass of gold or silver seal, and then, when our minds are refreshed, we'll move on to the other beverages."

"See, I knew it!'

"Don't worry, Sashenka, we'll drink a cup of tea, too—with brandy in it—to your health."

"Well, that's perfect!" she cried, clasping her hands. "It's China Black Tea, six rubles a tin. The merchant made a gift of it three days ago. And you want to pour brandy in it! Do not listen to him, Ivan Petrovich. I will pour you a cup and you shall discover for yourself how fine tea should taste."

And she busied herself at the samovar.

It was clear that they both intended to keep me there the entire evening. Alexandra Semyonovna had been anticipating visitors for a year and she was prepared to give me a year's worth of hospitality. This did not fit in with *my* plans.

"Listen, Masloboyev," I said, sitting down. "I've not come to pay a visit. You invited me here because you had something to tell me."

"Well, business is business, but there is time for a friendly conversation, as well."

"No, my dear friend, do not count on me. At half past eight I will have to say good-bye. I have an appointment, and I gave my word..."

"I do not think so. Good heavens, what are you doing to me? What are you doing to Alexandra Semyonovna? Just look at her, she is dumbfounded. Why did she take the trouble to pomade me? I'm drenched in bergamot!"

"You're making jokes again, Masloboyev. My dear Alexandra Semyonovna, I swear that next week, or perhaps Friday, if you like, I will come for dinner. But this evening I have given my word to be… at a certain place." I turned to Masloboyev again. "It is best that you give me the news that you wanted to report."

"So you really must leave at half past eight?" Alexandra Semyonovna asked in a timid and plaintive voice. She was almost in tears as she handed me a cup of tea.

"Don't worry, Sasha, that's all nonsense," Masloboyev said. "He'll stay. That's nonsense. But tell me, Vanya, what is so important that you have to run out on us? Where are you going? What are you doing? May I know? Because every time I see you, you're running off somewhere. You don't work..."

"Why do you want to know? Perhaps I'll tell you later. But I would like you to explain why you came to visit me yesterday when I had told you I would not be home?"

"I only remembered afterwards but had forgotten at the time. I really wanted to talk with you, but most of all I wanted to please Alexandra Semyonovna. 'There is a man,' I told her, 'an old friend I have rediscovered. Why not invite him over?' And let me tell you, brother, she has been pestering me for the last four days to get you over here. Perhaps I will be forgiven forty sins in the next world for having to deal with the bergamot in this, but is it such a terrible thing for you to spend an evening in friendly conversation with us? I went about it strategically; I wrote to say that if you did not come, my ship would be sunk."

I implored him not to do so again, but just to speak to me directly. However, his explanation did not entirely satisfy me.

"Well, why did you run away from me this morning?" I asked.

"Oh, this morning I really did have business. That was not a lie."

"Not with the prince?"

"Do you like our tea?" Alexandra Semyonovna asked in a honied tone.

She had been waiting five minutes for me to praise her tea, but I had been oblivious.

"Splendid, Alexandra Semyonovna, excellent! I'm not used to such quality tea."

Alexandra Semyonovna blushed with delight and hurried to pour me another.

"The prince!" cried Masloboyev, "the prince. That fellow is a rogue, a rascal! I admit, brother, that I am a bit of a rogue myself, but out of sheer decency I would not want to be in his skin! But enough. My lips are sealed! That is as much as I can tell you about him!"

"But, among other things, I have come here *specifically* to ask about him. But that can wait 'til later. What I'd like to know *now* is why you gave Elena candy yesterday and danced in front of her? And what could you have found to talk about with her for so long?"

Masloboyev turned suddenly to Alexandra Semyonovna. "Elena is a little girl of eleven or twelve who is currently living with Ivan Petrovich." He turned back to me with a finger pointed at her. "Look, Vanya, look. See how jealous she became when she heard that I was visiting an unknown girl and bringing her sweets. She's flushed and trembling as if we had suddenly fired a pistol at her! Her little eyes are smoldering like burning coal. You can't pretend you weren't a little jealous, Alexandra Semyonovna, it's clear as day! Jealous, Vanya. If I hadn't explained to her that the girl is an eleven-year-old, she would have pulled out my hair and the bergamot wouldn't have saved me!"

"Nothing will save you now!"

And with these words, Alexandra Semyonovna leapt from the tea-table, and before Masloboyev could shield his head, she grabbed a fistful of his hair and pulled.

"That's for you, for you! Don't you dare tell a visitor that I was jealous, don't you dare, don't you dare, don't you dare!"

She was blushing and laughing at the same time, but Masloboyev still caught a dose of her anger.

"He says all sorts of shameful things!" she added, seriously, turning to me.

"Well, Vanya, you see what life is like for me? Is it any wonder I enjoy a drop of vodka?" Masloboyev straightened his hair and almost ran to the decanter. But Alexandra Semyonovna reached for it first and poured a glass. She then handed it to Masloboyev and patted him on the cheek. Masloboyev proudly winked at me, clicked his tongue, and solemnly drank his vodka.

"As for the sweets, it's difficult to say," he said, sitting down beside me on the couch. "I bought them the day before—while I was drunk—at the greengrocers. I don't know why. Perhaps to support the local tradesmen, can't say for certain, but I do remember walking down the street, very drunk, and falling in the mud. I tore at my hair and cried out that my life was worthless. Of course, I forgot about the candies, so they stayed in my pocket until yesterday when I sat down on them on your couch. The same thing happened with the dancing, another symptom of inebriation. I was quite drunk again yesterday and when I'm drunk, I sometimes love to dance. That's really all there was to it, except that this little orphan girl excited pity in me, and when she refused to talk because of her anger, I danced to cheer her up, and gave her the candies."

"And you were not trying to bribe her to wean some information from her? I suspected that *that* was your real motive when you came to my house, knowing I would not be home, in order to chat with her one-to-one and learn something or other. Because I know you spent an hour-and-a-half with her, assured her that you had known her dead mother, and asked her questions."

Masloboyev narrowed his eyes and smiled slyly.

"It certainly would have been a clever thing to do," he said. "But no, Vanya, it's not true. But what would have been so bad if I *had* done that... although I didn't. Look, old friend, I am now quite drunk again, as usual, but know that Philip Philippich would never with evil intent lie to you... with evil intent, that is."

"Yes, but would you lie to me *without* evil intent?"

"Well... even without evil intent. But to hell with it, let's have a drink and then take care of business! It's not insignificant to note," he continued, drinking, "this Bubnova woman had no legal right to keep the girl, I found out. There was no adoption or official agreement. The mother owed her money, so she took hold of the girl. Bubnova is a wicked crone and a scheming hag, but she is also a fool, like all women. The deceased woman had a legitimate passport, so everything is quite legal. Elena is free to live with you, though it would be better if some benevolent family would take her in and give her a proper home. But meanwhile, let her stay with you. It's a simple matter, I'll take care of it. Bubnova dare not lift a finger. As for Elena's mother, I've learned a few pertinent facts. She is the widow of someone by the name of Saltzman."

"Yes, Nellie told me that."

"Well, Vanya" he began with a certain solemnity, "that takes care of that matter. But now I have a certain favor to ask of you and it is important that you grant it. Tell me what you have been up to recently, where you go when you disappear for whole days at a time. Though I've heard rumors, and you've given me scattered clues, I need to know much more."

Such solemnity surprised me and even made me uneasy.

"Why do you ask? Why is it so important? You make it sound so solemn."

"Look, Vanya, without mincing words, I want to do you a service. You see, my friend, if I weren't being honest with you, I could learn what I need to know without the solemnity. But you've suggested that I'm trying to deceive you—asking about the candy just now—I understand that. But I'm being serious with you now so you'll understand that it is not for myself I ask this, but for you. So do not hesitate to be blunt and answer truthfully."

"But what kind of service? Listen, Masloboyev, why won't you answer any of my questions about the prince? That's why I came here. *That* would be a service."

"About the prince? Hmm. Well, so be it. But first I have to ask *you* a few questions about the prince."

"Why?"

"I'll tell you why, my friend. It's become clear to me that the prince is somehow mixed up in your affairs. Among other things, he asked me about you. How he found out that we know each other... is none of your business. The only important thing is that you be on your guard against the prince. He is a treacherous Judas and worse. So when I saw that he was involved in your affairs, I trembled for you. But I don't yet understand *how* he is involved. That's why I beg you to tell me everything you know. That's why I asked you here today. That is the important business I needed to discuss with you."

"At least tell me something, anything, about why I should be afraid of the prince."

"Well, so be it. You should know, brother, that I am sometimes employed in certain matters of a confidential nature. If I am trusted, it is because my clients know that I am not a chatterbox. That makes it difficult for me to reveal what I know, so you'll understand if I speak in general, very generally, about how I know what a scoundrel he is. But first, I need to hear your own story."

I decided that I had no reason to hide my personal business from Masloboyev. Natasha's situation was clearly not a secret, and it seemed reasonable to believe that Masloboyev's assistance could benefit me. Of course, I left out certain points in my story that I didn't want to share, but gave him as much as possible. Masloboyev listened attentively, especially to anything that concerned the prince, stopping me several times and asking me to repeat what I had said in greater detail. My story went on for half an hour.

"Hmm! That girl has quite a brain," decided Masloboyev. "If she hasn't quite guessed what the prince is up to, she recognized early on that he is a threat and broke off relations with him. Well done, Natalia Nikolayevna! I drink to her health!" He took a drink. "It's not only her brain, but her heart that served her well. Her heart saw that she was being deceived. Of course, she'll still lose in the end. The prince will insist on getting his way and Alyosha will let her go. I feel especially sorry for her father. Ichmenyev will have to pay ten thousand rubles to the scoundrel! But who has taken up his case, acted on his behalf? No one. I'm betting he represented himself. Ech! These noble, exalted creatures are worthless in matters of the law. That's not how to fight the prince. I would have found a first-rate lawyer for Ichmenyev, kaboom!" And he angrily banged on the table.

"So, tell me now about Prince Valkovsky."

"You're still going on about Valkovsky? What else can I say? I'm sorry I made the offer. I just wanted to warn you, Vanya, about this scoundrel... to protect you, so to speak, from his influence. Anyone who gets mixed up with him is not safe. So keep your eyes open, that's all. You've probably been imagining, God knows what, about some secrets I've uncovered in Paris. I can see you are, indeed, a novelist! But what else do you need to know about the scoundrel? A villain is a villain. But here is one example. I'll tell you one bit of business, without giving any names or places or towns, and without accurately dating the incident. You may have heard that when he was a young man, when he was still forced to live on a clerk's salary, he married a rich merchant's daughter. He treated his wife in a most uncivil manner, and though it does not matter now, I will note, Vanya, that he has always managed to turn such affairs to his financial advantage. Here's another example. He went abroad. There..."

"Wait, Masloboyev, which trip abroad are you describing? In what year?"

"Exactly ninety-nine years and three months ago. Well, there he seduced the daughter of a certain father and took her with him to Paris. Well, something happened there. The father was some sort of merchant or involved in some business enterprise. I don't know the details. I'm just telling you what little I've been able to deduce from available information. The prince cheated the man and weaseled his way into his business. He destroyed the company and absconded with the money. The old man had documents, of course, that proved he had been swindled, but the prince had no intention of giving the money back. In simple Russian, he stole it. Well, as I said, the old man had a daughter who was very beautiful, and this beauty was in love with her ideal man, one of the Schiller brotherhood, a poet, and at the same time, a merchant, a young dreamer—in a word, a German, a Pfefferkuchen."

"That was his name? Pfefferkuchen?"

"Well, maybe not Pfefferkuchen, for God's sake, it does not matter. But the prince made a move on the daughter and she fell foolishly in love with him. The prince wanted two things: first, to possess the girl, and second, to obtain the documents her father had proving his deception. The keys to the old man's strong box were in the daughter's keeping. The old man loved his daughter with so much passion that he did not want her to marry. Seriously. He was jealous of every suitor and would not consider parting with her. He drove Pfefferkuchen away. He was an eccentric Englishman, the father..."

"An Englishman? But where did all this happen?"

"I only used Englishman hypothetically and you caught me on it. Well, it happened in Santa-Fe-de-Bogota, or perhaps in Krakow, but it was most likely in Nassau, like the label on the bottles of seltzer water—yes, it was certainly in Nassau—does that satisfy you? Well, the prince seduced the girl and stole her away from her father and, at the insistence of the prince, she brought with her the incriminating documents. There is, after all, that kind of love, Vanya, may God help us! She was an honest girl, noble, principled. It's true, she probably had no idea of the significance of the papers, but she feared only one thing—her father's curse. The prince reassured her by making a legal promise, on paper, that he would marry her. In this way, he was able to convince her that they were only going abroad for a little while, on a honeymoon, and when the old man's anger subsided, they would return as man and wife and the three of them would live the good life ever after, and so on *ad infinitum*. They ran away, the father cursed her and then went bankrupt. They were followed to Paris by Frauenmilch, who threw away everything, including his business, he was so much in love."

"Stop! Who is Frauenmilch?"

"Well, that fellow… what was his name? Feuerbach, then... ugh, damn it. Pfefferkuchen! Well, the prince, of course, could not marry her. What would society think? So he had to deceive her. He did so in a very cruel fashion. First, he almost beat her, and secondly, he purposefully invited Pfefferkuchen to visit them. Pfefferkuchen came and was welcomed as a friend. He would sit alone with the girl many an evening and they would whimper and bemoan their fate, comforting each other. They were simple, loving souls. The prince arranged all of this on purpose, so he could eventually walk in on them and invent an intrigue, find fault with something they were doing, claiming he had witnessed it with his own eyes. Well, he gave them both the gate, and moved to London, where he lived for a time. Not much later, she gave birth to a daughter… wait… did I say daughter? I meant to say a son. That was the prince's son, whom she christened Volodka, and Pfefferkuchen was made the godfather. So she went off with Pfefferkuchen. He had a little money. They toured Switzerland, Italy... all of the poetic locations. She cried a lot and Pfefferkuchen whimpered, and so many years passed by, and the baby grew into a little girl. And everything was going well for the prince except for one thing. He had never retrieved his written obligation to marry the woman. 'You're a terrible man,' she had said when she left him. 'You robbed me and defiled me and then deserted me. Goodbye! But I will not give you the written commitment. Not because I ever want to marry you, but because you are afraid of this document. So it will never leave my possession.' She lost her temper, but the prince remained calm. Generally, his type of scoundrel always triumphs over so-called exalted beings who are so noble they are easily deceived. They almost always choose sublime and noble contempt over the more practical application of business law, even when it is on their side. Well, here at least, the young mother escaped with her proud disdain, and even though she kept the document, the prince knew that she would rather hang herself than use it to take him to court, so he was at peace for a time. And although she spat in his vile face, she still had Volodka in her possession and if she should die what would happen to him? But she didn't concern herself with this. Bruderschraft, too, encouraged her not to talk about it. He read her Schiller. Finally, Bruderschraft became ill and died..."

"You mean Pfefferkuchen?"

"Whatever the hell… Then she..."

"Wait a minute! How many years had they been traveling?"

"Exactly two hundred. Well, she came back to Krakow. Her father refused to see her, cursed her, she died, and the prince crossed himself with joy. I was there, too, and let me tell you, the whisky flowed like a waterfall, with plenty of liquor for one and all. Let us drink, brother Vanya!"

"I suspect that you have had a hand in this case, Masloboyev."

"You would certainly have it so, it seems."

"But I do not understand just what your involvement is!"

"Well, you see, when she moved back to Madrid, after a ten-year absence, under an assumed name, someone had to verify the information about Bruderschraft and the old man and the child, and determine if the mother had died, and whether or not the papers still existed, and so on and so forth. Yes, and even more than that. The prince is a dreadful man, Vanya, beware of him, but don't ever think that Masloboyev is a scoundrel! Though he *is* a scoundrel—because, in my opinion, there is no man who isn't—Masloboyev is never a scoundrel in his dealings with you. I'm drunk, but listen... If ever, near or far, sooner or later, now or next year, you should think that Masloboyev has in any way bamboozled you—and please do not forget that word, bamboozled—you should know that it is not with evil intent. Masloboyev is watching over you. So do not believe your suspicions, but rather come to Masloboyev and talk to him candidly and like a brother. Well now, will you have a drink?"

"No."

"Something to eat?"

"No, brother, I'm sorry..."

"Well then, get a move on. It's a quarter to nine and you have commitments. Now you have to go."

"Well, what next?" Alexandra Semyonovna cried, almost in tears. "He gets drunk and drives away our guest! It's always like this! He's shameless!"

"A walking man is poor company for an equestrian, Alexandra Semyonovna. But you and I shall be left alone to adore each other. This general... No, Vanya, I lied. You are not a general, but I am certainly a scoundrel! What do I look like now? What am I to you? Forgive me, Vanya, do not condemn me, but let me vent..."

He hugged me and burst into tears. I started to leave.

"Oh, my God! And we've prepared dinner for you!" said Alexandra Semyonovna with a terrible moan. "But you *will* come to us on Friday, won't you?"

"I will, Alexandra Semyonovna, honestly. I promise."

"Perhaps you look down on him because he is such a... drunk," she added. "Do not condemn him, Ivan Petrovich, he is a kind man, very kind, and he loves you so much! You are all he talks about day and night, nothing but you. He went and bought your book for me, though I haven't read it yet. I'll start tomorrow. And how happy I will be when you come! No one ever comes to visit us and we have so much to share and yet I sit all alone. But tonight, I have been sitting here listening, listening to everything you've said, and how good it feels. So, until Friday..."

Chapter Thirty-Three

I hurried home with Masloboyev's words burning in my ears. All manner of thoughts filled my brain. As luck would have it, an event awaited me at home that would shock me like a lightning bolt.

Above the gates of the house where I lodged was a streetlamp. Just as I approached the gate, the light of the lamp illuminated a strange figure as it darted towards me. Half-crazed and trembling with fright, it screamed as it clutched my hands. Horror gripped me. It was Nellie!

"Nellie! What is it?" I cried. "What's the matter?"

"There, upstairs... He's in our rooms... He..."

"Who is? Come along, come with me."

"I won't! I don't want to see him! I'll wait until he leaves... on the staircase... I won't!"

I went up to my room with a strange foreboding. I opened the door and saw… the prince. He was sitting at the table reading my novel. At the very least, the book was open before him.

"Ivan Petrovich!" he cried with apparent delight. "I'm so glad you've finally returned. I was just about to leave. I've been waiting for more than an hour for you. I gave my word to the countess that I would bring you to see her this evening. She begged me most emphatically as she is most eager to meet you! So, as I had already given my promise to call on you, I thought I would come by early, before you had a chance to go anywhere, and invite you to tag along with me. Imagine my sadness when I learned from your servant that you were not at home. What could I do? I had given my word of honor to come to you, so I sat down to wait, thinking I would stay no more than a quarter of an hour, but it has been a very long quarter of an hour. I opened your novel and quite forgot about the time! Ivan Petrovich, it's a masterpiece! Your talent has not been properly recognized! Your writing actually brought tears to my eyes, and I do not cry very often."

"So you want me to come with you? I confess that at this moment… Not that I wouldn't want to, but..."

"For God's sake, let's go! What's wrong with me that you should refuse? After all, I have been waiting more than an hour and a half! Besides, I do need to talk with you—you know what about. You understand this business better than I do. Together, we may resolve the situation, find a solution! For God's sake, do not refuse me!"

I figured that sooner or later I would have to go. Natasha was alone now and needed me, but she herself had asked me to get to know Katya as soon as possible. Besides, someone else might be there—Alyosha! I knew that Natasha would not be satisfied until I brought her news of Katya, so I decided to go. But I was worried about Nellie.

"Wait," I said to the prince, and went out to the stair landing. Nellie was hiding in a dark corner.

"Why won't you come in, Nellie? What did he do? What did he say to you?"

"Nothing… I don't want to… I don't want to..." she repeated. "I'm afraid..."

I tried to reassure her, but nothing helped. I then told her I was going out and that, after we'd left, she should come back into the room and lock herself in.

"And do not let anybody in, Nellie, no matter how much they beg."

"Are you going with him?"

"Yes, I am."

She shuddered and grabbed my sleeve as if to beg me not to go, but did not utter a word. I decided I would question her in detail the following day.

Apologizing to the prince, I began to dress. He assured me that I needn't dress formally. "Perhaps just freshen up a bit," he added, looking me over from head to toe. "You know, we all cling to these old traditions... one cannot completely get rid of them. It will be a long time before we reach a state of perfection in this world," he concluded with pleasure when he saw that I owned a dress-coat.

We went out, but I left him on the stairs and darted back into the room into which Nellie had already slipped. I once again said good-bye to her. She was terribly agitated. Her face was so feverish with anger, I was afraid for her. It was hard for me to leave.

"That's a strange servant you have," the prince said to me as we descended the stairs. "I assume that little girl is your servant."

"No... she's just... she is living with me for the time being."

"A most peculiar little girl. I suspect she is a bit mad. Imagine, when she first opened the door, she was quite civil, but she suddenly cried out and rushed at me, trembling and clinging to my coat... She seemed to want to say something… but didn't. I admit I was a bit alarmed and was tempted to retreat but, thank God, she ran out first. I was astonished. How do you manage to get along with her?"

"She has epilepsy," I answered.

"Ah, so that's it. Well, it's not surprising then...if she has attacks."

I immediately thought about Masloboyev's visit of the previous day when he knew I would not be home, and my visit to Masloboyev that morning when he said he was drunk and invited me to return at seven o'clock, his urging me to not think I was being bamboozled by him and, finally, the prince waiting an hour-and-a-half for me when he probably knew that I was with Masloboyev, and Nellie rushing away from him into the street, and it struck me that all of these facts were somehow connected. It was something to think about.

Prince Valkovsky's carriage was now waiting at the gate. We got in and drove off.

Chapter Thirty-Four

It was not a long ride to the Torgovy Bridge. During the early moments, we were silent. I kept wondering what he would have to say to me. I felt certain that he would feel me out at first, probe me, but when he finally spoke, he went straight to business.

"I am very concerned about one thing now, Ivan Petrovich," he said, "and I want to talk with you first and ask for your advice. I long ago decided to forgo my winnings in the court settlement and return the ten thousand to Ichmenyev. What should I do?"

"It's not possible that you really don't know what to do," flashed through my mind, and I wondered if he was having a laugh at my expense.

"I don't know," I answered as simply as possible. "If it were anything else—that is, with respect to Natalia Nikolayevna—I am prepared to offer you any advice that could possibly benefit you or us, but on this matter, you certainly know more than I do."

"No, no, I don't know very much at all. You know the Ichmenyevs and, perhaps, even Natalia may have aired her thoughts on this subject, and that for me would be my primary guide. You could help me a great deal. It is an extremely difficult situation. I am willing to make a concession, you understand, no matter how other matters may play out. But how and in what form to make this concession, that is my question. The old man is proud, stubborn, and may insult me for my generosity. He may well fling the money back in my face."

"But let me ask, do you consider this money yours or his?"

"I won the lawsuit, so the money is mine."

"But in your conscience?"

"Of course, I have no doubt it is mine," he replied, somewhat taken aback by my impertinence, "but it seems that you may not understand all of the details of this case. I do not blame the old man for deliberately deceiving me, and I confess I have never accused him of such. *He* chose to take it as a personal insult. He was guilty of careless oversight in his handling of my business, and, according to our agreement, he was responsible for some of those losses. But even that was not the principal reason for our quarrel during those days of mutual recrimination. It was, in fact, our mutually wounded pride. I might have given scant attention to that paltry ten thousand rubles were it not for what it represented and how the whole disagreement started. I agree, I was suspicious and I was probably wrong—that is, wrong at first, though I didn't realize it at the time—but it was my irritation and resentment towards his rudeness that prompted me to get back at him by initiating the lawsuit. You may, perhaps, find my behavior ignoble—I do not justify it—but

I would note that anger and, more importantly, wounded pride, have nothing to do with nobility, but are natural and human. And I confess, I repeat again, I knew very little about Ichmenyev at the time, and completely believed those rumors about his daughter and Alyosha, so I truly believed that he stole the money intentionally. But putting that aside, the big question is, what do I do now? If I refuse the money, but still maintain that my claim is just, it surely means that I am making a gift of the money to him. And when you add in this ticklish situation with Natalia Nikolayevna, he is certainly likely to fling the money back in my face."

"You see, you yourself say he'll fling the money back at you, which proves you consider him an honest man, and therefore you can be quite sure that he did not steal your money. And if so, why don't you go to him directly and just announce that you consider your claim illegal? It would be the noble thing to do, and Ichmenyev would not find it so difficult to accept the return of his money."

"Hmm... his money, that's just the point. What position are you putting me in? Go and tell him that I consider my claim illegal. 'Then why did you take him to court if you knew your claim was unjustified?' That's what others will say to my face. And I don't deserve that because my claim *was* legitimate. I have never said nor even written that he stole from me, but I do believe he was indiscrete and careless in the way he conducted my business. This money is positively mine, and therefore it would be slanderous to make a false claim against *myself*. And finally, I repeat, the old man brought this on himself, and you want me to beg *his* forgiveness for his own offenses? That's hard."

"I think if two people want to reconcile, then..."

"You think it's easy?"

"Yes."

"No, it is sometimes very difficult, especially..."

"Especially if it brings up other circumstances related to it. There I agree with you, Prince. The situation with Natalia Nikolayevna and your son should be settled by you to whatever degree you have control and settled to the satisfaction of the Ichmenyevs. Only then can you convince Ichmenyev that you were sincere in your handling of the lawsuit. Until then, with *nothing* settled, you have only one path—to admit the injustice of your claim, and to admit it openly, and if necessary, publicly. That is my opinion. I'm being straight with you because you, yourself, asked for my opinion and would probably prefer my candor. It also gives me the courage to ask you why you are so concerned about returning the money to Ichmenyev. If you think you are right in this claim, why give it to him? Forgive my curiosity, but the circumstances compel it."

"What do you think?" he asked suddenly, as if he had not heard my question. "Do you really believe the old man would refuse the ten thousand, even if I gave him the money without reservation and... and... free of any conditions?"

"Of course he would refuse!"

I shuddered with indignation as my face turned crimson. This shamelessly brazen question struck me in much the same way as the prince spitting in my eye. My resentment was multiplied by the coarse, aristocratic manner in which he ignored my own question, as if it were unworthy of his notice. I have always detested this sort of phony, snobbish behavior and had tried in the past to steer Alyosha away from it.

"Hmm... you are too impulsive. Not everything in this world can be accomplished as easily as you imagine," the prince said quietly in response to my outburst. "However, I think that Natalia Nikolayevna may be able to resolve this situation. You should ask for her advice."

"I don't think so," I answered rudely. "You were not the least bit interested in what I had to say a moment ago but interrupted me instead. Natalia Nikolayevna will realize that your return of the money without any, as you say, conditions, is really an insincere attempt to compensate the father for the loss of his daughter, and her for the loss of Alyosha. In a word, bribery."

"Hmm! So that's how you see me, my clever Ivan Petrovich," the prince laughed. Why did he laugh?

"And yet," he continued, "we still have so much, so very much to talk over together. But not just now. I implore you to understand one thing. Natalia Nikolayevna's future happiness depends, in part, on how we resolve this issue. Your participation is essential, as you shall see for yourself. So, if you remain devoted to Natalia Nikolayevna, you must not refuse to discuss these matters, however little sympathy you may feel for me. But we've arrived. Come."

CHAPTER THIRTY-FIVE

The countess lived well. Her rooms were furnished comfortably and with style, although not lavishly so. Everything, however, bore the character of a temporary residence, rather than the permanent home of a rich, aristocratic family with all of the accoutrements and extravagances that the nobility seems to find essential. There was a rumor afloat that the countess would return in the summer to her once fashionable country estate, now in ruins and heavily mortgaged, in the province of Simbirsk, and that the prince would accompany her. I had heard the murmurings and thought, with anguish, what would Alyosha do when Katya went away with her stepmother? Natasha and I had not discussed it (she seemed afraid to do so), but there were indications that she, too, had heard the rumors, and had chosen to suffer in silence.

The countess received me graciously, politely offered me her hand, and confirmed that she had long wished to meet me. She poured tea from a beautiful silver samovar, around which we all sat—the prince and I, and a very elegant middle-aged gentleman who wore a star on his coat and had the well-starched manners of a diplomat. This guest was treated with the utmost respect. The countess, only recently returned from abroad, had not had sufficient time that winter in St. Petersburg to establish her position in society and develop the contacts she had anticipated and expected. Other than this one guest, there were no other visitors that evening. I looked in vain for Katarina Fedorovna, who was in another room with Alyosha, but when she heard of our arrival, she immediately came to greet us. Prince Valkovsky kissed her hand graciously and the countess waved her towards me. The prince immediately introduced us. I eagerly studied her appearance. She was a delicate and petite blonde, dressed in a white dress, with a quiet and serene expression on her face and very blue eyes, just as Alyosha had described them, but her beauty was solely that of youth. I had expected to see the very personification of perfection, but that was not the case. The gently contoured shape of her face, her regular but unremarkable features, the curly mane of hair fashioned in a simple, everyday style, and her quiet, attentive stare were such that had I met her in passing on a street somewhere, I would not have paid any special attention to her. But that opinion was formed by only an initial glance. I would get to know her better later that evening. The one thing that impressed me the most in that moment was the way she took my hands, staring at me with a kind of naive but strange intensity that made me smile in spite of myself. I felt immediately that I had before me a creature of the purest heart. The countess followed her closely with her eyes. After shaking hands with me, Katya moved quickly across the room with Alyosha and sat down next to him. Alyosha greeted me in passing with a whispered, "I am here only for a moment, but I'll be over there."

The "diplomat" (I never learned his name but call him that simply to identify him) spoke calmly and majestically, pontificating on some idea. The countess listened to him attentively. The prince smiled in a flattering and encouraging manner, so the man often turned to him, perhaps appreciating him as a worthy student. They gave me some tea and left me in peace, for which I was most grateful. Meanwhile, I looked at the countess. Despite my initial reluctance, I found her fascinating. She was, perhaps, no longer young, but she seemed to me no more than twenty-eight years old. Her face was still fresh, and once, in early youth, must have been very beautiful. Her dark brown hair was still quite thick. Her expression was friendly, but had a mischievously mocking playfulness to it, although she seemed to be restraining herself at the moment. There was an air of great intelligence about her, but even more of kindness and good humor. I also sensed an overwhelming combination of frivolity and hedonism just beneath her calm facade. She was clearly under the command of the prince, who had an extraordinary influence over her. I knew that they had been lovers during their stay abroad, but it seemed to me now that they were bound by something much more than their former relationship, by something quite mysterious, perhaps based on a mutual commitment to some unspoken goal. It was clear that the prince had grown weary of her yet maintained their relationship principally because of their mutual plans for Katya, an enterprise initiated undoubtedly by the prince. On this basis, the prince had narrowly avoided marriage to the countess by persuading her to focus on a marriage between Alyosha and her stepdaughter. All of these details I had deduced from the careless hints dropped by Alyosha, who couldn't help but pick up on the scheming machinations of his father. I also gathered from past rumors about the prince that, in spite of his obvious control over the countess, he had some reason to be afraid of her. Even Alyosha noticed this. I learned later that the prince had also been anxious to get the countess married to someone else, one reason why he was planning to send her to Simbirsk, hoping to find a suitable husband for her in the province.

I sat quietly and listened, not knowing how I could quickly arrange a face-to-face conversation with Katerina Fedorovna. The diplomat responded to a question about the countess's current financial situation, and how the ongoing political reforms were affecting her. He talked long and hard, calmly and with great authority. He developed his ideas in a subtle and clever way, but I found them repulsive. He insisted that the whole spirit of reforms and improvements would bring about results that all too soon would reveal their failings, and that society (or, at least, a certain part of it) would soon come to its senses and return to the old ways with vigor. The experience, however unfortunate, would prove beneficial because it would demonstrate the inevitability of the old ways, and he looked forward to the current recklessness reaching its zenith as soon as possible. "They cannot," he concluded, "get along without *us*. No society has ever stood its ground without *us*. We shall lose nothing, but on the contrary, grow even stronger. Our motto at this moment should be 'the worse things get, the better it is for *us*!'"

The prince smiled at him with a pathetic empathy. The man was clearly quite pleased with himself. I was so angry that I was tempted to protest, but I was stopped by a poisonous glare from the prince. He had moved in closer to me and I suspected that he might be waiting for me to make some peculiar and childlike outburst so he could enjoy my discomfort. I was, however, firmly convinced that the diplomat would not have paid any attention to my objection, if he was even aware of my existence. I was very uncomfortable sitting with them, but Alyosha came to my rescue. He quietly approached me and touched my shoulder. He wanted a few words with me, he said, although I suspected that he was actually delivering a message from Katya. I was right. A minute later I was sitting next to her. At first, she just looked at me intently, as if thinking: "Who exactly is this man?" We were both unable to find the words to say, but I was convinced that once she began to speak, she wouldn't stop, at least until morning. The "five or six hours of intimate conversation" that Alyosha had mentioned suddenly flashed in my mind. Alyosha was sitting right there waiting for us to begin.

"Why don't you say something?" he asked with a smile directed at both of us. "They finally meet and say nothing."

"Ah, Alyosha, why do you... We will begin directly," Katya replied. "Ivan Petrovich and I have so much to say to each other that I hardly know where to begin. We are a bit late in getting to know each other, but I feel as though I have known you for ages. I was so looking forward to meeting you, I even considered writing you a letter."

"About what?" I asked, smiling involuntarily.

"So many things," she answered intently. "At the very least to find out if Alyosha told me the truth about Natalia Nikolayevna, how she is not offended when he leaves her alone for such long stretches of time? How is it possible for anyone to behave as he does?" She turned to Alyosha. "For example, why are you here now, tell me, please?"

"Oh, my God, I am just leaving. I told you that I would only stay for a minute, to see the two of you talking together, and here you are... together... talking."

"Yes, we are together and talking, so why are you still here? He is always like this," she added, blushing slightly and pointing her finger at him. "'One minute,' he says repeatedly, 'just for a minute,' but look at him. He'd stay until midnight if he could, and then it would be too late to go to her. 'She won't be angry,' he tells me, 'she's kind.' That's how he explains himself, but is that an honorable way to behave?"

"Yes, I guess I'll be going," Alyosha answered mournfully, "only I would really like to stay with the two of you..."

"What do you want with us? We, by contrast, have a great deal to talk about alone. But listen, don't be peeved at me. It is important that you understand that completely."

"Well, if I have to, I'll go now. Why should I be peeved? I'll just take a minute to see Levenka, and then I'll go immediately to Natasha. Oh, one thing, Ivan Petrovich," he continued, taking his hat, "did you know my father wants to refuse the money he won in his lawsuit with Ichmenyev?"

"Yes, I know. He told me."

"I think that's a very honorable thing to do, but Katya doesn't think what he's doing is the least bit honorable. Talk to her about it. Good-bye, Katya, and please do not doubt my love for Natasha. And why do you impose all these conditions on me, blame me, check up on me? It feels like you're spying on me! Natasha knows how much I love her, and she believes in me. I'm sure she believes in me. I love her more than anything, without any obligation to do so. I do not know *how* I love her, just that I love her. So there's no reason for you to interrogate me and make me feel guilty. Just ask Ivan Petrovich, he's here now, and he can confirm to you that Natasha is jealous, and although she's terribly fond of me, it's a kind of selfish love, because she isn't willing to sacrifice anything for me."

"What's that?" I asked in amazement, not believing my ears.

"What are you saying, Alyosha?" Katya cried, clasping her hands.

"Well, why is that so surprising? Ivan Petrovich knows. She's always demanding that I stay with her. She doesn't exactly say that, of course, but it's clear that that's what she wants."

"Are you not ashamed, ashamed of yourself?" Katya said, turning crimson with anger.

"But what is there to be ashamed of? How silly you are, Katya, really! I love her more than she can possibly imagine, but if she loved me equally, she would be willing to sacrifice *her* pleasure for *mine*. It's true that she encourages me to come here, but I can see in her face how difficult it is for her, so it's really the same as her not wanting me to come."

"No, this is no accident!" Katya cried, turning again to me with flashing, angry eyes. "Own up, Alyosha, confess it now! You've been talking to your father, haven't you? He's the one who put these ideas into your head! And don't bother to deny it, for I will know immediately! It's true, isn't it?"

"Yes, he spoke to me," Alyosha answered, confused. "What of it? He spoke to me today in such a kindly, friendly manner, and he did nothing but praise Natasha, which surprised me, considering all the terrible things she has said about him."

"And you, you believed him," I said. "You, to whom she has given everything she possibly could, even today when she has been so anxious about you, not wanting you to be bored, not wanting to deprive you of the possibility of seeing Katerina Fedorovna! She told me this today. And suddenly, you're willing to believe such a treacherous slander! Aren't you ashamed?"

"Ungrateful fool! That's the problem, he's never ashamed of anything!" Katya said, waving her hand as if to dismiss him as a hopeless cause.

"Really, the things you say, Katya," Alyosha went on in a plaintive voice. "But you're always like that. Always suspecting me of doing something bad. I'm not talking about you, Ivan Petrovich! You think I don't really love Natasha. I didn't mean to suggest that Natasha was selfish. I just meant that she loves me too much, so much out of proportion that it's impossible for me to live up to it. And I never let my father sway me, even though he tries to, I won't let him. He didn't mean to suggest that Natasha was selfish in a bad way. I understood what he meant. He said it in exactly the same way I did a moment ago. That she loves me so overwhelmingly that it amounts to a kind of egoism, which makes it difficult for me and difficult for her, and then later even more difficult for me. Well, it's the truth, and he only said it because he loves me, and he didn't mean to insult Natasha. On the contrary, he admires the power of her love, a love without measure, a love without reason..."

But Katya interrupted him and would not let him finish. She reproached him bitterly and insisted that the prince had only praised Natasha to mask his true intention, which was to break up their relationship, but to do so in such a subtle and imperceptible manner as to turn Alyosha against her. She cleverly and passionately argued that Natasha loved him, but even so strong a love could never excuse the way he was treating her, and that if anyone was being selfish, it was Alyosha. Little by little, Katya drove him to a state of complete anguish and remorse, and he stared at the floor with a pained expression, completely destroyed. But Katya was relentless. I studied her with the greatest fascination. I wanted to get to know this strange girl. She was certainly a child, but a remarkable one, with strong convictions and a passionate, innate love of goodness and justice. If she was, in fact, a child, she belonged to that class of cultured, educated children, that are so prevalent among Russian families. It was evident that she had an insatiable curiosity. It would be interesting to peep into that skull and study the mixture of childish images and fancies with the serious impressions and observations gained from life (because Katya had certainly lived), but also the unformulated, abstract ideas born of her lack of worldly experience and her emersion in books, although she probably mistook these ideas for actual knowledge. During that evening, and afterwards, I studied her carefully and got to know her quite well. Her heart was ardent and receptive. She seemed unconcerned about self-control, for being true to herself was of paramount importance, and every effort of society to place restraints on people like her was just conventional prejudice. She took pride in that conviction, a trait not uncommon in people of ardent temperament, even among those who are not quite so young. It was that attitude, in fact, which provided her peculiar charm. She loved to think and to seek the truth, but not in some stuffy pedantic way, but with such a youthful exuberance that you loved her at first sight and appreciated her originality. I thought of Levenka and Borenka, and it seemed to me that all of this was consistent with their philosophy of the natural order. And, strangely, as I studied her face, which had initially seemed not particularly remarkable, Katya became more beautiful and attractive by the minute. This dichotomy of naive child and thinking woman, childishness combined with a genuine thirst for truth and justice and an unwavering faith in her impulses, lit up her face with a glow of sincerity that gave her a higher, spiritual beauty. It seemed impossible to measure the full range of possibilities encapsulated in such beauty, the significance of which is lost on those who offer little more than a cursory, indifferent glance. And I realized why Alyosha was so passionately attached to her. If he, himself, was incapable of thought and reason, he would naturally be drawn to someone who could do his thinking and, perhaps, even wishing for him, and Katya has already taken him under her wing. His heart was open and generous, and he surrendered immediately to all that was fair and beautiful, and Katya had already spoken to him with a sincerity and sympathy that appealed to his childlike view of life. Alyosha had not a drop of his own will, and Katya had a persistent, strong and fiery-minded determination, and Alyosha would bind only to one who could dominate and even command him. It was partly because of this that Alyosha attached himself to Natasha at the beginning of their relationship, but Katya had a great advantage over Natasha in that she was still a child and seemed likely to remain a child for a long time. This childishness, combined with a brilliant mind and, at the same time, a certain lack of judgment, was something more akin to Alyosha. He sensed this and grew more and more attracted to Katya. I am sure that when they spoke together in private, enmeshed in one of Katya's discussions on "propaganda," that their conversation would quickly veer into childish trivialities. And though Katya probably often lectured Alyosha and held him in the palm of her hand, he was undoubtedly more comfortable with her than with Natasha. They were more like equals, which meant a lot.

"Stop, Katya, that's enough, enough. You are always right in these matters and I am always wrong, but that's because your heart is purer than mine," Alyosha said, getting up and giving her his hand in parting. "I will go to her right away, and I won't even stop in on Levenka."

"There is nothing for you to do at Levenka's, but you are very sweet to obey me and go to her now."

"And you are a thousand times sweeter than anyone," Alyosha responded sadly. "Ivan, I have a word or two I need to say to you."

We moved a few steps away.

"I behaved shamelessly today," he whispered to me. "I've sunk so low, I'm guilty before the entire world, but most especially the two most important people. After lunch today, my father introduced me to Mademoiselle Alexandrine, a charming French girl. I was... carried away and... But what can I say, I am not worthy to be with any of them... Goodbye, Ivan Petrovich!"

"He is very kind-hearted and generous," Katya began hurriedly after I sat down beside her again, "but we'll talk more about him another time. For now, we need to come to an understanding. How do you feel about the prince?"

"I think he is a very bad man."

"As do I. So, we agree on that point. Now, about Natalia Nikolayevna. You know, Ivan Petrovich, I am quite in the dark and have been waiting for you to enlighten me. At present, I can only guess about her from the little information I have received from Alyosha. There is no one else from whom I can learn anything. Now, tell me, first and foremost – and this is the chief point – do you think Alyosha and Natasha will be happy together or not? That is what I need to know first, before I can decide on my own course of action."

"But how can I answer that with any certainty?"

"Of course, you can't be certain," she said, "but tell me what *you* think about it. You are a clever man, I know that."

"My opinion is that they can never be happy together."

"And why is that?"

"Because they are not suited to each other."

"That is what I suspected," she said uneasily, and sat awhile with her hands folded.

"Tell me more," she continued. "Listen, I am most anxious to meet Natasha because we have a great deal to talk about, and I believe we shall be able to settle the matter between us. I always imagine Natasha to be highly intelligent, serious, honest, and very pretty. Is it so?"

"It is."

"I was sure of it. But if she truly is all those things, how could she possibly fall in love with Alyosha, who is such a child? Please explain this to me! I often wonder!"

"I can't explain it, Katerina Fedorovna. Love has no reason. True, he is a child, but you know how easy it can be to love a child."

My heart softened towards this girl, with her serious, deep-blue eyes fixed intensely on me.

"And the less like a child Natasha is," I continued, "the more seriously and quickly she could fall in love with him. He is honest, sincere, unsophisticated, and sometimes charmingly naive. Perhaps she fell in love with him out of a sort of pity, who knows? Sometimes higher leveled creatures love lower beings out of compassion. But I cannot explain the matter, and therefor turn the question back to you. You love him yourself, don't you?"

I put this question to her boldly and felt confident that by the openness of it, I could avoid disturbing the absolute purity of this young and vulnerable soul.

"I can't really be sure yet," she answered, very quietly, gazing serenely into my eyes, "but I think I love him very much."

"There, you see. And can you explain why *you* love him?"

"There is nothing fake about him," she replied, thoughtfully, "and I like it when he looks straight into my eyes and says something. It feels extremely sweet to me. But listen, Ivan Petrovich, here I am talking to you like this. I'm a girl and you're a man. Is it proper behavior for me to talk to you like this or isn't it?"

"Why, what is the harm in it?"

"I don't see any harm myself, but they…" nodding at the countess and the group gathered around the samovar, "would certainly say it's wrong. Are they right, do you think?"

"No. Doesn't your heart tell you when you're doing something wrong?

"Yes, that's how I usually decide," she said. Evidently, she was anxious to confide in me as much as possible. "Whenever I feel disturbed about anything, I always ask my heart, and if my heart tells me it's all right, then I know I'm safe. That is how one ought to act, I'm sure, and I am speaking to you openly like this because, first of all, I know you to be a good man, and secondly, because I have learned about you and Natasha *before* Alyosha came, and I cried when I heard about it."

"Who told you about us?"

"Alyosha, of course, and he too cried when he spoke about it. That was genuinely nice of him, and I especially like that about him. I think he likes you better than you like him, Ivan Petrovich. It is one of the things about him I admire most. Another reason why I feel comfortable speaking with you so openly is because you are a wise and clever man who can advise me about a great many things."

"But how do you know that I am clever enough to teach you?"

"Well, never mind about all that. Let's consider the chief point *now*. I can't help knowing, Ivan Petrovich, that I am Natasha's rival and I don't know how I should act? That is why I asked you whether they would be happy together. I think about that day and night. Natasha's position is frightful, frightful! I think he has ceased to love her and loves *me* more and more, isn't that so?"

"I'm afraid you're right."

"And yet he isn't actually deceiving her, because *he* doesn't know this about himself, although *she* knows it all too well. How she must be suffering!"

"Well, what do you propose to do, Katerina Fedorovna?"

"I have several ideas," she said with determination, "but in the meantime, I get more and more confused. That is why I have been so anxious to meet you, so you might help me to decide. You know so much more about these things than I do, which is why I think of you as a kind of god. At least, that's how I pictured you at first. If they love one another, they must be happy and should remain so, and I should help them by sacrificing my own happiness."

"I know you *have* sacrificed yourself."

"Yes, I did. But when he kept coming to see me time after time, and his love grew stronger and stronger, I began to think to myself, shall I sacrifice myself or not? That's very wrong, isn't it?"

"It's natural," I said, "and to be expected, so you are not to blame!"

"I'm not so sure! You say that because you are kind-hearted, but I'm afraid *my* heart is not quite so pure in this matter. If it were truly pure, I should know how to behave. However, after I learned more about their relationship from the prince, from Mama, and from Alyosha himself, I concluded that they were *not* suited to one another, which you have now confirmed. Which makes me even *more* confused. What shall I do now? If they're going to be unhappy, it's better that they separate, so I decided to ask you for more information and then to pay Natasha a visit myself and settle it all with her."

"But how will you settle it? That's the question!"

"I shall tell her, 'You love this boy more than anything, so you should value his happiness above your own. Therefore, you must release him from his commitment and break it off.'"

"Yes, that's all very well, but how do you think she's going to take that, and even if she agrees with you, will she have the strength to carry it out?"

"That's what I think about day and night, and…"

And she suddenly burst into tears.

"You don't know how sorry I am for Natasha!" she sobbed, her lips trembling with emotion.

There was nothing more to be said, so I remained silent. As I looked at her, I too felt inclined to cry, although I wasn't sure why. Perhaps out of sensitivity to her predicament. What an adorable child she was! I no longer felt obliged to ask her why she thought she was more likely to make Alyosha happy than Natasha was.

"Are you fond of music?" she asked me suddenly, still sobbing.

"Yes," I said, with some surprise.

"If there were time, I would play you Beethoven's Third Concerto. That's what I'm working on now. There are all these confusing emotions to be found in that piece, just like I'm feeling. But I'll show you another time, we must go on talking now."

We began to discuss how best to arrange for Katya to see Natasha. She felt very well looked-after by her stepmother, but even though the woman was fond of and very kind to her, she would never think of allowing Katya to befriend Natasha, so the meeting would have to be arranged in secret. She went out walking every day with the countess, she told me, and if the countess couldn't go because of a headache or something, then the old French companion would accompany her, but the companion was ill just now, so the next time her stepmother had a headache, she might manage to get away. She could easily get around the old French woman, who was very loving to her, but because the plan depended on the stepmother's health, it was impossible to let Natasha know in advance on which day Katya would come.

"If you do get to meet Natasha," I said, "you will certainly not regret it. She, herself, is very anxious to meet you, and she *should* meet you, if only to see for whom she is giving up Alyosha. Do not disturb yourself about all this too much. Time will resolve it all for you, if necessary. You are going to the country, are you not?"

"Yes," she said, "in a month. The prince insists upon it."

"Do you think that Alyosha will go with you?"

"I was just thinking about that myself," she said, gazing fixedly at me. "I suppose he will go, won't he?"

"Oh yes, he is sure to go!"

"Good heavens, I wonder what's going to happen. Listen, Ivan Petrovitch, I shall write and tell you about everything—long letters and frequent ones. I shall weigh you down with correspondence. You'll come and see us here often, won't you?"

"I can't promise that, I'm afraid. It depends upon circumstances. Perhaps I shall not be able to come at all."

"Why?"

"Well, there are several factors that may affect my coming, most of all, my relations with the prince."

"Oh! That dishonest creature!" Katya said with decision. "I'll tell you what, Ivan Petrovich, how about if I come to see you? Will that be a good idea?"

"How do you feel about that?"

"All right, I think," she said, smiling. "I could call on you, you know. I must tell you, that besides admiring you very much, I am very fond of you, and I could learn so much from you. Oh, yes, I like you very much. It's not shameful to speak like this, is it?"

"Why should it be shameful? You are as dear to me already as one of my own family."

"Then you do want to be my friend?"

"Oh, yes, yes!" I replied.

"Of course, those good people would certainly say it is shameful and dreadfully wrong for a young girl to behave like this," she said, nodding towards the others.

I should remark here that I believe the prince left us together on purpose to talk to our heart's content.

"I know very well," she continued, "that the prince wants my money. They think me a mere child, and, in fact, tell me that in no uncertain terms, but I am of a different opinion. I am not a child. They are strange people and behave just like children themselves. What on earth are they always fussing about?"

"Katerina Fedorovna," I said, "I forgot to ask you who are Levenka and Borenka, whom Alyosha visits so often?"

"Distant relations of mine, very clever and very honest, but they talk much too much. I know them!"

And she laughed.

"Is it true that you intend to give them a million rubles some day?"

"Oh, I don't know. We shall see. Why do I need all this money? Everyone is always worrying themselves about my money till it becomes unbearable, and I assume that I will want to donate some to useful causes at some point in the future. They are already hard at work dividing, distributing, determining how it should be spent— they are both in such a hurry. Yet they are honest, good-hearted, and intelligent fellows. They are learning to be useful and that's better than the way most other people live their lives, isn't it?"

And we talked a great deal more. She gave me a detailed history of her own life and listened with the greatest eagerness to what I had to tell her about mine. She continually begged me to tell her more and more about Alyosha and Natasha. It was midnight when the prince came up and informed me that it was time to go. I said good-bye. Katia pressed my hand very warmly and looked at me most expressively. The countess asked me to come again, and I took my leave, going out with the prince.

I cannot refrain from making a strange and, perhaps, quite inappropriate remark here. I carried away from my three-hour conversation with Katya the full and deep conviction that she was so absolutely a child that she had no idea whatever of any mysterious connection between men and women. This gave an unusual and comical aspect to some of her arguments and deductions and to the serious tone which she adopted in speaking of many important subjects.

Chapter Thirty-Six

"I'll tell you what," Prince Valkovsky said, as he settled himself next to me in the carriage, "Let's have a late supper, shall we? What do you say?"

"I really don't know, Prince," I answered, hesitatingly, "I never take supper..."

"Well, of course, we'll talk while we eat," he added intently, looking me straight in the eye.

I could not misinterpret his meaning. He wanted to speak to me, and since that was what I wanted, too, I agreed.

"Good. To B's on Bolshaya Morskaya," he called to the driver.

"Is that a restaurant?" I asked with some surprise.

"Yes, of course. I rarely have supper at home. Surely you will not refuse to be my guest?"

"But I've told you already that I never take supper."

"Once in a while is acceptable. After all, I have invited you."

Which meant that he was paying, I was sure he added to emphasize the point. I agreed to go with him but decided that I would pay for my own meal. We arrived at the restaurant and the prince engaged a private room and knowledgeably and expertly chose two or three dishes. The meals were expensive, as was the bottle of fine table wine he ordered. All of this was well beyond my means. I looked at the menu and told the waiter to bring me a glass of Lafite and a partridge. The prince objected fiercely.

"You don't want to be my guest? That's ridiculous. Pardon me, my friend, but this self-righteousness is tedious. The pettiest form of vanity. If this is a matter of class distinction, I assure you, I find it insulting."

But I repeated my order.

"Whatever you say," he responded. "I won't force you." When the waiter left, he continued. "Tell me, Ivan Petrovich, may I speak to you as a friend?"

"I should like that."

"Well, in my opinion, this display of scruples on your part does you no good. On the contrary, it is positively harmful. People like you are your own worst enemies, standing in the way of your own progress. You are an intelligent man, a writer, who should get to know the world, and yet you shun it. I'm not talking about the partridge now, but your unwillingness to associate with a group of higher-class people of whom you disapprove. In addition to losing a great many things—well, a career for one—you lose a firsthand knowledge of things any writer must understand, for novels certainly include stories of counts, and princes, and boudoirs. But what am I saying? Poverty seems to be the latest fashion in literature, with tales of lost coats, quarrelsome inspectors, impoverished clerks, dissenters, clouded visions of days gone by. I know, I know."

"But you are wrong, Prince. If I choose not to move in the exalted circle you refer to as the 'higher class,' it is because, first of all, they are so boring, and secondly, there is nothing for me to do among them! I have ventured among them on occasion…"

"Yes, I know, at Count Nainsky's party every year. I was there and met you. And the rest of the year, you wallow in your democratic pride and waste away in drafty attics or sordid garrets, though not all of your crowd live like that. Some are daring adventurers who positively make me sick…"

"I would ask you, Prince, to change the conversation and not return to our attics and garrets."

"Oh, my God, I have offended you. But you did give me leave to speak to you as a friend. But I am sorry, I have done nothing yet to deserve your friendship. The wine is very good, try it."

He poured me half a glass from his bottle.

"You see, my dear Ivan Petrovich, I am well aware that it is bad manners to impose one's friendship upon another. We are not all as rude and insolent to your class as you imagine, and I also understand very well that you are sitting here with me not out of affection, but because I promised to talk with you. That's true, isn't it?" He laughed. "And as you are always watching over the interests of a certain person, you *want* to hear what I have to say. Right?" he added with an evil smile.

"You are not mistaken," I interrupted impatiently. I understood that he was one of those men who, discovering that he has even a modicum of power over another man, cannot resist making him feel that power. And as I could not leave without hearing all he intended to say, I was in his power, and he knew it. His tone had changed, and he had become more brazenly familiar and mocking. "You are not mistaken, Prince," I said again. "That is precisely why I am here. Otherwise, I would not be supping here… so late."

I wanted to say under no circumstances would I be supping here with *you*, but I didn't say that, and finished my sentence differently—not from fear but from my cursed weakness and delicacy. But really, how could a person look someone straight in the eye and say such a rude thing, even if that person deserved it and you wanted to be rude? I think the prince could see that conflict in my eyes and was mocking me as I tried to finish my sentence, as if enjoying my timidity and egging me on with his own eyes: "Afraid to speak your own mind, are you, brother?" At least, that's the impression I got, because when I finished, he laughed, and then gave me a condescending pat on the knee.

"Can't stand up to me, can you?" I read in his eyes. "Just you wait!" I thought to myself.

"I have had a most entertaining evening!" he said, "and really don't know why. Yes, yes, my boy! It was that certain young person that I wanted to talk to you about. We should speak openly and candidly until we reach a proper conclusion, and I hope that this time you will understand me perfectly. Not long ago I spoke with you about that money and that foolish father of hers, that sexagenarian child. Well, it's not worth rehashing now. I wasn't really serious! Ha-ha-ha! You are a literary man; you must have figured that out."

I looked at him in amazement. He didn't seem to be drunk.

"Well, as for this girl, I really do respect her, even like her, I assure you. She's a bit of a pepperbox, but then 'there is no rose without thorns,' as they used to say fifty years ago, and it was well said, too. Thorns prick. But that is what makes her so enticing, and even though Alyosha is a fool, I've already forgiven him to a certain extent—for his good taste. In short, I love these kinds of girls and I…" He pursed his lips. "…have interesting opinions of my own. But more about that later."

"Prince! Listen, Prince!" I cried. "I do not understand this sudden change of… but please change the subject, I beg you!"

"You're getting excited again! Well, well... I'll change the subject! Only now I want to ask you, my good friend, do you have a strong regard for her?"

"Of course," I answered with impatience.

"Well, well… and do you *love* her?" he said, baring his teeth lasciviously and narrowing his eyes.

"You forget yourself!"

"Oh, well, I won't do that, I won't! Calm yourself! I am just in a playful mood today. It's been a long time since I have had so much fun. Shall we have some champagne? What do you think, my poet?"

"I will not drink it! I don't want any!"

"Ah, don't say that! You must definitely keep me company this evening. I feel ever so jolly and quite sentimental, and I cannot bear to be happy alone. Who knows, we might even drink to our undying friendship! Ha-ha-ha! No, my young friend, you really don't know me. I'm sure you'll love me when you do get to know me. I want to share with you tonight both my joy and sorrow, my laughter and tears, though I certainly hope I do not shed any tears tonight. Why not, Ivan Petrovich? After all, you should understand that if I don't get what I want, then all my inspiration may disappear, evaporate, and you will hear nothing, and you know you are here solely in the hope of hearing *something*. Aren't you?" he added, winking at me insolently again. "So, make your choice."

The threat was significant, so I agreed. "I hope he does not intend to get me drunk," I thought. By the way, this is the place to mention a rumor about the prince that I had heard sometime before. It was said of him that, although he was always elegant and decent in society, at night he had a habit of drinking like a fish and engaging in the most disgusting debauchery and mysterious vices. I had heard terrible rumors about him. The talk was that Alyosha knew his father sometimes drank, and tried to hide it from everyone, especially from Natasha. One day he inadvertently let slip something to me in conversation, but immediately changed the subject and would not answer any of my questions. However, it was not from him that I heard the rumor, and I confess that I did not believe it at the time. Now I was waiting to see what would happen.

The champagne arrived, and the prince filled two glasses, one for himself and one for me.

"She is a dear, sweet girl, despite having scolded me," he said, savoring the wine, "but these lovely creatures are particularly sweet just at such moments... And she probably thought she had shamed me mercilessly. Do you remember that evening when she crushed me into dust? Ha-ha-ha! And how she blushed! Are you a connoisseur of women? Sometimes a sudden flush is wonderfully attractive to a pale cheek. Have you noticed that? Oh, dear God, you seem to be angry again!"

"Yes, I am angry!" I cried, no longer able to restrain myself, "and I won't have you speaking about Natalia Nikolayevna... that is, in such a tone. I... I will not allow you to do that!"

"Ah ha! Well, if it will make you happy, I shall change the subject. I am as yielding and soft as bread dough. Let us talk about *you*. I like you, Ivan Petrovitch. If you only knew how friendly, how sincere I am where you are concerned."

"Prince," I interrupted, "wouldn't it be best to stick to the matter at hand?"

"About our little *situation*, you mean. I understand you without words, my friend, but you do not realize how close we touch on the matter by just talking about you, and if, of course, you do not interrupt. So, I will continue. I wanted to tell you, my invaluable Ivan Petrovich, that to live the way you are living is a type of slow suicide. Oh, you must let me touch on this delicate matter, as I am speaking to you as a friend. You are poor, you take money in advance from your publisher and pay off some small debts and then live on tea for the next six months, shivering in your attic, struggling to finish your novel and see it in your publisher's magazine. Am I right?"

"That is true, but it's..."

"More honorable than stealing, servitude, taking bribes, intriguing, and so on and so forth. I know, I know what you want to say, for all of that has been printed long ago."

"And, consequently, you have no reason to talk about my affairs. Surely, I need not, Prince, give you a lesson in delicacy."

"Well, certainly you needn't. But what should I do if that indelicate matter is precisely what we must focus on? It is not possible to bypass the subject. But, yes, let us, indeed, leave garrets out of it. I, myself, am not at all fond of them—except in certain cases," he added with a disgusting laugh. But what surprises me is that you are so willing to play second fiddle. Of course, I remember a writer once said that it might be the greatest feat of a human being to be able to limit his role in life to a secondary role... or something to that effect! I've heard similar talk somewhere else, but it's a fact that Alyosha has stolen away with your bride, and you, like some Schiller, are quite willing to be crucified for them, happy to serve them, almost at their beck and call. You must excuse me, my dear fellow, but this noble act of yours is rather nauseating, even shameful, and I should think you would be sick of it by now. If I were in your shoes, I believe I would die of mortification and, worse, of the shame of it, the shame!"

"Prince! You seem to have purposely brought me here to insult me!" I cried, beside myself with anger.

"Oh no, my friend, no! I am at this moment, simply an ordinary person who wishes for nothing but your happiness. In short, I want to right the situation. But let us set that aside for a moment, and have you hear me to the end, trying not to get angry, if only for two minutes. Come, what do you think of the idea of you getting married? You see, I am now talking about a completely peripheral matter. Why do you look at me with such amazement?"

"I'm waiting for you to finish," I answered, really looking at him with astonishment.

"But there is nothing more to add. I just wanted to know what you would say if one of your friends, wishing you a true, permanent happiness, not some ephemeral thing, were to offer you a girl, young and pretty, but... perhaps a bit tampered with by someone else… I am speaking allegorically, but you'll understand that I mean someone *similar* to Natalia Nikolayevna, but, of course with a decent sum of money. Please note that I am speaking of some unrelated case, not *our* affair. Well, what would you say?"

"I would tell you that you were... crazy."

"Ha-ha-ha! Bah! Yes, you look like you want to hit me!"

I really was ready to throw myself at him. I could not hold back much longer. He impressed me as some type of reptile, some huge spider, which I urgently wanted to crush. He enjoyed taunting me, and he played me like a cat with a mouse, assuming that I was completely in his power. It seemed to me, and I understood it, that he found great fun and, perhaps, even a lustful gratification in the callousness, in the insolence, in the cynicism with which he finally tore off his mask in front of me. He wanted to enjoy my surprise, my horror. He sincerely despised me and was laughing at me.

I had sensed from the very beginning that this had all been intentionally conceived in advance, with dubious motives, but I was in no position to stop him as I needed to listen to him no matter what happened. It was for Natasha's sake that I had to accept anything and everything, because the whole affair might be resolved at any moment. But how could I listen to these mean, cynical insults at her expense and remain calm? Even worse, he fully understood that I could not avoid listening, which doubled his offensiveness. But he needed me at the same time, I thought, and I began to answer him sharply and rudely. He figured that out.

"Listen, my friend," he began with a serious expression, "we can't continue like this, so perhaps we should come to an understanding. I am trying, you see, to say something important to you and you are obliged to listen to me no matter what. I wish to speak as I choose and say what I want to say, and in the present circumstances that is how it should be. So, my young friend, will you be patient and hear me?"

I controlled myself and remained silent, despite the fact that he was looking at me with such a mocking expression that he seemed to be challenging me to protest strongly. But he realized that I had already agreed to listen, so he went on.

"Do not be angry with me, my friend. You are angry, are you not? At some surface matter perhaps? But the truth is that you did not expect to hear anything of substance from me, so I could have spoken with a perfumed courtesy, or as I am now, it would have made no difference. You despise me, don't you? And yet you can see how much of me is this sweet simplicity, this frankness, this *bonhomie.* I confess to you everything, even my childish attitudes. Yes, *mon cher*, a bit more *bonhomie* on your part, too, and we shall get along famously and finally understand each other completely. No need to wonder about me. I am so completely exhausted by all of this virtuousness, by all of Alyosha's innocent pastoral fantasies, all of the poetic images connected to this damned intrigue with Natasha—who is a very appealing young woman—that I am glad, so to speak, to have the opportunity to stick out my tongue at it all. Well, that opportunity is now. And finally, I am anxious to pour out my heart and soul to you. Ha-ha-ha!"

"You surprise me, Prince, and I barely recognize you. You are sinking to the level of a Punchinello doll with such unexpected frankness..."

"Ha-ha-ha, that is partly true! A very apt comparison! Ha-ha! I am on a spree and having a marvelous time. I am happy and contented, and you, a poet, should certainly allow me all possible leniency. But let us drink," he concluded, filling up his glass, quite pleased with himself. "I'll tell you what, my friend, that foolish evening at Natasha's, do you remember, nearly finished me off completely. Her strength was very appealing, I'll admit, but I came away from there with a terrible rage and I do not want to forget that. Neither forget it nor conceal it. Of course, our time will come, and it is fast approaching, but let's dismiss that for now. And by the way, I wanted to tell you that I have one personality trait with which you may not be aware, and that is a hatred for all that vulgar and worthless pastoral nonsense, and one of my greatest pleasures has always been to pretend to go along with such idiocy, putting on that tone and style myself, egging on any young Schiller and then suddenly ripping my mask off and crushing him in one blow, changing my enthusiastic smile into a grimace, sticking out my tongue at precisely the moment when he least expects such a surprise. What? You don't understand that, and think it is an ugly, ridiculous, dishonorable thing to do, is that it?"

"Of course it is."

"You are honest, I dare say, but what am I to do if they torture me? I am foolishly honest, too, but that is my nature. However, I want to tell you some interesting moments in my life which will help you to understand me better, and it will be very interesting. Yes, I really can be a bit like a Punchinello, but a Punchinello is candid, is he not?"

"Listen, Prince, it's late now, and perhaps..."

"What? My God, what impatience! Why the rush? Stay and let us talk in a friendly manner over a glass of wine, like two good friends. Do you think I'm drunk? Well, what does it matter? Ha-ha-ha! Really, these friendly chats are always recalled long afterwards with great pleasure. You are not a pleasant man, Ivan Petrovitch. You have no sentimentality and no sensitivity. You don't even have one hour to spare for a friend like me? In addition, you must know that this has a bearing on a certain matter… Of course, you must realize that. You are a writer, so you should bless this opportunity. You might, after all, use me as inspiration for a character in your writing, ha-ha-ha! God, how amiably candid I am today!"

He was evidently drunk. His face changed and took on a nasty expression. He was obviously being sarcastic, hoping to sting, to bite, to mock. "It's probably better if he is drunk," I thought. "Drunks tend to reveal more." But he knew what he was doing.

"My young friend," he said, apparently enjoying himself, "I made a confession to you just now, perhaps even an inappropriate one, that I sometimes have an irresistible desire to stick out my tongue to people in certain situations. For my naive and artless frankness, you compare me to Punchinello, which genuinely amuses me. But if you blame me or marvel at me for being rude to you just now, and perhaps even as boorish as a peasant, or for having suddenly changed my tone with you, then you are being quite unfair. First of all, it pleases, and secondly, I am not at home, I am with *you*… that is to say, we are out on the town together as good friends, and thirdly, I'm awfully fond of acting on my whims. Do you know that I once had a fantasy of becoming a metaphysician and a philanthropist, and found myself entertaining many of the same ideals as you? But that was long ago, in the golden days of my youth. I remember going back to my village with the best of intentions and, of course, was utterly bored. And you would not believe what happened to me then. Out of boredom, I began to make the acquaintance of several pretty young women... Oh, you're not making faces already, are you? Oh, my boy, we are speaking as friends now. One must party on occasion and let oneself go! I am a Russian with an authentic Russian temperament, a patriot who loves to throw open the doors of life and grab the moment. We all will die, and what then? So, I chose to flirt with a few girls. I remember one was a shepherdess with a husband, a handsome young fellow. I gave him quite a beating and planned for him to wake up as a soldier—past pranks, my poet—but I didn't follow through with it. He died in my hospital... I had built a little hospital in the village with twelve beds, beautifully arranged, clean, with parquet floors. I closed it down long ago, but I was proud of it at the time. I was a philanthropist! Well, I almost flogged that peasant to death for having such a pretty wife... There you go again, making faces! You are disgusted by my story? It hurts your noble feelings? There now, don't upset yourself! All this took place years ago, during my romantic phase, when I wanted to be a benefactor to mankind, to establish a philanthropic society... that was the rut I was in at the time. Then I was into thrashing husbands. Now I would never do it. Now everyone would be grimacing—such are the times we live in... But more than anything else, what makes me laugh now is that fool Ichmenyev. I am sure he knew all about that incident with the peasant... but what do you think? Out of the kindness of his heart, made up, it seems, of molasses, and the fact that he loved me and was anxious to please me, he decided not to believe any of it and, in fact, did not believe it, standing firmly by my side for twelve years, until the shoe pinched his *own* foot. Ha-ha-ha! Well, all of that is nonsense! Drink up, my friend. Listen, are you fond of women?"

I did not answer. I just listened to him. He had already started on the second bottle.

"I like to talk about them over supper. I could introduce you when we finish to a Mademoiselle Phileberté, an acquaintance of mine. Eh? What do you think? But what is wrong with you? You won't even look at me... Hmm!"

He seemed thoughtful. Then he suddenly raised his head, looked at me with a significant glare, and continued.

"I'll tell you what, my poet, I want to reveal to you a secret of nature of which you seem to be unaware. I am sure that you are calling me a sinner at this moment, maybe even a scoundrel, a monster of depravity and vice. But here is what I want to tell you. If it were possible—which, given the laws of human nature, could never be—for every one of us to reveal all of our secret thoughts, but without hesitating to disclose what he is generally afraid to say, that which he is afraid to tell other people, afraid to tell even his best friends, perhaps even afraid to admit to myself, then surely the world would be filled with such a stench that we would all have been suffocated. That is why I must say, in parenthesis, that our social proprieties and societal conventions are so essential. They have a profound value, I won't say for morality, but simply for self-preservation, for comfort is, of course, even better, since morality is essentially the same comfort, that is, invented solely for the sake of comfort. But we'll talk about proprieties later—I'm straying from my point—remind me about them when I'm done. In summation, you accuse me of vice, depravity, immorality, and I am, perhaps, more to blame only because I am more open than others, and nothing more, for I do not conceal what others hide even from themselves, as I said before... It's a terrible habit, but it's precisely doing right now because I want to. However, do not fret about it," he added with a sarcastic smile, "I said 'to blame,' but I do not apologize. Note this too: I am not putting you on the spot. I am not asking whether you have the very same secrets in order to justify my own, and I... I am behaving quite properly and nobly. Actually, I always play the game..."

"You are talking gibberish," I said, looking at him with contempt.

"Gibberish, ha-ha-ha! And shall I tell you what you are thinking now? You are wondering why I brought you here and am suddenly, for no apparent reason, opening my heart to you? Am I right?"

"Yes."

"Well, I'll let you know… later."

"The simplest explanation is that you have drunk nearly two bottles and... and are not sober."

"You mean I am drunk. That could be true. 'Not sober!' That is so much more dignified than drunk. Oh, youth, full of delicacy! But... we seem to have started abusing each other again, and we were talking about such an interesting subject. Yes, my poet, is there anything left in the world prettier and sweeter than women?"

"You know, Prince, I still do not understand why you have chosen me as your confidant in your secrets and romantic... aspirations."

"Hmm... But I told you I will tell you later. Don't worry about it, and even if I haven't any reason, you're a poet, you will understand me, but I already told you that. There is a special gratification in suddenly ripping off the mask, in the cynicism with which a person suddenly exposes himself in front of another with no regard to shame or decency. I will tell you an anecdote. In Paris, there was a crazy bureaucrat who was later put into a madhouse, where it became clear that he was crazy. Well, when he went mad, this is the game he invented for his own pleasure. He undressed at home, totally, like Adam, except for his shoes and socks, and threw on a long cloak that fell to his toes, wrapping himself in it with a serious, majestic demeanor and walked out into the streets. Well, looked at from the side, he was just an ordinary man in a broad cloak out for a stroll for his own pleasure. But as soon as he came across a passer-by in a private place, with no one else about, he would walk silently up to them, and with the most serious and thoughtful expression, stop in front of them, throw open his cloak, and expose himself in all his... authenticity. It lasted for a minute, then he would cover himself up again and, in silence, without moving a muscle in his face, walk smoothly by the stunned spectator, gliding like the ghost in *Hamlet*. Well, he did this with everyone, men, women and children, and it was his sole pleasure in life. Some part of that pleasure can be experienced when you suddenly flabbergast a romantic poet by sticking out your tongue at him when he least expects it. 'Flabbergast'—what a word! I discovered it in the works of one of your contemporary writers."

"Well, that man was crazy, but you..."

"I'm in my right mind?"

"Yes."

The prince laughed.

"You judge rightly, my boy," he added with a most insolent expression.

"Prince," I said, angered by his impudence, "you hate us all, including me, and avenge yourself on me for everyone and everything. It all stems from your petty vanity. You are evil and petty in your spite. You have been angered, and perhaps most of all you are angry about that evening. Of course, you have no better way to repay me than with this absolute contempt. You toss aside even the everyday and obligatory politeness we all owe to each other. You clearly want to show me that you regard even common decency unworthy of me by throwing off your vile mask and exposing your moral cynicism..."

"Why are you saying all this to me?" he asked, rudely and angrily staring at me. "To display your insight?"

"To show that I understand you and say it openly to you."

"What an idea, my boy," he continued, suddenly reverting to his former cheerful, talkative, and good-natured tone. "You have just rescued me from the subject. Let's drink, my friend, I'll pour. And I just wanted to tell you about a very charming and interesting adventure. I'll tell it to you in general terms. I was once acquainted with a lady, she was not in her first youth, about twenty-seven or twenty-eight. Her beauty was of the first rank, with a formidable bust and an outstanding carriage! She had the piercing eyes of an eagle, but always stern and foreboding, dignified but unapproachable. She was reputed to be as cold as snow, and intimidated everyone by her unattainable, menacing virtue. Menacing's the word. There was not in all the town a more intolerant judge than she. She punished not only vice, but even the slightest weakness in other women, and punished it permanently, with no appeal. In her circle, she had the greatest influence. The proudest and most virtuous old women revered her and even fawned over her. She stared impassively at all of them, as cruel as an abbess in a medieval convent. Young women trembled before her harsh glances and critical judgment. A single remark, a mere allusion from her was enough to destroy a reputation. So powerful was her influence in society, that even men were afraid of her. Finally, she threw herself into a sort of contemplative mysticism, but also calm and dignified... And what do you suppose? It turned out that there was no one more corrupt and sinful than this wicked woman, and I had the good fortune to earn her trust. In short, I became her secret and mysterious lover. Our rendezvous were engineered so deftly, in such an expert manner, that none of her own household could have had the slightest suspicion. Only her maid, a comely young Frenchwoman, was made privy to all of her secrets, but one could rely on this maid's absolute discretion. She, too, took part in our activities; just how I will not say at this moment, but her mistress's decadence was such that the Marquis de Sade could have taken lessons from her. But the strongest, the most poignant and startling excitement in this sensual activity was its secrecy and the sheer audacity of the deception. This mockery in private of all that the countess preached in public as noble, transcendent, and inviolable, this diabolic inner laughter and deliberate defiance of all that was held sacred, and all performed with such unrestrained depravity which even the most feverish imagination could not contemplate. Yes, *that* above all else accounted for the most gratifying aspect of this debauchery. Yes, she was the devil incarnate, but an irresistibly charming devil. Even now I cannot think about her without excitement. In the heat of flaming pleasures, she would suddenly laugh like a mad woman and I understood, I understood why she was laughing, and I laughed, too... I'm still short of breath from laughter at the memory of it, and that was many years ago. A year later, she cast me out. Even if I had wanted to, I couldn't have hurt her. Who would have believed me? With her reputation? What say you, my young friend?"

"Phew, how disgusting!" I answered with revulsion after hearing his confession.

"You would not be my friend if you had answered any other way! I knew you would say that. Ha-ha-ha! Just wait, *mon ami*, stick around a bit longer and you will understand, but for now you still need icing on your gingerbread. But you're not really a poet if you feel that way. That woman understood life and knew how to live it fully."

"Why should one descend to such atrocities?"

"To what atrocities?"

"To which this woman descended, and you with her."

"And you call this an atrocity? A sign that you are still tethered by strings. Of course, I recognize that independence can be displayed in opposing ways, but... if we speak truthfully, my friend... you must admit that it is all nonsense."

"But what *isn't* nonsense?"

"What isn't nonsense is personality—me. All is for me and the world was created for me. Listen, my friend, I still believe that one can live well in this world. And that is the best faith, because without faith, it is impossible to live even unhappily. There would be nothing left but to poison oneself. I've heard that that is what one fool did. He philosophized until he had destroyed everything, everything, even the legitimacy of all normal and natural human duties, until at last he had nothing left, and so he declared that the best thing in life was hydrogen cyanide. You say that is the plot of *Hamlet*. That terrible despair. In fact, something so majestic that we could not even dream of it. But you are a poet, and I am a simple man, so I say that we must look at the matter from the simplest, most practical point of view. For example, I long ago freed myself from all shackles, and even obligations. I recognize obligations only if they might benefit me in some way. You certainly cannot look at things that way because your legs are fettered, and your taste is morose. You yearn for the ideal, for virtue. Well, my friend, I am very willing to accept anything you want me to, but what can I do if I know that the basis of all human virtue lies in the most profound egoism. And the more virtuous any action, the more egoism there is. Love yourself—that is the one rule that I recognize. Life is a commercial transaction, don't give away your money for nothing, but if you pay for your indulgences, you will fulfill all your obligations to your neighbor. Those are my morals, if you really want to know, although I confess to you, in my opinion, it is better not to pay your neighbor if you can get him to do it for free. I have no ideals and I do not want them. I have never felt a need for them. One can have so much fun, and live so nicely without ideals... in short, I am incredibly happy that I get along *without* the hydrogen cyanide. After all, if I were more virtuous, I might perhaps require it, like that fool philosopher, undoubtedly a German. No! There is still so much that is good in life! I love substance, rank, a fine home, a huge stake in a card game—I'm awfully fond of cards—but the primary thing is... women! Women of every kind. I love lust—dark, depraved and original—and even a bit of perversion just for variety... Ha-ha-ha! I look at your face and see the contempt you feel for me now!"

"You are right," I answered.

"Well, even assuming you are right, isn't a bit of perversion better than hydrogen cyanide? Don't you think?"

"No, hydrogen cyanide is decidedly preferable."

"Ah, I purposely asked you that in order to enjoy your reply, which I knew beforehand. No, my friend, if you are a true lover of mankind, then wish that all the smart people share my tastes, even to the point of perversion, or the wise man will soon have nothing left to do in the world and only fools will remain. How lucky for *them*! There is, in fact, some proverb about fools being lucky, and you know there is nothing more pleasant and profitable than to live with fools! It should not be surprising that I value convention, cherish prejudices, and hold certain traditions in high regard, because I live in a worthless world, but I am comfortable in it, assent to it and stand firm in it, although I *would* be first to leave it if the occasion arose. I know all your modern ideas, though I have never suffered from them and have no desire to. I never have pangs of conscience about anything. I agree to everything, as long as I come out all right, and there are legions of others like me. All things can be lost, but we will never perish. As long as the world exists, we shall exist. All the world may sink, but we shall float, we shall always float to the top. By the way, have you noticed how full of life people like me are? We are, above all, phenomenally tenacious. We live to be eighty, ninety. Nature itself protects us, heh-heh-heh! I definitely want to live to be ninety years old. I am not fond of death, and I'm afraid of it. After all, God alone knows what death is like! But why talk about it! It was that philosopher who poisoned himself that set me on this track. To hell with philosophy! Let us drink! We had started to talk about pretty women... Where are you going?"

"I'm going home, and it's time for you to do the same."

"Nonsense, nonsense! I have, so to speak, opened my heart to you, and you do not seem to appreciate what strong evidence this is of my friendship. Heh-heh-heh! There is not much love in you, my poet. But wait, I want another bottle."

"A third?"

"A third! As for virtue, my young pet—you will allow me to call you this sweet name—who knows, maybe my teachings will come in handy one day. So, my pet, about virtue, I have already told you, 'the more virtuous virtue is, the more egoism there is in it.' I want to tell you a very pretty anecdote apropos of that: I once loved a girl, and I think I may have actually loved her for real. She even sacrificed a lot for me..."

"Is that the one you robbed?" I asked rudely, not willing to restrain myself any longer.

Prince Valkovsky started, his color changed, and he fixed his bloodshot eyes on me. He was both perplexed and furious.

"Wait a minute," he said, as if to himself, "wait, let me think about... I'm really drunk, and I find it difficult to..."

He paused and looked searchingly at me with that same malevolent stare, grasping my hand in his, as if afraid that I would get away. I was sure at that moment that he was trying to understand how much I knew and where I might have learned something that almost nobody knew, and whether there was any danger in my knowledge. This went on for a full minute, but suddenly his face changed quickly. The old mocking, good-humored expression appeared again in his eyes. He laughed.

"Ha-ha-ha! You're as craftily diplomatic as Talleyrand! Yes, I actually did stand in front of her once when she spat upon me and blurted out that I had robbed her. Oh, she screamed and cursed me something awful. She was like a mad woman and... all for nothing. But judge for yourself. First of all, I did not rob her, as you put it just now. She gave me the money herself, which was mine to begin with. Suppose you were to give me your best dress coat..." (As he said this, he looked at my ugly, badly worn coat made for me three years earlier by a tailor named Ivan Skornyagin.) "I am grateful to you and wear it. Suddenly, a year later you quarrel with me and demand it back after I had already worn it out. This would be ungentlemanly. Why give it to me at all? Secondly, despite the fact that the money was mine, I certainly would have returned it to her but, as you must admit, where could I suddenly raise such a sum? And most importantly, I cannot stand pastorals and Schillerizing, as I told you so before, and that was the cause of our fight. You would not believe how she looked, standing there in front of me, screaming that she gave me what was in fact my money. Well, I grew angry and suddenly had the presence of mind to recognize that if I gave her money, I would make her even more unhappy. I would deprive her of the satisfaction of being miserable *because of me* and deny her the pleasure of cursing me for the rest of her life. Believe me, my friend, there *does* exist in misfortune a very real and exalted condition of the mind which finds relief and consolation in believing in one's complete innocence and high-mindedness, and having earned the right to call your abuser a scoundrel. This infatuation with evil natures is found frequently among admirers of Schiller, of course, and although she may have soon found herself homeless, with nothing to eat, she would certainly be happy. I did not want to deprive her of that happiness by sending her money, so I kept it. All of this justifies my rule that at the root of all high-mindedness and virtue lies the most abominable selfishness. Is that clear to you now? But... you wanted to trip me up, ha-ha-ha! Well, admit it, you wanted to catch me... Oh, Talleyrand!"

"Good-bye!" I said, rising.

"Wait a minute! Two final words," he cried, suddenly changing his tone from angry to a deadly serious. "Hear my final words. From everything I have told you, it should be clear and unmistakable—I think you would have noticed—that I never give anything to others unless it benefits me. I love money and I need it. Katerina Fedorovna has plenty, her father held a monopoly on vodka for ten years. She has three million rubles and that three million will be very useful to me. Alyosha and Katya are a perfect pair, both complete fools, which is ideal for me. So, it is certainly my wish that their marriage be consummated as soon as possible. In two weeks, the countess and Katya are going to the country. Alyosha must accompany them. Warn Natalia Nikolayevna that there must be no idyllic nonsense, no Schillerisms. She had better not fight me on this. I can be malicious and vengeful when crossed, and I am not afraid to stand up to her. I will have my way, so my warning to her is really for her sake. See that she does nothing stupid, that she behaves prudently. Otherwise it will not end well. She should be grateful that I have not treated her as I could have, since the law is on my side. Know, my poet, that laws protect family tranquility. They guarantee that a son will obey his father, and those who attempt to seduce children from their most sacred duties to their parents are not looked upon kindly by the courts. Remember, too, that I have influential connections and she has none. I am sure you can imagine what I *could* do to her, although I have not done so because she has acted wisely so far. You need not worry. Every move they have made and every action they have taken for the past six months has been observed with my keen eyes, and I remember every detail. I have calmly waited for Alyosha to tire of her and end the relationship on his own, and that process has begun. But meanwhile she has been a nice little distraction for him. Most importantly, I have remained in his eyes a kind, humane father, and I intend to keep it that way. Ha-ha-ha! When I remember that I complimented her that evening for being so generous and selfless as to not marry him, I wonder that she could have even considered marrying him! As to my visit to her then, it was solely because it was time to end their relationship. But I need to convince myself with my own eyes, my own experience. Well, is that enough for you? Or perhaps you still want to know why I brought you here, and why I have revealed so many of my deepest secrets to you, when I could have made my point without any such frank confessions—right?"

"Right."

I controlled myself and listened eagerly. I had nothing more to say to him.

"It is only because, my friend, that in you I have recognized a great deal more common sense and clear sightedness than in either of our two young fools. You may have studied my past and drawn some conclusions about me, but I wanted to make it easier for you and decided to show you face to face precisely with whom you are dealing. A first-hand experience is a great thing, so hear me, my friend: You understand what I am capable of, and you love her, so I hope now that you will use all of your influence—and you still do have influence with her—to save her from *certain* awkward and unpleasant circumstances. Otherwise there will be trouble, I assure you, and it will not be anything to joke about. And finally, the third reason for my honesty with you—but of course you have guessed it, my dear boy—is that I really wanted an opportunity to spit on this whole business a little, and especially to spit in your face."

"Well, you've achieved your goal," I said, trembling with rage. "I agree that you could not have better revealed your hatred and contempt for me and all of us better than by these revelations. Not only are you not bothered that your disgusting confessions may compromise you in my eyes, you are not even ashamed to expose the depth of your depravity to me. You really are like that madman in the cloak. You do not regard me as a human being."

"You have guessed right, my young friend," he said, getting up. "You are very perceptive. It's no wonder you're a writer. I hope that we are parting amicably. Shall we have a final drink to brotherhood?"

"You are drunk, and the only reason I cannot answer you as I would like..."

"Again, a figure of silence! You haven't said all you might have said. Ha-ha-ha! And you won't allow me to pay for you?"

"Don't worry, I'll pay for myself."

"I have no doubt about that. But aren't we both going the same direction?"

"I'm not coming with you."

"Farewell then, my poet. I hope you've understood me..."

He went out, walking unsteadily and not turning back to me. The footman helped him into his carriage. I went my own way on foot. It was nearly three o'clock in the morning. It was raining and the night was dark.

Chapter Thirty-Seven

I won't attempt to describe my rage. I had been expecting pretty much anything, but the prince still managed to astonish me. He had appeared before me, quite unpredictably, in all his loathsome ugliness. I remember, though, that my sensations were confused, as if I had been beaten and bruised, with a black dread gnawing at my heart. I was afraid for Natasha. I could see great suffering ahead for her and I hoped to find some way to avoid it, to soften the blow before the final catastrophic ending. The inevitability of that catastrophe was not in doubt, and it was easy to see that it was approaching fast!

I have no memory of how I made it home that night, but I arrived drenched from the rain. It was after three in the morning. Before I could knock on the door of my apartment, I heard a groan and Nellie hurriedly opened the door, looking like she had never gone to bed, but had been watching the threshold for my arrival. A candle was burning, and I was shocked to see the change in her face. Her eyes burned with a fever that gave her a wild appearance, as if she did not recognize me.

"Nellie, what's wrong, are you sick?" I asked, leaning in to hold her in my arms.

She clung to me anxiously, clearly afraid of something, and started to speak quickly and erratically, as if she had waited all night to tell me something. But her words were incoherent and strange, and I did not understand. She was delirious.

I led her quickly to her sofa bed, but she rushed back to me and clung tightly, as if begging me to protect her from someone. And even after I had tucked her in, she continued to clutch my hand tightly, perhaps afraid that I might leave her again. I was so shocked and my nerves so frayed that I began to cry. Seeing my tears, she gazed long and fixedly at me as if trying to grasp and understand something. This evidently took a great deal of effort on her part. Finally, something similar to an idea lit up her face. After a strong epileptic attack, she usually took a long time to gather her thoughts clearly before being able to speak coherently. And so it was now. After making an extraordinary effort to say something to me, and realizing that I did not understand, she held out her little hand and began to wipe away my tears, then she hugged my neck, drew me down to her, and tenderly kissed my cheek.

It was clear that she had had a seizure in my absence, and it had happened at precisely the moment she was standing at the door. Rousing herself from the fit had probably taken quite some time. During that period of recovery, reality often mixed with delirium, and she sometimes imagined something terrible, some horror. At the same time, she must have been vaguely aware that I would be back soon and would be knocking at the door, and so, lying in the doorway on the floor, she keenly awaited my return, and got up on my first knock.

"But why had she been at the door in the first place?" I wondered, and suddenly noticed with astonishment that she was wearing the old weathered coat I had acquired for her from an old woman peddler who occasionally visited my apartment and gave me old goods in recompense for money I had lent her. So, she must have been planning to go out and had already unlocked the door when she was surprised by the epileptic incident. Where could she have been planning to go? Was she already suffering delusions?

Meanwhile, the fever did not pass, and she soon fell back into delirium and unconsciousness. She had previously had two fits in my apartment, but they had passed without incident. But now she had a high fever. After sitting beside her for half an hour, I pushed a chair next to the sofa and settled into it, fully dressed, so that I would be able to wake up immediately if she called for me. I did not even snuff out the candle. I watched her for some time before I, too, fell asleep. She was pale, her lips were parched with fever and stained with blood, probably from falling on her face. That face still held a look of terror and a kind of wounded sorrow that continued to haunt her even as she slept. I decided that if she did not improve, I would go first thing in the morning to the doctor. I was afraid Nellie might end up with actual brain fever.

"She must have been frightened by the prince," I thought, with a shudder, and I recalled his story about the woman he had abandoned who threw money in his face.

CHAPTER THIRTY-EIGHT

Two weeks later, Nellie's health was improving. Although she had not developed brain fever, she was still seriously ill. She was able to get out of bed on a bright, clear day at the end of April. It was Holy Week.

The poor creature! I cannot continue my story in the same order. A great deal of time has passed since the events I am describing, but I still recall that period with a heavy heart as I think about her pale, thin face, and the long, piercing glances from those dark eyes when we were occasionally alone together. She would gaze at me from her bed, watching for long periods of time, as if challenging me to guess what was on her mind. But once she realized that I was still confused, she would give me a gentle smile and stretch out her hot little hand with its thin, withered fingers. Now everything is past and all is understood, but to this day I still do not know all of the secrets of that exhausted, wounded little heart.

I feel that I am straying from my story, but at this moment I'd like to think only of Nellie. Strange, now that I'm lying here alone in a hospital bed, abandoned by all whom I have loved so warmly and intensely, some half-forgotten incident that was barely noticed at the time will come suddenly to mind and take on a whole new significance, revealing to me a meaning that I had failed to grasp at the time.

For the first four days of Nellie's illness, the doctor and I were terribly worried about her, but on the fifth day the doctor pulled me aside and told me that we had nothing to fear, that she would undoubtedly recover. This was the same doctor I had known for so long, a kindly and eccentric old bachelor whom I had brought in the first time Nellie had been sick, and who had so impressed her with his huge Stanislav cross hanging from his neck.

"So there's no reason to worry," I said, greatly relieved.

"No, she will recover this time, but she will die soon after that."

"Die! But why?" I cried, overwhelmed by such a prediction.

"Yes, she will die very soon. The patient has an organic heart defect and even the least adverse circumstances could lay her up again. She may recover once again but, inevitably, she will die."

"And there is nothing we can do to save her? That can't be possible!"

"But it is a fact. And yet, if you remove the adverse circumstances and give her a calm and quiet life and keep her happy, the patient may still be kept from death for a while, and there are even cases… unexpected... unusual and exceptional… when a patient may be sustained by a series of favorable circumstances. But radically cured, never."

"But, my God, what do I do now?"

"Follow my advice, lead a quiet life, and get her to take her medicine regularly. I've noticed that this girl is capricious, with an uneven temperament, and a disdainful sense of humor. And she does not like to take her powders regularly. In fact, she has just now flatly refused to take them."

"Yes, Doctor, she is strange, but I attribute that to her erratic history. Yesterday she was very obedient, but today when I brought Nellie her medicine, she shoved the spoon as if by accident, and it spilled all over. When I wanted to mix another powder, she grabbed the box from me, threw it on the floor, and then burst into tears. And yet, I don't think it was solely because I tried to force her to take her medicine," I added, after a moment's thought.

"Hmm! Insecurity. Still her greatest obstacle."

I had told the doctor, fully and frankly, Nellie's history, and my story had impressed him greatly.

"Everything in her past has certainly contributed to her illness," he continued. "But for the time being the only remedy is to take the powders I gave you, and it must be those powders. I'll go talk with her again and try to impress on her the need to follow medical advice and... that means, generally speaking... taking her medicine."

We both came out of the kitchen, where our consultation had taken place, and the doctor again approached Nellie's bedside. I think the sick girl had overheard at least part of our conversation, as she had raised her head from the pillow and turned her ear in our direction, listening intently the whole time. I had noticed this through a crack in the half-opened door, and when we returned to her the little scamp had slipped back under the covers and was grinning at us with a playful smile. The poor thing had grown even thinner during those four days of illness. Her eyes were sunken, and her fever had not yet passed, so the mischievous smile and the playful, provocative look on her face surprised the doctor, one of the most good-natured Germans in St. Petersburg. He was somber but tried to soften his voice as best he could. In a tender and gentle tone, he explained the need for the powders, and how it was the duty of every patient to accept them. As the doctor moved the spoon towards her, Nellie opened her mouth, but a sudden unexpected movement of her arm, seemingly unintentional, knocked the doctor's hand, causing him to spill the medicine on the floor yet again. I was sure that she did it on purpose.

"This is a very unpleasant carelessness," the old man said quietly, "and I suspect that you have done it on purpose, which is inexcusable. But... We can remedy this by preparing another powder."

Nellie laughed in his face. The doctor shook his head methodically.

"This is very wrong," he said, opening a new box, "completely inexcusable."

"Don't be angry with me," Nellie said, vainly trying not to laugh again. "I will certainly take it... But do you like me?"

"If you conduct yourself admirably, I will like you very much."

"Very much?"

"Very much indeed."

"But don't you like me now?"

"Yes, I like you even now."

"And will you kiss me if I want you to?

"Yes, if you deserve it."

This amused Nellie and she could not help but laugh again.

"The patient has a cheerful disposition, but right now she is suffering from nerves and caprice," the doctor whispered, turning to me with a serious expression.

"All right, all right, I'll drink the powder!" Nellie cried suddenly, her voice weak, "but when I grow up will you marry me?"

Evidently the invention of this new game delighted the girl. Her eyes shone brightly, and her lips twitched with laughter as she awaited an answer from the astonished doctor.

"Well," he answered, smiling involuntarily at Nellie's latest whim. "Yes, if you grow up to be a good, well-mannered young lady who will follow instructions and..."

"Take my medicine?" she finished his sentence.

"Ah ha! Yes, take your medicine. Good girl!" he said. He turned to me again and whispered, "There are many wonderful things… she is kind and clever, but… to propose marriage... What a strange notion."

And he turned again to offer her the medicine on a spoon. But this time she made no pretense of clumsiness and simply pushed the doctor's hand up, splashing the medicine directly on the poor man's shirt front and face. Nellie laughed aloud, but not the cheerful, good-humored laughter from before. This time there was something cruel and malevolent in her expression. During all this time she had avoided my gaze, looking only at the doctor with derision, through which glimpses I could detect an uneasiness, as if she were waiting to see what the "ridiculous" old man would do.

"Oh! You've done it again. How unfortunate! But... I can mix you another powder," the old man said calmly, wiping his face and shirt-front with a handkerchief.

This made a strong impression on Nellie. She had expected an angry outburst, followed by a scolding and reproval. Perhaps, unconsciously, she had been looking for an excuse to cry, to sob hysterically, to upset more spoons of medicine, and even break something in her vexation, all to satisfy her capricious and aching heart. Such whims are found not only in sick people and not only in Nellie. I had often walked up and down the room with an unconscious desire to have someone insult me or say something that I could interpret as an insult so I would have an excuse to vent my anger on someone. Women, venting their anger in that way will cry, shedding genuine and sincere tears, and the more sensitive of them may even go into hysterics. It is a simple and everyday experience, and happens most often when there is some other, often unrevealed, sadness in the heart, to which one would like to give voice but can't.

But suddenly struck by the angelic kindness of the old doctor and the patience with which he set to work preparing a third powder, without uttering one word of reproach to her, Nellie's petulance suddenly subsided. The ridicule vanished from her lips, the color returned to her cheeks, and her eyes grew moist. She glanced briefly at me and immediately turned away. The doctor again offered her medicine and she quietly and timidly swallowed it, grasping the old man's plump red hand, and slowly looking up into his eyes.

"You... are angry... I was horrible," she started to say, but did not finish. She ducked under her covers and hid her head before bursting into loud hysterical sobs.

"Oh, my child, don't cry. It's nothing... It's just nerves, have a drink of water."

But Nellie did not hear him.

"Be comforted... do not upset yourself," he went on, almost whimpering over her, for he was an extremely sensitive man. "I forgive you, and will marry you if, like a good, well-mannered young woman, you will..."

"Take my powders!" came from under the covers with a nervous laugh that sounded like the tinkle of a bell interspersed with sobs—a laugh I knew well.

"Good-hearted, grateful child," said the doctor triumphantly, almost with tears in his own eyes. "A sweet little girl!"

From that day on he and Nellie began a strange and wonderful friendship, but with me, Nellie became even more sullen, nervous and irritable. I had no idea why this was happening, and I puzzled over it at the time. Most surprisingly, the change seemed to have occurred overnight. During the early days of her illness, Nellie had been extremely gentle and affectionate with me. Indeed, it seemed like she could not get enough of me and never wanted me to leave her side. She would clutch my hand in her feverish little grip and sit beside me whenever possible. If she noticed that I was moody or anxious, she would try to cheer me up by making jokes, playing games, and smiling endlessly at me, all of which evidently helped to suppress her own suffering. She did not want me to work at night or to sit up to look after her, and she lamented when I would not listen to her. Sometimes she would notice a worried look on my face and she would begin to question me to find out why I was sad, what was on my mind, but strangely, when I mentioned Natasha, she immediately fell silent or wanted to talk about something else. In fact, she seemed to avoid talking about Natasha entirely, which puzzled me. When I came home, she was happy, but when I took up my hat to go out, she would become sad and look at me strangely, following me with her eyes, reproachfully.

On the fourth day of her illness, I spent the whole evening at Natasha's and stayed out passed midnight. Natasha and I had something we needed to talk about. As I left my apartment, I had told my little invalid that I would return very soon, which I had fully expected at the time. When I was delayed at Natasha's, I didn't worry about Nellie because Alexandra Semyonovna was looking after her. She had learned from Masloboyev after he had stopped by, that Nellie was sick, and I was having so much trouble because I had no one to help me. My God, how the pious Alexandra Semyonovna fussed upon hearing that. "So, of course, he won't come to dine with us anymore! Oh, my lord! He is all alone, poor fellow, all alone. Well, now we must show Vanya how we feel about him. Such an opportunity, we must not fail him."

She immediately appeared at my door with a stack of parcels, having arrived by cab. Her first words were that she had come to help me and that she was going to stay. Then she untied the parcels. There were syrups and jams for the invalid, chickens and other fowl for when the patient began to recover, apples for baking, oranges, dry Kiev preserves (in the event the doctor would allow them), and finally, linen sheets, napkins, ladies' underwear, bandages, compresses, enough to outfit a whole hospital.

"We have everything!" she said to me, articulating each word in her haste to make herself understood. "Well, you live like a bachelor. You do not have enough of anything. So let me... as Philip Philippich suggested… Well, what now... quickly, quickly! Tell me what I should do first! How is she? Is she conscious? Oh, how uncomfortable she must be lying there. I will fix her pillow so her head will be lower, but what do you think… would a leather cushion be better? Leather is cooler. Oh, what a fool I am! It never occurred to me to bring… I'll go get one... Shouldn't we light the fire? I will send you my old woman. I have a friend who is an old woman. Because you have no female servants, have you? Well, now what do I do? What is this? Herbs? The doctor prescribed them? For some herb tea, perhaps. I'll go and light the fire."

But I reassured her, and she was surprised and even a bit saddened to learn that there was very little that needed to be done. This, however, did not discourage her completely. She immediately made friends with Nellie and helped me a great deal during the remainder of Nellie's illness. She visited us almost every day, and always arrived looking as though she had lost something, or it had gone astray and she had to hurry to catch it. She always added that Philip Philippich had told her to come. Nellie liked her very much. They loved each other like two sisters, and I think that Alexandra Semyonovna was as much a child as Nellie. She would tell the child stories to amuse her, and Nellie often missed Alexandra Semyonovna when she had returned home.

Her first appearance had surprised my patient, but Nellie immediately guessed why the uninvited guest had come and, as usual, frowned and became silent and ungracious.

"Why did she come to see us?" Nellie asked, with what seemed like an air of displeasure, when Alexandra Semyonovna had gone.

"To help you, Nellie, and to look after you."

"But why? What for? I've never done anything for her."

"Good people don't wait for that, Nellie. They like to help people in need without expecting anything in return. Truly, Nellie, the world is full of many good people. Unfortunately, you and your mother did not meet any of them when they could have helped the most."

Nellie was silent, and I walked away from her. But a quarter of an hour later she called me to her in a weak voice, asked for something to drink and then suddenly hugged me, clinging to my chest for a long time. The next day, when Alexandra Semyonovna arrived, Nellie greeted her with a joyful smile, although she still seemed a bit ashamed for her previous behavior.

Chapter Thirty-Nine

It happened on that day when I was at Natasha's apartment the whole evening. I had come home late, and Nellie was asleep. Alexandra Semyonovna was sleepy, but she was still awake, sitting next to the sleeping invalid and waiting for me. As soon as I entered, she hurriedly whispered to me that Nellie had been quite cheerful at first, even laughing a lot, but when I failed to come home, she grew bored and then became silent and thoughtful. "Then she began to complain that she had a headache and started to cry. She sobbed so much that I didn't know what to do," Alexandra Semyonovna added. "She started asking me questions about Natalia Nikolayevna, but I told her I didn't know anything, so she stopped the questions and eventually fell asleep in tears. Well, goodnight, Ivan Petrovich. She is better now, I think, and I must go home. Philip Philippich ordered it. I must confess to you that he only wanted me to stay for two hours, but then I decided to stay on my own. But don't worry about me. He doesn't dare get angry with me. Only now he… Oh, my God, my dear Ivan Petrovich, what do I do? He always comes home drunk now! He seems busy with some matter, but he won't tell me anything about it. He has important business on his mind, I can see that, and yet he comes home drunk every evening. Think about that. When he comes home tonight, someone will have to put him to bed. Well, I'm going, I'm going. Goodnight, Ivan Petrovich. I noticed how many books you have. You must be very smart. I'm such a fool, I never read anything. Well, until tomorrow…"

The very next day Nellie woke up sad and gloomy and only responded to me reluctantly. She did not want to speak to me, it seemed, because she was angry with me. I noticed her taking a few sideward glances in my direction, but they were done stealthily, on the sly. In those pained looks I saw much concealed heartache, and yet still some indications of tenderness, which she never revealed when she looked directly at me. It was on that day that the incident with the doctor and her medicine occurred. I did not know what to think.

But where I was concerned, Nellie had changed completely. Her eccentricities, her whims, and her apparent hatred towards me continued right up to the day when she ceased to live with me, till the catastrophe that was to end our close relationship. But more about that later.

It happened sometimes, however, that for an hour or so she would suddenly become as affectionate towards me as she had been at first. Her tenderness seemed doubled at such moments, most often when she was weeping bitterly. But those hours ended all too soon and she would sink back into the old misery and again look at me with hostility, or with the petulance she had displayed with the doctor, or notice suddenly that I did not appreciate some new mischief of hers, and begin laughing and almost always end in tears.

She quarreled even with Alexandra Semyonovna and told her that she wanted nothing to do with her. When I began to scold her in front of Alexandra Semyonovna, Nellie got angry, replied with an outburst of accumulated spite, and then suddenly stopped talking for two days, not uttering a single word to me. She would not take any of her medicine and refused to eat and drink. Only the old doctor could appeal to her conscience and bring her around.

I have mentioned already that since the incident with the medicine, she and the doctor had established a warmly sympathetic relationship. Nellie was very fond of him, and always greeted him with a cheerful smile, no matter how sad she had been before his arrival. For his part, the old man began to visit us every day and sometimes twice a day, even after Nellie had recovered enough to walk around on her own. He seemed so bewitched by her that he could not live a day without hearing her laugh and make fun of him, usually in very funny ways. He began bringing her picture books, all with underlying educational properties, and sweets and chocolates in pretty boxes. At such times he usually arrived with an earnest look, pretending it was his birthday or a similar event, and Nellie immediately guessed that he had come with a gift. But he wouldn't show her the gift, just laughed slyly, seating himself beside Nellie and hinting that if a young girl knew how to behave properly and earn his appreciation in his absence, then that young lady would deserve a proper reward. At the same time, he would look at her in such a good-natured and innocent way that Nellie would laugh at him with honest and sincere affection that showed in her little eyes. Finally, the old man would rise solemnly from his chair, take out a box of candy and hand it to Nellie, invariably adding "for my gracious and charming future wife." At that moment he was probably happier than Nellie.

After that, they would talk seriously, and he would always try to persuade her to protect her health, and he would give her strong medical advice.

"Above all one must take care of one's health," he would say in a dogmatic tone, "firstly and most importantly, in order to stay alive, and secondly, to always be healthy and thus achieve happiness in life. If you have, my dear child, any sorrows, forget them, or better yet, try not to think about them. If you don't have any sorrows, well then... you still shouldn't think about them, but try to think about pleasant things… something cheerful and amusing."

"And what should I think about that is cheerful and amusing?" Nellie would ask.

The doctor would have no immediate answer. One time he answered, "Well... of some innocent game, appropriate for your age or, well... something like that."

"I don't want to play games, I do not like games," Nellie said... "I like new dresses better."

"New dresses! Hmm. Well, that's not so good. We must be content with modest things in life. And yet... maybe... you can still love new dresses."

"And will you make me a lot of new dresses when I am married to you?"

"What an idea!" the doctor said with a frown. Nellie smiled slyly, and forgetting herself for a moment, turned and smiled at me. "And yet," the doctor continued, "I might *buy* you a dress, if you earn it by your good behavior."

"And must I take my medicine every day when I'm married to you?"

"Well, maybe by then you won't need to take your medicine as often," the doctor answered with a smile.

Nellie interrupted the conversation with laughter. The old man laughed with her and enjoyed seeing her so happy.

"A playful creative mind!" he observed, turning to me. "But still visible signs of caprice and whimsicality along with some irritability."

He was right. I really did not know what was happening with her. She seemed utterly unwilling to talk to me, as if I had treated her badly in some way. I couldn't help feeling bitter. I frowned and didn't speak to her for the rest of the day, but the next day I felt ashamed. She would cry a great deal, and I really had no idea how to console her. However, on one occasion she broke her silence with me.

I had returned home just before nightfall and saw Nellie quickly hide a book under her pillow. It was my novel, which she had taken from the table and begun to read in my absence. "Why did she feel she needed to hide it from me? As if she were ashamed," I wondered, but I showed no sign of having seen anything. Fifteen minutes later, when I went into the kitchen for a moment, she quickly jumped out of bed and put the novel back in its place. When I returned, I saw it back on the table. A minute later she called me to her. There was a note of excitement in her voice. For the previous four days she had hardly said a word to me.

"Are you... today... going to visit Natasha?" she asked me in a broken voice.

"Yes, Nellie, I really need to see her today." Nellie was silent.

"You... are very... fond of her?" she asked again, in a weak voice.

"Yes, Nellie, I'm very fond of her."

"And I love her, too," she added quietly. Then there was silence again.

"I want to go and live with her," Nellie began again, shyly glancing at me.

"That's impossible, Nellie," I answered, somewhat surprised. "Are you so unhappy with me?"

"Why is it impossible?" Her face flushed crimson. "You were trying to persuade me to go live with her father, and I didn't want to go there. Has she a servant?"

"Yes."

"Well, let her send her servant away, and I will serve her. I'll do everything for her and she won't have to pay me. I'll love her and do her cooking. You tell her that today."

"But what a strange fantasy, Nellie. Do you really think that she would agree to take you instead of her cook? If she did let you live with her, it would be as a sister, as an equal."

"No, I do not want to be an equal. I don't want it like that..."

"Why not?"

Nellie was silent. Her lips twitched. She was about to cry.

"The man she loves is going away from her and leaving her alone?" she asked finally. I was surprised.

"Yes, how do you know about that, Nellie?"

"You told me about it yourself, and the day before yesterday when Alexandra Semyonovna's husband came in the morning, I asked him, and he told me everything."

"Masloboyev came here in the morning?"

"Yes," she answered, staring at the floor.

"Why didn't you tell me that he had been here?"

"I don't know."

I thought for a moment. Why in the world was Masloboyev meeting secretly with Nellie? What had they talked about? I knew that I had to go see him.

"Well, how does it concern you, Nellie, if he leaves her?"

"Because you love her very much," Nellie said, still not looking me in the eye. "And if you love her, you will marry her when he leaves."

"No, Nellie, she does not love me like I love her, and I... No, that's not going to happen, Nellie."

"And I can work for you both as your servant, and we would all live together and be happy," she said, almost in a whisper, still not looking at me.

I wondered what had happened to her to give her these strange ideas, and my soul was knotted in confusion. Nellie was silent again and did not say a word the rest of the evening. When I left, she began to cry and Alexandra Semyonovna told me later that Nellie never stopped crying and eventually fell asleep in tears. That night, she cried in her sleep and even spoke out loud in her delirium.

From that day on, she became even more morose and silent, and never spoke to me at all. There were two or three moments when I caught her toss a furtive glance in my direction and there was great tenderness in her eyes. But these moments passed quickly and the rest of the time she was as gloomy as ever. She was even moody with the doctor, who was surprised at the change in her character. Meanwhile, her health was almost completely restored, and the doctor allowed her to finally take a walk in the fresh air, but only for a short time. The weather was bright and warm. It was Holy Week, Easter having come later than usual that year. I went out early in the morning to visit Natasha but planned to return in time to take Nellie for a walk. Meanwhile, I had left her alone.

But I cannot express what a tremendous shock awaited me at home. I hurried home and saw the key sticking out of the lock in the door. I went in and she was gone. I froze. There on the table was a pencil and a piece of paper that said, in a large, uneven hand:

"I have gone away and will never come back to you. But I love you very much. Your faithful Nellie."

I uttered a cry of horror and rushed out of the apartment.

Chapter Forty

I had not even had time to run out into the street or consider what I should do next, when I saw an open carriage stop at the gate of our building. Alexandra Semyonovna was stepping out of it, leading Nellie by the hand. She held her tightly, as if afraid that she might run away again. I rushed over to them.

"Nellie, what's the matter?" I cried. "Where did you go. Why did you leave me?"

"Wait a minute, don't rush her," Alexandra Semyonovna twittered. "Let us hurry upstairs and you'll learn everything there. I have so much to tell you, Ivan Petrovich," she whispered as we climbed the stairs. "You'll be surprised. Come, you shall hear all."

Her face suggested that she had extremely important news.

"Go on, Nellie, go and lie down for a while," she said when we walked into the apartment. "You must be so tired, running around after so great an illness. Lie down, my dear, lie down. Ivan Petrovich and I will be in the kitchen. We will talk quietly so you can sleep." And she winked at me and preceded me into the kitchen."

But Nellie did not lie down. She sat on the sofa and covered her face with both hands.

In the kitchen, Alexandra Semyonovna gave me a quick summary of what had happened. I would learn more details later. Here is the story:

Nellie had gone out about two hours before my return home, leaving the note on the table. She ran first to the old doctor, whose address she had found among my papers. The doctor later told me that he had almost fainted when she arrived at his door and was unnerved the whole time she was with him. "I couldn't believe my eyes. I still don't believe it," he said as he concluded his story. And yet Nellie had been there with him. He was sitting quietly in his room, wearing a dressing gown and sipping coffee, when she burst in and threw her arms around his neck. Before he could recover, she was crying, kissing his hands, and trying, almost incoherently, to convince him to take her into his home, saying she could not—and would not—live with me any longer and had, therefore, left me. She was very unhappy and promised that she would not laugh at him anymore or talk to him about new dresses, and she would wash and iron his shirts—she had probably rehearsed the speech in her head on the way to his home—and that, most importantly, she would obey his instructions and always take her medicine when he gave it to her. And she said that she did not really expect him to marry her, that it had been a joke, and that she would never talk about it again. The old German was so stunned, he sat with his mouth hanging open and completely forgot about the cigar he was holding until it had burned itself out.

"My dear child," he said at last, once he had recovered the powers of speech, "if I understood you correctly, you're asking me to give you a job in my home. But that is… impossible! You can see I am very cramped here and I do not have a significant income... And for you to leap into something like this without thinking... is terrible! And it seems that you have run away from his home, which is reprehensible and quite unacceptable... And while I have approved your taking a short walk, on a clear day, under the supervision of your benefactor, you have now abandoned your benefactor and come to me, when you should be home taking care of yourself and... and... taking your medicine. And finally... finally, I do not understand what…"

Nellie did not let him finish. She began to cry and implored him again, but nothing could persuade him. The old man was more and more confused and less and less understanding. Finally, Nellie gave up, muttered "Oh, dear God!" and ran out. "I was sick the whole day," the doctor concluded, "and I had to take an herbal decoction in the evening."

Nellie rushed off to Masloboyev's house. She had taken his address, too, and managed to find it, though not without some difficulty. Masloboyev was at home. Alexandra Semyonovna clasped her hands in amazement when Nellie begged them to take her in. When asked why she was looking for a room, what had happened, and was she unhappy with me, Nellie had no answer and flung herself sobbing into a chair. "She was sobbing so violently, so violently," Alexandra Semyonovna told me, "that I thought she would die." Nellie begged to be taken in, if only as a cook or a maid. She said she would sweep the floor and learn to wash clothes. She seemed to think that washing clothes, for some reason, would be a powerful inducement for hiring her. According to Alexandra Semyonovna, she had wanted to let Nellie stay until the matter could be cleared up, meanwhile letting me know she was there. But Philip Philippich strongly opposed the suggestion and ordered her to bring the runaway back to me immediately. Dear Alexandra Semyonovna then kissed Nellie, which made Nellie cry even more. Looking at her, I could see that Alexandra Semyonovna had been crying, too. In fact, both of them had been crying during the entire carriage ride.

"But why, Nellie, why don't you want to continue living with Ivan Petrovich? What has he done? Was he unkind to you?" Alexandra Semyonovna asked her, once again in tears.

"No, he didn't do anything."

"Well then, why?"

"I just don't want to live with him... I can't... I'm always so mean to him... and he's so nice... But with you, I won't be mean, I'll be working," she said, sobbing hysterically.

"Why are you so mean to him, Nellie?"

"Well..."

"And 'well' was all I could get out of her," sighed Alexandra Semyonovna, wiping away her tears. "Why is she such an unhappy little thing? Is it the epilepsy or what? What do you think, Ivan Petrovich?"

We returned to Nellie. She was lying with her face hidden in the pillow, still crying. I knelt in front of her, took her hands and began kissing them. She snatched her hands back from me and sobbed even harder. I simply did not know what to say. At that moment the old man, Ichmenyev, came in.

"I've come to see you on business, Ivan Petrovich, how are you?" he said, looking at the three of us and surprised to see me on my knees. The old man had been ill of late. He was pale and thin, but, putting on a brave front, he neglected his illness, refused to listen to Anna Andreyevna's exhortations, and went about his daily business, refusing to take to his bed.

"Good-bye for now," Alexandra Semyonovna said, staring at the old man. "Philip Philippich told me to return as soon as possible. We have much to do. But this evening, around sunset, I'll come back and sit with Nellie for an hour or two."

"Who is she?" the old man whispered to me, apparently thinking of something else. I explained.

"Hmm. Well, I've come on business."

I knew what business he was referring to and had been expecting his visit. He had come to talk with me and Nellie, and to implore her to come live with him. Anna Andreyevna had finally agreed to take in the orphaned girl. This had been a result of my private talks with her. The fact that Nellie's mother had been cursed by *her* father had helped to turn the old woman's heart around. I had also suggested that taking in an orphan girl might soften her husband's heart to other feelings. From that point on, she had urged him to take in the orphan. The old man eagerly set to work, first, to please his Anna Andreyevna, and second, because he had his own motives. But all this, I will explain later and more fully.

I have already mentioned that Nellie had taken a dislike to the old man on his very first visit. Since then there had been a look of hatred in her face at the mere utterance of Ichmenyev's name. The old man began to work immediately without beating around the bush. He went straight up to Nellie, who was still lying down, hiding her face in the pillows, and took her hand in his. He asked if she wanted to go to live with him instead of his daughter.

"I had a daughter, I loved her more than myself," the old man added, "but she is no longer with me. She is dead. Would you be willing to take her place in my house… and in my heart?"

And in his eyes, dry and inflamed from his recent fever, gleamed a tear.

"No, I wouldn't," Nellie answered, without raising her head.

"Why, my child? You have no one else. Vanya cannot keep you with him forever, and with me it will be like you have your own home."

"I don't want to because you're wicked. Yes, wicked, wicked," she added, raising her head and looking at the old man. "I am wicked, we're all wicked, but you're more wicked than anyone!"

As she said this, Nellie turned pale, her eyes flashed, and even her trembling lips turned pale, distorted by the rush of strong feelings. The old man looked at her, perplexed.

"Yes, more wicked than me because you refuse to forgive your daughter and you want to forget her altogether and replace her with me. How can you forget your own child? How can you love me? Whenever you look at me, you'll see a stranger and remember that you once had a daughter of your own whom you'd forgotten, because you're a cruel man. I don't want to live with cruel people. I won't!" Nellie sobbed and glanced at me. "The day after tomorrow is Easter. All the people will be kissing and embracing one another. They will all make peace and bad deeds will be forgiven... But not by you. Only you will refuse… ugh, cruel man! Go away!"

She burst into tears. I'm convinced that she had prepared that speech in advance, learned it by heart, just in case the old man ever asked her again to live with him. The old man was devastated and pale. The pain he was feeling was reflected in his face.

"And why, why, why is everyone so worried about me? I don't want them to be!" Nellie cried, suddenly in a frenzy. "I'm going to go and beg in the streets!"

"Nellie, what's the matter? Nellie, my darling!" I cried involuntarily, but my exclamation only added fuel to the fire.

"Yes, I'll be better off begging in the streets. I won't stay here," she shrieked, sobbing more than ever. "Mama begged in the streets, and when she was dying, she told me it's better to be poor and beg than... It's not shameful to ask for money. Instead of asking one person, I'll ask everyone. I'm not ashamed! Because I'm small, no one will give me a job, so I'll beg! I don't want to, I don't want to, I don't… I'm wicked, wickeder than anyone!"

And suddenly Nellie quite unexpectedly seized the cup from the table and threw it on the floor.

"There, now it's broken," she shouted, with a defiant look of triumph directed at me. "There are only two cups," she added, "and I'll break the other! And then how will you drink your tea?"

She seemed possessed by some demon and took delight in her rage, as if aware that it was shameful and wrong, but at the same time, spurring herself on to greater fury.

"She was sick with you, Vanya, that's what," the old man said, "or... I really don't understand this child. Good-bye!"

He took his cap and shook my hand. He was stiff with rage. Nellie had insulted him terribly, and I felt his anger build in me.

"Have you no pity, Nellie?" I cried as soon as the old man had stormed out. "Aren't you ashamed, ashamed for what you said! No, you're not good, you really are wicked!"

And just as I was, without a coat or hat, I ran after the old man. I wanted to escort him to the gate and say at least a few words to console him. As I ran down the stairs, I could still see Nellie's face, pale white from my reproaches.

I quickly caught up with the old man.

"The poor girl has been hurt and turned her grief against me," he said, smiling bitterly. "I tried to tell her of my own pain, but I touched on a sore spot. They say the well-fed cannot understand the hungry, Vanya, but I would add that the hungry do not always understand the hungry. Well, good-bye!"

I wanted to change the subject and say something, but the old man just waved me off.

"No need to comfort me. It would be better if you see to it that she doesn't run away from you. She looks like she may," he added with some bitterness, walking away from me with rapid steps, brandishing his stick and tapping it on the pavement.

He had no idea that he was a prophet.

Imagine my horror, when I climbed the stairs back to my attic apartment and discovered that Nellie had once again disappeared. I rushed out onto the landing, hoping to find her on the stairs, and even knocked on my neighbors' doors and asked if anyone had seen her. I could not and would not believe that she had run away again. How could she have run away? There was only one gate out of the house, and she would have had to slip past me while I was talking to my old friend. But soon, much to my sorrow, I realized that she could have been hiding somewhere above me on the stairs to the roof and hurried down the stairs at the moment I went into my apartment, thereby making her escape. In any case, she could not have gone far.

In great anxiety I ran back down to the street to search for her, leaving the apartment unlocked just in case she returned.

First of all, I went to Masloboyev's and found neither Masloboyev nor Alexandra Semyonovna at home. I left them a note to inform them of this new crisis and to ask them to let me know immediately should Nellie appear. I also went to the doctor but he, too, was out. The building's doorman told me that there had been no visitors since the day before. What could I do? I even went to Madame Bubnova's and learned from my friend the coffin-maker's wife that her landlady had been sitting for two days in the police station for some unspecified crime, and Nellie had not been seen there since the *incident*. Tired and worn out, I ran back to the Masloboyevs, only to discover that they had not yet returned, and no one had seen the girl. My note still lay on the table. What was I to do?

In mortal anguish, I started for home. The sun had already set. I should have been with Natasha, who had asked me that morning to return, but I had not even tasted food the entire day, so worried was I about Nellie. My soul was in turmoil. "What could have happened?" I wondered. "Could this be some consequence of her disease? I don't think that going mad is a symptom of epilepsy, but, my God, where is she? Where should I look?"

I had just completed that thought, when I spotted Nellie only a few steps from where I was walking on the Anichkov Bridge. She was standing under a streetlamp and could not see me. I wanted to run to her but stopped myself. "What is she doing here?" I asked myself in disbelief, and confident that I would not lose her again, I decided to wait and watch her. Ten minutes passed and she was still standing there, looking at passers-by. Finally, a well-dressed older gentleman approached, and Nellie went up to him. Without stopping, he pulled something from his pocket and handed it to her. She curtsied to him. I cannot express what I felt at that moment. An agonizing pain tore at my heart, as if something precious that I loved, cherished and embraced had been tossed in the gutter and spat upon in front of me. At that moment, tears welled up in my eyes.

Yes, tears for poor little Nellie, but at the same time I felt an irreconcilable resentment. She was not begging out of monetary need or hunger, nor because she had been forsaken or abandoned to her fate. She was not fleeing from cruel oppressors, but from friends who loved and cherished her. It was as if she wanted to shock or frighten others with her exploits, showing off in front of someone to make a point. But there was something secret maturing in her mind. The old man had been right. She had been ill-treated and her wound could not be healed, and yet she seemed to be deliberately trying to aggravate the wound by this mysterious behavior, this mistrust of us all. She was enjoying her pain, her suffering in a selfish Christ-like kind of egoism, if I may express it that way. This aggravation of pain and suffering, the taking of pleasure in it, was something I could understand. It is the suffering of those who have been used and abused by their oppressors, smarting under the injustice thrust upon them by destiny. But what sort of injustice could Nellie protest? She wanted to surprise and frighten us with her whims and wild antics, but I felt as though she were really asserting herself against me. But no! She was alone now on that bridge, so she couldn't have known that I would see her begging. She must have found pleasure in it just for her own sake. Why did she require charity? For what did she need the money?

After her most recent transaction, Nellie left the bridge and went up to the brightly lit window of a shop. There she began to count her newly acquired capital. I was standing just ten paces from her. From the amount of money in her hand, it was clear that she had been begging for much of the day. Squeezing her fist tightly, she crossed the street and went into another shop. I immediately went to the wide-open door of the shop and looked to see what she was going to do.

I saw her put the money on the counter and watched as the merchant handed her a cup, a simple teacup, very similar to the one she had broken that morning to demonstrate to Ichmenyev and me that she was wicked. A cup of no great value, perhaps fifteen kopeks or less. The merchant wrapped it in paper, tied it with a string and gave it to Nellie, who hurried happily out of the shop.

"Nellie!" I cried when she came near me. "Nellie!"

She started, glanced up at me, the cup slipped from her hands, fell to the pavement and broke. Nellie was pale but looked at me and quickly realized that I had seen everything and understood what she had done. She suddenly blushed, clearly from a combination of embarrassment and unbearable, agonizing shame. I took her hand and led her home. We did not have far to walk and neither of us uttered a word on the way. When we got home, I sat Nellie down in front of me. She seemed anxious and confused, still pale, her eyes fixed on the floor. She could not look at me.

"Nellie, were you begging in the streets?"

"Yes!" She whispered, and her head dropped even lower.

"You wanted to earn money to buy a cup to replace the one you broke this morning?"

"Yes."

"But did I reproach you or scold you about that cup? Surely you must see, Nellie, what a naughty and unkind thing you did. Am I right? Are you ashamed? Surely..."

"Yes," she whispered in a barely audible voice as a tear rolled down her cheek.

"Yes?" I repeated after her. "Nellie, dear, if I have wronged you, please forgive me and let me make amends."

She looked at me, tears streaming from her eyes, and threw herself at my chest.

At that moment Alexandra Semyonovna rushed in.

"What? She is home? Again? Oh, Nellie, Nellie, what is the matter with you? Well, well, at least you are home now. Where did you find her, Ivan Petrovich?"

I signaled to Alexandra Semyonovna not to ask any more questions and she understood me. I gently said good-bye to Nellie, who was still crying, and begged the kind-hearted Alexandra Semyonovna to sit with her until my return. I then ran to Natasha. I was late and in a hurry.

That evening, our fate was being decided. Natasha and I had a great deal to discuss, but I did mention Nellie and told her everything that had happened, with all the details. Natasha was very interested in my story and, I think, even a little impressed.

"You know what, Vanya," she said after a long pause, "I believe that Nellie is in love with you."

"What? How could that be?" I asked in surprise.

"Yes, this may be the beginning of love, a real grown-up love."

"Why do you say that, Natasha, it's complete nonsense! She is just a child!"

"A child who will soon be fourteen years old. This behavior on her part may be because she is confused by her feelings, she may not even realize she has these feelings. There is a lot of childish behavior, but the emotions are real… and very painful. But most importantly, she is jealous of your feelings for me. You love me so much that you probably talk about me at home. You're always worrying about me, thinking and talking about me, and she probably feels that you are ignoring her. She notices… and she is hurt. Perhaps she has tried to talk to you about her feelings, to open her heart to you, but she doesn't know how. She is ashamed because she isn't even sure herself about these feelings. She is waiting for an opportunity, but each time she is almost ready, you pull away from her, run off to see me. What's even worse, when she was sick you left her alone for days on end. She cries about you, misses you, and worst of all, you don't seem to even notice. And now, at a moment such as this, you have left her alone again… for me. Yes, she will be sick tomorrow because of this. How could you just leave her? Go back to her now."

"I shouldn't have left her, but..."

"Yes, I know, because I asked you to come. But now… go.

"Of course, I'll go, but I don't believe any of this."

"Because she is so different from other people. Think about her story and it will begin to make sense. She didn't grow up like you and I did."

I returned home, but it was late. Alexandra Semyonovna told me that Nellie had cried herself to sleep again, just as she had the night before. "And now I am going home, Ivan Petrovich, as Philip Philippich has instructed me to. He is waiting for me, the poor dear."

I thanked her and sat down by Nellie's pillow. I felt terrible for having left her at such a serious moment. For a long time, throughout most of the night, I sat thinking about the situation. It was a crucial time for all of us.

But I must now describe what had been taking place during those two weeks.

CHAPTER FORTY-ONE

After that memorable evening with Prince Valkovsky at the restaurant, I spent several days in constant fear for Natasha's well-being. "What kind of revenge was that damned prince threatening when he spoke of her?" I asked myself constantly, and my mind was overwhelmed by the many possibilities. I finally concluded that the threat was all too real and not just empty talk, and that as long as she was living with Alyosha, the prince could really make her life difficult. "He is petty, vindictive, evil and calculating," I thought. It was impossible for him to forget any insult, and he would take advantage of any opportunity for revenge. In any case, he had been adamant about one point in particular. He was determined that Alyosha end his relationship with Natasha, and he expected me to prepare Natasha so there would be no "scenes, no idyllic nonsense, and no Schillerisms." Of course, the prince was also determined that Alyosha not hold him responsible for anything but remain on good terms with his "loving" father. This was essential if the prince was going to get his hands on Katya's money. And so, I was assigned the task of preparing Natasha for the impending separation. But I noticed a major change in Natasha's attitude towards me. Her usual frankness was missing and she seemed almost to distrust me. My attempts to console her worried her, and my questions puzzled and frequently angered her. I was used to sitting in her room and watching her pace the floor with her arms folded across her chest, her face pale and gloomy, as if in a trance, often forgetting that I was there. When she did look at me, sometimes avoiding my eyes, I caught glimpses of irritation and impatience in her expression, and she would quickly turn away. I realized that she might, perhaps, be contemplating her own plan for the upcoming breakup, and how best to avoid the pain and bitterness. And I was convinced that she had already resigned herself to the separation. Although I was tormented and frightened by her gloomy demeanor, I was also hesitant to comfort or console her, but instead lived in terror of the pending resolution.

As for her stern and unapproachable attitude with me, it tormented me, but I had faith in Natasha's heart. I could see that it was difficult for her, too, and she was similarly upset. But any outside interference frustrated and angered her. In such cases, it was particularly annoying to her when close friends, who were conversant with her secret thoughts, attempted to influence her. But I knew all too well that, at the last minute, Natasha would return to me and seek comfort in my affection for her.

About my conversation with the prince, I, of course, remained silent. My story would have excited and upset her even more. I only mentioned, in passing, that I had been with the prince at the countess's, and that I was convinced he was a terrible scoundrel. She did not even question me about him, which pleased me, but she eagerly listened to everything I had to say about my conversation with Katya. After listening, she again said nothing, but the color returned to her cheeks and she displayed an unusual excitement for the rest of the day. I did not hide anything about Katya and admitted that she had made an excellent impression on me. Yes, and what would be the point of hiding that? Natasha would have guessed that I was hiding something and would only get angry with me. So I deliberately told her everything as accurately as possible, trying to anticipate each of her questions, knowing that if I were in her position, these questions would be difficult for me to ask. It couldn't have been easy, in fact, pretending to be indifferent while learning about her rival's perfection.

I thought it unlikely that she knew the prince had insisted Alyosha accompany the countess and Katya to the country, so I was determined to soften the blow as much as possible by breaking the news to her gently. Imagine my amazement when Natasha stopped me immediately and said there was no need to comfort her, as she had known about that for five days.

"Oh, my God!" I cried, "but who told you?"

"Alyosha."

"What? Alyosha has already told you?"

"Yes, and I have already made up my mind about everything, Vanya," she added with an impatient look that clearly warned me not to continue the conversation.

Alyosha often visited Natasha, but only briefly before running off. One time only he stayed with her for several hours, but I was not there at the time. He was usually sad and looked at her shyly and tenderly, but Natasha was so kind and gentle to him, he immediately forgot his sorrow and brightened up. He frequently visited me, too, almost every day, in fact. He was very tormented and couldn't stand being alone with his sorrow for more than a few minutes at a time, so he kept running to me for comfort.

What could I say to him? He accused me of coldness, of indifference, even of holding spiteful feelings toward him. He grieved, he cried, and then hurried to Katya, where he received the comfort he required.

On the same day Natasha told me she knew about Alyosha's pending visit to the country—it was a week after my conversation with the prince—Alyosha visited me in despair. He embraced me forcefully and sobbed like a child. I kept silent and waited to hear what he had to say.

"I'm a cruel, wretched creature, Vanya," he said to me. "Save me from myself. I'm not crying because I'm low and vile but, because of me, Natasha will be miserable. When I leave, she will suffer terribly. Vanya, my friend, tell me… decide for me. Which of the two do I love most: Katya or Natasha?"

"I can't decide that for you, Alyosha'" I answered. "You ought to know better than I do."

"No, Vanya, that's not it. I'm not so stupid as to ask such a question, but… the point is… I do not want to be compelled to answer. I can ask… but

I cannot answer. But you are good at looking at things from the outside and may know more than I do. Well, even if you don't know the answer, how do you *feel* about it?"

"I think you and Katya have more in common."

"You think so? No, no, absolutely not! You've guessed wrong. I absolutely adore Natasha! I could never leave her! I've already told Katya that, and Katya agrees with me completely. Why are you silent? There, I saw you smile just now. Ah, Vanya, you never comfort me when I am miserable, which I am now... Good-bye!"

He ran from the room, leaving an extraordinary impression on the astonished Nellie, who had listened to our conversation in silence. This was during the period when she was sick in bed and taking medication. Alyosha never said a word to her and usually ignored her during his visits.

Two hours later he appeared again, and I was surprised by his joyous expression. He threw himself into another strong embrace and grinned at me.

"It's all settled!" he cried, "all misunderstandings have been resolved. I just went from you to Natasha. I was upset! I could not live without her! Once inside, I fell on my knees before her and kissed her feet. I needed to do that. I have been *longing* to do that! It just seemed like the perfect thing to do. She didn't say anything, but she hugged me and cried. Then I simply told her that I love Katya more than her..."

"What did she say?"

"Well, she didn't say anything. She just caressed and comforted me. Me, after what I had just told her. She really knows how to comfort me, Vanya! I simply wept away all my grief and told her everything. I just said straight out that I love Katya, but be that as it may, I couldn't live without Natasha, I would simply die if she left me, I know that, so, Vanya, I have decided to marry her immediately, although we can't do it prior to my departure because it is Lent, and we can't get married during Lent, so it will have to wait until my return, which should be by the first of June. My father will approve, I have no doubt about that. And as for Katya, what of that? I cannot live without Natasha, as I said... So, we'll be married, and then we'll be off at once to Katya's..."

Poor Natasha! How difficult it must have been for her to comfort this silly boy, to sit beside him and hear his confession, and then comfort the naïve egoist by inventing the tale of a speedy marriage. Alyosha was comforted for a few days. He had always run to Natasha because his fragile heart could not bear heartache alone. But still, as the time approached for their separation, he again fell into fretting and crying, and would return to me to pour out his sorrow. Recently, he had become so attached to Natasha that he could not leave her for a single day, much less six weeks. He was completely convinced, however, at least until the very last minute, that he would be leaving Natasha for only a month-and-a-half, and that upon his return there would be a wedding. As for Natasha, she fully understood that her life was about to change permanently, that Alyosha would never come back to her, and that this was how it was meant to be.

The day of their separation was approaching. Natasha was ill, pale, with bloodshot eyes, and parched lips. Sometimes she talked to herself, and other times she threw quick and piercing glances at me. She did not cry, did not answer my questions, and shook like a leaf on a tree when she heard Alyosha's tremulous voice. She lit up like an ember and hastened to him, hugging and kissing him, and laughing almost hysterically. Alyosha gazed at her and inquired anxiously about her health. He tried to comfort her by insisting that he would not be gone for long, and that they would be married when he returned. Natasha made a visible effort to control herself and suppress her tears. She did not cry in front of him.

He said he would leave her enough money to cover the time he would be gone, and that she needn't worry because his father promised to give him a lot of money for the journey. Natasha frowned. When we were alone, I told her I had a hundred and fifty rubles available to her if she needed it. She did not question where the money came from. That was two days before Alyosha's departure, and one day before Natasha's first and last meeting with Katya. Katya had sent Alyosha to deliver a note asking Natasha for permission to visit her the following day, and she sent me a separate note imploring me to be present at their meeting.

I determined to be at the noon meeting, the time having been set by Katya, in spite of any difficulties or delays. In addition to Nellie, I had to take into account any time conflicts with the Ichmenyevs. Anna Andreyevna had sent for me the week before, begging me to drop everything and rush to her immediately to discuss a very important matter. When I arrived, I found her alone, pacing the room in a fever of excitement and fear, trembling, awaiting the return of Nikolai Sergeich. As usual, it took me a long time to pry from her the reason for her anxiety, and why it was absolutely necessary for my immediate presence. Finally, after several heated and unwarranted reproaches—Why had I grown so indifferent to their troubles?—Anna Andreyevna told me that for the last three days Nikolai Sergeich had been in a state of extreme agitation, "impossible to describe."

"He hasn't been himself," she said. "He's in a fever. At night he secretly prays on his knees before the ikons. He murmurs in his sleep, and he acts crazy when he is awake. Yesterday we were having soup and he couldn't find the spoon that was sitting right next to the bowl, and when I ask him a question, he will respond with a completely unrelated answer. He has taken to dashing out at all hours. He says he has business or legal matters to see to, and this morning he locked himself in his study. 'I have to write an important paper relating to the legal business,' he told me. Well, I'm thinking, how is he going to write an important statement when he can't find a spoon next to his bowl? But I peeked through the keyhole and he was sitting at his desk writing something and crying his eyes out. What sort of legal document is that? Perhaps he was thinking about losing Ichmenyevka!

Does that mean our property is lost? Well, as I was thinking this, he suddenly jumped up, threw down his pen, wiped his eyes, grabbed his cap, then rushed out past me. 'I must go out, Anna Andreyevna. I will return soon,' he said. He left and I immediately went to his desk. There are stacks of papers about our litigation which he never lets me touch. How many times have I begged him, 'Please just once let me lift up the papers so I can dust,' and he waves his arms and shouts, 'Don't you dare!' He has grown so angry since we have been in St. Petersburg, yelling about everything. So, I am standing at his desk trying to find the paper he was writing, because I know for sure that he did not take it with him but buried it under the other papers when he got up. Well, see here, Vanya, what I found."

And she handed me a sheet of notepaper half covered with writing, but with so many ink blots that in some places it was impossible to read.

Poor old man! From the first lines I could guess what, and to whom, he was writing. It was a letter to Natasha, his beloved Natasha. He began warmly and tenderly, asking her to forgive him and begging her to come visit him. It was difficult to make out the whole letter, so clumsily and fitfully was it written, and with countless ink splotches. The intensity of feelings that compelled him to grab a pen became evident only after the first few gentle comments morphed into something quite different. The old man began to reproach his daughter, describing her wicked behavior in vivid terms, indignantly reminding her of her obstinacy, and reproaching her for her cruelty towards her m other and father. He threatened her with retribution and cursed her for her pride, and closed by demanding that she immediately and obediently return home, and then, only then, perhaps, as a reward for her "humble and exemplary new life in the bosom of your family, we may decide to forgive you," he wrote. It was evident that he regarded the first few tender comments as a sign of weakness, became ashamed of it, and allowed his tormented feelings and wounded pride to take control and he finished with angry threats. Anna Andreyevna stood before me with hands clasped over her heart, waiting in suspense for my reaction to the letter.

I told her truthfully what I thought, namely that her husband cannot bear to live any longer without Natasha, and that I was certain that a speedy reconciliation was inevitable, but that everything depended on circumstances. I suggested that the bad outcome to the lawsuit had upset and shaken him to the core, not to mention how his pride was wounded by the prince's triumph over him, and his resentment had been revived by the final decision in the case. At such moments, the soul cannot help but to seek sympathy, and he was reminded of the one person he loved more than anything else in the world. Finally, he undoubtedly knew (because he was following Natasha and knew everything about her) that Alyosha would soon be deserting her. He could not help but understand what she was going through now, and her need for comforting. But still he could not overcome the feeling that he had been insulted and humiliated by his daughter. He, no doubt, had come to believe that she would not come to him first. Perhaps she wasn't even thinking about her parents and felt no need for reconciliation. "That's what he must be thinking," I concluded, "and why he was unable to finish the letter. He may have realized that Natasha would consider these comments yet another offense, even stronger than the first, which would make reconciliation even more difficult, perhaps even postpone it indefinitely."

Anna Andreyevna was crying as she listened to me. Finally, when I said I needed to go at once to Natasha and that I was late, she roused herself and announced that she had forgotten the main thing. When removing the letter from his papers, she had accidentally knocked over the inkwell. Indeed, the whole corner of his desk was filled with ink, and Anna Andreyevna was terribly afraid that her husband would immediately realize that she had been rummaging through his papers and had read his letter to Natasha. Her fear was well founded. Once he knew that we had learned his secret, his shame and vexation could prolong his anger and his wounded pride might make him even more stubborn and unforgiving.

However, having reconsidered the matter, I persuaded my old friend not to worry. Nikolai Sergeich had been so agitated when he got up from his letter, he might conclude that he had knocked over the inkwell himself. Having comforted Anna Andreyevna, we carefully put the letter back in its place, and before leaving I took a moment to talk seriously about Nellie. It seemed to me that the poor abandoned orphan, whose mother had also been cursed by an unforgiving father, might, owing to her sad, tragic story and the death of her mother, touch the old man's heart and move him to more generous feelings. Everything was ready, his heart was primed, the longing for his daughter was already overpowering his pride and wounded vanity. All that was lacking was a slight push, a convenient opportunity, and that opportunity might be Nellie. The old woman listened to me with extreme attention. Her whole face lit up with hope and enthusiasm. She immediately began to reproach me for not having pointed this out before. She eagerly began to question me about Nellie and finished with a solemn promise that she would urge her husband to take the orphan girl into their home. She had already started to feel a genuine affection for Nellie, was sorry to hear that she was ill, asked me for more information about her, and insisted that I take Nellie a jar of jam, for which she ran to a storeroom. She also brought me five rubles, assuming that I had no money for doctors, but when I declined her generous offer, she took comfort in knowing that Nellie would need clothes and underwear, so she could still be useful. She instantly began a search through her chests and closets and lay out all the clothes that she could give to the orphan.

I then left for Natasha's. Mounting the last staircase, which I previously noted curved around in a spiral, I noticed a man at her door who was about to knock, but paused when he heard my steps. Finally, after some hesitation, he suddenly abandoned his intentions, and started down the staircase. I ran into him at the final turn of the stairs. You can imagine my surprise when I recognized Ichmenyev. Even in daylight, it was very dark on the stairs, but he leaned back against the wall to let me pass, and I remember a strange gleam in his eyes as we exchanged glances. He seemed to be blushing from embarrassment, or at least from confusion and shock.

"Ah, Vanya, yes it's you!" he said in an uneven voice. "I am here to see someone… a clerk... on legal business… he recently moved... around here somewhere... but not here, it seems… I have a wrong address. Good-bye."

And he quickly ran down the stairs.

I decided not to tell Natasha about this meeting, at least until Alyosha had gone and she was alone. At present, she was so distraught, that even if she had understood and comprehended the full importance of this fact, she would not have been able to take it in emotionally during this period of overwhelming grief and despair. This was not the right moment.

I could have returned to the Ichmenyevs later that day, and I was tempted to, but I did not go. I fancied my old friend would be uncomfortable at the sight of me, and he might think that I had purposely run to him as a result of our meeting on the stairs. I went to him two days later and the old man was depressed, but he greeted me quite casually and spoke of nothing other than business.

"By the way," he said suddenly, "who was it you were going to visit so high up when we met… do you remember… the day before yesterday, I believe." He tried to sound casual, but still avoided looking me in the eye.

"A friend of mine lives there," I replied, also turning my eyes away from him.

"Ah! And I was looking for a clerk named Astafiev. I was directed to that house... but it was a mistake..." He then rambled on for a minute about unrelated matters, but when he mentioned the court case, he turned positively crimson.

I told Anna Andreyevna this story during that same visit, but implored her not, under any circumstances, to look at him with an odd expression, or sigh, or drop any hints, that might betray in any way that she knew about his covert visit to Natasha. The old woman was so astonished and delighted that, at first, she did not believe me. For her part, she told me that she had already hinted to Nikolai Sergeich about the orphan, but he said nothing in reply, despite having pleaded with her numerous times to take the girl in to their house. We decided that the next day she would ask him about it directly, without any hints or evasiveness. But the next day we both had a terrible fright.

Ichmenyev had had an interview in the morning with an official in connection with his case, and the official told him that he had spoken with the prince's lawyer and although the prince intended to keep Ichmenyevka, he had decided, "due to some family circumstances," to compensate the old man with the sum of ten thousand rubles. Ichmenyev had run directly to my house immediately after this meeting in a terrible state of excitement, his eyes flashing with fury. He pulled me out of my apartment onto the landing, shut the door, and demanded that I go immediately to the prince and present him with his challenge to a duel. I was so overwhelmed that for a long time I could not think of a response. I then attempted to dissuade him, but the old man became so enraged that he collapsed on the stairs. I rushed into my apartment to get a glass of water, but when I returned, Ichmenyev was no longer there.

The next day I went to see him, but he was not at home. He disappeared for three whole days.

On the third day we learned what had happened. From me, he had rushed straight to the prince, discovered he was not at home, and left a note. In the note he said he had learned of the prince's intentions and considered them a deadly insult. He looked on the prince as a lowly scoundrel, and challenged him to a duel, warning him that if he dared to decline the challenge, he would be publicly disgraced.

Anna Andreyevna told me that he had come home so dejected, he went straight to bed and collapsed. He was very gentle with her but would not answer her questions and was evidently waiting for something with a feverish impatience. The next morning a letter arrived via post. Reading it, Ichmenyev roared his displeasure and clutched at his head. Anna Andreyevna was numb with fear. But he immediately grabbed his cap and walking stick and rushed out.

The letter was from the prince. Dryly, briefly and politely he informed Ichmenyev that he, Valkovsky, was not obliged to discuss anything he had communicated to his lawyer and, while he felt great sympathy for Ichmenyev for the loss of his case, he did not feel it justified the losing party seeking revenge by challenging the winner to a duel. As to the "public disgrace" which Ichmenyev had threatened, the prince advised Ichmenyev not to concern himself with it. There would be and could be no public disgrace since Ichmenyev's threatening letter would be sent immediately to the police, and they would probably be able to take the appropriate measures to ensure peace and order.

Ichmenyev, with the letter in his hand, immediately rushed to the prince. Again, he was not at home, but the old man learned from the footman that the prince was with Count Nainsky. Without stopping to think, he ran to the count's mansion, where the doorman stopped him on the front steps. Infuriated to the utmost, the old man hit him with his stick. Ichmenyev was immediately seized by guards, dragged to the bottom of the steps and handed over to a police officer, who escorted him to the local police station. The count received word of the incident and the prince, who was with him at the time, explained to the proud, haughty count, that the intruder was Ichmenyev, the father of the very Natalia Nikolayevna who had been a playmate to his son Alexey Petrovich since childhood. Nainsky, who had once been a benefactor to the boy, laughed and agreed to temper justice with a little mercy. The order was given that Ichmenyev should be released, although it was not until two days later that the order was carried out, possibly due to interference from the prince. Upon his release, however, the old man was informed that the prince had begged the count for leniency.

The old man returned home in a mental state bordering on insanity. He rushed to the bed and lay there for an hour without moving. When he finally got up, he went to Anna Andreyevna and made the startling announcement that he was cursing his daughter forever and would never again offer her his fatherly blessing.

Anna Andreyevna was horrified, but she had to look after the old man, and she did so day and night, bathing his temples with vinegar and soothing his forehead with ice. He was feverish and delirious. It was two hours past midnight by the time I left them. But the next morning, Ichmenyev had recovered enough to come to me to take Nellie home with him for good. I have already described his conversation with Nellie when she refused to go with him. Feeling shell-shocked from that encounter, he returned home and again took to his bed. That was on Good Friday, the day agreed upon for the meeting between Natasha and Katya, and one day before Alyosha and Katya were to leave St. Petersburg. The meeting occurred early in the morning, even before the old man's visit to me, and before Nellie ran away from me for the first time.

Chapter Forty-Two

Alyosha arrived an hour early to prepare Natasha for the meeting. I arrived at precisely the moment that Katya's carriage stopped in front of Natasha's building. Accompanying Katya was an old Frenchwoman, who consented to the assignment only after a great deal of hesitation and persuasion. She even agreed to wait in the carriage and let Katya go upstairs to meet Natasha without her, but only if the girl was accompanied by Alyosha. Even before getting out of her carriage, Katya caught my eye and beckoned me over to her. She asked me to call Alyosha down. When I had climbed the stairs, I found Natasha in tears. In fact, she and Alyosha were both crying. Hearing that Katya had arrived, she got up from her chair, wiped her tears, and with great excitement stood facing the door. She was dressed that morning all in white. Her dark brown hair was combed smoothly back and tied with a thick knot. I liked her hair that way. After Alyosha headed down the stairs, Natasha looked at me and told me to go with him to greet her guest.

"I could not visit with Natasha before now," Katya said to me as we started up the stairs. "I have so many people spying on me it's frightening. I have been working on Madame Albert for two weeks, trying to persuade her to let me come and she finally agreed. But you, Ivan Petrovich, have never returned to see me! I could have written to you, but I didn't really want to because there are some things you just cannot say in a letter. And I so much wanted to see you... My God, my heart is beating so fast…"

"These stairs are steep," I answered.

"Well, yes... the stairs... but tell me what you think. Will Natasha be angry with me?"

"No, why?"

"Well… of course… why should she be? I'll see for myself in a moment, so there's no need to ask questions."

I gave her my arm. She turned pale and looked very scared. At the base of the final flight, she stopped for breath, but then looked at me, smiled, and resolutely started up again.

She stopped again at the door and whispered to me, "I'll just go in and tell her that I had so much faith in her, I wasn't the least bit frightened to come. But why am I saying that? I am sure that Natasha is the noblest of creatures. Don't you think?"

She entered timidly, as if guilty of something, and looked wide-eyed at Natasha, who immediately smiled at her. Then Katya ran quickly to her, grabbed her hand, and pressed her puffy little lips to Natasha's. Then, without saying a word to Natasha, she turned to Alyosha with a stern expression and asked him to leave them alone for half an hour.

"Don't be upset, Alyosha," she added, "it's only because I have a great deal to talk with Natasha about, important and serious issues that you shouldn't hear. Try to understand… and go away. But you must stay, Ivan Petrovich. You must hear our entire conversation."

"Let us sit down," she said to Natasha when Alyosha had left the room. "I'll sit here opposite you. I would like to look at you first."

She sat almost directly in front of Natasha and gazed intently at her for a long time. Natasha responded with an involuntary smile.

"I have seen your photograph," Katya said. "Alyosha showed it to me."

"Well, am I like my portrait?"

"You are even better," Katya replied firmly and seriously. "Yes, I thought you would be."

"Really? And I can't help staring at you. How pretty you are!"

"What are you saying? How could you… But you are a darling!" she added, taking Natasha's hand in her own, which was visibly trembling. They both fell silent again, staring at each other.

"I must tell you, my angel," Katya said, breaking the silence, "we have only half an hour together. Madame Albert agreed only to that, and we have so much to discuss. I want to... That is... Well, I just want to ask you if you care about Alyosha."

"Yes, very much."

"And if so... If you care very much for Alyosha... then... you must want him to be happy..." she added timidly and in a whisper.

"Yes, I want him to be happy."

"Ah, but here is the question: Will I make him happy? Am I right to ask that, since I will be taking him away from you? If you think, and we decide now that he will be happier with you, then... then..."

"That has already been decided, dear Katya. You can see for yourself that it is all settled," Natasha answered softly, and bowed her head. It was, apparently, very difficult for her to continue the conversation.

Katya had been prepared, it seems, for a lengthy discussion on the topic of who would make Alyosha happy, and which of them would have to give him up. But after Natasha's immediate answer, there was nothing left to be said. With her pretty lips half parted, she looked with sadness at Natasha, who was still holding her hand.

"Do you love him very much?" Natasha asked suddenly.

"Yes, and there is something else I specifically wanted to ask you. Tell me, what exactly do you love about him?"

"I don't know," Natasha answered, with what seemed like bitter impatience.

"Is he clever, do you think?" Katya asked.

"No, I just love him."

"I do too. I always seem to feel sorry for him."

"Me too," Natasha replied.

"Well, what do we do with him now? I simply cannot understand how he could leave you for me!" Katya said. "Now that I see you, it simply makes no sense!"

Natasha looked at the ground and did not answer. Katya was silent for a while and then suddenly rose from her chair and quietly hugged Natasha. The two embraced each other and wept. Katya sat on the arm of Natasha's chair, not ending the embrace, and began to kiss Natasha's hand.

"If you only knew how much I love you!" she said, still weeping. "Let us always be sisters and always write to each other... I shall love you forever... I'll be so loving, so loving..."

"Did he speak to you about our wedding in June?" Natasha asked.

"He did. He said that you had consented. That was just to comfort him, wasn't it?"

"Yes, of course."

"That's what I assumed. I will love him very much, Natasha, and write to you about everything. It seems that he will soon be my husband. They all say so. Darling Natasha, does this mean that you will now... go home?"

Natasha did not answer, but silently kissed her cheek. "Be happy!" she said.

"And you... and you, too!" said Katya.

At that moment, the door opened and Alyosha came in. He could not wait the full half hour. Seeing them both in each other's arms and crying, he fell to his knees in helpless anguish before the two women.

"What are you crying about?" Natasha asked him. "Because you are parting from me? It's not for long. Won't you be back in June?"

"And then your wedding will happen," Katya added through her tears, trying to comfort Alyosha.

"But I cannot… I can't leave you, even for one day, Natasha. I will die without you. You don't know how much I love you! Especially now!"

"Well, here's what you must do then," Natasha said, suddenly taking charge of the situation. "The countess will be going to Moscow, won't she?"

"Yes, for almost a week," Katya replied.

"A week! Well then, here is what you will do," Natasha said to Alyosha. "You will escort them to Moscow tomorrow, then immediately return here. That is just one day. When they are ready to leave Moscow, you will go back there to accompany them to Simbirsk for a month."

"Yes, yes, that's it!" Katya cooed with delight, exchanging meaningful glances with Natasha. "Then you will have an extra four days together with your fiancée!"

I cannot describe Alyosha's delight at this new itinerary. He was at once completely comforted, and his face beamed with joy. He embraced Natasha, kissed Katya's hands, and hugged me. Natasha, with a sad smile, looked at him, but Katya could not stand it. She exchanged glances with me with feverish, sparkling eyes, embraced Natasha, and rose from the chair to go. As luck would have it, at that moment the Frenchwoman's footman arrived with a request from her to end our conversation as soon as possible, indicating that the agreed-upon half hour had passed.

Natasha got up. She and Katya stood facing each other and held hands, as if trying to convey with their eyes all that had collected in their souls.

"It is likely that we shall never see each other again," Katya said.

"Very true, Katya," replied Natasha.

"Well, then, let us say good-bye."

They embraced each other.

"Do not curse me," Katya whispered hurriedly, "I'll… always... you can be sure... he will be happy... Come, Alyosha, take me down!" She took his hand and left quickly.

"Vanya," Natasha said to me, exhausted and concerned when they had gone. "Go after them and… don't come back until later. Alyosha will be with me this evening till eight o'clock. He won't be staying late because he is leaving in the morning. I shall be left alone.... Come back at nine o'clock, please!"

That was the evening when Nellie broke the teacup. I left her with Alexandra Semyonovna and hurried to Natasha, who was alone and anxiously expecting me. Mavra prepared the samovar and Natasha poured me a cup of tea. She sat on the sofa and beckoned me to join her. "So, everything is over now," she said, looking at me intently. Never shall I forget that look.

"Our love is over, too. Only six months out of my life… and yet it feels like a lifetime!" she added, clutching my hand. Her hand was feverish. I tried to persuade her to dress warmly and go to bed.

"Soon, Vanya, soon, my dear friend. Let me talk a bit and remember... I feel broken... shattered into pieces. Tomorrow at ten o'clock shall be the last time I see him… the last time!"

"Natasha, you have a fever. Soon you will be shivering. If nothing else, please take pity on yourself."

"Well, I have been waiting for you, Vanya. It's been half an hour since he left for good. And what do you imagine I have been thinking about? What do you think I have been puzzling over? I've been asking myself, 'Did I love him? Or didn't I? And, if so, what kind of love was it?' Isn't that laughable, Vanya, that only now am I asking myself that?"

"Don't upset yourself, Natasha..."

"You see, Vanya, I've decided that I never did love him as an equal, as a woman usually loves a man. I loved him like… almost like… a mother. I am starting to believe that in all the world, there is no such thing as a love in which two people love each other as equals. What do you think?"

Her question made me very uneasy. I was afraid that her illness might develop into brain fever. Something was compelling her to speak, but her sentences didn't always follow in a logical order, and her words were often incomprehensible. I was worried for her.

"He was mine," she went on. "Almost from our first meeting, I had an irresistible urge to make him mine, mine immediately, before any other woman could claim him. Katya expressed it very well this morning. I loved him because he always found a way to make me feel sorry for him. I have always had an intense desire, a perfect anguish when I was alone, that he should always be happy, extremely happy. I could never look at his face—well you know that expression of his, Vanya—without being moved. No one else has such an expression, no one, and when he laughed, I turned cold and shivered. Really!"

"Natasha, listen..."

"People would say," she interrupted, "and you yourself have said it often enough, that he has no character, no will of his own. That he has the mind of a child. Well, that's what I loved about him more than anything. Can you believe that? I don't know if I loved just that one thing, I simply loved him as he was. If he had been somehow different, stronger willed or smarter, I might not have loved him so. You know, Vanya, I'll confess one thing to you. Do you remember the quarrel we had three months ago, when he had been to see that… what's her name… that Minna? Well, I heard about it and, would you believe, I was terribly hurt, yet at the same time rather pleased. I'm not sure why... but the thought that he was amusing himself… no, not just that. That he was enjoying himself like a grown-up man together with other men, running after pretty girls… that he, too, had a Minna! What a pleasure it was for me to quarrel with him… and then forgive him... he was so adorable!"

She looked into my eyes and laughed oddly. Then she appeared lost in thought, as if recalling memories of Alyosha. She sat for a long time, with a smile on her lips, reliving their time together.

"I'm very fond of forgiving him, Vanya," she said. "You know that when he left me alone, I would sometimes pace the room, fretting and crying, and realize that the poorer he treated me, the happier I felt. Yes! And you know, I always imagine him as a little boy. I'm seated, and he puts his head on my knees and falls asleep, and I gently stroke his head softly and caress him. I always imagined him like that when he was not with me. Listen, Vanya," she added suddenly, "isn't Katya a lovely person?"

It seemed to me that she was intentionally picking at her own wounds, compelled by an inexplicable yearning, a yearning for despair and suffering... as is often the case with a heart that has suffered great loss.

"Katya, I think, could make him happy," she continued. "She has character and strong convictions, and when she speaks to him, she sounds serious and significant. She says such clever things, just like a grown-up, but she is really a child herself, just like Alyosha… A sweet, adorable baby! Such a darling! I hope they will be happy! I hope so, I hope so."

And her tears and sobs gushed from her heart in a torrent. For half an hour she was unable to stop, but ultimately managed to recover some self-control.

My dear angel, Natasha! Despite her own grief that evening, she was still able to sympathize with my anxieties. When I saw that she was a little calmer, or perhaps merely exhausted, I decided to tell her about Nellie, thinking it might distract her. I finally departed late that evening, but only after she had fallen asleep. On my way out, I asked Mavra not to leave her sad, suffering mistress all night.

"Oh, if only this misery would end!" I said to myself as I walked home. "Let it happen soon, whatever the outcome may be!"

The next morning at exactly ten o'clock, I was with Natasha again. Alyosha arrived at the same moment, this time to say good-bye. I will not describe that scene; it is something I would prefer to forget. I think Natasha was determined to show a brave face, to appear happier and indifferent to the situation, but she was unable to stick to that intention. She put her arms around Alyosha and embraced him passionately, even obsessively. She said very little, but stared at him with a wild-eyed, almost insane fanaticism. She hung on his every word, and yet seemed to understand nothing. I remember that Alyosha begged her to forgive him, to forgive him for his love, for the pain he had caused her, for his infidelities, for his love for Katya, for leaving her... He spoke incoherently, choking on his own tears. He attempted to comfort Natasha by reminding her that he was only going away for a month or, at most, five weeks, and that he would return to her in the summer, when they would be married with his father's blessing and, finally, most importantly, that he would be returning from Moscow the day after tomorrow, giving them four full days together, so they would really only be separated for one day!

It was strange. He was so completely convinced that he would be coming back the next day from Moscow, I couldn't understand why he was so tormented and unable to stop crying.

When the clock finally struck eleven, I could hardly persuade him to go. The Moscow train left at precisely midday. There was only one hour left. Natasha later told me she couldn't remember how she looked when she said good-bye to him. I told her she had made the sign of the cross over him, kissed him, and then covered her face with her hands and rushed back into the room. I decided to walk Alyosha down the stairs and put him in his carriage. If I didn't, I felt certain he would run back up again and never reached the bottom.

"You are our one hope," he said to me, as we descended to the street. "My dear friend, Vanya! I am guilty before you and could never win your love, but you will always be a brother to me. Love her, Vanya, and do not abandon her. Write to me about everything, with as much detail as possible, as much as you can. The day after tomorrow I will be here again for certain, for certain! But, afterwards, when I leave, then you should write!"

I helped him into his carriage.

"Until the day after tomorrow!" he shouted to me from the road. "Absolutely!"

With a sinking heart I went back upstairs, back to Natasha. She was standing in the middle of the room with her arms crossed, looking at me with a puzzled expression, as if she did not recognize me. Her pinned hair had fallen on one side, her eyes were dull and unfocused. Mavra stood in the doorway, looking nervously at her.

Suddenly Natasha's eyes flashed.

"Ah! It's you! You!" she screamed at me. "So, only you remain. You hated him! You never could forgive him for my loving him! Now you are with me again! Have you come to comfort me, to persuade me to return to my father, who threw me out and cursed me? I knew to expect this yesterday, even two months ago! I don't want to go, I won't. I curse him, too! Go away! I can't bear the sight of you! Go away!"

I realized that she was in a frenzy, and that the sight of me stirred her anger to near insanity. I had half expected that and thought it best to leave. I sat on the top stair outside… and waited. Occasionally, I rose, opened the door and beckoned to Mavra to question her. She was in tears, too.

So passed an hour and a half. I cannot pretend that it wasn't extremely painful for me during that time. My heart sank and ached with infinite pain. Suddenly the door opened, and Natasha ran onto the stairs wearing her cape and hat. She seemed oblivious to everything, and later told me that she couldn't recall where she wanted to go, or for what purpose.

I didn't even have time to jump up from my seat and hide when she saw me and stopped in front of me, as if suddenly struck by some thought. "I suddenly remembered," she told me later, "that in my cruelty and madness I had actually thrown you out, you, my friend, my brother, my savior! And when I saw that you, poor boy, after being assaulted by me, had not gone away, but were still there, sitting on the stairs, waiting until I might call you back… My God! If you knew, Vanya, what I felt then! It was like a knife through my heart…"

"Vanya! Vanya!" she cried, holding out her hands. "You're here!" And she fell into my arms.

I caught her up and carried her into the room. She had fainted! "What should I do?" I thought. "She'll have brain fever for certain!"

I decided to run for the doctor. He would have some way to stop her fever. I knew I had to hurry because the old German was usually at home until about two o'clock. Before hailing a cab, I begged Mavra not for a moment, not for one second, to leave Natasha's side, and not to let her go out. God was watching out for us. Had I been a minute later, I would not have found my old friend at home. He had already left his apartment and was standing in the street. I quickly helped him into my cab before he had a moment to object or ask questions, and we hurried back to Natasha.

Yes, God was good! During my thirty-minute absence there was an incident that could have killed Natasha had the doctor not arrived in time. Less than a quarter of an hour after my departure, Prince Valkovsky walked in. He had just been seeing the others off and had come to Natasha's straight from the railway station. He had probably been planning this visit for a while. Natasha told me later that when he first appeared, she was not even surprised. "My mind had come unhinged," she said.

He sat down opposite her, giving her a look that combined pity with affection.

"My dear," he said with a sigh. "I understand your grief. I know how hard it must be for you at this minute, so I felt it was my duty to visit you. Be comforted, if possible, by the fact that by giving up Alyosha, you have secured his future happiness. But you understand that better than anyone, for you have used this situation to your advantage."

"I sat and listened," Natasha told me, "but at first I wasn't sure if I had understood him correctly. I only remember staring at him dumbfounded. He took my hand and started pressing it in his. He seemed to take great pleasure in this. I was so beside myself, it never even occurred to me to pull my hand away."

"You understood," he continued, "that had you become Alyosha's wife, he would soon grow to hate you, and your noble pride wouldn't accept that, so you made up your mind to let him go… I haven't come here to praise you. I only came to say that you have never had nor will you ever have a truer friend than me. I sympathize with you and feel sorry for you. My participation in this unfortunate business was entirely involuntary; I was merely performing my duty. Your tender heart will understand that and bond with my own. But it has been more difficult for me than it has for you, believe me!"

"Enough, Prince," said Natasha. "Leave me in peace."

"Certainly, I will leave in a moment," he answered, "but I love you like a daughter, and you must allow me to come visit you. Look to me now as a father and let me be useful to you."

"I do not need anything from you. Leave me alone," Natasha interrupted again.

"I know you are proud... But I am speaking sincerely… from my heart. What do you intend to do now? Make peace with your parents? That would be a good thing, but your father is unjust, proud, and a tyrant… forgive me, but it's true. If you went home now, you would be met with new reproaches and fresh suffering. But you need to be independent, and it is my obligation, my sacred duty to take care of you now. Alyosha begged me not to leave you, but to be your friend. But apart from me, there are people who are deeply loyal to you. You will, I hope, allow me to introduce you to Count Nainsky. He has an excellent heart and is a relative of mine. One might even say he has been a benefactor to my whole family. He has done a great deal for Alyosha. Alyosha has the greatest respect and love for him. He is a very powerful man with great influence, already an old man, and it would be quite beneficial for a girl like you to receive him. I've already told him about you. He can establish you and, if you like, secure you an excellent position... with one of his relations. I gave him a full and frank account of our *affair* of long ago, and he was so stirred by generous and noble feelings that he has implored me to introduce you to him as soon as possible. He is a man sympathetic to everything beautiful, believe me. He is a generous and highly respected old man, able to appreciate a person's true worth. Not long ago he behaved most nobly to your... *father,*" indicating himself, "in a certain matter."

Natasha jumped up as if stung. Now, at last, she fully understood him.

"Leave me alone, leave now!" she cried.

"But, my dear, you forget that the count could be useful to your *actual* father, as well."

"*My* father will not take anything from you. Will you leave now?" Natasha cried again.

"Oh, you're so impatient and mistrustful! How have I deserved this?" asked the prince, looking around uneasily. "You will allow me at least," he continued, taking a large roll of money from his pocket, "to leave you with this proof of my sympathy, and especially the sympathy of Count Nainsky, on whose suggestion I am acting. This roll contains ten thousand rubles. Wait, my dear," he said quickly when he saw Natasha rise in anger. "Listen patiently to everything. You know your father lost a lawsuit against me. This ten thousand rubles will serve as compensation for..."

"Go away!" Natasha screamed. "Take your money away! I see through you! Oh, you vile, vile, vile man!"

Prince Valkovsky rose from his chair, pale with anger.

Perhaps he had come to test the waters, feel her out, discover where he stood, undoubtedly relying on the strong effect ten thousand rubles would have on a destitute and abandoned young woman. The base and brutal prince had often been of service to Count Nainsky, an immoral old sinner, in enterprises of this nature. But he hated Natasha, and realizing that things were not going smoothly, he immediately changed his tone and with an evil joy hastened to insult her, so as not to *leave with nothing*.

"It is not a good idea, my dear, for you to lose your temper," he said in a voice that vibrated with an eagerness to enjoy the results of his insults. "That's not useful here. You are being offered protection, and you turn up your nose... The truth is you ought to be grateful to me. As the father of the young man you corrupted and led astray, I could have easily had you imprisoned long ago, but I didn't do that... heh-heh-heh!"

But by this point the doctor and I had come in. We were still in the kitchen when we heard another voice. I stopped the doctor for a moment and listened to the prince's last sentence. Then came that hideous laugh of his and a desperate cry from Natasha.

"Oh, my God!"

At this moment I opened the door and rushed at the prince.

I spat in his face and struck him on the cheek with all my might. He was about to fling himself on me, but seeing that there were two of us, he ran for the door instead, grabbing the roll of money off the table on his way.

Yes, he did that. I saw it myself. I grabbed a rolling pin off the kitchen table and threw it after him. When I ran back into the room, I saw the doctor was supporting Natasha, who was writhing and struggling to break free of him as if suffering convulsions. For a long time, we could not calm her down. Finally, we were able to get her in bed, but the delirium continued.

"Doctor, what's wrong with her?" I asked, breathless with fear.

"Wait," he answered, "I need to study her more closely to diagnose her condition... but, generally speaking, things are very bad. It could even end in brain fever... But we will take action..."

I had a sudden thought and begged the doctor to stay with Natasha for another two or three hours, making him promise not to leave her for a minute. He gave me his word, and I ran home.

Nellie was sitting in a corner, sullen and depressed, and she looked at me strangely. I must have looked strange myself.

I took her in my arms, sat on the couch with her on my lap, and kissed her gently on the cheek. She blushed.

"Nellie, my angel!" I said, "do you want to be our salvation? Do you want to save us all?" She looked at me in amazement.

"Nellie! You are my one hope now! There is a father, you have seen him and know him. He cursed his daughter and came here yesterday to ask you to take his daughter's place. Now she, Natasha… you told me you love her… has been abandoned by the man she loves, for whose sake she left her father. He is the son of that prince who came here… you remember… one evening to see me and found you alone. But you ran away from him and then were sick afterwards... You know him, don't you? He is an evil man!"

"I know," said Nellie, shuddering and turning pale.

"Yes, he is an evil man. He hated Natasha because his son Alyosha wanted to marry her. Today Alyosha left and an hour later his father was already at Natasha's, insulting and threatening to put her in prison, and he laughed at her. Do you understand me, Nellie?"

Her black eyes sparkled, but she immediately dropped them.

"I understand," she whispered almost inaudibly.

"Now Natasha is alone and sick, and I left her with our doctor, and came running to you. Please, Nellie, let us go to Natasha's father. You don't love him, and you don't want to live with him, but we'll go to him together. We'll go and you'll tell him that you want to take the place of his daughter, Natasha. The old man is sick now, too, because he has cursed Natasha and because Alyosha's father mortally offended him recently. He does not want to hear about his daughter now, but he loves her, Nellie… he loves her… and wants to make peace with her. I know that. I know everything! It's true! Do you hear me, Nellie?"

"I hear you," she said in the same whisper.

I spoke to her with my tears flowing. She looked at me timidly.

"Do you believe it?" I asked.

"Yes."

"So, we'll go together. I will take you to them and they will welcome you and hug you and begin to question you. Then I'll turn the conversation to what *your* life was like before, about *your* mother and *your* grandfather. Tell them, Nellie, just the way you told me, simply and not hiding anything. Tell them how your mother was abandoned by a bad man, how she lay dying in a cellar at Madame Bubnova's, how you and your mother used to beg in the streets, what she said and what she asked you to do when she was dying... Then tell them about your grandfather, how he did not want to forgive your mother, and how she sent you to him in her dying hour. But when he finally arrived to beg her to forgive him, he was too late. She had died. Tell them. Tell them everything. And when you tell the old man, he will feel it in his heart. You see, he knows that Alyosha has left her and that she is feeling used and abused, alone and helpless, with no one to protect her from allegations by her enemy. He knows all this... Nellie, save Natasha, save her! Will you go?"

"Yes," she answered, gasping for breath, and staring at me with a strange, prolonged gaze. There was reproach in her eyes, and I felt it in my heart.

But I could not give up on my idea. I had too much faith in it. I took Nellie by the hand and we went out. It was past three o'clock in the afternoon. A storm was moving in and the clouds were darkening. All the recent weather was hot and stifling, but now there was a rumbling of early spring thunder. Wind swept through the dusty streets.

We got into a cab. Nellie was silent the whole way, but she looked at me occasionally with those same strange and mysterious eyes. Her chest was heaving, and I put my arm around her to prevent her from falling out of the carriage. I could feel the pounding of her heart with my hand, thumping so hard it felt as though it would leap out of her body.

CHAPTER FORTY-THREE

The cab ride seemed endless to me. Finally, we arrived at the Ichmenyev's and I went in to see my old friends with a sinking feeling in my heart. I did not know how things would be when I left their home, but I knew that I had to do whatever was necessary to leave with forgiveness and reconciliation.

It was nearly four o'clock. The old couple were sitting in separate chairs, as usual. Nikolai Sergeich was irritated and sick and lay stretched out on his reclining armchair. He was pale and exhausted, his head bandaged with a handkerchief. Anna Andreyevna was sitting beside him in a padded chair, occasionally moistening his temples with vinegar, and incessantly studying his face with a curious and pained look, something which seemed to worry and annoy the old man even more. He stubbornly remained silent, and she dared not speak. Our sudden arrival surprised them both. Anna Andreyevna, for some reason, seemed especially surprised at the sight of Nellie, and for the first few minutes stared at us with an oddly guilty expression.

"I have brought you my Nellie," I said upon entering. "She has made up her own mind and now wants to live with you. Welcome her and love her..."

The old man looked at me suspiciously, and from his expression I could see that he knew his Natasha was now alone, deserted, and abandoned, and had, perhaps, even been threatened. He wanted to penetrate the mystery of our arrival, and he looked questioningly at both Nellie and me. Nellie was trembling and tightly clutched my hand in her own. She was staring at the floor but would occasionally glance around the room like a small wild animal caught in a trap. But Anna Andreyevna soon recovered her composure and understood the situation. She rushed to Nellie, kissed her, caressed her, even wept over her, and then lovingly had her sit beside her, still holding her hand in her own. Nellie looked at her with curiosity and not a little astonishment.

But after having warmly embraced and seated Nellie next to her, the old woman did not know what to do next. She looked at me with naive expectation. The old man frowned, perhaps guessing why I had brought Nellie. Realizing that I had noticed his disgruntled expression and furrowed brow, he raised his hand to his forehead and said, "I have a terrible headache, Vanya."

We all sat in silence again and I thought about how to begin. The room was dim as black clouds gathered outside, and once again we heard the distant rumble of thunder.

"We're getting thunder early this spring," the old man said. "But I remember 1837 when the storms arrived even earlier."

Anna Andreyevna sighed. "Shall we have the samovar?' she asked timidly, but no one answered, so she again turned to Nellie.

"What is your name, my dear?" she asked. Nellie answered in a tiny, weak voice, and looked down even more. The old man looked at her intently. "It is also Elena, right?" Anna Andreyevna continued, with growing enthusiasm.

"Yes," Nellie said, and again there was silence.

"Anna Andreyevna's sister, Praskovia, had a niece named Elena," Nikolai Sergeich observed. "She was also called Nellie, I remember."

"And have you no family, my darling? No father, no mother?" Anna Andreyevna asked.

"No," Nellie responded abruptly in a hoarse whisper.

"That's what I had heard... had heard. Has it been a long time since your mother died?"

"No, not long."

"You poor, darling little orphan," the old woman continued, looking with compassion at her. Nikolai Sergeich impatiently drummed his fingers on the table.

"Your mother was a foreigner, wasn't she? Isn't that what you told me, Vanya?" Anna Andreyevna asked, with some hesitation.

Nellie glanced at me with her black eyes, as if imploring me to help. Her breath was coming in heavy, uneven gasps.

"Her mother was the daughter of an Englishman and a Russian woman," I said to Anna Andreyevna, "so she was probably more of a Russian. Nellie was born abroad."

"Oh, did her mother go to live abroad when she married?"

Nellie suddenly flushed. The old woman instantly guessed that she had been indiscreet and trembled under an angry glance from her husband. He looked at her sternly then turned toward the window.

"Her mother was deceived by an evil and mean-spirited man," he said, suddenly turning back to Anna Andreyevna. "She left her father and went with him, giving her father's money to her lover. He had lured her abroad and then robbed and abandoned her. A good friend remained true to her and helped her until his death. And when he died two years ago, she came back to Russia, to her father. Wasn't that what you told me, Vanya?" he asked abruptly.

Nellie became very agitated. She stood and tried to get to the door.

"Come here, Nellie," the old man said, holding out his hand at last. "Sit here, sit down beside me, here... sit down!"

He bent over to her and kissed her forehead, then he slowly began to stroke her hair. Nellie was trembling visibly but checked her instinct to run. Anna Andreyevna was filled with joyful hope when she saw that Nikolai Sergeich's heart was beginning to warm to the orphan.

"I know, Nellie, that a wicked man, an evil and immoral man hurt your mother, but I also know that your mother loved and honored her father," the old man said, still stroking Nellie's head. He could not resist throwing in this piece of information as a challenge to us. His pale cheeks flushed, and he tried not to glance our way.

"Mother loved Grandpa more than he loved her," Nellie said timidly, yet firmly. She, too, tried to avoid anyone else's eyes.

"How do you know?" the old man asked sharply, sounding more like a child than an adult, but he seemed embarrassed by his outburst.

"I know," Nellie answered testily. "He refused to see my mother and... drove her away..."

I saw that Nikolai Sergeich wanted to say something, to come to her grandfather's defense, but he looked at us and said nothing.

"How do you know that?" Anna Andreyevna asked. "Where were you living when he refused to see your mother?" She seemed determined to continue the conversation in this direction.

"When we arrived, we searched for my grandfather a long time," Nellie said, "but we couldn't find him. Mother told me then that Grandpa had once been very rich and wanted to build a factory, but now he was very poor because the man my mother had run away with had taken all of Grandpa's money and refused to return it. She told me that herself."

"Hmm..." said the old man.

"And she also told me…" Nellie continued, now more vigorously, as if wishing to answer Nikolai Sergeich but addressing Anna Andreyevna. "She told me that Grandpa was very angry with her, and that she blamed herself for betraying him with that other man, but that now she had no one else on earth except Grandpa. And when she said this to me, she cried. 'He will never forgive me,' she said when we first arrived here, 'but perhaps he will see you and love you, and for your sake forgive me.' Mother was very fond of me and would always kiss me when she said this. But she was very much afraid of trying to see my grandfather. She taught me to pray for him, and she prayed for him, too. She even told me about how she had lived with Grandpa in the old days when he loved her very much, more than anyone else. She played the piano for him and read books to him at night, and he would kiss her and give her lots of presents. He used to give her everything, but they once had a falling out over Mama's birthday gift, because Grandpa didn't know that Mama knew what his gift was going to be, but she had learned long before. Mama wanted earrings, but Grandpa purposely tried to fool her by saying it would be a brooch, but when he gave her earrings and saw that she already knew his gift would be earrings and not a brooch, he became angry and wouldn't speak to her for half the day, but then he went and kissed her and asked for her forgiveness."

Nellie spoke with a sudden passion, and there was even a flush of red on her pale, ashen cheeks.

It was clear that Nellie's mother had often huddled with her little girl in their corner of the cellar, and spoken about her previously happy life, while hugging and kissing the child, who was the only thing left to comfort her in life. She would frequently weep while telling the stories, not suspecting what a powerful effect they had on the morbidly sensitive and precocious heart of her sickly child.

After her sudden outburst, Nellie fell silent and returned to her previously sullen state, looking at the others with misgivings. The old man frowned and drummed his fingers on the table again. Anna Andreyevna silently wiped a single tear from her eye with a handkerchief.

"Mother came here very ill," Nellie finally added, speaking softly, "with terrible chest pains. We had been looking for Grandpa a long time and couldn't find him, so we moved into a small corner of a woman's cellar."

"A sick woman in the corner of a cellar!" cried Anna Andreyevna.

"Yes... in the corner..." Nellie said. "Mama was poor. Mama told me," she added, with renewed enthusiasm, "there is no sin in being poor, but there is sin in being rich and hurtful... and God was punishing her for that."

"Was it on Vasilyevsky Island that you lodged? With Madame Bubnova?" the old man asked, turning to me and trying not to show his growing concern with his question. He spoke as if he were embarrassed to sit in silence.

"No, not there... the first was on Meshchanskaya Street," Nellie said. "It was very dark and damp there," she added after a pause, "and Mama got very sick, although she was still able to walk then. I did the laundry for her and she was always crying. There used to be an old woman who lived there, too, the widow of a captain. And then there was a retired clerk who always came home drunk at night screaming and roaring. I was dreadfully afraid of him. Mama used to take me into her bed and hug me, and she would tremble all over when he would shout and swear. Once he nearly beat the captain's widow to death. She was an old lady and walked with a cane. Mother felt sorry for her, and she stood up for her. The man hit my mother, too, and then I hit him..."

Nellie stopped. The memory upset her. Her eyes were blazing.

"Oh, my God!" cried Anna Andreyevna, completely absorbed in the story and keeping her eyes on Nellie, who seemed to be speaking primarily to her.

"Then my mother left that place," Nellie went on, "and took me with her. We started in the morning and were wandering about the streets until evening. Mama was holding my hand tightly and couldn't stop crying. I was so tired, and we hadn't eaten anything all day. And Mama kept mumbling to herself and said to me, 'Be poor, Nellie, and when I die, don't listen to anyone or anything. Don't ask anyone for help, just work and be poor and alone. And if you can't get work, beg on the street, but never, ever go to *him*!' It was just after sunset when we came to a large street and Mama cried out, 'Azorka! Azorka!' And suddenly a large hairless dog ran up, whining and leaping up to her. Then Mama was terribly frightened. She screamed and turned pale. Then she threw herself on her knees in front of a tall old man who had just walked up to us carrying a cane and looking at the ground. And this tall old man was my grandfather. He was so thin and pale and wearing such shabby clothes. That was the first time I ever saw Grandpa. He was scared, too, and when he saw my mother kneeling at his feet and grabbing at his legs, he pushed Mama back, broke away, and struck the pavement with his stick as he walked away. Azorka stayed behind, whining and licking mother, then ran to catch up with the old man, grabbed him by the coattails and tried to pull him back. And Grandpa hit her with his stick. Azorka was going to run back to us, but Grandpa called her, so she followed after him and kept whining. And Mama lay on the pavement as if dead. A crowd of people gathered around and the police came. I kept screaming and trying to get Mama up. She finally stood up, looked around, and followed me. I led her home as people stared and shook their heads at us."

Nellie stopped to take a breath before going on. She was very pale, but there was a determined gleam in her eyes. It was evident that she had made up her mind to tell everything. There was something defiant about her at this moment.

"Well," Nikolai Sergeich said in an unsteady, rough voice, "your mother insulted her father so he was justified in rejecting her..."

"That's what Mama told me," Nellie snapped back. "As we walked home, she kept saying, 'That's your grandfather, Nellie, and I sinned against him, so he cursed me, and now God is punishing me.' And all that evening and the next day she kept repeating that, although she talked as though she had no idea what she was saying."

The old man remained silent.

"And then how was it you found another apartment?" Anna Andreyevna asked, continuing to cry softly.

"That same night Mama became ill and the captain's widow found us lodging at Bubnova's, and on the third day we moved. The captain's widow came with us. After we moved, Mama grew even sicker and lay in bed for three weeks while I looked after her. All of our money was gone and we were helped by the captain's widow and by Ivan Alexandrovich."

"The coffin-maker," I said in explanation.

"And when Mama got out of bed and began to walk, she told me about Azorka."

Nellie paused. The old man seemed pleased that the conversation had turned to Azorka.

"Well, what did she tell you about Azorka?" he asked, scrunching down even lower in his seat to further hide his face and look at the floor.

"She kept talking to me about my grandfather," Nellie said, "and when she was sick, she kept talking about him, and when the delirium set in, she did the same. When she began to recover, she told me of her life before... and then she told me about Azorka. Some horrid boys had dragged her to the river outside the town and threatened to drown her. Mama gave the boys money and bought Azorka. When Grandpa saw the dog, he laughed. But then Azorka ran away and Mama couldn't stop crying. Grandpa was frightened and offered a hundred rubles to anyone who found Azorka. On the third day, someone brought her back and Grandpa gave him a hundred rubles. From that day on he grew to love Azorka. And mother loved her so much she let her sleep on her bed with her. She told me that Azorka had been trained to perform in the streets with strolling actors and knew how to play her part. She used to carry a monkey on her back and learned to shoot a gun and do so much more. And when Mama ran away from Grandpa, he kept Azorka. So, when Mama saw Azorka on the street, she knew Grandpa was nearby."

The old man had not been expecting this story when he asked about Azorka and he scowled more and more. He asked no more questions.

"So you didn't see your grandfather again?" asked Anna Andreyevna.

"No, when Mama began to recover, I met him again. I went to the shop for bread and suddenly saw a man with Azorka. I looked closer and saw that it was Grandpa. I stepped aside and pressed up against the wall. Grandpa looked at me. His look was so long and terrible that I was terrified and let him pass by. Azorka remembered me, though, and began to jump around me and to lick my hands. I immediately started for home, looked back, and saw my grandfather go into the shop. Then I thought, he's sure to ask about me, which frightened me even more, so when I came home, I didn't tell Mama about seeing him because I didn't want her to get sick again. I didn't go to the shop the next day. I told Mama I had a headache. When I went on the third day, I didn't see him, but I was so scared I ran all the way home. Then, the next day I came around a corner and there he was standing in front of me with Azorka. I ran and turned into another street and came back to the shop by a different route. But I suddenly came across him again and was so frightened that I immediately stopped and couldn't move. Grandpa stood in front of me and stared at me for a long time, then he patted me on the head, took my hand and walked with me, with Azorka following behind wagging her tail. Then I saw that my grandfather couldn't walk upright, but had to lean on his stick, and his hands were trembling the whole time. He took me to an outdoor stall on the corner where a man was selling cakes and apples. Grandpa bought a gingerbread cock and a fish, and a candy and an apple. When he took the money from his leather purse, his hands were shaking so dreadfully that he dropped a penny, which I picked up for him. He gave me the penny and the two gingerbread cakes and patted me on the head, but he still said nothing and just walked away.

"Then I went to Mama and told her all about Grandpa and how at first I was afraid and hid from him. At first, Mama didn't believe me, but then was so happy that she questioned me all night, kissed me and cried. After I had told her everything, she told me never to be afraid of my grandfather, and that he probably loved me because he had purposely come up to me. And she told me to be nice to him and speak with him. The next day, she sent me out several times, even though I told her that Grandpa only came to the shops in the evening. She followed me from a distance and hid just around the corner. The next day she did the same thing, but Grandpa didn't come. It had rained on each of those days and my mother caught a very bad cold coming down to the shops, and again she fell ill.

"Grandpa came again a week later and again bought me a gingerbread fish and an apple, and again he said nothing. And when he walked away that time, I quietly followed him, because I had decided beforehand that I would find out where my grandfather lived and tell mother. I was walking quite a distance behind him on the other side of the street, so he didn't see me. And he lived very far away, not where he lived later when he died, but on the fourth floor of a big house on Gorokhovaya Street. I learned all that and it was late when I got back home. Mama was very scared because she didn't know where I was. When I told her, Mama was again very happy and wanted to go see Grandpa the very next day, but the next day she thought about it and became frightened again, so she didn't go for three days. And then she called me to her and said, 'Listen, Nellie, I am sick now and cannot go, so I've written a letter to your grandfather. Go to him and give him the letter. And see, Nellie, how he reads it, what he says, and what he will do, and you kneel down before him, kiss him, and beg him to forgive your mother.' And Mama cried dreadfully and kept kissing me, making the sign of the cross, and praying. Then she made me kneel in front of the ikons with her, and even though she was very sick she walked me as far as the gate. When I looked back, she was still watching me.

"When I got to Grandpa's there was no latch on the door, so I just pushed it open. Grandpa was sitting at the table eating bread and potatoes. Azorka stood watching him and wagging her tail. The windows were low and let in very little light, and there was only one table and one chair. He was clearly living alone. I went in and he was frightened and started to tremble. I was frightened too and didn't say a word. I just went to the table where he was sitting and put the letter on it. When he saw the letter, Grandpa was so angry he stood up and started shaking his stick at me. But he didn't hit me. He just led me to the stair landing and gave me a push. Before I was halfway down the first flight of stairs, he opened his door again and tossed the letter after me. He hadn't even opened it. I went home and told Mama what had happened. After that, she was sick and in bed again."

Chapter Forty-Four

At that moment there was a large clap of thunder and the rain pounded on the windowpanes. The room was growing darker. The old woman seemed scared and crossed herself. We were all startled.

"The rain will stop soon," the old man said, glancing out the window. Then he got up and paced back and forth across the room.

Nellie watched him with a sidelong glance. She was in an extreme state of morose excitement. I could see that, even though she managed to avoid looking at me.

"Well, what next?" asked the old man, moving back to his chair. Nellie looked around timidly. "You didn't see your grandfather again, I suppose," he said.

"Yes, I did..."

"Yes, yes! Tell us, my darling, tell us," Anna Andreyevna chimed in.

"I didn't see him again for three weeks'" Nellie began, "and not before winter had arrived. It was cold and the snow had fallen. When I saw Grandpa again, at the same shop, I was very happy... because Mama was very depressed that he hadn't visited her. When I saw him, I purposely ran across the street, so that he could see me running away from him. Once I looked back and saw that he was following me quickly, but then he started to run and called out to me. 'Nellie, Nellie!' And Azorka was also running after me, too, and I felt sorry for her, so I stopped. Then my grandfather caught up, took me by the hand and started leading me. But when he saw that I was crying, he stopped, looked at me, bent down and kissed me. Then he saw that my shoes were old and worn out. He asked if I had other shoes. I immediately told him that Mama had no money and that the people where we were lodging only gave us food to eat out of pity. Grandpa did not say anything, but he took me to the market and bought me new shoes and told me to put them on at once. Then he took me to his house on Gorokhovaya, but first stopped at a shop to buy a pie and two pieces of candy. When we got to his room, he told me to eat the pie and then watched me as I ate it. Then he gave me the candy. Azorka put her paws on the table and asked for some pie, too. I gave her some, and Grandpa laughed. Then he had me stand in front of him, stroked my hair, and asked if I had had any schooling and what I knew. I answered him, and he said that whenever I could, I should come back there every day at three o'clock and he would teach me himself. Then he told me to turn my back until he said it was all right to turn around again, so I turned and looked out the window. I did what he said but took a peep on the sly and saw him reach into the bottom corner of his pillow and take out four rubles. Then he brought them to me and said, 'These are only for you.' I started to take them, but then I thought about it and said, 'If they're only for me, I don't want them." Suddenly, Grandpa became terribly angry and told me, 'Well, do what you want with them, but go away!' I left and he didn't kiss me.

"When I got home, I told Mama everything. And Mama's health kept getting worse and worse. A medical student who occasionally visited the coffin-maker, brought Mama some medicine and told her to take it.

"I started going to see Grandpa often because Mama wanted me to. Grandpa bought a New Testament and a geography book and began teaching me. And sometimes he would tell me about the earth and the different countries on it, and how different people lived. And he talked about the oceans and seas, and how the world was in olden days, and even how Christ forgave us all. When I asked him questions, he was very happy, so I asked him a lot of questions and he answered them. And he talked a lot about God. And sometimes we didn't study but played with Azorka instead. Azorka began to love me very much, and I taught her how to jump over a stick, and Grandpa would laugh and pat me on the head. Grandpa laughed very little. One time he might talk a lot and then suddenly stop talking and sit, as if asleep, with his eyes open. And then he would sit like that until dark, and when it was dark, he would become a scary old man. Another time I would come to him and find him sitting in his chair thinking and he would hear nothing, and Azorka would be lying near him. I would wait and wait and cough, but still Grandpa wouldn't look around, so I would go away. And at home Mama would be waiting for me. She would lie there and I would tell her everything... everything... and night would come and I would still be telling her and she would still be listening about Grandpa; what he'd done that day, what he'd said to me, and the lessons he had given me. And when I told her how I had made Azorka jump over a stick and made my grandfather laugh, she suddenly started to laugh, too, and she would laugh and be happy a long time. Then she would ask me to repeat the story and she would begin to pray. And I kept thinking that mother loved Grandpa so much, and Grandpa didn't love her at all, and once I went to see Grandpa on purpose to tell him how much Mama loved him and how she was always asking about him. He listened, looking so angry, but he listened without saying a word. Then I asked him why it was that Mama always asked about him, but he never asked anything about Mama. Grandpa got angry and threw me out of his room, but I waited on the other side of the door until he suddenly opened it and called me back in. But still he was angry and silent. And later, when we began reading the Gospel, I asked him again why Jesus said, 'love one another and forgive trespasses,' and yet he wouldn't forgive my mother? Then he jumped up and shouted that my mother had taught me to say that, and he threw me out and told me never to dare to come see him again. And I said I never wanted to come back again anyway, and I left. And the very next day Grandpa moved out of that apartment."

"I told you that the rain would soon pass, and see it's gone and the sun has come out. Look, Vanya," Nikolai Sergeich said, turning to the window.

Anna Andreyevna looked at him in utter bewilderment, and suddenly there was a flash of anger in the eyes of that hitherto meek and frightened old woman. Silently she took Nellie's hand and pulled the girl onto her lap.

"Tell me, my angel," she said, "I'll listen to you. Let those who have hardened hearts..."

She burst into tears without finishing her thought. Nellie looked questioningly at me, as if in disbelief and dismay. The old man looked at me and seemed about to shrug his shoulders but turned away instead.

"Go on, Nellie," I said.

"For three days I didn't go to see Grandpa," Nellie began again, "during which time Mama was feeling even worse. All of our money was gone and we had nothing to buy medicine with, and nothing to eat, because the coffin-maker and his wife had nothing either, and they began to reproach us for living at their expense. Then on the third day I got up and began to dress. Mama asked where I was going. I said to Grandpa's to ask for money, and she was glad, because I had told Mama how he had turned me out and how I had told him I didn't want to return even though my mother had cried and begged me to go. So I went and discovered that my grandfather had moved, and I went searching for his new address. As soon as I had climbed the stairs to the attic where he had moved, he jumped up and rushed to me, stamping his feet dramatically, but I told him right away that my mother was very ill and that we needed fifty kopecks for medicine because we had nothing. Grandpa yelled and pushed me towards the stairs and closed the door behind me. But when he pushed me out, I told him that I would sit on the stairs until he gave me the money. So I sat on the stairs. A little later, he opened the door and saw that I was still sitting there and closed the door again. Then, after a long time had passed, he opened the door, saw me again and shut the door again. And he did that a few more times. Finally, he came out with Azorka, locked the door, and walked past me without saying a word, and I didn't say a word, but I remained sitting there until it got dark."

"My dear," cried Anna Andreyevna, "but it must have been so cold on the stairs!"

"I was wearing a heavy coat," Nellie said.

"But how warm could it have been? My darling, how you have suffered! What did your grandfather do then?"

Nellie's lips began to quiver, but she made an extraordinary effort to stay strong.

"He came back after it was dark and stumbled into me on the stairs. 'Who's there?' he shouted. 'It's me,' I said. He probably thought I had left long before that, but when he saw that I was still there he was very surprised. He stood in front of me for a moment and then suddenly hit the stairs with his stick, ran and unlocked his door and came out with some copper coins which he threw to me on the stairs. 'Here,' he shouted, 'take it all from me, that's all I have, and tell your mother that I curse her,' and then he slammed the door. Some of the coins had rolled down the stairs and I started to crawl around in the dark to find them. Grandpa apparently realized that I would have trouble finding all the coins in the dark, so he opened his door again and brought out a candle. And by candlelight Grandpa and I managed to find all of the coins. He told me that there should be seventy kopecks altogether, and then went back into his room. When I got home, I gave the money to Mama and told her what had happened. But Mama became even worse, and I myself was sick with a fever all night and the next day, but I had only one thought, because I was so angry with Grandpa, and when mother had fallen asleep, I went to my grandfather's apartment, but before I got there I stopped on the bridge and then *he* passed by…"

"It was Arkhipov," I said. "That disgusting man I spoke to you about, Nikolai Sergeich. The merchant who had paid Madame Bubnova to have his way with Nellie. This was the first time Nellie had seen him since Masloboyev rescued her. Go on, Nellie."

"I stopped him and asked for money, a silver ruble. He looked at me and said, 'A silver ruble?' I said, 'Yes.' Then he laughed and said, 'Come with me.' I wasn't sure if I should go with him, when suddenly a little old man in gold-rimmed spectacles came along. He had heard me ask for the silver ruble. He leaned down to me and asked why I wanted so much. I told him that my mother was sick and needed it for medicine. He asked me where we lived and wrote down the address, and then gave me a piece of paper, a silver ruble. When the fat man saw the gentleman in spectacles, he left and didn't try to take me with him. I went into a shop and got change for the ruble. I wrapped thirty kopecks in paper and set it aside for Mama, but seventy kopecks I didn't wrapped in paper but deliberately squeezed in my hand and went to Grandpa's. When I got there, I opened the door, stood in the doorway, and tossed all the money into the room so that it rolled on the floor.

"'There, take your money!' I told him. Mama doesn't want it from you because you cursed her. Then I slammed the door and ran all the way home."

Her eyes sparkled, and she looked with naive defiance at the old man.

"The right thing to do," said Anna Andreyevna, not looking at Nikolai Sergeich but tightly hugging Nellie in her arms. "It served him right. Your grandfather was a wicked and hardhearted man!"

"Hm!" Nikolai Sergeich grumbled.

"Well, so what happened then?" Anna Andreyevna asked impatiently.

"I stopped going to see Grandpa, and he stopped meeting me at the shops," Nellie said.

"Well, how did you get on then, your mother and you? Oh, you poor, poor things!"

"Mother got even worse, and seldom got out of bed," Nellie went on, her voice trembling and broken. "We had no more money, so I started taking walks with the captain's widow, who would go from house to house or stop good people in the street asking for help. And that was how she survived. She told me she was not a beggar. She had a paper that showed her dead husband's rank and another that said she was poor. She would show people these papers and they would give her money. She told me that there was no shame in asking for help. I went with her and people gave us both money, and that's how we lived. Mama found out about it because the other tenants reproached her for being a beggar, and Bubnova herself came to Mama and said that she should have me work for *her* rather than be a beggar. She came to Mama and offered her money for my services, but Mama refused to take it. The Bubnova said, 'Why are you so proud when I am offering you money for food?' When she talked about me, Mama began to cry. She was so frightened when Bubnova began to scold her because the old crone was a drunk. She told Mama I was already begging in the streets with the captain's widow, and that same evening she kicked the captain's widow out of the house. When Mama heard about it, she began to cry and struggled out of her bed, dressed, grabbed my arm, and led me out. Ivan Alexandrovich tried to stop her, but she wouldn't listen to him, and we went out into the street. Mama could scarcely walk, and she had to sit down every few minutes, even with me supporting her. Mama kept saying that I should take her to Grandpa's but by then it was quite late. Suddenly we came to a big street with carriages stopped in front of several of the houses. People were coming in and out of the houses and the windows were all lit up and I heard music. Mama stopped me and grabbed my arm. 'Nellie, be poor,' she told me. 'Be poor all your life. Do not go with him, no matter who calls on you. Even if he is rich and dressed in fancy clothes, I do not want you to go with him. He is evil and cruel, and those are my instructions to you. Remain poor, work, and beg if you have to, and if someone comes after you, say, "I do not want to go with you!"' That's what my mother said to me when she was half out of her mind with illness, and I intend to obey her all my life," Nellie said, trembling with emotion, her little face glowing. "I will work and be a servant all my life. And that's why I've come to you, to be your servant and work hard. I do not want to be like a daughter."

"Hush, hush, my love, that's enough!" cried the old woman, hugging Nellie warmly. "Your mother was ill when she said that."

"She was out of her mind," the old man said sharply.

"So what if she were…" Nellie cried sharply, turning to him. "Even if she was crazy, that's what she told me to do, so that's how I'll be all of my life. Right after she said that to me, she fell on the ground and fainted."

"Good Lord!" cried Anna Andreyevna. "Sick... in the street… in winter?"

"They would have taken us to the police, but one gentleman came forward and asked where we lived, gave me ten rubles, and ordered his driver to take us home in his carriage. After that, Mama never left her bed again, and she died three weeks later."

"And her father? He still didn't forgive her after all this?" cried Anna Andreyevna.

"He didn't forgive her," Nellie answered, trying to hold herself together. "A week before her death, Mama called me to her and said, 'Nellie, go again to your grandfather one last time, and asked him to come to me and forgive me. Tell him I am going to die within a few days and leave you alone in the world. And tell him, too, that it is hard for me to die...' I went and knocked on Grandpa's door. He opened it and when he saw it was me he immediately tried to shut it, but I jumped at the door with both hands and shouted to him, "Mama is dying and is calling for you. You must go!' But he pushed me away and slammed the door. I came back to mother, lay down beside her, put my arms around her, and said nothing. Mama hugged me, too, and asked no questions."

At this point, Nikolai Sergeich leaned heavily on the table with his hands and stood up, but after looking at us with his strange, dull eyes, he sank helplessly back into his chair. Anna Andreyevna no longer looked at him. She was sobbing over Nellie.

"Late in the afternoon of her last day, Mama called me to her, took my hand and said, 'I shall die tonight, Nellie.' She wanted to say more but didn't have the strength. I looked at her, but she didn't seem to see me, but she held my hand firmly in hers. I gently pulled my hand away and ran all the way to Grandpa's. When he saw me rush through his door, he jumped up from his chair and looked pale and terrified. His whole body was trembling. I grabbed his hand and said only one thing: 'She is dying now.'

"He suddenly grabbed his stick and ran after me, even forgetting to take his hat, and it was cold. I grabbed his hat and put it on his head, and we ran off together. I hurried him down the stairs and told him he should hire a cab because Mama was going to die, but Grandpa only had seven kopecks in his pocket. He stopped a cab driver and tried to bargain with him, but the man just laughed at him and laughed at Azorka, who had run after us. We started running and we ran on and on. Grandpa was breathing hard and he was so exhausted, but he kept running. Suddenly he fell and his hat fell off. I helped him up, then picked up his hat and put it on his head. Again, we started to run, with me pulling him along by the hand, and just before dark we made it home. But my mother was already lying dead. When he saw her, Grandpa clasped his hands together and trembled as he stood over her. He said nothing. Then I went to my dead mother and grabbed Grandpa's hand and shouted at him, 'See, you cruel, evil man! Look! Look!' Then Grandpa screamed and fell to the floor as if dead."

Nellie leapt up, freed herself from Anna Andreyevna's arms, and stood in front of us, pale, exhausted and frightened. But Anna Andreyevna flew to her side, again hugging her, and crying out as if spiritually inspired.

"I… I'll be a mother to you now, Nellie, and you shall be my child! Yes, my darling, come away with me and we'll rid ourselves of these cruel, evil people who mock others and laugh at God. God will punish them. Come, Nellie, come away from here, come!"

I have never, before or since, seen Anna Andreyevna so agitated and willing to stand up to her husband. Nikolai Sergeich sat up in his chair, then stood and asked in a broken voice, "Where are you going, Anna Andreyevna?"

"To her, to my daughter, to Natasha!" she screamed and pulled Nellie to the door.

"Wait, stay! Stay!"

"There is no need to wait, you cruel and heartless man! I have waited much too long, and Natasha has waited, and Nellie has waited. It is time to say good-bye!"

Saying this, Anna Andreyevna turned around and looked at her husband. She was stunned. Nikolai Sergeich was standing before her, his trembling hands pulling on his overcoat and reaching for his hat.

"And you? You are coming with us?" she cried, incredulously, clasping her hands over her heart, not daring to believe in such happiness.

"Natasha, where is my Natasha? Where is she? Where is my daughter?" poured at last from the old man's lips. "Give me back my Natasha! Where, where is she?" And, seizing the stick which I passed to him, he rushed to the door.

"He has forgiven! Forgiven!" Anna Andreyevna cried joyfully.

But the old man did not reach the threshold. The door opened suddenly and Natasha ran into the room, pale, with flashing eyes, as if in a fever. Her dress was crumpled and soaked with rain. The kerchief which had covered her head had slipped down to her neck and the thick strands of her dark hair glistened with raindrops. She saw her father, ran to him, and with a great cry fell on her knees and stretched out her arms to him.

CHAPTER FORTY-FIVE

But he was already holding her in his arms!

He lifted his daughter like a child, carried her to his chair, sat her down, and fell on his knees before her. He hurriedly kissed her hands and feet and gazed at her as though he could not believe that she had returned to him, that he could once again see and hear her. Natasha, his beloved daughter, his Natasha.

Anna Andreyevna, still sobbing, stood by her daughter's side, embracing her and pressing her head to her own bosom. She was so overcome by the embrace that she was unable to utter a word.

"My darling! My life! My joy!" the old man murmured incoherently, clinging to Natasha's hand and gazing like a lover at her pale, thin, but still lovely face, and into her eyes that sparkled with tears. "My joy, my child!" he repeated again and again and then stopped to gaze rapturously at her once more. Still on his knees, he turned to us with a childlike smile. "Why did you tell me she was so much thinner? She's lost a little weight it's true, but look at her, she is prettier than ever!" he added, his voice cracking unintentionally from a combination of joy and anguish, two emotions that seemed to be battling for his soul.

"Get up, father, please stand up!" Natasha implored, rising from the chair and pulling at him, "because I want to kiss you, too!"

"Oh, the little darling! Do you hear, Annushka, do you hear how sweetly she said that?" and he flung his arms around her legs convulsively.

"No, Natasha, I need to lie at your feet until my heart convinces me that you have forgiven me, because I can never, ever do enough to earn your forgiveness! I rejected you, cast you out, and cursed you, do you hear me, Natasha? I cursed you! How could I do that? And you… you, Natasha, can you believe that I cursed you? You should never have believed it, you should not have believed that I could curse you! Cruel little heart! Why didn't you come to me? You must have known that I would take you back! Because you remember how much I loved you before. Well, I have loved you all this time, twice as much… no, a thousand times more than I ever loved before! I love you with every drop of my blood! I would have torn my heart out and laid it at your feet. Oh, my joy!"

"Well then, kiss me, you cruel old man. Kiss me the way Mama kisses me!" Natasha implored in a gentle, patient voice, almost overwhelmed by joyful tears, as he kissed her cheek.

"And on your beautiful eyes, too. Your wonderful eyes! Remember how I used to kiss your eyes?" the old man continued after a long, sweet hug with his daughter. "Oh, Natasha! Did you sometimes dream about us where you were? I dreamed of you almost every night and every night you came to me and I cried over you. Once you came to me as a tiny little thing—do you remember when you were ten years old and were just learning to play the piano?—you came in a short dress and pretty little shoes and tiny red hands... she had red hands then, do you remember, Annushka? She came to me and sat on my knee and hugged me... And you, you, you wicked girl! You could imagine that I would curse you and not welcome you if you came to me. But I... Listen, Natasha, your mother didn't know, no one knew, but I often went to see you… I would stand under your window, sometimes waiting half a day, sometimes on the pavement near your gate, hoping for an opportunity just to see you in the distance! Often in the evening I would see a candle burning in your window, and I returned many times, Natasha, in the evenings just to see you light a candle that would cast your shadow on the windowpane. I blessed you at night. Were you blessing me at night? Did you think of me? Did your heart tell you that I was there, below your window? And how many times late at night in the winter did I climb your stairs and stand on the dark landing outside your door, listening for the sound of your voice. Don't you think it's funny? That I could curse you? Why, I came to you one evening, planning to forgive you, but I turned back at the door. Oh, Natasha!"

He stood up, he lifted her from the chair and tightly pressed her to his heart.

"She is here again, next to my heart!" he cried. "Oh, Lord, I thank Thee for everything… everything… for Thy wrath and for Thy mercy! And for the sun, which is shining on us now after the thunderstorm! For this minute now, I thank you! We may be humiliated and debased, but we are together again now and triumphant over the proud and arrogant people who have used and abused us! Let them throw stones at us! Do not worry, Natasha... We will walk hand in hand and I will tell them, "This my darling, my beloved daughter, my blameless daughter whom you have used and abused, but whom I love and bless forever and ever!"

"Vanya! Vanya!" Natasha cried in a weak voice, reaching out to me from her father's arms for an embrace.

Oh, I shall never forget that at that moment she remembered me and called to me!

"Where is Nellie?" the old man asked, looking around.

"Ah, where is she?" cried the old woman. "My darling! We're leaving her out!"

But she was not in the room. She had quietly slipped back into her bedroom. We all went in there. Nellie was standing in the corner behind the door, timidly hiding from us.

"Nellie, what's the matter with you, my child?" the old man cried, reaching out to hug her, but she just stared vaguely at him for a long time.

"Mama, where is Mama?" she muttered as if delirious. "Where… where is my mother?" she cried again, stretching out her trembling hands to us. Then, suddenly, a terrible, unearthly cry burst from her chest, the muscles in her face quivered, and she fell on the floor with dreadful muscular tremors.

Chapter Forty-Six

Final memories.

It was early in June. The day was hot and stifling. It was nearly impossible to remain in the city of dust, plaster, construction, red-hot pavements, and noxious fumes. But now, oh joy! Thunder roared in the distance and little-by-little the sky darkened and the winds kicked up, driving before them clouds of city dust. A few large drops fell heavily on the ground and moments later the sky opened and a river of rainwater engulfed the city. Within half an hour, the sun shone again, and I opened the small windows of my garret and eagerly filled my lungs with fresh air. In my elation, I would have happily thrown aside my pen, my work and my publisher, and hurried to my friends on Vasilyevsky Island. But even though the temptation was great, I managed to resist and whipped myself into a sort of fury once again, attacking my paperwork, knowing that I had to fulfill my commitment to my publisher, who would not pay until my assignment was completed. He was waiting for my manuscript, but that evening I knew I would be free, completely free as the wind, my reward for the past two days and two nights of laborious writing in which I had completed three-and-a-half printed pages.

And now the work was done and I threw down my pen and stood up. There was a pain in my back and chest and my head felt heavy. I knew that at that moment my nerves were knotted tightly, and recalled the last words spoken to me by my old German friend the doctor: "No, no man's health could withstand such stress, because it's impossible!" Well for the time being, however, it was possible! My head was spinning, I could hardly stand on my feet, but the joy in my heart was limitless. My novel was finished and my publisher, even though I had told him about it many times, would be delighted to have it in hand and would pay me at least fifty rubles, an amount I had not seen in a long time. Freedom and money! Excitedly, I grabbed my hat and with my manuscript under my arm, ran headlong to catch my treasured publisher, Alexander Petrovich, at home.

I found him just as he was heading out. He, too, had just completed a highly profitable business arrangement, though not a literary one, after some two hours of conversation in his study. He eagerly gave me his hand, and in a soft, gentle, bass voice asked me about my health. He is one of the kindest men I have ever known, and it is far from hyperbole when I say that a great many writers owe him a debt of gratitude. It is not his fault that despite his devotion to literature his whole life, he is just a publisher. He realized long ago that literature needed an entrepreneurial individual to promote it, and he has earned his honor and glory in that pursuit.

He smiled pleasantly when he learned that my novel was done and that the next several volumes of his journal would thus be provided with a main section, but charmingly quipped that he was surprised that I was able to finish anything. Then he went to his iron chest and provided me with the promised fifty rubles. As he did this, he passed me a thick magazine of literary criticism and pointed out a column which offered a few words about my last story.

It was an article written by "Scribe." I was glad to see that while he didn't praise my work, neither was he overly abusive. But "Scribe" did write that, among other things, my work generally "smelled of sweat," meaning that he could discern the toil and meticulous labor that went into its creation and that my obvious efforts to write, rewrite and polish each line resulted in a finished product that was cloying.

Alexander Petrovich and I laughed over the comment, especially after I pointed out that the story in question had been written in two nights, and that in the previous two days and two nights I had completed three and a half printed pages. If only "Scribe" knew *that*, he certainly wouldn't have accused me of slow, laborious work.

"But it's your own fault, Ivan Petrovich," the publisher said. "Why do you get so far behind in your work that you have to work at night?"

Alexander Petrovich is, of course, a dear man, but he has one special weakness—to show off his literary judgment to those who, like himself, he suspects share his passion for literature. But I did not want to chat with him about literature, so I took the money and picked up my hat. Alexander Petrovich was on his way to his cottage on Vasilyevsky Island and when he heard that I, too, was on my way there, generously offered to take me in his carriage.

"I have a new carriage," he said, "that you haven't seen yet. Very pretty!"

Moments later, we descended the stairs to the street. The coach really was very pretty and Alexander Petrovich, being newly in possession of it, derived great pleasure in offering rides to his friends.

In the coach, he again tried several times to enter into a discussion of contemporary literature. In my company, he was not embarrassed to casually repeat the second-hand opinions of writers in whom he trusted, and whose judgment he respected. This practice of his occasionally led him to make some astounding statements. He would misinterpret other people's opinions or misapply them in such a way that the result made little or no sense at all. I sat in silence and marveled at the variety and capriciousness of human passions.

"Well, here's a man," I thought to myself, "who has built up a small fortune and forged a successful career as a publisher, who nevertheless aspires to fame and literary glory as an editor and critic!"

At that moment he was trying to elaborate on a complex literary theory that he had first heard three days before from *me*, and while he had originally argued *against* it, he was now presenting it as his own original idea. But with Alexander Petrovich such forgetfulness occurs frequently, and it is treated as an innocent idiosyncrasy among his friends. At that moment he was happy, proudly discoursing in his own carriage, pleased with his own good fortune and the pleasures of life. He delighted in conversation which was erudite and sophisticated and even his pleasant, gentle bass added weight to his scholarship. Little by little his dissertation drifted to the innocently skeptical conclusion that no one in literature could ever proceed with honesty and humility, especially with the growing trend toward "mutual whipping" exemplified by the unattributed articles by contemporary critics. I thought to myself that Alexander Petrovich regarded even honest and sincere men of letters as little more than simpletons, if not outright fools. Of course, such a judgment was likely the product of Alexander Petrovich's extreme innocence.

But I had not really been listening. On Vasilyevsky Island, he let me out of his carriage and I ran to the Ichmenyev's house on the Thirteenth Line. Upon seeing me, Anna Andreyevna shook her finger in front of her lips and waved her arms to keep me quiet.

"Nellie has just fallen asleep, poor thing!" she whispered to me hurriedly. "For God's sake, do not wake her up! She's very weak, the little darling. We are so worried about her. The doctor says it's nothing to worry about for now, but what information can you get from that doctor of yours? And you should be ashamed of yourself, Vanya. We've been waiting for you, expecting you for lunch, but for two days we've seen nothing of you!"

"But I told you *two days ago* that you wouldn't see me for two days!" I whispered to Anna Andreyevna. "I had to work to finish my book."

"But you promised to join us for lunch today. Why weren't you here? Nellie purposely got out of her little bed and we put her in a comfortable chair to wait for you. We had to carry her in to lunch. 'I want to wait for Vanya,' she said, but our Vanya never came. And it will be six o'clock soon! Where have you been hiding out, you sinner you! You're the only one who can calm her when she's upset. I didn't know what to say. Fortunately, she's asleep now, the little darling. And Nikolai Sergeich has gone off to the city, but he'll be back in time for tea. I'm struggling here all alone. It looks like a post may have opened up for him, Vanya, but when I think about moving to Perm, it sends a cold chill through me…"

"Where is Natasha?"

"In the garden, dear, in the garden! Go to her. Something is troubling her too and I can't figure out what it is. Oh, Vanya, I ache to my very soul! She claims that she is happy and content, but I do not believe her. Go speak with her, Vanya, and then quietly let me know what is wrong. Do you hear?"

But I was no longer listening to Anna Andreyevna and ran into the garden. The garden belonged to the house and was twenty-five paces in length and the same in width and was overgrown with vegetation. There were three old spreading trees, several young birch trees, a few bushes of lilacs and honeysuckle, a patch of raspberries in a corner, two beds of strawberries, and two narrow paths that wound through the garden. The old man delighted in the garden and declared that there would soon be mushrooms. The most important thing was that Nellie loved the garden and would often be carried out in a chair to sit on the garden path.

I found Natasha and she greeted me happily and gave me her hand. How thin and pale it was! She, too, had barely recovered from her illness.

"Did you finish it, Vanya?" she asked me.

"Absolutely, absolutely! And my evening is completely free."

"Well, thank God! You didn't rush it, did you? You haven't spoiled it?"

"It came out well; nothing to worry about. The nervous stress I feel when under pressure makes me work harder, and I think more clearly, more vividly and deeply. Every syllable seems to be under my control and the result is that I write better. So, all is well."

"Ah, Vanya, Vanya!"

Natasha had recently revealed a devoted and possessive attitude toward my literary success, basking in my glory. She had read everything I had typed in the past year, constantly inquired about my future plans, took an interest in every critical comment (becoming angry at some), and wanted me to advance in the literary world. She expressed this desire so strongly and persistently that it sometimes surprised me.

"You're working too hard, Vanya," she said to me. "The stress is not good for you and you'll ruin your health." She mentioned one acclaimed writer who had written only one novel in the previous two years, and another who had yet to write a second novel ten years after his first was published. "But see how elegant and polished their writing is," she noted. "Neither would permit a single careless error."

"Yes, but they are both prosperous and don't need to write to survive, while I am just a hack! Well, it's useless to talk about it! Let's leave it, my friend. Is there anything new with you?"

"A lot. First, I got a letter from him."

"What again?"

"Yes, again."

And she handed me a letter from Alyosha. It was the third she had received since their separation. The first, sent from Moscow, seemed to have been written in a frenzied passion. He notified her that circumstances in Moscow prevented him from returning to St. Petersburg, as they had originally planned when they parted. In the second letter, he hastened to inform Natasha that he was planning to arrive in a few days, and he was anxious to marry her as soon as possible, and nothing could prevent it. And yet the tone of the letter clearly suggested that he was in despair, that some foreign influence was weighing heavily on him and that he really did not believe what he was writing. He mentioned, among other things, that Katya was his "providence," and that only she provided him with comfort and support. I eagerly opened the third letter in my hand.

It was on two pages, written in scattered fragments, randomly, quickly and indiscriminately, marred by ink smudges and tear stains. It began by Alyosha renouncing Natasha and trying to persuade her to forget him. He tried to explain how their alliance was not possible; that foreign, hostile influences were too strong to repel, and that, finally, it was clear that he and Natasha would be miserable together because they were not equals. But he could not sustain the noble performance and suddenly abandoned his arguments and evidence and, without tearing up and discarding the first half of the letter, switched his tactics completely, admitting that he had been reprehensible in his treatment of Natasha, that he had killed any chance of a relationship, and that he was not man enough to rebel against the wishes of his father, who had joined him in the country. He wrote that he could not express his anguish, admitted among other things, that he was confident he could make Natasha happy, and suddenly presented the argument that they were quite equal, angrily refuted the arguments of his father against their marriage, and desperately drew a picture of the lifelong wedded bliss he and Natasha would have had, if only he were not such a coward, and bid her farewell forever! The letter was written with great anguish and it was evident that he had been crying when he wrote it. Natasha then handed me another letter... from Katya. This letter came in the same envelope with Alyosha's but bore its own seal. Katya, in a brief, concise letter of only a few lines, informed Natasha that Alyosha was really very sad, crying a lot, and almost sick with despair, but that she was with him and that he would soon be happy. She quickly added that Natasha should not think that Alyosha could be easily comforted, that his was a serious grief. "He will never forget you," Katya added, "and, indeed, could never forget you because his heart would not permit it. He loves you infinitely, will always love you, and if he ever did stop loving you or ceased even for a second to grieve at the thought of you, I, myself, would stop loving him immediately."

I returned both letters to Natasha, and we looked at each other without saying a word. It had been the same with his two prior letters and, indeed, we had begun to avoid talking about the past as though by silent agreement. She was suffering unbearably, I could see, but she would not speak even to me about her despair. After returning to her parents' home three weeks earlier, she had stayed in bed, sick with a fever, and was only now showing signs of recovery. We talked very little about the upcoming changes in our lives, even though she knew that her father had acquired a new position which would soon take her away from me. In spite of that, she remained tender, attentive, and actively engaged in my concerns, always giving me her insistent, persistent attention, listening to everything I had to tell her about myself, and at first I felt guilty about it, thinking that she was merely trying to make up for her past behavior toward me. But this burden quickly disappeared when I realized that there was quite another reason for her change in attitude—she simply loved me, had loved me forever, and could not live without me or without taking an interest in everything that concerned me, and I felt that no sister had ever loved a brother to the extent of Natasha's love for me. I knew the thought of our parting weighed heavily on her, and that she was suffering, for she understood, too, that I could not live without her either. But we did not talk about any of these things. Instead, I asked her about Nikolai Sergeich.

"He'll be home soon, I think," Natasha responded. "He promised to come for tea."

"He's busy making arrangements for his new job?"

"Yes, indeed, there is no doubt about the job now. But he really didn't need to leave today," she added. "He could have gone tomorrow."

"Then why *did* he go?"

"Because I got the letter… He is making himself sick over me." After a pause, Natasha added, "It's difficult for me to watch, Vanya. He seems to dream about me in his sleep and I'm the only thing he sees when he's awake. He's only concerned about what is happening to me, how I live, what I think. That's all he *ever* thinks about. My slightest anxiety causes him grief. Oh, he tries to pretend that he isn't worried about me by feigning cheerfulness and laughing out loud, so I laugh along with him. My mother, too, is not herself at such moments and she doesn't believe his laughter is real either, she just sighs... She's so awkward… a noble soul!" she added with a laugh. "So when I received the letter today, he had to run away, so as not to have to look me in the eyes... I love him more than myself, Vanya. More than anyone in the world," she added, lowering her head and squeezing my hand. "Even more than you..."

We paced through the garden twice before she spoke again.

"Masloboyev was here today, and yesterday as well," she said.

"Yes, he has gotten into the habit of visiting you quite often."

"And do you know why he comes here? My mother believes in him beyond anything I can imagine. She thinks he knows everything—well, about laws and all that—that he can handle any transaction. You would not believe the ideas that ramble through her brain. She is terribly hurt and sad that I did not became a princess. She cannot get that idea out of her head and I think she's been completely open about it with Masloboyev. She was afraid to talk about it with my father, but I imagine she thinks Masloboyev might be able to help, manipulating the laws, perhaps? Masloboyev, it seems, doesn't want to contradict her because she pampers him with plenty of wine," Natasha added with a grin.

"He's a mischievous fellow. But how do you know all this?"

"Why, my mother has let it slip to me… with little hints."

"What about Nellie? How is she?" I asked.

"I'm surprised at you, Vanya, that it has taken you so long to ask about her!" Natasha said, reproachfully. Nellie had become the idol of the whole house. Natasha had grown terribly fond of her and had finally given her heart to the poor child! Nellie had never in her life expected to find such loving people, and I was pleased to see that her embittered little heart was softening and her soul was opening to us all. It was painfully difficult, at first, for her to respond to the universal love which surrounded her, as opposed to her unhappy past, which had made her distrustful, angry and stubborn. However, for a long time, Nellie deliberately concealed from us her tears of reconciliation until, finally, she gave in and surrendered to us all. She grew to love Natasha, Anna Andreyevna and, finally, Nikolai Sergeich. I became so important to her that her health deteriorated if I stayed away for a long time. I had a difficult time persuading her to spare me for two days so I could finish my novel. But, of course, Nellie made a show of her indifference, embarrassed as she was to reveal her feelings openly.

She had all of us very worried. Silently and without any discussion, it was agreed that she would remain forever with Nikolai Sergeich and his family, and yet with their impending departure approaching quickly, Nellie was getting worse and worse. She had been sick from the day I first took her to the Ichmenyevs, on the day Natasha and her father finally reconciled. But if truth be told, she was always sick. The disease had been slowly building in her for years, but now began to grow with extraordinary speed. I do not understand, nor can I precisely describe her illness. Her seizures were recurring more frequently than before, but, more importantly, her symptoms included diminishing strength, a general loss of energy, and a perpetual state of fever and emotional distress, all of which culminated in her inability to even rise from her bed for the past few days.

The odd fact was that the more overcome by illness she became, the softer, sweeter and more open with us all she grew. Three days before, she caught my hand when I walked past her bed and pulled me to her. We were alone together in the room. She had grown terribly thin, her face was flushed, and her eyes burned with fever. She frantically, passionately reached out to me, and when I leaned over her, she firmly grabbed my neck with her dark slender arms and kissed my cheek and then immediately demanded I bring Natasha to her. I called for Natasha and when she appeared, Nellie had her sit next to her on the bed.

"I want to look at you," she said. "I had a dream about you last night, and I will dream about you again tonight... I often dream about you... every night..."

She clearly wanted to say something, but she was overcome with an emotion that she did not understand and didn't know how to express.

She loved Nikolai Sergeich more than almost anyone, except me, and I must say that Nikolai Sergeich was almost as fond of her as Natasha. He had the amazing ability to make Nellie laugh. He only had to come near her and she would soon be laughing and playful. The sick girl was a carefree child again, flirting with the old man, laughing along with him, and revealing her dreams or inventing some story to entertain him, while encouraging fresh stories out of him, as well. Nikolai Sergeich was happier than he had been in years, admiring his "little daughter, Nellie," and growing more and more delighted with her every day.

"God has sent her to us as a reward for our years of suffering," he told me once, after making the sign of the cross over her bed and leaving her to sleep.

Every evening, we would all gather together in the main room. Masloboyev would also come most nights, and sometimes the old doctor, who had grown fond of the Ichmenyevs, would join us as well. Nikolai Sergeich would carry Nellie in and place her in an easy chair at the big round table. The door to the veranda would be opened and the green garden, lit by the rays of the setting sun, would provide a lovely backdrop for a lively conversation. The smell of fresh herbs and newly blossoming lilacs filled the air. Nellie sat cozily in her chair and watched each of us affectionately as she listened to our conversation. Occasionally, however, her energy would revive and she would shyly ease her way into our chat. At such moments, we would all listen to her intently, although sometimes with anxiety, because her memories might touch on aspects of her life that we were uncomfortable discussing. Natasha, her mother and father, and I would relive the guilt we felt on the day Nellie, trembling and exhausted, first told us her story. The doctor, particularly, hated hearing the story repeated and he generally tried to change the direction of the conversation. At such moments, Nellie would pretend that she didn't see our discomfort and quickly find a way to make the doctor or Nikolai Sergeich laugh.

And yet, her health grew worse and worse and her struggle affected us all greatly. Her heartbeat was irregular and the doctor confided in me that she might not have long to live.

Not wanting to distress him, I said nothing about this to Ichmenyev. He was quite convinced that Nellie would recover in time for their relocation to Perm.

"I hear papa's voice," Natasha said. "He's home. Come, Vanya."

Nikolai Sergeich had barely crossed the threshold when his voice, as was his custom, thundered throughout the house. Anna Andreyevna quickly waved her hands to quiet him. The old man immediately calmed down and when he saw Natasha and me, he began in a fervent whisper to recount his recent adventure, the places he had traveled to, and the new life that awaited them. He seemed very pleased.

"We can be off in two weeks," he said, rubbing his hands and glancing cautiously at Natasha. But she answered him with a big smile and hugged him warmly, which instantly dispelled his doubts.

"Let us go, go, my dear ones, let us be off," he said jubilantly, and then added, "It is only when I think about leaving you that it hurts, Vanya." I should note that he never even suggested that I go with them, which he might very well have done under other circumstances, had he not been aware of my love for Natasha.

"Well, what is there to be done, my friend? It can't be helped! It hurts me, Vanya, but a change of place is a wonderful thing. A change of place will mean a whole new life for us," he added, again glancing at his daughter.

He believed wholeheartedly that that was true.

"And Nellie?" said Anna Andreyevna.

"Nellie? Well, the little darling is still sick, but by the time we are ready to leave she should be much better. She has already improved a great deal, don't you think, Vanya?" he asked me anxiously, but his frightened look suggested that he was hoping I might relieve him of his concerns.

"How is she? Has she slept? Is anything wrong? Is she awake now?" he asked his wife. "Do you know what, Anna Andreyevna, we should move the table out to the terrace and set up the samovar there, and when our friends arrive, Nellie will join us for tea. That will be nice. But is she awake yet? I'll go in to her, just to take a look and see. I won't wake her, don't worry," he added as he spotted Anna Andreyevna waving her hands at him.

But Nellie was already awake. Within fifteen minutes we were all gathered around the table, as usual, for our evening tea.

Nellie had been carried to her chair. The doctor arrived, as did Masloboyev, who brought a large bouquet of lilacs for Nellie, but he seemed somewhat distracted and concerned about something. Masloboyev was in the habit of stopping by almost every day now. I have already mentioned that the family, especially Anna Andreyevna, loved him dearly, but no one ever brought up the subject of Alexandra Semyonovna, nor did Masloboyev mention her himself. Anna Andreyevna, having learned from me that Alexandra Semyonovna had not yet become Masloboyev's lawful wife, decided that she could not receive the young woman (nor even speak her name) in their home. This declaration was honored by all as it was consistent with Anna Andreyevna's character. However, I suspect that had it not been for Natasha's current emotional state, Anna Andreyevna might not have been so finicky.

Nellie seemed particularly unhappy that evening and disturbed about something, as if she had had a bad dream and was thinking about it. But Masloboyev's gift made her very happy and she observed the flowers, which had been placed in front of her in a glass vase, with great pleasure.

"So you're very fond of flowers, Nellie," said the old man. "Just wait!" he added eagerly. "Tomorrow... Well, yes, you'll see for yourself!"

"I love them," Nellie said, "and remember how we would often surprise Mama with flowers when we were living abroad. She was sick once for four weeks during that time. Me and Henrik had agreed that when she first set foot out of her bedroom, which she didn't leave for a whole month, we would surprise her with a whole room filled with flowers. So we did. Mama told us one night that she would join us for breakfast in the morning, so we got up very early and Henrik and I filled the apartment with colorful blossoms and green leaves and garlands. There was even ivy, and something with broad leaves—I don't know what it's called—and still other leaves that clung to *everything*, and huge white flowers and colorful daffodils, which are my favorites, and such glorious roses, and so many other kinds of flowers. We hung them in wreaths or put them in pots, and there were some flowers that were as big as whole trees which we placed in large tubs in the corners and next to Mama's chair, and when she came out of her bedroom she was surprised and very happy, and Henrik was pleased. I remember that now."

That evening Nellie was especially weak and unsettled. The doctor studied her anxiously, but she insisted that she wanted to talk. And by the time dusk had arrived, she had already told us of her early life abroad and we did not interrupt her. She, along with her mother and Henrik, had traveled extensively, and the old memories were still vivid in her mind. She excitedly told us about the blue skies and high mountains with snow and ice, and waterfalls which they had driven past, then on to the lakes and valleys of Italy, the flowers and trees, the rustic villagers with their exotic clothes and dark faces with black eyes. She told us about the various events and adventures they had participated in and described tombs and palaces and a tall domed church which was suddenly illuminated with brilliant colored lights, and a hot, southern city with blue skies and a blue sea. Never before had Nellie revealed so many detailed, happy memories. We listened to her with rapt attention. Until then, we had heard her speak only of a dark, gloomy town, with its pressing, stupefying atmosphere and infected air, with once valued houses now soiled with dirt and grime, a dull, hazy sun, and evil, half-crazed people, at whose hands she and her mother suffered so much. And it seemed to me that I could picture the two of them in a dirty basement in the damp, gloomy evening, clinging to each other in bed and reminiscing about their lost Henrik and the wonders of other lands. I also pictured Nellie, living alone without her mother, and Madame Bubnova brutally beating her and trying to coerce Nellie into joining her abhorrent profession.

But, finally, Nellie felt faint and she was carried back to her bed. The old man was alarmed and upset that we had all permitted her to talk for so long. Nellie's subsequent seizure seemed a kind of "death experience" and it was repeated several more times. When they had past, Nellie demanded to see me and told me she had something to say to me alone. She was so adamant that the doctor himself insisted that they fulfill her wish and herded the others out of the room.

"Look, Vanya," Nellie said when we were at last alone. "I know they think I'm going with them, but I am *not* going, because I can't, and I will stay with you as I should have all along."

I tried to dissuade her from this decision by telling her how much the Ichmenyevs loved her and had grown to regard her as a daughter. They would be very sorry to lose her. I, on the other hand, had nothing to offer her except poverty and a hard life. As much as I loved her, it was better for all concerned that she leave me.

"No, it's impossible!" Nellie answered forcefully, "because I often see mother in my dreams and she tells me not to go with them, but to stay here. She says that I sinned terribly by leaving my grandfather alone and she always cries when she says that. I want to stay here and look after Grandpa, Vanya."

"But your grandfather is dead, Nellie, you know that," I said, listening to her with astonishment.

She thought for a moment and stared at me.

"Tell me again, Vanya," she said, "how my grandfather died. Tell me everything and don't leave anything out."

I was amazed at her request, but then began to describe the events leading up to Smith's death, leaving out none of the details. I suspected that she was delirious or, at the very least, that her head had not yet cleared after the attack.

She listened carefully to my story, and I remember her black, shiny, feverish eyes staring relentlessly at me as I spoke. The room was dark now.

"No, Vanya, he's not dead!" she said firmly after I had finished. "Mama often speaks about Grandpa and when I told her yesterday that Grandpa had died, she was very upset. She cried and told me that it wasn't true, that I had been told that on purpose, and that even now he walks the streets, begging, 'as we used to do,' she said, 'and he keeps walking around where we first met him when I fell down before him and Azorka knew me...'"

"That was a dream, Nellie, the kind that comes when you're sick, because you are very ill now," I told her.

"I kept thinking that it might be just a dream," Nellie said, "so I didn't tell anyone about it. You were the only one I wanted to tell. But today when I fell asleep, after you didn't come, I saw Grandpa himself in my dream. He was sitting at home waiting for me and he was so terribly thin. He had been waiting two days for me, he said, and had eaten nothing. Azorka, too, was very hungry and Grandpa was angry with me and scolded me. He also told me that he had no tobacco and that he couldn't live without tobacco. It's true, in fact, Vanya, that he told me that once before, after Mama died, when I first went to visit him. He was very sick then and I didn't understand much of what he was saying. So when I heard him say it again today, I thought I should go and stand on the bridge and beg for money, and then I could buy him bread and boiled potatoes and tobacco. So I did that, and I saw my grandfather walking around. He hesitated a moment, then came up to me and looked to see how many kopecks I had received, and he took them from me. 'That's enough for bread,' he told me, 'now get me money for tobacco.' So I begged some more and he came and took that, as well. I told him he could have everything, I wouldn't hide anything from him, but he said 'No, you're stealing from me. Madame Bubnova said you were a thief and that's why I will never let you come live with me. Where is the rest of the money?' I cried because he didn't believe me and wouldn't listen to me, but kept shouting 'You stole a kopeck!' and he began to beat me, right there on the bridge, and he hurt me. And I kept crying, Vanya, until I came to realize that he must be alive somewhere, walking around, waiting for me!"

I tried again to comfort Nellie and convince her that she was confused and, finally, she seemed to believe me. She told me she was afraid to go to sleep now, because she would see her grandfather again. She hugged me tightly. "And that's why I can't leave you, Vanya!" she whispered, pressing her face to mine. "Even if it weren't for Grandpa, I could never leave you."

Nellie's recurring seizures worried all of us. I quietly told the doctor about her dreams and asked him to be honest with me about her illness.

"There's really nothing I can say," he answered. "All we can do for the time being is watch her and keep her comfortable. Beyond that I don't know what else to do. A full recovery is, I think, unlikely. She will probably die. I'm only telling you this because you wanted me to be truthful. I'll come by again tomorrow and check on her. Perhaps the disease will take a different turn after that. I feel very sorry for this girl, she is like a daughter. Such a dear, sweet child, with such a playful mind!"

Nikolai Sergeich was particularly distressed.

"Look, Vanya," he said, "I know she loves flowers. Here's what we should do. Tomorrow morning when she wakes up, I want to fill the house with flowers, just like she and Henrik did for her mother. She was so excited when she spoke about it today."

"Maybe a little too excited," I answered. "Excitement may not be good for her right now."

"Ah, but pleasant excitement is another matter! Believe me, my boy, in my experience happy emotions may even help cure her, they are good for the health."

In short, the old man was so excited by his idea that he was positively giddy with delight. It was impossible to talk him out of it. I asked the doctor for *his* advice, but before he could even speak, the old man had grabbed his cap and was about to run off to make the arrangements.

"Look," he said at the door, "there is a greenhouse nearby, a fantastic place. The growers sell their flowers directly to the public and you can buy them surprisingly cheap. Make sure you tell Anna Andreyevna that or she will be angry with me over the expense. Well, then... Yes! Here is another thing, my friend. Where are you off to now? You've finished your work, after all, so why should you be in a hurry to get back home? Spend the night here, upstairs in the attic. You've slept there before, remember? And your bed is still there, untouched. You'll sleep like the king of France! Eh? Stay the night. Tomorrow we will wake up early, they'll bring flowers, and by eight o'clock, we will have filled the room completely. And Natasha will help—she has much better taste than we have. Well, do you agree? Will you spend the night?"

I agreed to stay and Ichmenyev went off to make the arrangements. When he returned, the doctor and Masloboyev said their good-byes and left. The family went to bed early, at eleven o'clock. As he was leaving, Masloboyev was deep in thought and looked like he wanted to tell me something, but he postponed 'til another time. But after I bid the family good-night, I climbed the staircase to the attic and, to my surprise, I saw him again. Masloboyev was waiting for me at the table, leafing through a book.

"I turned and came back, Vanya, because it's better that I tell you this now. Sit down. You see, it's a very stupid bit of business, annoyingly so..."

"What is it?"

"That bastard of a prince of yours got me very angry two weeks ago, so angry, in fact that I'm still furious about it."

"What? Why? Are you still doing business with the prince?"

"Well now, there you go with your 'What, why?' as if God knows what has happened. You, brother Vanya, are exactly like my Alexandra Semyonovna and every other insufferable woman. I cannot stand females! If a raven squawks, it's always, 'What's the matter? What's happened?'"

"Don't be angry."

"It's all right, I'm not angry, but in a matter such as this it is necessary to look at things calmly, reasonably, and not exaggerate... that's what I say."

He paused, as if still mad at me. I did not interrupt him.

"You see, brother," he began again, "I was on the trail of something... that is, I stumbled upon a clue… Perhaps not really a clue, but it struck me that… considering the facts… that Nellie may be... Well, to put it simply, Nellie *is* Prince Valkovsky's *legitimate* daughter."

"What are you saying?"

"Now there you go again, roaring 'What are you saying?' I swear, you just can't talk to some people!" he howled, waving his hand frantically. "Have I not just told you something positive, you feather-head? I've told you that it is a proven fact that she is the prince's daughter? Did I not just say that?"

"Listen, my old friend," I interrupted him excitedly, "do not shout, for God's sake, but just explain to me clearly and precisely… Honestly, I'll understand. But you must understand how important this information is. And how great the consequences..."

"Consequences indeed… but from what? Where is the evidence? Things are not as simple as that, and I am telling you a secret right now. I have a reason for saying what I'm saying and I will explain later. So, shut up and listen and know that everything is a secret. Here are the facts. Last winter, even before Smith died, the prince returned from Warsaw and started this search. But it actually started much earlier last year. But at that time he was looking for one thing and then he began to look for another. The main thing is that he suddenly lost the thread. It's been thirteen years since he abandoned Smith's daughter—Nellie's mother—in Paris, but for all those thirteen years, he has steadily kept track of her. He knew she was living with Henrik—the man Nellie told us about today—he knew about her daughter, he knew that she had become sick; well, in a word, he knew just about everything. But suddenly he lost the thread. It happened, it seems, soon after Henrik died, when she came to St. Petersburg. In Petersburg, of course, he would have found her easily no matter what name she was living under, but the fact is that his agents abroad deceived him by providing false information. They assured him that she was living in some God forsaken little town somewhere in southern Germany, but they themselves were deceived through their own negligence—they had been pursuing the wrong woman. This went on for a year or more. Well, after a year, the prince began to wonder if some of the facts he'd been given were wrong and maybe this was not the right woman. So the question arose, where was the *real* Smith woman? And then it occurred to him, although he had no real information to go on, that she might be living right here in Petersburg. For the time being, he kept up the investigation abroad, but when he began his search here, for some reason, he didn't want to go through official channels. And that's when he met with me. He had heard that I was doing some detective work on the side, tracking down missing persons, lost lovers and so on. So, this evil son-of-a-bitch explains to me—but only in the vaguest, most ambiguous terms—what he wants me to do. His story had a lot of holes in it and he repeated himself several times, with the facts coming out differently each time he told it, but no matter how cunningly you try to hide things, you can't bury all the tracks. Of course, I pretended to be all guileless and subservient, in short, slavishly devoted to him, but there is a rule that I accepted long ago as a law of nature—for it is, in fact, a law of nature—and I considered, first of all, if he had told me what he really wanted of me and, second, if maybe he wasn't actually hiding something he didn't want me to know? In the latter case, it is likely that you with your poetic mind can understand the possibilities of this. Perhaps he was offering me one ruble for information for which he would happily pay someone else four rubles! Of course, I would be a fool to accept one ruble if I could get four. So I began to investigate the matter and determine what information I could get, first, from him, then what I might learn from a third party and, finally, what I might gather using my own wits. You may ask why I even bother? My answer is that the prince seems entirely too keen about acquiring information that he is afraid might become public knowledge. But, I ask, why should he be so frightened? A man steals a young virgin away from her father, gets her pregnant and then deserts her. There is nothing unusual or remarkable about that. A spirited little prank and nothing more. Certainly nothing for a man like a prince to be concerned with! And yet he was definitely afraid of... what? It made me suspicious. I learned some interesting facts, my brother, by following, among other things, the trail left by Henrik. Of course, he is dead, but from one of his cousins—now married to a baker here in Petersburg, but who had been passionately in love with Henrik before, and continues to love him fifteen years later, despite having inadvertently borne eight of the fat papa baker's children—from this cousin, I say, I managed through various maneuvers to learn an important piece of information: Henrik had developed the German habit of writing letters and keeping diaries and before his death he sent her a collection of these papers. She was a fool and had no understanding of the importance of these letters.

She loved when he wrote about the moon, or *du lieber Augus*tin, or *Weiland der Schmeid*, it seems, but through these letters I was able to trace a new path. I learned, for example, about the wealthy manufacturer Mr. Smith, and the daughter who was stolen from him, along with his money, by the prince, and finally, after wading through layers of allegorical references and wide-ranging wordplay, I hit upon the crux of the matter, and it's not good, Vanya, not good at all. Henrik purposely concealed the truth, only hinting at it, but I pieced these clues together until I reached a heavenly harmony in my mind: the prince was legally married to Smith's daughter! When or where he married her, whether abroad or here, I have found no documents. It is a complete mystery. In fact, brother Vanya, I have torn my hair out in frustration, searching everywhere, day and night, with no success.

"I finally managed to track Smith down, but he went and died before I had time to even get a look at him. Then, by chance, I learned about a woman, one of my prime suspects, who had recently died on Vasilyevsky Island. I rushed to Vasilyevsky and, as you well remember, ran into you. Then the pieces began to fall into place. In short, Nellie has tied the whole thing together."

"Listen," I interrupted him, "do you really think that Nellie knows?"

"What?"

"That she is Prince Valkovsky's daughter?"

"But you yourself know that she is the prince's daughter," he answered, looking at me with a sort of angry reproach, "so why do you ask idle questions like a foolish person? That is not the important thing. What matters is not that she is the daughter of the prince, but that she is his *legitimate* daughter! Do you understand what that means?"

"It can't be!" I cried.

"I told myself, at first, that it was impossible and even now I sometimes think 'Can it be true?' But the point is that not only is it *not* impossible, in all probability, it *is* true."

"No, Masloboyev, it's not. Your imagination is running away with you," I cried. "Not only does Nellie know nothing about this, but she is, in fact, the prince's *illegitimate* daughter. If the mother had any kind of documentary evidence in her hands, would she have endured such a harsh life here in Petersburg, and would she have abandoned her child to such a cruel fate? Enough! It cannot be!"

"I, myself, wondered about that, and even standing her now, I am puzzled. But the thing to understand is that Nellie's mother may have been the most impetuous and foolishly naïve woman in the world. She was an extraordinary woman, but her idealized view of romance—all of this nonsense about the transformative powers of love—ultimately drove her insane. Right from the beginning she dreamt only of a heavenly paradise of cherubs and angels, unselfish and unlimited love, and I believe that when the prince stopped loving her she threw all sanity aside, not only because had she been deserted, but because her romantic idol had deceived her, crushed her fantasy, tossed her in the dirt, spat upon and humiliated her. Her silly, starry-eyed view of life had been distorted overnight. She had been used and abused in the most insulting manner; can you envision such an insult? In her horror, and, most importantly, the affront to her pride, she recoiled from him with infinite contempt. She severed all ties, destroyed all documents, spat upon his money—forgetting completely that the money was not really his, but her father's—refused it, like so much dust, in order to crush her deceiver by her own spiritual grandeur. He was no better than a thief and she determined to despise him for life, and reject the dishonor of being called his wife. We do not have divorce in Russia, but she saw their separation as a *de facto* divorce. After all this, how could she return to him and beg for help? On her deathbed, this crazy woman told Nellie, "Do not go to him. Work, beg, perish, but do not go to him, no matter who tries to make you." Even at that moment, she was dreaming of crushing the man's fatherly expectations with her contempt. In short, she nourished her final weeks on earth with dreams rather than bread. I have elicited a great many facts from Nellie in our conversations and have even more to reveal. Of course, her mother was dying of consumption and the disease made her particularly irritable and seething with resentment, but I learned from a crony of Bubnova's that the mother actually wrote to the prince. Yes, to the prince, the prince himself."

"Wrote! And did she receive a reply?" I asked impatiently.

"That's just it. I don't know whether he got it or not. Do you remember that painted woman who lived in Bubnova's house? She is now in prison, but she was there when the mother addressed a letter to the prince and gave it to her to deliver. But then she took it back from the woman and refused to send it. That was three weeks before her death. But what is significant is that she may have changed her mind and decided to send it again, although, of course, she might have taken it back a second time. So, if she sent the letter or not, I don't know, but there is reason to believe that she didn't, because the prince only learned about her whereabouts in St. Petersburg after her death. He must have been delighted!"

"Yes, I remember Alyosha telling me about a letter that made his father very happy, but that was very recently, only about two months ago. Well, tell me more, what about your dealings with the prince?"

"My dealings with the prince? Well, understand that I had an unqualified moral certainty, and yet no positive evidence, not even a shred, no matter how hard I struggled. The situation was critical! I had to make inquiries abroad, but where overseas? I had no idea. Of course, I had a real battle with myself. I couldn't just frighten him with hints, pretend that I knew more than I really did."

"Well, what then?"

"He wasn't convinced, although he was scared. So scared that he's *still* a bit nervous. We had a few meetings and once he seemed restored to life and began to tell me the whole story. This is when he thought that I already knew everything. He told the story frankly, with great feeling, but, of course, he lied shamelessly. That's when I realized the extent to which he was afraid of me. I pretended to be an outright simpleton in front of him to convince him I actually believed what he was saying. I was awkward, that is deliberately awkward, and rude, which threatened him, I think—all to make him uncomfortable so he might slip up. But he figured out what I was doing, the scoundrel! Another time I pretended to be drunk, but that didn't work either. He's much too clever! You can understand, my friend Vanya, that I needed, first, to know exactly how afraid of me he was, and, second, to convince him I knew more than I really did..."

"And what was the final outcome?"

"Well," he shrugged, "it didn't work. I needed hard facts, evidence, and I didn't get them. But he realized that I could still make quite a scandal and, of course, a scandal is the one thing he is most afraid of, since he has started to make connections here that he dare not jeopardize. You know he's planning to marry again?"

"No..."

"In the coming year! He found himself a bride last year who was then only fourteen years old! She is fifteen now, but it seems still wearing pinafores, the poor thing. Her parents are thrilled! You can well understand how important it was for the prince to know if his wife was living or dead. This girl is a general's daughter, with a lot of money, stacks of money! You and I, brother Vanya, will never find such a rewarding marriage. There is just one thing, however, for which I will never forgive myself as long as I live," Masloboyev shouted, banging his fist hard on the table. "I allowed the prince to get the better of me two weeks ago... the bastard!"

"What happened?"

"Oh, I could see that he was starting to realize I had nothing concrete against him and decided that if I stretched this out much longer, he would finally recognize my weakness. So I agreed to take his two thousand."

"You took two thousand!"

"In silver, Vanya! I was reluctant, but I took it. I was, of course, embarrassed to take only two thousand for a job that was worth so much more! I felt humiliated. It was as if he stood there and spat upon me. He told me, 'Masloboyev, I have not yet paid you for your previous work,' when in fact he had already paid me, some time ago, a hundred and fifty rubles, the amount we had agreed on. 'I am planning to go away,' he added, "so here is two thousand rubles and I trust all of our business is now settled.' And I answered, "Completely settled, Your Highness," but I didn't dare look him in that deceitful face of his because I knew he was thinking, "It's way too much, but I'm giving it to this fool because I am so generous!" I can't even remember how I got out of that room!"

"But that's despicable, Masloboyev!" I cried. "What about Nellie?"

"It wasn't just cowardly, it was disgraceful, it was scandalous... It... it... yes, there are no words to express it!"

"Oh, my God! At the very least, he could have done something to provide for Nellie!"

"That would have been the proper thing to do. But how could I force him? Intimidate him? I doubt he could be intimidated at this point. I've taken his money. I openly admitted that the most he had to fear from me was worth two thousand rubles, I even set the price myself! What have I left to intimidate him with?"

"Can it really be that all hope for Nellie is gone?" I cried, almost in despair.

"Not at all!" he exclaimed with fervor, his energy building again. "I'm not that easily defeated! I'll start the whole business over again, Vanya. So, I took his two thousand. What of it? I consider that minimal compensation for the way he used me and the abuse I suffered. He cheated me and then laughed at me. Cheated, and even laughed! I will not allow people to laugh at me. I'll start all over again, Vanya, with Nellie. I am quite certain that she is the key to unlocking this whole case. She knows everything... Her mother told her, in the heat of anguish, as she was dying. There was no one else there she could confide in so, perhaps, she told Nellie. Or maybe we will find the necessary documents," he added in sweet delight, rubbing his hands. "Do you understand now, Vanya, why I am always hanging around here? First, out of friendship for you, it goes without saying, but the most important thing is to keep an eye on Nellie, and finally, as my friend, Vanya, like it or not, you must help me because you have the most influence on Nellie!"

"Certainly, I swear," I cried, "and I hope, Masloboyev, that you will do this, above all, for Nellie, for the sake of a poor abandoned orphan, and not simply for your own financial gain..."

"Why should it matter for whose benefit I do this, you dear blessed man, as long as the deed is accomplished? To get it done, that's the main thing! Of course, most importantly, for the sake of the orphan, that's just simple humanity. But you, Vanya, do not condemn me too harshly if I also take care of myself. I am a poor man, and that bastard should never dare to offend the poor. When he cheats one of us, he cheats us all. So I, in your opinion, should I not pursue retribution from such a villain? See you tomorrow morning!"

But our flower festival the next morning failed. Nellie became worse and she could not leave her room.

And, in truth, she never again came out of her room.

She died two weeks later. During those two weeks of agony she never completely returned to her senses, nor escaped the bizarre fantasies that haunted her. Her mind was clouded. She was firmly convinced, until her death, that her grandfather was calling to her, angry that she had stopped visiting him and begging for bread and tobacco. She often cried in her sleep and when she awoke, she told me she had seen her mother.

Occasionally, her reason seemed to return, at least partially, and once when we were alone, she reached out and grabbed my hand with her thin, feverishly hot fingers.

"Vanya," she said, "when I die, marry Natasha!"

I believe that she had come to this decision quite some time before. I silently smiled at her. Seeing my smile, she too smiled and mischievously shook her slender finger at me, then immediately showered my face with kisses.

Three days before her death, on a lovely summer evening, Nellie asked me to raise the curtain and open the window in her bedroom. The window looked out into the garden, and she stared at the thick greenery, the setting sun, and suddenly asked to be alone with me.

"Vanya," she said, her voice barely audible because she was already very weak, "I'm going to die soon... very soon... and I want to tell you... I want you to remember me... I leave you this memento," and she showed me a tiny little bag that hung around her neck along with a cross. "My mother left me this when she was dying. So, when I die, I want you to remove the scroll and read what it is says. I'm going to tell everyone today that when I die, they are to give this bag only to you. And when you read what is written on it, then go to *him* and tell him that I am dead and that he has not been forgiven. Tell him also that I have recently read the Gospel. It says that we should forgive all our enemies. Well, I read it, but I still won't forgive him, because when my mother was dying and could still speak, the last thing she said was: "I curse him!" Well, I curse him now, not for myself, but for my mother. Tell him also that when my mother died, I was left all alone with Madame Bubnova. Tell him that you saw me there and saw what they wanted me to do... tell him everything. And then tell him... that I would rather have worked for Madame Bubnova than live with him."

As she said this, Nellie turned pale, her eyes flashed and her heart began pounding so hard that she fell back on the pillow and for two minutes could not utter a word.

"Call them, Vanya," she said at last in a weak voice, "I want to say good-bye to them all. Good-bye, Vanya!"

She hugged me tightly one last time. The others all joined me around Nellie's bed. The old man refused to acknowledge that she was dying; he simply could not accept the idea. Until even that last day he had argued with all of us, maintaining that she would most certainly recover. He was quite worn out by anxiety, but he sat beside Nellie's bed for days on end and even nights. The night before she died, he literally did not sleep at all. He tried to anticipate her slightest whim, eager to please her in any way, but when he finally left her room he wept bitterly, only to recover a moment later and assure us that her health would return. He had been filling her room with flowers. One time he had walked a great distance and returned with a whole cluster of lovely red and white roses for his little Nellie. Similar endeavors on his part delighted Nellie and she could not find the words in her heart to respond to such unconditional love. That evening, on the evening of her farewell to us, the old man did not want to say good-bye to her forever. Nellie smiled at him and the whole evening tried to appear gay, joked with him, even laughed. We left her room almost hopeful, but the next day she could not speak. Two days later she died.

The old man covered her coffin with flowers and gazed in despair at Nellie's emaciated little face. There was a deathly smile on her lips and her arms were crossed on her chest. He wept over her as if she were his own natural child. We all tried to console him, but nothing could comfort him, and he became seriously ill after Nellie's funeral.

Anna Andreyevna herself gave me the little bag which she had taken from around Nellie's neck. In the little bag was a letter to Prince Valkovsky from Nellie's mother. I read it on the day Nellie died. She cursed the prince and told him she could not forgive him. She then described the hardship she had endured for the past few years and the horror that lay ahead for their little girl and begged him to do something for the baby. "She is yours," she wrote. "She is your daughter and you know that to be true. When I die, I have told her to go to you and put this letter in your hand. If you do not reject Nellie, then maybe I will forgive you, and on the Day of Judgment I will go before the throne of God and beg him to forgive you for your sins. Nellie knows the contents of this letter. I read it to her and told her everything. She knows everything... everything."

But Nellie had not fulfilled her mother's dying request. She knew everything, but she had never visited the prince and she died without forgiving him.

When we returned from Nellie's funeral, Natasha and I went into the garden. The day was hot and sunny. In another week they would be leaving. Natasha gave me a long, strange look.

"Vanya," she said. "It was all a dream, you know!"

"What was a dream?" I asked.

"All, all…" she answered. "This entire past year, Vanya. Why did I ruin your happiness?"

Then, her expression changed ever so slightly, and in her eyes I read, "We might *still* be happy together… forever!"

Author's Note

How did an American playwright and novelist who can neither read nor speak Russian come to write an English language adaptation of a classic (albeit lesser known) novel by the great Fyodor Dostoyevsky? The sequence of events leading up to the publication of *The Used and Abused* began in March of 2009 when I first contacted the Russian composer Alexander Zhurbin about collaborating with him on a musical play. I had met Zhurbin in 1988 during a period when he was living and working in New York City and was unaware that he had since returned to Moscow and had become the foremost composer of musical theater and opera in Russia, with more than fifty works to his credit. After an exchange of emails, Zhurbin sent me several audio recordings of musical productions that he felt might be suitable for an American production. One of these was an epic musical adaptation of Dostoyevsky's novel *Oonizhyenniye i oskorblyenniye,* which Zhurbin and his librettist had called *Vladimir Square* (a title only peripherally related to the novel), the score of which included more than fifty musical numbers and production requirements on a scale comparable to *Les Misérables*. Without understanding a word of the lyrics or dialogue, I fell in love with the music and sought out an English language translation of the novel to find out what was actually happening in the story.

It was at that point that I discovered just how rare Dostoyevsky's novel was in America and why I had never heard of it. Although still extremely popular and never out of print in Dostoyevsky's homeland, until a few years ago it was difficult to find an English language version in the United States. Unlike Dostoyevsky's masterpiece, *Pryestupleniye i nakazaniye,* which is always referred to in English as *Crime and Punishment, Oonizhyenniye i oskorblyenniye* has never, until recently, been translated twice under the same title.

The first English translation by Frederick Whishaw was published in London in 1886 by Vizetelly & Co. under the title *Injury and Insult*. As far as I have been able to determine, it was never published in the United States and, until the advent of public domain reprints, has been virtually impossible to find except in antiquarian bookshops.

The one readily available translation in America during the early 20th Century was *The Insulted and Injured* by the English writer Constance Garnett, whose prolific output of published translations introduced countless English speaking readers to the works of not only Dostoyevsky, but Tolstoy, Pushkin, Turgenev, Chekhov, and others. *The Insulted and Injured* was first published in England in 1915 and although it was subsequently published in America, it was out-of-print for decades.

A third translation, *The Insulted and Humiliated* by Olga Shartse, was published in Moscow in 1956 by Foreign Languages Publishing House and can occasionally be found on eBay or from booksellers specializing in Russian literature.

I was able to download pdf or text files of the Whishaw and Garnett translations, both of which are now in the public domain. After reading both, I determined that their narrative language and, especially, their dialogue, were stylistically unsuitable for my purposes. There were also large portions of the Russian text which had simply been ignored by both writers, including a large section of the scene in Mueller's pastry shop which plays an important part in the musical. Taking advantage of the electronic translation tools available from Google, Yahoo and Babylon, I began to piece together my own version of Dostoyevsky's novel, rewriting and expanding upon each of the different public domain translations available to me.

Although remnants of the Whishaw and Garnett translations may still be found scattered throughout this adaptation, I have endeavored to remain as faithful to the story, characters and spirit of Dostoyevsky's original text as I could, while still bringing my own writing style to the project. But, most importantly, I wanted to write an entertaining book, and if my retelling of Dostoyevsky's novel fails to impress a few Russian literary scholars, that is precisely why I chose the cover attribution "Retold by Robert Armin" rather than "A New Translation by Robert Armin."

In 2010, after I had completed more than a hundred pages of translation, I suddenly discovered that a new translation (the first in more than half a century) by Ignat Avsey had recently been published in paperback by Oneworld Classics under yet another new title, *Humiliated and Insulted*. I bought a copy and read the first few pages to assure myself that our writing styles were sufficiently diverse as to warrant yet another translation. Once I was sure that I was not stepping on Avsey's toes, stylistically speaking, I set his book aside and never referred to it again. Since my primary motivation for writing my own translation was to assist me in writing the musical, I wanted to make sure that I never inadvertently "borrowed" any of Avsey's language for my own dialogue and lyrics. A few years later, I discovered that yet another new translation, this time by Boris Jakim, was published in 2011 by Eerdmans Publishing Company under the title *The Insulted and Injured*, marking the first time a title had been used twice.

As I was preparing the final manuscript of *The Used and Abused* for publication, I decided to divide the book into two separate parts in order to give myself time to move forward with the musical adaptation of the complete work, while giving the reading public a tantalizing preview of what lay ahead. Dostoyevsky and his literary inspiration, Charles Dickens, both published during a period when novels were serialized in periodicals prior to their complete edition. Dostoyevsky, himself, divided his original novel into four separate "books."

In 2016, I combined my version of the first two books and published them as *Dostoyevsky's The Used and Abused, Volume One* (releasing at the same time a companion audiobook splendidly narrated by theater and television actor Philip Hoffman), fully expecting to publish *Volume Two* within six months of the first. Unfortunately, as often happens, life intervened, and I switched to several other writing projects, including a musical adaptation of Vladimir Nabokov's *Kamera Obscura,* with music once again by Alexander Zhurbin, which had its first public reading in the fall of 2018. The following year, I returned to my Dostoyevsky adaptation and managed to complete most of book three. When the worldwide pandemic of 2020 struck, and all other endeavors screeched to a grinding halt, I finally committed myself to finishing the final quarter section of *The Used and Abused*, and publishing the entire work in one complete volume, the results of which you have, presumably, just completed reading. Given the current uncertainty about live theater, in general, the future of the big Broadway musical that inspired this reimagined version of the story remains clouded in mystery. We shall see.

As for my title, *The Used and Abused,* I recognized early on that the original Russian title consisted of two words that rhyme, and I decided to find two English words that accomplished the same task. My initial working title was *Humiliation and Degradation,* but I could not imagine a big Broadway musical selling out with such a somber and depressing title. After long deliberation, I finally hit upon the idiomatic expression "used and abused" as a perfect title for my American adaptation of *Oonizhyenniye i oskorblyenniye*. *The Used and Abused* is, in fact, no less an accurate description of the contents of Dostoyevsky's novel than *Injury and Insult*, *The Insulted and Injured*, *The Insulted and Humiliated*, and *Humiliated and Insulted*. And it certainly "sings" better.

Robert Armin
New York City
November 2020

Also Recommended

The Flash of Midnight

By Robert Armin

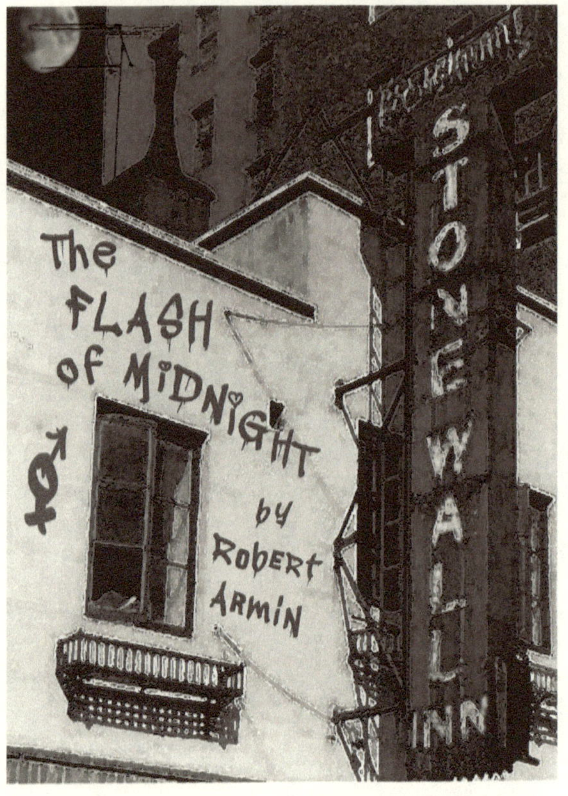

Taking its inspiration from Voltaire's *Candide,* Robert Armin's novel *The Flash of Midnight* recounts the bisexual escapades of Laurie Norber, a young woman who steadfastly believes that true love is just around the corner, never imagining that in June of 1969 she will become the spark that ignites a sexual revolution at a Greenwich Village bar called the Stonewall Inn.

Also Recommended

Sherman Yellen

In *Spotless,* two time Emmy Award-winning writer Sherman Yellen lovingly recreates the world of his impoverished forebears before World War I; his troubled, prosperous, mendacious father; his beautiful, willful fashion-model mother, and especially his own New York childhood in the 1930s and 40s. Yellen witnessed both great events and the everyday life of a city boy in an embattled family, viewed through the eyes of an observant little boy waiting impatiently for his body to catch up to his all-seeing consciousness. Yellen summons up this lost world of a New York Jewish-American family with candor and love.

Trade Paperback ISBN-13: 978-0996016926 Paperback $19.95

Also Available in **Kindle eBook**

MORECLACKE  PUBLISHING

Also Recommended

"Yellen has given us the Jewish-American immigrant experience more vitally and persuasively than any writer since Isaac Bashevis Singer." Christopher Davis

Cousin Bella – The Whore of Minsk recounts the life of a young Jewish woman in Tsarist Russia who was sold into prostitution, rescued by the author's indomitable grandmother, and then immigrated to America where the most extraordinary drama of her life was yet to unfold. Written by Tony® nominee and two-time Emmy® winning screenwriter, Sherman Yellen. Also included is Yellen's holiday classic, *A Christmas Lilly*, a tender, poignant memory of a Jewish family's first Christmas tree in 1939, celebrating the author's wise and compassionate mother.

Trade Paperback ISBN-13: 978-1495290435 Paperback $8.95

Also Available in **Kindle eBook** and **Unabridged Audiobook**

MORECLACKE  **PUBLISHING**

www.ingramcontent.com/pod-product-compliance
Lightning Source LLC
LaVergne TN
LVHW091112080826
845145LV00008B/1882

* 9 7 8 0 9 9 6 0 1 6 9 7 1 *